P9-CBZ-970

The Bikini Car Wash

JUL 1 3 2010

HAYNER PLD/DOWNTOWN

HAYNER PUBLIC LIBRARY DISTRICT
ALTON, ILLINOIS

OVERDUES 10 PER DAY, MAXIMUM FINE
COST OF ITEM
ADDITIONAL $5.00 SERVICE CHARGE
APPLIED TO
LOST OR DAMAGED ITEMS

Also by
Pamela Morsi

RED'S HOT HONKY-TONK BAR
LAST DANCE AT JITTERBUG LOUNGE
BITSY'S BAIT & BBQ
THE COTTON QUEEN
BY SUMMER'S END
SUBURBAN RENEWAL
LETTING GO
DOING GOOD*

*Reissued in April 2010 as
THE SOCIAL CLIMBER OF DAVENPORT HEIGHTS

PAMELA MORSI

The Bikini Car Wash

If you purchased this book without a cover you should be aware
that this book is stolen property. It was reported as "unsold and
destroyed" to the publisher, and neither the author nor the
publisher has received any payment for this "stripped book."

MIRA

Recycling programs
for this product may
not exist in your area.

ISBN-13: 978-0-7783-2781-3

THE BIKINI CAR WASH

Copyright © 2010 by Pamela Morsi.

All rights reserved. Except for use in any review, the reproduction or
utilization of this work in whole or in part in any form by any electronic,
mechanical or other means, now known or hereafter invented, including
xerography, photocopying and recording, or in any information storage or
retrieval system, is forbidden without the written permission of the publisher,
MIRA Books, 225 Duncan Mill Road, Don Mills, Ontario, Canada M3B 3K9.

This is a work of fiction. Names, characters, places and incidents are
either the product of the author's imagination or are used fictitiously, and
any resemblance to actual persons, living or dead, business establishments,
events or locales is entirely coincidental.

MIRA and the Star Colophon are trademarks used under license and registered
in Australia, New Zealand, Philippines, United States Patent and Trademark
Office and in other countries.

For questions and comments about the quality of this book please contact us
at Customer_eCare@Harlequin.ca.

www.MIRABooks.com

Printed in U.S.A.

First Printing: July 2010
10 9 8 7 6 5 4 3 2 1

F
MOR

b19218552

The author wishes to acknowledge
the help of friends
Rebecca Waldman,
on this and other books,
and
John Litton
Retail Renaissance Man
both of whom would look excellent
in a bikini.

The appetizing scent of roast chicken drifted down the stairs into the basement rumpus room, perhaps encouraging the growling stomach of the occupant of the room, known to friends and family by the nickname Jelly. It was getting close to dinnertime. Jelly knew that because Lenny Briscoe had already fingered the perp, and Assistant D.A. Claire Kincaid was getting ready for the Prosecution.

When a commercial for a cholesterol drug momentarily filled the television screen, Jelly retrieved a photo album from the nearby shelf that held some of her collection. Returning to her seat on the couch, she opened it to exactly the page she wanted. A friendly, smiling woman gazed back at her. A sad little sigh escaped her lips as she ran her fingers along the face portrayed in the photo. Jelly looked into those eyes that she knew so well. They were now very far away, farther away than Jelly knew how to go. And there was no bus to get there. Jelly had asked.

With a distinctive chime, her favorite TV drama was back on the screen. Jelly paid attention as a disagreement flared up between the characters. Then she began offering advice.

"Don't listen to Mike Logan," Jelly warned Claire. "He's a hothead."

Jelly knew that from vast experience. She had watched every episode of Law & Order *ever filmed. And many of them she'd seen dozens of times.*

She glanced down again at the beloved photo and then held it up to face the screen.

"Ladies and gentlemen of the jury, this is my mom," she announced. *"She's dead. Natural causes. No investigation necessary."* Jelly sighed again heavily. *"I'm trying not to be sad anymore. I'm trying to be happy. Andi's home, that should make everybody happy."*

Chapter 1

ANDREA WOLKOWICZ REALIZED almost immediately that she'd made a mistake. She'd worn her bright blue Escada dress because she looked so good in it. And it gave her confidence. Confidence was something she was going to need in this next round of interviews. She was on her sixth month of job hunting. So far, she'd been unable to convince any local business that five years of helping an international corporation give away money meant she was more than qualified to help a small company make some.

The designer dress was a serious miscalculation.

Miss Kepper, the person who did the hiring at Guthrie Foods, had given only a cursory glance at her résumé, but she'd looked Andi up and down as if she were the prized beef contender at the county fair.

And it didn't seem to Andi that her interest was fashion. The puny, dour woman with a bad haircut was wearing a gray suit so many years out of style that its gigantic shoulder pads would have put the female cast of *Dallas* to shame. And her shoes, flats in basic black, looked more like something that would be worn in the gym than in the office.

Andi was explaining herself, with a mix of understatement and Midwest modesty. She had a graduate degree from one of the nation's top business schools. She'd done an internship on the Miracle Mile. And she'd walked away from a successful career as a corporate contributions professional for a Fortune 500 company in Chicago. The question Miss Kepper rightly ought to ask, Andi thought, was: *Why would such a dynamic professional with a bright future possibly be interested in a crummy part-time job like this?*

Miss Kepper did not, of course, ask that question.

But Andi had asked it of herself often enough these past few months. When her mom died last October, moving home to live with Pop had seemed like the perfect decision, and she had rushed to make it happen. Now, flat broke and out of work, the logic of giving up a good job in a bad economy and moving back to the wilds of the rust belt, didn't seem quite so brilliant.

"My responsibility at Milo Corp meant targeting charitable foundations whose mission clearly aligned with the goals and values of our overall corporate direction. This involved maintaining clear, up-to-the minute assessments of both the operations and the ground level accomplishments of philanthropic organizations worldwide."

Miss Kepper did not look impressed.

"Please contact my former employer," Andi urged. "They have great respect for my work and were very sorry to see me leave."

The woman pursed her lips and made a noncommittal sound that was not at all promising.

"Well, thank you for coming in. We'll certainly keep you in mind," she told Andi, her words dismissive.

Andi wasn't ready to be dismissed. The pencil-pushing Miss Kepper would never have gotten out of the mail room at Andi's former employer. "This is a great opportunity for Guthrie Foods," she stated firmly. "A person with my credentials and breadth of experience doesn't walk into a small local business like this every day. I could be a real asset to this company."

"Yes, well," the woman hedged. "This is a very competitive job market and many, many people have applied for this position, most of them longtime residents of our community. We have plenty of our own looking for work. We don't necessarily need an influx of outsiders."

"I'm not an outsider," Andi insisted quickly. "I grew up right here in town. My dad had a business on this street. I went to high school with Pete Guthrie. We...we were on student council together."

This last comment was a bit of a stretch and Andi made a special effort to look Miss Kepper directly in the eye. Pete Guthrie had been *president* of the student council. Andi had represented the math club on the council's advisory committee. She had never been one to pad her résumé. She'd never needed to. But that had been high school, it had been ten years ago and she needed this job now.

Miss Kepper's right eyebrow raised slightly, a guarantee she suspected a lie.

"Well, then," she said, too pleasantly. "As Mr. Guthrie

makes the final decision, I don't suppose you'll have any problem. Thank you so much for coming."

The woman rose to her feet and Andi had no choice but to do the same. She was escorted out into the hallway where she was directed toward the stairs. She hadn't gotten the job. She knew that all ready. After perhaps a hundred unacknowledged résumés and two dozen fruitless interviews, Andi recognized a door slamming in her face, even when it occurred only figuratively.

As she headed down the corridor, her eyes scanned the scuffed and dingy beige walls, unrelieved by even so much as an advertising poster.

Sheesh! What a miserable place to work, she thought. Not getting this job might be a blessing in disguise, she consoled herself.

That thought lasted until she got downstairs. The store itself was much cleaner, and more modern and cheerful than the office space. And the place was full of food. Even in the worst of economic times, people still bought food.

Even Andi did, but not today. Today she was on her two-dollar diet. That's what she called it. To avoid spending, she'd taken to carrying only two dollars in her purse. That was enough to get her bus fare home, but not much else.

She walked past the line of checkout lanes and the rows of shopping carts, through the sliding glass doors into the parking lot. Going from the air-conditioning to the outdoors was a bit of a shock.

Andi made a huff of surprise, willing herself not to perspire in her best dress.

Was it always this hot in May?

She couldn't remember. It had been a long time since she'd been here for anything but Christmas vacation. But now she was here indefinitely.

She walked across the parking lot toward the sidewalk. Guthrie Foods was a fixture on Grosvenor Avenue, Plainview's commercial main street. And Andi was as familiar with it as she was with her own childhood. At the edge of Guthrie's parking lot, on the corner of Grosvenor and Fifth Street, was a small empty building with a large covered drive-through. On the face of its brick front overhang, the sign was still vividly readable. PLAINVIEW WASH & WAX. Andi smiled as she read it. This had been her father's business. And she'd made a point of spending her childhood here instead of at home. As she walked past the boarded-up windows and the scuffed walls thick with graffiti, she marveled at how much smaller it seemed from the busy, exciting place she remembered.

Now that she thought about it, almost everything in town was smaller and less exciting.

At the corner she waited for the light, surveying the sidewalk ahead of her. The crab apple trees that lined the street were in bloom, their pink flowers a vivid contrast to the un-relieved gray of concrete, and they added a freshness to the line of aging brick buildings.

When the light turned green Andi crossed the street as quickly as her sensible but stylish pumps would take her. Plainview was not so different from when she'd lived here as a young girl. Somehow there was comfort in that.

Taking up much of the next block and looking much as it always had, was Joffee's Manhattan Store. Andi was pretty sure that the word Manhattan had been included in the name to give the locals a sense of foreign sophistication. It must have worked, for the date over the doorway read 1888. Joffee's was to Plainview what Macy's was to New York, as much a tradition as a shopping destination. Andi glanced at the merchandise in the windows. Sundresses and beach umbrellas seemed a long way from her hometown. In the corner of the display were three torso mannequins in swimsuits. The red thong bikini caught Andi's eye and she smiled. A woman *would* have to be headless to wear something like that in this town, she thought.

On down the street she passed Schott Pharmacy and then the hardware store. Yes, Plainview was much as it had always been. But if you looked closer, it had changed. The buildings that had once housed little dress shops and five-and-dimes now sold used furniture and cheap electronics. The old men who sat on the sidewalk benches looked more unkempt and a lot more uninterested than the seniors of twenty years ago.

Andi walked past them, making her way to Connor's Diner at the end of the street. Connor's at least, was still spick-and-span. Its blue vinyl decor was original but still in good condition.

"I'm meeting someone," she told the hostess as she stepped inside.

Andi scanned the room until she spotted the person more dear to her than anyone in the world.

The young woman looked much like Andi herself, except her light brown hair was cut in a cute bob that perfectly framed a chubby big-eyed face. She had headphones in her ears and was rocking in place in the narrow booth where she sat thumbing through a photo album. As Andi approached, she noticed the misbuttoned red Christmas sweater. Andi scooted into the bench facing her. She reached over and pulled out her earbuds, unable to stop herself from commenting.

"Jelly, why are you wearing that winter sweater? It's practically summer, way too hot outside for that."

The bright smile of greeting immediately turned into an expression of patient concern.

"Andi," she said in a very serious, almost incredulous tone. "This is Frosty the Snowman. He's a jolly, happy soul."

"Yeah, well maybe so," Andi agreed. "But you need to save him to wear in December."

Jelly frowned. "That doesn't make sense," she said. "We need to have happiness all year round."

Andi didn't argue. "Where's Pop?" she asked instead.

"He had an appointment," Jelly answered.

"He left you here by yourself?"

"It's okay, Andi," Jelly assured her quickly. "He gave the waitress a tip and told her to watch me. I've been sitting right here looking at my picture book and she's been watching me."

As if on cue, the waitress arrived at the table. Jelly was all smiles for her.

"This is my sister, Andi," she told the woman. "We're twins. Andrea and Angela. But you can call us Andi and Jelly. She's the smart one and I'm the funny one."

"Well, I guess you're both the lucky ones to have each other," the waitress said.

Andi eyed the woman suspiciously looking for sarcasm, but she seemed sincere.

"Would you like something? Cup of coffee? Pie?"

"No, no thanks," Andi said.

"She wants coffee," Jelly corrected.

Andi raised her head to protest.

"Don't worry," Jelly said. "I've got money. It's my treat."

As the waitress headed toward the coffeepot, Andi whispered to Jelly. "Why did you do that? I don't need any coffee and you don't need to buy me anything."

"You do need coffee," Jelly answered. "You drank it all the time when you had a job. I have a job. I can buy you coffee."

Andi watched as her sister set her backpack on the table and began rifling through it. To get to her wallet Jelly first had to unload several wads of crumpled paper, a half-eaten candy bar, a flashlight with two extra batteries, a dozen pieces of plastic jewelry and a baseball cap.

"Why do you carry so much stuff?" Andi asked.

Jelly looked at her blankly. "I might need something," she answered.

"When I get a job I'm going to get you a really nice little purse," Andi told her. "It will be a lot easier to carry around, it won't get filled up with stuff and it'll look a lot more stylish, more grown-up."

"No little purse, Andi," Jelly said. "I gotta have my backpack, 'cause I gotta carry my picture books."

Andi hesitated for a moment and then relented with a sigh. Her younger sister, her twin, was born when Andi was just twelve minutes old. Andi's birth had somehow created a kink in the umbilical cord that her sister relied on for oxygen. Twelve minutes equaled a lot of brain damage. And any amount of brain damage can equal a much different life.

Andi pulled out the remains of the Sunday employment section of the paper and spread it across her side of the table. With a definitive X she marked though the ad for Guthrie

Foods and began looking more carefully at the other items she'd circled.

The waitress set a cup of coffee beside her. The woman began to move away and then hesitated. Andi glanced up.

"Don't bother with that one," she said, pointing to one of the ads circled. "It's not really a job, they want you to buy products from them that you can go out and sell."

"Okay," Andi said, crossing it off as well.

"And this one is a night shift in a really slimy-looking motel. I felt like I was in danger just being there for the interview."

Andi nodded. "So why are you looking?" she asked. "You've got a job."

The waitress shook her head. "This one is my sister's," she answered. "She's off on maternity leave and she was afraid of letting anyone else fill in 'cause they might get to replace her. She'll be coming back in another week or so, so I'm looking all over town for something."

"Yeah," Andi said. "Me, too."

"I have a job!" Jelly piped in. "I deliver meals on wheels."

"Good for you," the waitress said. "Next week your sister and I both may need for you to buy the coffee."

Andi watched Jelly smile proudly.

"I'm Tiff," the waitress said. "Tiff McCarin."

"I'm Andi. And thanks for watching my sister."

Tiff shrugged and then flashed a smile at Jelly. "She's just sitting here looking at photographs not being any trouble to anybody."

"Still, thanks," Andi said. "And good luck on the job search."

"You, too."

★ ★ ★

Pete Guthrie made his way down Aisle Seven, canned fruits, dried fruits, pickles and condiments, his cell phone pressed against his ear. He was a tall guy, three inches over six feet. His long limbs had finally stopped growing, but he retained a lean lankiness that seemed youthful, a contrast from the lines of worry that now appeared permanently etched in his face.

"You've got to give me a better price than that," he said into the phone. "You know I'm being strangled to death by ShopMart and Superbuy."

The response on the other end of the call was apparently less than hopeful. With his free hand, Pete was nervously tugging at a hank of his expensively trimmed brown hair.

"Greg," Pete said, gravely. "You've got to see that we're in this together. Do you honestly think those national chains are going to stick with you if I stumble?"

"Guthrie! Guthrie!" A well-dressed older woman called out for his attention.

Pete stopped in his tracks, gave her a quick half smile and held up his hand as a polite request for her to wait.

"You have to give me a fighting chance here," he continued to admonish over the phone. "I'm not asking for a better deal. I'm just asking for the same deal you'd give to them. Our companies have been doing business together for years."

"Guthrie!" the woman said again, impatiently.

This time Pete completely ignored her.

"If you can give me another percentage point, it will do us both a lot of good, Greg," he continued. "When times are tough, we local yokels have got to stick together."

The woman began snapping her fingers annoyingly.

"I'm waiting!" she pointed out loudly.

Pete interrupted his conversation. "Let me call you back, Greg. I've got a customer." He clapped the phone shut and, forcing a well-practiced smile on his face, turned to the well-heeled, well-coifed and seriously frowning older woman.

"Yes, Mrs. Meyer," he said politely. "What seems to be the problem today?"

"*Mr.* Guthrie," she began with great emphasis on the title. "I want you to know how disappointed I am with the apple-sauce section."

"Something's wrong with the applesauce?"

Mrs. Meyer gestured broadly taking in the entire canned fruit section. "Where is the Sweet Moon Applesauce?" she asked. "I have looked high and low on these shelves and it is nowhere to be found."

Pete didn't even have to look at the shelf to know the answer. "We don't carry that brand anymore," he told her.

"You don't carry it?" Her tone was incredulous. "When was that decision made?" she asked haughtily.

"Ah…I'm not sure exactly," answered. "Maybe last year."

"Well, I certainly didn't hear anything about it."

"Mrs. Meyer, this is a supermarket. We make a lot of product decisions that the typical shopper might not be aware of."

"One would think that the management of this store would have the decency to inform a loyal customer about any changes that might directly affect her."

Pete was at a loss at how to answer that.

"I'm very sorry, Mrs. Meyer," he tried. "If I'd realized that it was important to you, I certainly would have let you know."

"Well, it certainly is important to me," the woman stated.

"I only want applesauce once or twice a year, but today I want it and it's not here."

Pete glanced up at the shelf in question. "We have four, no, five other brands of applesauce available," he said. "How about trying one of those?"

The woman made a disdainful huffing sound.

"I can't imagine how you can just willy-nilly wake up one day and decide to change everything in the store," Mrs. Meyer complained. "I've been shopping here my entire adult life."

"I know you have," Pete agreed. "But we haven't changed everything, we're making small, tiny, minuscule changes."

She raised an eyebrow in disbelief.

"I don't see why you need to make any changes at all."

Pete cleared his throat and tried giving her the logical explanation. "Sweet Moon is packed in the Far East," he said. "These days we're limiting ourselves to local producers and national brands. It saves our customers money as well as the unseen costs of international shipping on items that we make right here."

"That means nothing to me," Mrs. Meyer said. "I like Sweet Moon because it has larger pieces of apple in it. These are pureed to the point of baby food."

"That's how most people like it," Pete pointed out.

"I am not most people!" Mrs. Meyer declared, unnecessarily. Pete had weathered enough encounters with the woman over the years to have no doubt of that.

"Maybe you could write a letter to the applesauce companies and encourage them to come out with a line of product with bigger apple pieces."

That suggestion clearly appalled her.

"Young man, do you think I have nothing better to do with my time than to try to improve the products at your grocery store?"

What Pete thought was that the woman had nothing at all to do but frequent his grocery store, and nothing to say that wasn't a complaint. He glanced down at her basket to see that today's purchase was a small can of Le Sueur peas and a bottle of vitamins. That served to remind him that she was a lonely old woman and that maybe she didn't buy much from his store, but it was everything that she bought.

"I'm awfully sorry, Mrs. Meyer," he said with deliberate kindness. "I'll ask Miss Kepper to make sure that you are immediately informed of all the product changes in the store. And for today, maybe I can direct you to the produce section. We have some really nice looking Rome apples that you could cook this afternoon into exactly the perfect consistency."

Mrs. Meyer allowed him to show her, but she wasn't happy about it.

Once she had huffed off, Pete made his way back through the store. Keeping his eyes open, he spotted a leaking mayonnaise jar, an open bag of cookies, half-eaten and left on a shelf, and an inch long toy car, lost in exactly the perfect spot to cause a calamity for an unsteady senior citizen. When he reached the checkout area he forced the big friendly smile back on his face. His customers needed to see him looking cheerful. And he'd found that his employees made fewer mistakes if it seemed like he was happy with their work. As soon as he reached the door to the office stairway, the smile disappeared.

Pete Guthrie knew that most people in Plainview considered him a very lucky man. He'd grown up as the only son of one of the city's oldest families. In high school he'd been both a scholar and an athlete. He'd done well at the state university, graduating *cum laude*. And after a brief, and very flashy, marriage to a former beauty pageant winner, he had come home to be handed the family business.

He had a fine house, an expensive car and a number of local women stepping all over each other to get his attention. Pete hardly noticed. He didn't have time to notice. His life was consumed by the day-to-day challenge of a keeping a quirky, family-owned store viable in a world of big-box grocery magnets.

Upstairs he walked down the dreary, ill-lit corridor without even noticing it. The door to Miss Kepper's office was open, and he stopped at the entrance for a quick word. The aging spinster had worked for Guthrie Foods longer than Pete had been alive. She knew every aspect of the operation. And without her help, Pete was pretty sure he never would have made it through the first five years.

"Have you found someone to take on the advertising?" he asked.

Miss Kepper shook her head. "I've talked to several candidates, but no one is quite who we're looking for."

Pete nodded, acceding to her judgment. "Okay, well, keep at it. The right person is bound to walk though the door eventually."

The woman agreed.

"Do you have the mailing address for Mrs. Meyer?" Pete asked.

"Mrs. Meyer?"

"You know, the older lady who complains about everything."

"Oh, her. Yes, yes I think I do."

"Good. Could you make a note to yourself to send of copy of every product decision to her."

Miss Kepper looked horrified. "You're joking," she said. "We have about thirty 'discontinues' a week and at least that many new products."

Pete nodded. "Yeah," he said. "And Mrs. Meyer says she wants to hear about every decision we make. So I'm going to bury that old woman in mail," he said. "Send her notices until she screams for mercy. The last thing I need is another senior citizen looking over my shoulder."

As soon as the words were out of Pete's mouth, he wished he could call them back. *Way to go, Peterson,* he thought sarcastically to himself. *Why didn't you just call her a dried-up old maid?*

Miss Kepper was definitely a person in the over sixty-five age category. And she was fiercely loyal to Pete's father, who was, without question, the senior most likely to be looking over Pete's shoulder.

The woman's back stiffened slightly and Pete knew that he'd offended her. Unable to fix that, he instead gifted her with the one thing he knew she would truly be grateful for.

"Listen, I'm going to be working in my office for a while," he said. "Could you hold all my calls? And could you phone my dad and ask him if he could come by here tomorrow."

"Certainly," Miss Kepper answered evenly. The color in her cheeks was the only sign of what those words truly meant to her.

For decades the worst kept secret in the break rooms of

Guthrie Foods continued to be that Miss Doris Kepper was in love with Hank Guthrie, Pete's father.

The two had met in college in 1962. Hank had been a "big man on campus," football star and president of his fraternity. Miss Kepper had been a shy mouse hoping to complete an associate degree and land a job as a secretary. She had fallen for him; hook, line and sinker. It had been her homework, her term papers and her class notes that allowed him to make good grades while leading a wild social life. He'd grown so accustomed to taking advantage of her crush on him, that he'd just never stopped.

After graduation, the lovelorn young woman followed Hank to Plainview and he'd given her a job. The success of the grocery store chain in the 1970s and '80s was due in large part to her hard work. Pete's father had been appropriately grateful. But, it seemed, never inappropriately grateful.

After an extended period of merry bachelorhood, his dad had married socially prominent Madeleine Grosvenor. And she had, in due course, provided Hank with his son and heir.

All this, while Miss Kepper kept her nose to the grindstone and gazed longingly from the sidelines.

Pete, at one time, had thought this was funny. Certainly his father found it very amusing. He'd been making jokes among his friends at the woman's expense for years. Hank called Miss Kepper the Vestal Virgin of Guthrie Foods. He found it hilariously ludicrous that a woman would, for all intents and purposes, give up her own life and future to bask in the shadow of his personal glory.

Back in high school, Pete and his buddies, in that inordinately cruel way young teens find so irresistible, had devised their own unpleasant name for her. They'd called her "Miss Kepper-legs-closed." In hindsight, Pete realized that part of his animosity toward the woman stemmed from a misplaced sense of loyalty to his mother. As well as a big misunderstanding of who uses who in relationships.

Now, working with Miss Kepper on a daily basis, he'd come to like and admire her. And to feel sorry for her and guilty about her. Miss Kepper genuinely loved his father, without, as far as Pete knew, ever getting anything in return. And she treated Pete both with the respect of an esteemed employer and the inexhaustible protectiveness of a doting parent. For that, he could certainly put up with his father's snide interference for a few hours once in a while. Hank's infrequent trips to the store were now the only time that Miss Kepper ever saw him.

Pete continued on down to the corner office. Inside, the perpendicular banks of windows gave him a perfect view of the corner of Grosvenor and Fifth Street. He had seen it so many times, he no longer even noticed it. Behind the desk were the portraits of the three other men who'd run this company, their names on little brass plates below their photos. Henry Peterson Guthrie stood in front of a tiny clapboard store wearing an apron and holding a broom. Henry Peterson Guthrie, Jr. sat for a formal photograph that made him look portly and presidential in wide lapeled pinstripes. Henry P. "Hank" Guthrie, III looked tall and tan in a Guthrie Foods golf shirt with a professional grade titanium club slung casually over his shoulder.

Pete, otherwise known as Henry Peterson Guthrie, IV, didn't wonder what his own photo might look like. He was in no mood to waste his time, energy or his cold hard cash having his portrait taken. When his dad had this job, the money came rolling in. These days every dollar had to be tracked down, hogtied and practically dragged through the door. And it was Pete's responsibility to do most of the dragging.

He crossed the room to the small compact refrigerator in the corner of the room. Opening it, he pulled out a bag of chocolate Mallomars from his stash inside. Pete ripped open the bag and set it on the desk before fishing out a cookie and stuffing it in his mouth. He closed his eyes for a moment, savoring the taste. Then, with a sigh, he pulled the cell phone out of his pocket and sat down at his desk to make the return call to the distributor.

Chapter 2

ANDI'S BROW WAS covered with sweat, her T-shirt was smeared with grease and her hands now sported a number of minor burns as she sat the bubbling casserole in the middle of the kitchen table.

She had never been much of a cook, but how could she be? Andi had been her father's daughter. She'd spent all her after-school time helping him out at work. Jelly was the one who had stayed home with Mom. Now that it was too late, Andi really wanted to be able to feed the family the way they'd always been fed. She wanted to cook.

How hard could it be? she'd asked herself. She'd explored her mother's recipe box and found it to be full of unhelpful secrets, like "dash of complement spices" and "cook to cloudy." She was determined to fix at least a few of the dishes that were her mother's specialties. And this was one of them.

"Dinner!" she called out. She got no immediate response. With a long-suffering sigh she went down the basement stairs.

When they were still kids, her mother had sectioned out the laundry area from a place she called the rumpus room. With its worn furniture, television and Ping-Pong table, it was still the most likely spot to find members of her family any time of the day or night.

Her sister was sitting on the couch cross-legged, elbows on knees with her face in her hands. An open photo album lay on her lap, but her eyes were glued to the TV.

"Jelly, turn that off and go find Pop. Tell him it's time for dinner."

Jelly's brow wrinkled and she looked at Andi with confusion. "We've still got perps," she answered. "We don't eat until after all the perps are caught."

The *perps,* or perpetrators, were the bad guys on Jelly's favorite cop show, *Law & Order.* Without the ability to tell time, Jelly relied on cable programming to let her know when to eat, sleep and wake. Preemptions and changes in the schedule could cause great upheaval. As could apparently, a casserole being done too early.

"You've seen that one a hundred times," Andi told her sister. "Remember, that's the one where the ex-wife tried to frame the new wife to protect her son."

"I know," Jelly said. "But they haven't caught him yet."

"Believe me," Andi told her. "It always turns out the same way."

Jelly seemed skeptical.

"Go out in the garage and get Pop," Andi insisted. "I've fixed a great meal and I don't want it to get cold."

Andi headed back up the stairs. She'd set the table exactly as her mother had taught her. The same plates, the same flatware, the same meal, it was almost the same. But almost, of course, is never quite good enough.

It was nearly ten minutes before the three of them were finally seated around the table, the way families were supposed to be. The way they would have been if her mother was still there.

Her father, at age sixty-six, was still good-looking. He was of average height and described himself as "wiry." His hair, once dark brown, was now mostly gray, and it started a bit further back on his forehead these days. He was quick with a laugh or a joke, unfailingly generous to his friends and neighbors, and completely at ease with Jelly and those he called her "like-minded friends." Walt Wolkowicz had married late in life. He and Ella, Andi and Jelly's mother, had thought it might be too late for children. But they had been blessed with twins. If the reality of those daughters had ever been a source of grief to them, they never said. Her parents had had the perfect marriage. They were true soul mates, two halves of one fused history. Totally in love every day of their lives.

Andi had wondered, more than once, if her inability to find any man she could really settle for was because her parents had set the relationship bar way too high.

"You don't have to fix these meals, Andi," her father told her. "Jelly and I have gotten used to eating light in the evening."

"I wanted to do it," Andi assured him. "You two need a healthy home-cooked meal."

"The food at the center is very healthy," Pop assured her.

Her father, long since retired from his small car wash business, was a volunteer taking lunchtime meals to elderly persons stuck at home. Pop was the driver and Jelly delivered to the front door. It was a good job for both. The church charity that ran the service provided them with a hot lunch every day.

"I'm sure it's fine," she agreed. "But it's not the same as home."

Since the dish was hot, Andi dolloped out generous portions around the table.

"What is this?" Jelly asked, wrinkling her nose.

"It's Mom's chicken-asparagus casserole," Andi answered. "Remember, you always loved it."

Her sister shook her head. "It's something, but I don't think that's what it is."

"Jelly, just say grace," Andi ordered.

The three joined hands around the table and bowed heads.

"Dear God," her sister prayed. "Thank you for all the stuff we get. And please make Andi's cooking taste better than it does."

"Jelly!"

"Don't interrupt me, I'm praying."

At the head of the table, her father was loudly clearing his throat to stifle his laughter.

"And please make sure the D.A. sends that *perp* to Rikers Island for twenty-five to life. Amen."

Her father was still trying to hide his grin as the family began eating.

"Where did you go today?" Andi asked him. "I really don't think you should leave Jelly just sitting alone in a restaurant like that."

"I wasn't alone," Jelly piped in. "The waitress was watching me. Her name is Tiff."

"I had an appointment," Pop answered. "And your sister is perfectly safe sitting in a public place."

"I don't think so," Andi said. "And what kind of appointment did you have. I could have taken you."

"I can get around town on my own, thank you very much," he said. "And you and Jelly got to spend some girl time together."

"I'm perfectly happy to spend time with Jelly, but I don't want her being left on her own waiting for me," Andi said. "I don't think Mom would have allowed it."

She saw her father raise an eyebrow, but he didn't argue. Instead he changed the subject.

"How goes the job search?" he asked her. "Any luck?"

"Not yet," Andi answered. "My interview with Guthrie's was a complete waste of my time. I am so overqualified, they should have gotten on their hands and knees to thank me for applying. But the old biddy who was doing the hiring was just totally negative."

Her father nodded.

"Well, I want you to know that I admire you going out there day after day trying. I never cared for that sort of thing at all," he said. "It goes against my nature to make myself look good in somebody else's eyes. And that's what you've got to do if you want to get hired. I guess that's why I always worked for myself."

Andi sighed. "I'd be delighted to work for myself," she said. "I could be the first self-employed corporate contributions professional. All I'd need is fifteen or twenty million dollars and I could really find some wonderful charities to give it away to."

Her father laughed. Jelly did, too, just to be sociable. Andi was certain that she didn't get the joke, but getting it wasn't the point to Jelly, it was all about laughter.

"I walked by your old place today," Andi said. "I'm surprised that Guthrie hasn't used that corner for a gas station or something."

Her father hesitated as he finished a bite. He had a strange look on his face, before he set his fork on the edge of his plate and pushed it forward and out of his way. "He hasn't used it because he doesn't own it," Pop said.

"I thought you sold that property to them years ago."

"I thought I did, too," Pop said. "Hank agreed to everything but just never got around to signing the deal and paying me the money. So I still own it. I still pay taxes on it."

"Really." Andi was intrigued.

"Yeah, I don't know what happened. I called the man and his attorney both a dozen times over two years and nobody would ever say anything more than it was still 'in process.' I finally gave up. I guess they just changed their mind."

"They changed their mind? Pop, don't you know there are legal remedies for that kind of thing?"

Her father shrugged. "Sweetie, there are things worth fighting for in the world and there are things that are not. I try to have the wisdom to recognize one from the other."

Andi admired her father's honor and his willingness to turn the other cheek, but she knew people in town sometimes took advantage of that. He was a better man than Plainview often deserved.

"The Guthries are lucky you didn't sell it to someone else."

Her father shook his head. "Nobody else ever showed any interest. I guess there's not much anyone could do with it."

"What do you mean that there's not much anyone could do with it," Andi said. "It's on one of the busiest corners in the whole downtown area. Half the people in town drive past it every day."

Her father nodded. "Yeah, it does seem a shame that it's just sitting there costing me money."

"I should open up some kind of business there," Andi said, absently.

"Yeah, you probably should," her father told her. "When a person has a job and a regular check coming in, it's always hard to risk that by going off on your own. But when you're unemployed, well, what's that old saying, 'when you've got nothing, you've got nothing to lose.'"

Her father's words caught Andi's attention.

"You'd be okay if I opened some kind of business in that place?"

"Sure," he said. "If you can think of something to do with it, you ought to do it. You probably won't get rich, but it sure wouldn't hurt to have some cash in your pocket and to build back your savings. You'll need it to move back to the city one day."

"I'm not moving back," Andi reminded him. "I'm staying in Plainview."

"Well, then, you'll need an income even more," he said. "It may be a good long while before business in this town begins to pick up again. I'll let you have the building for free. You can pay me after you make your first million." He chuckled.

Andi did too. It seemed pretty unlikely.

"The building's way too small for a shop or a restaurant," she said. "It would be a good size for an office. But who needs an office with a drive-through?"

"That's been my problem with it all along," her father said. "I can't tear the place down because it's part of an architectural conservation zone. I can't expand, because the lot is undersized and pie-shaped. I couldn't add so much as a closet without getting into the easement of Guthrie's property. It was fine for what it was, but I could never figure what else to do with it."

"Maybe it could be a drive-through coffee place," Andi suggested.

"I don't know how much demand there is for that kind of thing," Pop said. "But it sure doesn't hurt to look into it."

"Great!" Andi said, feeling surprisingly pleased and optimistic. She forked a big bite of casserole in her mouth and discovered why her father had pushed his plate away and why her sister was playing with hers.

"Yuck, this is awful!"

Jelly and Pop nodded.

"You can't cook, Andi," her father pointed out. "You never could. And I don't know why you keep thinking you can, 'cause you're terrible at it."

"Mom was so good at it," Andi said.

"She was. But you're not," her father said. "So what do you girls think? How about some nice cheese and crackers? Maybe we can slice up an apple."

Jelly nodded enthusiastically.

Andi was still mourning her epicurean disaster as she carried the casserole to the garbage disposal. "I don't get it," she said. "I did everything I was supposed to do. And it looks just exactly the way Mom's used to look."

Her father chuckled with wisdom born of experience. "How things look, as often as not, completely fool us as to how things are."

★ ★ ★

The next morning Pete was sitting in front of the computer screen in his office, poring over a plan-o-gram from the distributor. The latest changes involved squeezing the books and magazines section to add more dietary supplements. The distributor was supposed to be doing constant research about what people wanted to buy. But Pete wasn't sure if, in this tough economy, his customers were truly more interested in organic gingko than they were in John Grisham.

He heard his father before he saw him. The booming voice that stood out in any crowd poured down the hallway. His father was talking with Miss Kepper, jovial to the edge of flirty, without ever quite pushing past what was acceptable between employer and employee.

"I wish I had you with me at City Hall, Doris," he heard his dad tell her. "Every two weeks they deliver a mountain of paper for me to go through and it's really cutting into my golf time."

His father laughed as if he were joking, but Pete knew there was more truth to his words than he wanted to admit.

Upon retirement, Hank Guthrie had run for, and been elected to, the Plainview city council. It was not that he had any great interest in politics or municipal governance. The day-to-day operations were run by a team of bureaucratic professionals. The five aldermen were elected ostensibly to oversee their work. The positions were compensated at the rate of one dollar per year. That meant, for the most part, the position of alderman was held by the affluent or the retired. Hank Guthrie qualified on both counts.

Naturally gregarious, and a glutton for attention, sitting on the council gave Pete's father an important position in the community, without any of the risk and headache of operating a business.

"If my boy gives you one moment of grief," Hank said to Miss Kepper. "Hand in your notice and come help me out. You know, I just don't feel like myself without you as my right-hand man."

Alone in his office, Pete rolled his eyes. Why did he have to do that? he wondered about his father, not for the first time. Why couldn't he just be kind to her without holding out this carrot that the two of them could be together? Pete sincerely hoped Miss Kepper didn't take the bait. He would hate to lose her but, worse than that, he would hate for his dad to once more put her into a position that drew public attention. He could imagine a tabloid headline: Lovelorn Old Maid Persists As Grocery Owner Groupie Well Into Retirement.

Pete could no longer concentrate on his work. He leaned back in his chair and waited. A sense of hunger swept through him and he glanced toward the refrigerator. He resisted the temptation. It was better not to be caught eating when his father came in. So he just sat there, tensely listening to the one-sided conversation between two people who'd known each other for more than forty years.

Finally his father made his way down to the corner office that had once been his own. Hank was almost as tall as his son, still in robust health, tanned and good-looking and always impeccably and expensively dressed.

"Hi, Dad," Pete said, rising to his feet to offer a handshake across the desk. "Thanks for coming down."

Hank ignored his son's outstretched hand. "What the hell is going on downstairs?" he asked gruffly and without preamble. "Why don't you turn on some lights? The place is too dark. Do you think you're running a stinking nightclub or something?"

His father's vehemence came as no surprise to Pete. Hank had never been the type to offer an *attaboy* to his only child.

"There's plenty of light, Dad," Pete replied evenly. "It's directed light, focused on the products and the aisles. There is no reason to light up the ceilings."

"Except that without it the whole store looks like a damn cave!"

"It saves energy and it saves money," Pete answered. "Our customers appreciate that saving being reflected in the price of their groceries."

"I don't like it," Hank said adamantly. "Guthrie's is not some bistro grocery, we're a family food market. I want it changed. And I want it changed now."

"No."

Pete's answer was not loud, or angry or even emphatic. It was matter-of-fact. It was his store. He made the decisions. And every time he talked to his father, he had to reinforce that fact.

The two men stared at each other across the width of the fancy mahogany desk. The passing of the Guthrie family torch had not been an easy one. Any success that Pete managed was hardly noted. And if up for discussion was usually noticed and discounted as pure luck. Setbacks, however, were placed squarely at Pete's door. No mitigating factors like an economic downturn, erosion of the local market base or increased pressure from national competitors were allowed as excuses. Hank took a strange pleasure that was almost delight in the problems his son faced. It wasn't that he wanted Pete to fail, but he certainly didn't want him to be too successful. Hank needed to be the "star" of the Guthrie Foods family, even if only in his own mind.

"So, how's Mom?" Pete asked, finally breaking the silence.

Hank leaned back in his chair, feeling more relaxed knowing Pete had been forced to speak first.

"Oh, you know your mother," Hank said. "She's just back from somewhere, headed somewhere else. I think she was in Mexico and now she's off to Japan."

Pete raised an eyebrow. "Actually she was in Peru and she's going on a five-week tour of China."

Hank shrugged. "Well, whatever. If you want her to stay home, you'll have to come up with some grandchildren. That's about the only thing I can think of that might keep her in town."

"She loves to travel," Pete said. "I think she should do that as long as she enjoys it. She spent a lot of years being the good company wife. This is her retirement, too."

"Retirement?" Hank offered a disdainful guffaw. "That woman never put in an honest day's work in her life. She lived off her old man, then she lived off me. What's she got to retire from?"

Pete didn't answer. It wasn't worth it to tell his father what he thought. He thought that if his mother had any sense at all she should "retire" from being Hank Guthrie's wife. She had certainly put up with enough already.

Instead, he said more congenially, "You know, she needs to get away from this town sometimes."

Hank shrugged. "It's all right by me," his father said. "But

I do get tired of eating at the country club. Where do you eat dinner?"

"At my house, in my kitchen," Pete replied.

Hank shook his head. "There's something wrong with that. I know you're gun-shy on marriage after your last fiasco, but couldn't you at least get some live-in girlfriend to cook and clean up."

"I can cook and clean up by myself," Pete told him.

"I suppose you can have sex by yourself, too," Hank said. "Though in my day they said that would make you go blind." The older man chuckled at his own joke.

After only the smallest hesitation, Pete's face broke into a wide grin. "Dad, you're the one who's complaining about the light downstairs," he pointed out.

Hank didn't enjoy having the joke turned on him. Within a couple of minutes he made an excuse to leave, without even bothering to find out why Pete had invited him down to the store.

Hank was in the doorway when Pete got around to his question.

"I want you to represent Guthrie's in the charity golf tournament," he said.

His father's brow furrowed. "Well, I'm playing, of course," he said. "But my intention was to represent myself as alderman."

"Could you wear a Guthrie's shirt and hand in my check?"

"You need to be out there yourself," Hank said. "You are Guthrie Foods now and it doesn't do the business any good for you to hide in here in the store."

"I'm not hiding, Dad. I'm working."

"Let Doris do that," Hank said. "People need to see you out in the community. They need to see you taking leisure time. That's the only way they'll think you're successful."

"I don't care if they *think* I'm successful, as long as I am successful."

Hank still didn't approve. "You're as pale as a night-shift clerk," he said. "And you're getting too fleshy around the middle. Your golf game has always been crap. It's not going to get any better if you're here at the store all day."

"Just do it for me, Dad," Pete said.

His father made a dismissive sound, but agreed. Then he left without even a parting word to Miss Kepper.

Pete stood at the corner windows just staring into the distance. He watched as his father left the building and walked over to his shiny new Lincoln that he'd illegally parked in a handicapped spot.

"Figures," Pete whispered to himself and shook his head.

As his father drove away, Pete congratulated himself on having thought to ask Hank to golf for the company. Pete was not a big participant in charitable events. He believed in charity and made a point to give, but the last thing he wanted to do with his time was attend a gala or a golf tournament. *Peterson, you're just not a party guy,* he reminded himself.

Suddenly out of the corner of his eye he saw something that just wasn't right. He stepped slightly closer to the window and squinted. There was someone moving around in the old car wash building. His first thought was to call the police. In his mind that idea was immediately followed by the curious question of "what kind of burglar breaks into an abandoned building in broad daylight?"

Undoubtedly, it had to be kids, he decided. He would just take care of it himself.

With a quick, "I've got my phone," to Miss Kepper, Pete headed down the hallway. He took the stairs two at a time and breezed through the front of the store and out the door without so much as a glance around.

He couldn't remember if there was anything stored inside the place next door, but even if it was empty, he didn't want anyone inside, perhaps vandalizing the place. Even if they were just trespassing, with his luck, they'd trip and break a leg and Guthrie Foods would be found liable.

He began loping across the parking lot. Always an athlete, he used to run every day. During his marriage, he'd gotten up to fifty miles a week. That time of his life was swiftly followed by what he thought of as the "divorce era" when he quit running completely. Now he jogged occasionally, but considering how winded he got just crossing the parking lot, he thought perhaps it wasn't occasionally enough.

Pete was breathing hard as he came around the corner of the little building. The windows were all boarded up. He glanced at the door, expecting to see evidence of it being forced open with a crowbar. Instead, it was casually ajar, with a key still hanging in the lock. That surprised him, but it didn't stop him. He pushed the door open more widely sending a larger shaft of light into the crowded, tightly packed space. He caught sight of a man in a ball cap and coveralls picking up a big brown box.

"Put that down!" Pete ordered in his most authoritative tone, sounding very much like his father.

The shocked thief immediately set the box back on the floor. Then, inexplicably, picked it back up.

"Who do you think you are? The packing police?" the thief asked.

Pete was taken aback by the voice, obviously that of a woman. And a woman who sounded not the least bit guilty of breaking and entering.

"I…uh…this is private property and you are trespassing," he explained firmly if more quietly.

The thief set the box back down and, stubbornly, put her hands on her hips. "It sure is private property," she said. "But you're the one trespassing. Bye-bye!"

The last comment was offered with a snarky little wave. The disrespect in the gesture was jaw-dropping. He couldn't imagine what this woman could be thinking.

"Do you know who I am?"

She huffed. "I'm sure you think you're God's gift to women, but I doubt if you'll be able to verify that."

That statement left him almost speechless, enough so that he stammered over his next words. "I…I…I am Pete Guthrie and this building is owned by Guthrie Foods."

"Wrong!" the thief said, moving closer and into the shaft of light. "This property belongs to Walt Wolkowicz. You Guthries just *think* you own the whole town."

Pete could see her face now, framed by a faded Pacers cap, and he recognized it. She was one of Wolkowicz's daughters. In high school Pete and his buddies had called them "the retard twins." There was the "math retard" and the "retard retard." Though he hadn't seen her in years, this was obviously Ms. Math, looking very much like she always had. Geeky, skinny and wearing men's clothes. What was her name? The question bounced around Pete's brain. It was a guy's name that could be used for a girl. Billie or Jamie? No it started with an *A*.

"You're…uh…you're Alex, right? Alex Wolkowicz."

"Andi," she answered, a steely annoyance evident in her voice. "And you're Pete Guthrie, just like you said. Though I wouldn't have recognized you. I guess all those Mallomars have finally begun to catch up with you."

Pete was startled. How could this person, whose name he hadn't been able to recall, remember his addiction to Mallomars? He decided to ignore that question in favor of something more pertinent.

"Where did you get this key and what are you doing inside here?" he asked. "Your family may feel attached to this place, but we own it."

"Nope," she answered. "Sorry, that's not true."

"Yes, it is," Pete answered. "It happened years ago. I was away at college…maybe you were, too. Your father sold it to my father. Ask him."

"I did ask him," Andi answered. "He says that your father never paid him and so the deal never went through, the deed was never transferred. We've been paying the taxes and so…and so it's ours."

Pete was surprised. And when it came to things that he ought to know, he really didn't like to be surprised. He was sure his dad had made a deal. Surely he wouldn't have just dropped it. He scanned his memory for some piece of evidence supporting what he'd always thought was, in fact, true. Nothing immediately came to mind.

"Well, if what you're saying is correct, and I don't know that it is, I'm sure it was an oversight," he told her.

"Yeah, oversight, I'm sure that's what it was," Andi replied, her tone ripe with inexplicable sarcasm. "It makes total sense that the high and mighty Guthries would completely overlook a regular guy like Walt Wolkowicz."

"Excuse me? The 'high and mighty Guthries'? What in the devil are you talking about?"

"You wouldn't have pulled a crappy business trick like this with one of your cronies from the country club," she answered venomously. "Because my pop's a decent hardworking guy who would never be any threat to you, you were totally free to treat him shabbily. Well, I'm not about to be as generous to you as he would. Get off my property!"

Chapter 3

IT WAS THE middle of the afternoon and Walt was in a hurry. They'd finished all the lunch deliveries at meals on wheels and he'd brought Jelly home. He'd planned to make a quick getaway, but his daughter had plans for laundry.

"This is Wednesday, wash day," she said, incredulous with his suggestion that it might wait until tomorrow. "It rhymes, Pop. My wash day is Wednesday. That's the rule."

Walt knew better than to try to go against a "rule." By necessity, in his daughter's life the three Rs were not reading, writing and 'rithmetic, all of which were beyond her grasp. Instead, her life worked due to regimen, routine and rules.

"All right," he agreed. "Let's get your laundry started, but let's hurry."

"We don't hurry, Pop," she reminded him. "We take our time and do it right."

With a sigh and a quick glance at his watch, he followed her downstairs without argument. Argument was futile. Arguments were for people who could change their mind. The reality of his daughter Jelly was that her mind could not, would not, ever change.

"I peg her IQ at about 50, maybe a little higher," the old family doctor had told them. "You can look at her yourself and see that she's totally vacant."

Walt had looked at his perfect little three-year-old with the big brown eyes and had not seen anything vacant about her. She was pretty and sweet and quiet. No, she was not like her sister, Andi. In that doctor's office Andi would have been into everything. She was curious about everything, climbing everywhere, and nothing in the room would have been safe. Jelly sat there, perfectly dressed with a bow in her hair. She wouldn't cause a problem for anybody.

"We can't always predict these outcomes. Adulthood is a long way off," the doctor continued. "But I'd say you'll be lucky if she's self-feeding and potty trained."

He heard his wife, Ella, gasp. He glanced over at her. Her face was pale, stricken. All he could think to say was, I'm sorry. I'm sorry I asked you to marry me. I'm sorry I got you into this mess. But it was not something a husband could say. He kept silent.

"It's up to you, of course," the doctor continued. "What I recommend, in cases like this, is to send them to a state institution. They usually don't live all that long anyway and it's harder if the family gets attached to them."

"We're already attached to her," Walt told the man. "We're not sending her anywhere."

The doctor shrugged. "A lot of the new thinking is that they do better at home with their families. And the law says now that they can't be kept out of public school. So if you want to take her home…well, just do the best you can."

And they had.

Downstairs in the laundry room, Jelly set her basket of dirty clothes on the floor and immediately began sorting the whites and the colors.

Walt opened the cabinet above the machine and retrieved a couple of plastic measuring cups and a bottle of detergent.

"How many loads do you think you have?" he asked rhetorically.

With a furrowed brow, Jelly assessed her laundry pile critically.

"About twenty," she answered.

Walt glanced at her dirty clothes and set two measuring cups on the counter. "I think you can make it all fit in one load for whites and one for colors," he said.

"Okay," Jelly agreed.

Walt poured the correct amount of detergent in each cup. Jelly had real issues with portion. Whether it was overfilling the milk glass, permeating the house with perfume or having an inch of sugar in the bottom of a cup of tea. If some was good, more was better. Walt had mopped up the laundry room too many times to allow her to pour her own laundry soap.

"One of these for each load," he reminded her. "Just like on your chart."

The chart he indicated was a homemade poster attached to the front of the washing machine. It showed seven blocks of color, red, yellow, blue, green, orange and purple, lined up left to right. These were interspersed with stick pictures of washing fundamentals. The colors matched up to splashes of the same color on buttons, dials and doors of the washer and dryer. A big black arrow on the left indicated where to start. And sitting atop it was a brown-haired girl magnet, representing Jelly herself. Moving the magnet through the steps would keep Jelly on task.

"Remember to look at your chart and follow your colors," Walt told her.

Jelly gave him a long-suffering look, more typically seen on the face of an average teenager.

"I know how to do it, Pop," she said. "I follow the chart. I don't need your help."

"Okay," he said. "Just concentrate on what you're doing. I have to go out to an appointment. Andi will be back soon, but I don't know exactly when."

Jelly nodded.

"What do you do if you hear something ringing?" he asked. It was a test question.

She answered smartly. "I can answer the phone, but don't answer the door."

He gave her a thumbs-up. "I've got my cell, so call me if you need me. What's my number on your speed dial?"

"You're number one!" she answered in the cadence of a pep rally.

Walt couldn't help but grin at her. "Good girl."

"Okay, Pop, don't worry," she said.

"I won't," he lied.

He took the stairs two at a time and rushed toward the front door. At the hall tree he stopped to grab his keys and hesitated a moment to glance at himself in the mirror. His face, he thought, was awfully grizzled from working outside all his life.

But he still had most of his hair. He was not as muscled as he once had been, but there wasn't an ounce of extra fat on him.

He noticed the edge of his collar was slightly frayed. He ran his thumb over the flaw. Maybe he should buy some new shirts, he thought to himself. It had been years since he'd bought a shirt. Ella always did that for him. He would never have bought one like this, he realized. It was a pale tan color with a very small brown stripe. His favorite color was blue. Maybe he would buy himself some blue shirts.

He stopped that train of thought abruptly.

"If it's about what color shirt you wear, you're doomed already," he told the mirror.

Shaking his head, he walked out the front door.

In the narrow driveway of the home he and Ella had purchased shortly after they married, his old truck awaited him. He kept the 1985 Ford in top condition. There were still a lot of them on the road. When he'd taken on meal delivery, he'd agreed to sport a decal on his doors. The truck was clearly identifiable as St. Hyacinth Senior Service Meals on Wheels. Every person in town who knew him would recognize his truck.

Walt climbed inside and carefully backed out into the street. He checked his watch again and winced. But he made it out to Fifteenth Street pretty quickly. He caught the light at Baltimore Avenue and turned left down Ridley Boulevard ahead of the Village Transit. He made it to the parking lot of the branch library where he locked the truck and ran to the bus stop, just in time to step on the *Mainline to Mt. Ridley.*

He showed his Senior Pass, but the driver didn't bother to look at it, just acknowledged Walt's familiar face with a nod.

Walt didn't want to be recognizable, but there was no help for that. He glanced around the bus and didn't see any faces that went with any names he knew. Relieved, he took a seat near the back door and watched the summer street go by. It was a busy thoroughfare these days with houses and sidewalks. When he'd driven this road as a teenager it had been a narrow lane that cut through a grove of trees. It had been well-traveled on Saturday nights as it led to the notorious Lovers Leap Overlook. The four of them crowded onto the bench seat of his '39 Chevy pickup. Paul, his best friend, could sometimes borrow his dad's car, but more often they were in the pickup.

"I don't mind," he'd teased the girls. "The less space you can put between us, the better."

The girls were both their "steadies" and could take a joke well enough not to be offended. Besides, Walt was pretty sure that even in those days, when nice girls waited until they had a ring on their finger, they hadn't wanted much distance either.

Remembering it all had him smiling by the time the bus reached the end of the line. The entrance to Mt. Ridley Park had changed considerably over the years. There was certainly no driving up to the overlook. Big metal balustrades guarded the drive and those entering were funneled through a ticket booth. Five dollars for adults, two dollars for children, Walt got a dollar off as a senior discount.

He walked slowly down the main pathway for several minutes, cautiously on the lookout for familiar faces. There were very few people at all in the middle of a Wednesday afternoon and none that he worried might know him.

Walt reached a set of rocky steps that ventured off into

the trees. The sign above it read Alternate View Trail Dead Ends. He glanced around one last time to make certain he hadn't been seen. Then he hurried up the steps and disappeared into the trees.

Andi considered Wednesday to have been a fairly productive day. The more she thought of having her own business, any business, the more she liked the idea. She had tossed and turned the night before, too excited to sleep. The prospect of finally doing something had her humming with optimism.

Her enthusiasm lasted through her crowded bus ride downtown and accompanied her arrival at City Hall. But after a long wait in an uncomfortable chair, her impromptu meeting with Mr. Gilbert, at the city's Code Compliance Office, had been full of pluses and minuses.

Mr. Gilbert was a big, happy gregarious man who seemed to love meeting people. But he was less enthusiastic about the intricate web of laws, regulations and ordinances, the enforcement of which comprised his job.

After some lengthy hemming and hawing, an inordinate amount of clicking around on his computer screen and a couple of consultations with the huge ledger books laid out on a crowded table at the far end of his office, he had this to tell her. "I've got some good news and some bad news."

He delivered the line in the cadence of a late-night TV comedian.

"Okay," Andi said. "How about the good news first."

"We've looked at that building in our overall downtown plan," he told her. "Structurally, it seems like it's in good shape. It was built in 1919 by a reputable construction firm.

It was, we think, the very first purpose-built gas station in the city. There were some grocery stores and other businesses that sold gas on the side. But this place on the corner of Grosvenor and Fifth Street was most likely the first of its kind in the city."

"Well, that's interesting," Andi said.

Mr. Gilbert nodded. "Which is why the city has it on the historic preservation list."

She nodded.

"The building itself appears sound," he continued. "And it's been kept up-to-date with electrical wiring and sewer drains."

Andi nodded. Her father had told her as much the night before.

"Then what's the bad news?" she asked.

Gilbert's face screwed into a pained expression. He obviously did not relish being the source of negative news. "The property has a lot of limitations," he said. "It won't work for most retail. I was thinking maybe it would be a good site for a minimum employee service business."

"A minimum employee service business?" Andi repeated. "What exactly is that?"

"A kind of one-man operation," he answered. "Maybe a watchmaker or a shoe repair."

Andi bit her lip as she tried not to roll her eyes. Watchmaking and shoe repair were not exactly the kind of cash cow she had in mind, at least not in the last hundred years! She managed not to say that.

"I was thinking of something more in the line of a drive-through coffee place," she told him. "You know, commuters grabbing a quick double-cream mocha latte before they get to the office."

Mr. Gilbert frowned. What he thought of that as a business prospect he didn't say. But he did understand its ramifications with city code.

"A place like that would fall under the statutes for restaurant operation," he told her. "You don't have nearly enough parking for that."

"But people won't be parking," Andi explained. "They'll just be driving through."

"The ordinances require parking anyway."

"But I won't need parking."

"It doesn't matter if you actually need it," he insisted. "It would still fall under the food service guidelines, so you'd still have to have it."

"That's crazy?"

"No, it's city government," Mr. Gilbert explained.

Andi couldn't tell if that answer was meant as sarcasm or not.

After several more minutes of unfruitful discussion, the code compliance officer finally gave her the wiggle room she needed.

"You can go to the city council and ask for a variance," he said.

"How do I do that?"

"You present a business plan and ask to be put on the agenda. You go before the council and answer questions. If you can make your case, they have the discretion to exempt you from specific regulations."

"How quickly can I do that?"

"Council meets every two weeks," Mr. Gilbert said. "The next meeting is on Monday, but that doesn't give you enough time to put anything together."

"Of course it does," Andi assured him. "I can put together a proposal this weekend."

She left the city offices feeling buoyed and headed over to the car wash. Her mind was already at work formulating the written presentation. However, once she arrived at the building, the amount of work she encountered dampened her enthusiasm tremendously.

Her father's deal with Guthrie involved both the building and the contents, so Pop had stacked everything left over from his car wash business neatly inside, boarded up the windows and locked the door. Now, years later, that had proved not to be the best idea.

She walked though the dank, dark little building, not quite as big as her bedroom. The place smelled moldy and dirty. It was going to take time and elbow grease. Since she was the one who was going to have to come up with both, there was no excuse not to get started.

In the closet that functioned as a unisex bathroom, she found her father's old coveralls still hanging on the hook on the back of the door. She smiled when she saw them. She'd once had a pair just like them. Car washing had been her after-school job. Maybe not as teenage glamorous as flipping burgers or taking tickets at the movie theater, but she'd enjoyed it. There was something very satisfying in making an old grimy car shine like it was brand-new. Recalling that, she told herself that cleaning the building, making it nice and new would surely give her a lot of the same sense of accomplishment.

With a huff of determination, she changed out of her good clothes into the old coveralls. Her dad was not a big guy, so they fit, more or less. A glance in the bathroom mirror indicated a fashion look that was significantly less than stylish and attractive. But it kept her good clothes from getting ruined by the accumulation of dust and dank in the place. And who would see her?

The implied answer of "no one" changed abruptly an hour later when Pete Guthrie showed up at the door, acting like the King of Plainview and talking to her like she was a criminal.

Andi was right in the middle of sorting the leftover supplies. There were cases of soap and wax, gallons of undercarriage rust prohibitors and sealed boxes of interior fragrance options. She'd stacked all that aside, hoping that she might be able to sell it for some start-up money. She then just began attacking the boxes of vending machine supplies. The ancient crackers and ten-year-old candy bars would simply have to go to the Dumpster. So she was in a less than congenial frame of mind when Pete arrived on the doorstep, looking clean and sharp, tanned and attractive in a way that he hadn't been, even in his high school heartthrob days.

She wasn't sure exactly what made her so angry. Of course, there was the crappy unfinished property deal with her father. And there was his unfounded accusation that she was trespassing. But Andi suspected it was more than just that. It was a lot of leftover resentment from high school.

Whenever she thought about those long-ago days, and she didn't think about them often, she saw herself as completely different from the geeky math girl she had been back then.

Andi had proved herself to herself. She knew she could be successful out in the big world. What people thought back in the little world of Plainview meant nothing to her, or almost nothing.

But Pete Guthrie had snuck up on her. He'd caught her looking unattractive and feeling unsuccessful. And suddenly all those long-ago insecurities had reared their ugly heads. Pete had brought it all back. It felt as if the happy, attractive in-crowd out in front of school, enjoying each other's company, laughing at those who weren't in their circle, were only a glance away.

And Pete Guthrie, Pete Guthrie was the worst of them!

That thought caught Andi up short. Pete had not been the worst of them. He'd simply been one of them. He'd been the one she'd liked. Pete had been her high school crush.

Acknowledging that fact, even after all these years, caused Andi considerable embarrassment. She'd spent three long years dreaming about him, sighing over him, watching him walk down the hallways, wishing he would speak to her. Which, of course, he never really did.

But he was speaking to her now. And her response was defensive, angry, full of everything it shouldn't be.

Mentioning the Mallomars had been a real mistake. What had brought that word to her lips? It had been a flaying shot intended to wound. She'd needed to insult him, but managed instead to suggest that she'd been paying attention to him. Having a good memory could be humiliating.

She had completely overreacted to his appearance. She knew it the minute he turned to walk away and admonished herself for that. Getting all miffed at him was stupid. If she really wanted to run a business on that corner, it would not be a good idea to start trouble with her next-door neighbor. The past was in the past. And if she was going to put her future on this corner, she'd need to get along with Guthrie Foods.

She'd do better next time. Next time when he would undoubtedly show up to apologize for mistaking her for a thief, she'd be magnanimous. That would be good. Magnanimous was always good.

It was nearly suppertime when she arrived home. She was dirty, tired and hungry. But she was excited, too. For the first time since she'd returned to Plainview, she felt as if she'd made the right decision. Not just the right decision for her sister and her father. Today, finally, she felt as if she'd made the right decision for herself.

In the driveway she noticed that her father's truck was gone. She felt a pang of disappointment. She wanted to talk to him about her day, about her plans. Inside, she found her sister, Jelly, in the basement meticulously folding up her laundry.

"Where's Pop?" she asked.

"He had an appointment."

"Another appointment?" Andi frowned to herself. Her father was almost never sick and visited the dentist maybe a couple of times a year. What kind of appointments could he be having?

She shrugged off the question.

"I went to City Hall today, Jelly," she told her sister. "I talked to a man there about starting up a business in Pop's old car wash."

"Who was the man at City Hall?" Jelly asked eagerly. "Was it Jack McCoy?"

Andi was momentarily confused, then remembered that Jack McCoy was a character from Jelly's favorite *Law & Order*.

"No," she answered with a sigh and a bittersweet smile for her sister. "It was somebody else."

Andi headed back upstairs to put together something for the family dinner. After the chicken-and-asparagus casserole fiasco, she'd decided maybe the light supper concept was not all that bad. Besides, she was going to be way too busy on her start-up business to invest the time needed to become a decent home cook.

Tonight she wanted to get to work on her drive-through coffee proposal. She didn't have enough background to get her mind completely around the possibilities, but she had no doubt she could get up to speed and wow the locals in time for the council meeting on Monday. She was eager for the challenge.

The last load was spinning noisily in the dryer as Jelly pulled out the white, satiny album of wedding photos. It was very important to keep it clean, Mom always said that. So Jelly took great pains to do so. She didn't look at it often, but Wednesday wash day was a good time. Nothing could be cleaner than laundry time.

As she opened it she could almost hear her mother's voice admonishing her to "be careful." Jelly glanced through the dozens of photos of the bride and groom's big day. The huge white dress with its cathedral train dominated each picture. And the pearl encrusted veil shimmered around her mother's face as if she were an angel. Jelly turned to the photo that she liked the best. The two stood in front of a three layer wedding cake, quiet, serious, not even glancing at the other, each of them with a hand on a silver knife slicing cleanly through the thin sweetness of buttercream frosting.

"Foreman, has the jury reached a verdict?" Jelly asked herself.

Chapter 4

SATURDAY MORNING, PETE woke up early and, rather than linger over coffee, decided he should try to get in a run. First, of course, he had to dig out some running gear and a decent pair of shoes. He found what he needed in an upstairs guest room still in a packing box. He rarely ventured upstairs except for sleeping. Everything he needed was on the first floor. But then, a single guy who spent all of his waking hours working didn't have many needs. Especially when it came to a house.

He'd bought this one, in the tony neighborhood where his parents lived, for his ex-wife. He had known that Minx liked wealthy people, wealthy parties and prominent social position. Plainview wasn't her hometown, but Pete had been sure that in Plainview, as his wife, she had a very good chance of being the most important hostess in the entire community. Pete had wanted very much to give her that.

He'd never really gotten a chance. She'd been with him

when they bought the house, she'd ordered the kitchen upgrades and the window coverings. But she'd never actually got around to moving in. She'd hesitated to leave her friends in the city. Pete hadn't realized, until it was way too late, that it had been a particular friend who kept her there. And that the person she ended up leaving was him.

He was very lucky. His father told him that all the time. Pete was lucky she'd insisted on a quick, no-muss, no-fuss divorce. Lucky that she was keener on snaring her new fish than cleaning the one she'd already caught.

His dad was right about that, of course. But Pete measured his good luck another way. He imagined, in horror, being trapped for decades in a marriage where the two principals could neither like nor respect each other. Or, to put a finer point on it, he didn't want the marriage that his parents had. He didn't relay that bit of insight to his dad.

In shorts, T-shirt and running shoes, Pete went out on his front porch bouncing and stretching. His next-door neighbor, Mrs. Joffee, was in her driveway dressed for synagogue and headed to her shiny blue Mercedes.

"Good morning!" he called out to her.

She smiled. "Hi, Pete."

He liked Mrs. Joffee a lot. And not just because she was one of the few of his mother's friends who hadn't had occasion to sleep with his father. She was funny and smart and still very attractive for a woman his mom's age. She'd married an older man and she'd been a widow for a decade or more. She was one of the wealthiest ladies in town, but there was no pretense about her at all. She was a homebody who liked puttering in her yard and listening to classical music. She was a quiet neighbor. No visitors except her two sons.

Pete took the porch steps two at a time.

"How's business?"

Mrs. Joffee shrugged. "You'll have to ask Dave or Seth," she answered. "I try to stay out of it."

Maybe that's what he *really* liked about her, Pete thought. She'd run the downtown department store for several years, but once she'd turned it over to the next generation, she'd stayed out of the way.

"Looks like it's going to be a beautiful day," she said.

"Yes, ma'am," he agreed.

With that he waved goodbye and was off running. The headphones in his ears played top forty tunes from his college days, keeping his pace strong and steady. He didn't have a regular route. Mainly, he just tried to stay off the streets with the most traffic as he made his way toward the soccer fields. The parks department had installed a low-impact jogging track around the perimeter. It was a popular place for runners from all over town. Unfortunately for Pete, it was two miles from his house. By the time he got to the field, he was breathing so hard he had to stop. Bent forward with his hands on his knees, he tried to catch his breath.

Wolkowicz might be right, he thought. The Mallomars sure weren't burning off like they used to.

Tomorrow morning he'd run the track, he decided. As soon as he was fit to move, he began walking back toward home, trying to keep a pace that was at least more than a lazy stroll. Instead of turning down his own street, he decided to stop by his parents' house. His mom had jetted off last night on her latest trip. He rarely visited the house when his dad was there alone. But remembering Wolkowicz, he found himself thinking about what she'd told him about the car wash property. He wanted to find out how the deal had fallen apart.

The home Pete had grown up in was a two-story brick Colonial set atop a sloped lot, the rise adding to its imposing curb appeal. The impression created was "somebody important lives here" and none of his mother's lovingly cultivated shrubs and flower beds could disguise the coldness, the exclusiveness, of that message.

He avoided the front door and went around to the tall, wrought-iron gate at the side. He keyed in the entry code and when the lock snapped open he let himself into the backyard. Here, too, his mother had pruned and planted and created little foliage grottos all over the yard. The gray stone swimming pool seemed almost, but not quite, natural in the setting. There was another keypad on the patio's French doors. Pete pressed in the correct numbers and walked in. The house was completely quiet.

He wondered momentarily if his father had spent the night elsewhere. But he saw the car keys lying on the counter next to the garage door. With a shrug he walked over to the coffeepot and began setting up a brew.

A few minutes later, as the smell began to waft its way through the house, Pete heard stirring overhead in the master bedroom. He'd already poured himself a cup and was seated in the breakfast nook overlooking the pool when his dad, disheveled and wearing only knit briefs, wandered into the kitchen.

He gave his son a critical glance. "Making yourself at home?" he asked sarcastically.

Pete smiled humorously. "Just making the morning coffee for my dear old dad," he answered.

"You ought not to wander in here," Hank said. "I might have had a woman with me."

Pete shook his head, disbelieving. "In my mother's house? In her own bed? She'd never forgive you for that," he pointed out. "And I'd be thrilled to testify when it came to court."

"You probably would, you S.O.B.," Hank muttered to himself as he poured a cup of coffee.

"Chip off the old block," Pete added.

His father grunted.

Hank seated himself across the table. Pete gave him time to settle in and absorb some caffeine. He was in no hurry. He eyed his father critically. Hank normally looked tan and vital, almost youthful. This morning he looked gray and old. Though he still prided himself on being fit and toned, the skin on his chest sagged and the ribs were more visible than the muscles. Just after he retired, Hank had gotten "his eyes done." The plastic surgery no longer pulled up the inside of his brows, the outside, however lifted sharply giving him a slightly demonic appearance, as if he was always a little bit angry. Then last year, he announced he'd decided to correct the problem by getting a complete face-lift. Neither Pete nor his mother had tried to talk him out of it. When Hank decided something, no one could ever dissuade him. For some reason, however, he hadn't gone through with it.

Pete thought it had probably been looking in the mirror on a morning like this that had given him the idea in the first place.

After a few moments the older man looked up at him.

"So, is this a workday or are you just planning to live off your inheritance."

"I'm going in at one," Pete answered. "I'm going to work until closing."

Hank gave a huff of disbelief and shook his head. "You're working the evening shift on a Saturday night," he said incredulously. "I guess you're never going to get laid."

"Guess not," Pete answered. "It's just that I find the idea of father-son sharing really creepy and you've already done most of the women in town."

Hank chuckled. "Only the good-looking ones, son," he said and then added, "You could always do Doris. I've never been that desperate."

Pete refused to laugh at Miss Kepper's expense. Instead he took another sip of coffee and said nothing.

"You've been out running?" Hank asked.

Pete nodded. "Yeah, I thought it might be about time to get back into it."

Hank shook his head. "If you played golf, you'd get plenty of exercise and do business at the same time."

"It's a myth that the greens are full of big-business deals," Pete countered. "Just a bunch of polo-shirted guys sneaking away from the office to try to improve their game."

"And the track is full of sweaty people humming to themselves," Hank said. "A pure waste of time."

Pete shook his head. "I get a lot of work done," he said. "All the planning and vision that are needed to grow a business, are things I don't have time to do in the store. I don't have a minute during the workday to get inside my own head. Running is perfect for that."

Hank gave a huff of pure disapproval. "It's crazy the way you look just like me on the outside. But inside you're completely your mother's child."

"Thanks," Pete said, though he knew the words weren't meant as a compliment.

"So what are you doing here," his father asked. "Lonely? Or have you got something to say?"

"I've got something to ask," Pete answered. "And it's business, if you think your head is clear enough to discuss it."

Hank nodded.

"Wolkowicz's daughter was in the car wash building yesterday," Pete said. "I thought we'd bought that building from her old man years ago."

His father raised an eyebrow. "His daughter? I thought she's like retarded or something."

"That's the other daughter," Pete said. "This one was an honor student and she said you never went through with the sale."

Hank shrugged. "She's right about that."

"Why not?"

Hank grinned. "Turn that question around completely," he said. "What you should be asking is, when it comes to that corner, why would I buy it?"

"Because it abuts Guthrie Foods property," Pete answered. "Guthrie Foods has a need to control what it looks like, whether it's kept up and what kind of business goes in there."

The smile on Hank's face was one of satisfaction. "We already do," he said, smugly.

Pete looked at him confused. "I don't get it," he said.

"Do you remember when those damn bitches that call

themselves the Conservation Committee were all up in arms about saving downtown buildings?"

Pete nodded. "Yeah, I remember something about it," he answered. Pete had been a teenager at the time, deeply involved in his own life of friends and sports. Mostly what he recalled was his father's ranting and raving.

"Well, I managed to keep us out of that mess," Hank said. "And it wasn't easy. They wanted to control the whole block. Our building was only fifteen years old and I managed, with some careful arm-twisting, to convince the council not to include our whole block, just the structures in the block older than fifty years."

"That makes some sense."

"It sure did to me," he said. "The only building on the block affected was Wolkowicz's. And that damn fool didn't even fight it. He said he *wanted* his building saved for future generations." Hank shook his head as he chuckled. "What an idiot. He was always like that. Even when we were kids he was all Mr. Responsible, the darling of the teachers, always doing the right thing. I was always the most popular guy in our class. But Wolkowicz was everyone's friend. What does that get you in the real world? Nothing you can take to the bank. In the world of business, it's the law of the jungle. The weak deserve what happens to them."

Pete gulped down the dregs of his coffee and got up to pour himself another cup. He'd heard his father's "law of the jungle" analogy too many times to count. And he was pretty sure that none of those dangerous jungle predators had had Miss Kepper to cover for them when they screwed up. But

Pete decided it was the better part of valor not to mention that to Hank.

On the way back to the table he opened the refrigerator and pulled out a package of Mallomars.

Pete ripped open the bag and each man took a cookie. As Pete took a casual bite, he critiqued his father's assessment. "I don't know Wolkowicz very well, but honestly, he never struck me as weak."

Hank's brow came down, angrily contorting his face. He didn't like to have his pronouncements questioned. His gruff words matched his expression.

"He's worse than weak! He's…he's ignorant of his own advantages," Hank said. "Do you know that bastard is hung like a horse. Every guy in gym class was jealous. Did he take advantage of that? Hell no. As far as I know, he never even had a date. He married Ella Passendorfer without so much as taking the gal to dinner. She was Paul Gillette's girl. Wolkowicz had never shown any interest in her. Then they get married and he's as faithful as an old dog for thirty years."

Pete chuckled. "Oh, so now I get it. You didn't buy the guy's car wash because he has a bigger penis than you. And he doesn't hound-dog around. That makes a lot of sense," Pete said facetiously.

"Don't be ridiculous," Hank said. "It wasn't personal, it was business."

"So, you didn't buy it because the building is in a conservation zone," Pete said.

"Even better than that," Hank said. "When Wolkowicz went out of business, his plan was to put the place up for sale. I heard the Joffees might be interested in it. So before he could even get a sign out, I went down there and offered for it. I had him close it up, lock the door, board it up. Then I stalled and ran circles around him for the next two years. It was brilliant. I had him turn a viable location into just another abandoned building."

Hank chuckled as if the memory was entertaining.

"You never intended to actually go through with the sale?"

"Why should I?" Hank asked. "There's not really much anyone can do with that building. You can't tear the place down because it's part of the conservation zone. You can't expand. The lot is undersized and pie-shaped. You couldn't add so much as closet without getting into the easement of our property. Guthrie Foods owns all the land on three sides. All we needed was to control it. I killed the deal for anyone else and saved the company the money we would have paid to buy it."

Hank was so obviously proud of himself, that Pete was left speechless.

"I doubt the damn fool ever even realized that I'd screwed him," Hank said.

Pete remembered the hostility in the voice of Wolkowicz's daughter. She knew all right.

Andi was pretty sure that most women of twenty-eight years of age got to make their own decisions about Sunday mornings. She did not. Her family got up early and attended services at St. Hyacinth's. On a cranky, bad-hair-day morning, Andi had made her one halfhearted protest to her father.

"Why do I have to do this?"

Pop's expression was not judgmental, but it didn't suggest any flexibility either.

"It's what your mother would have expected of us."

So they went to church as a family. The three of them crammed together in the front seat of the pickup truck.

St. Hyacinth's was a beautiful old building, with its towering stained-glass windows and Gothic revival architecture. Andi had grown up in this church, as had both her parents. The creaking wood floors and well-worn pews were as familiar as anything in her own home.

The founders of the parish, grandparents of today's congregation, had immigrated from Poland in 1892. The entire village had left together and settled en masse in Plainview. They were a tight-knit community, wary of strangers and quick to stick their noses in each other's private lives. Everyone knew everyone and everything anyone had ever said or done. And they were all completely comfortable with allowing whatever entered their minds to come right out of their mouths.

"You look very nice today, Andi," Mrs. Pietras told her. "Doesn't she look nice, Margaret?"

Margaret, aka Mrs. Zawadzki, a heavyset woman of a certain age, was dressed in vivid purple, wearing an overblown hairdo first made popular in the mid-80s. She turned to give Andi an assessing glance.

"Yes, very nice," she agreed. "It's such a shame that you've never married. Is there still hope?"

Andi was momentarily taken aback. Both women's eyes were on her with expressions of sympathetic concern.

"Uh…what do you mean?"

"Is there someone special on your horizon?"

"I couldn't say," Andi answered, her tight smile disguising

the annoyance she felt. "I haven't really had time to look out on my horizon lately."

"Oh, you really must," Mrs. Zawadzki said. "I mean with your sister as she is, well you are the only one that your father might be able to count on for grandchildren."

It was all Andi could manage not to roll her eyes.

"Thanks for the heads-up," she told the women and moved on as quickly as possible. She took her seat in the pew and deliberately kept her head down.

The guys from her childhood catechism class who were still unwed were not what she would think of as potential mates. The girls from St. Hyacinth's married in their early twenties and what they hadn't snapped up seemed pretty much picked-over.

Andi hoped to appear absorbed in her prayer book, as she privately steamed. That kind of nosiness was what she couldn't stand about her hometown. Everybody thought they had a right to be in your private life, critiquing your choices. It was infuriating. Anonymity had been one of the great lures of the outside world. In Chicago nobody knew or cared if she was dating or who it might be.

When the service finally started it was comfortingly familiar. And it was great to sit next to Jelly who sang out boldly on every hymn. In the places where she didn't recall the words, her "ums" and "ahs" were voiced as passionately as the actual lyrics. Of course, Andi imagined that um and ah were as meaningful to Jelly as a line like "then let the world obeisance due perform." It was meant to be a joyful noise. Her Jelly certainly managed that. If her sister's singing bothered the other worshippers, at least no one complained.

Andi remembered a Christmas concert when they were

girls, when the choir director had publicly hushed Jelly in the middle of a song. Angered, Andi, who was slightly left of completely tone deaf, had belted out the remainder of the tune, horrendously drowning out better voices, embarrassing the teacher, the chorus and basically the entire student body. She had not one regret about that. In fact, just remembering it had her smiling.

People had a right to their expectations. But they didn't have a right to insist that other people live up to them. Growing up with Jelly had taught her that.

After the final benediction, she hoped to make a quick and silent exit. Unfortunately that was not to be. Before the last reverberations of "Amen" bounced against the walls, her father was immediately surrounded by a flock of women, each of whom seemed to have some silly question for him, or problem she needed to discuss. It was this way every Sunday.

Normally, Andi would remain with her father and sister as Pop made his responses and offers to help as he slowly worked his way down the aisle. Today, however, Andi went out the other end of the pew and made her way back to the church door.

Outside, in the cool shade of a giant sycamore, she waited, eager to get home and get busy on her project.

Todd Kozlowski, a guy she'd known since kindergarten, came over. His wife, Bekka, was shepherding their toddler.

"You are looking so hot these days," he told Andi. "I'm sure my talking to you makes my wife jealous."

Andi gave a little laugh, not sure if one should accept jealousy as a compliment. Todd had asked her out a couple of times when they were both in the high school math club. While he had always seemed like an okay guy, she had never felt they had much in common. Math formulas alone did not make for successful dating discourse.

"You're looking great, too," Andi told him, then added quickly. "And so is Bekka." She waved at the woman across the lawn.

He glanced back in his wife's direction. "Oh no, she looks like a total whale," he said with stark honestly. "But it's my fault. She's not really fat, she's pregnant again."

"Oh! That's wonderful."

Todd shrugged and shook his head. "It's not wonderful yet. She's still in the 'I think I could throw up any minute' phase. It should start being wonderful in a few more weeks."

Andi smiled vaguely and nodded. She didn't know that much about having children.

"Well, congratulations a little ahead of time then."

"Thanks," he said. "I love kids and Bekka's a great mom. With the economy like it is, we probably wouldn't have decided to have another kid just now, but stuff happens." He shrugged sheepishly. "I think that's good. Bekka says all the best things are those we don't plan."

Andi nodded. "Maybe so."

"So what are you doing out here alone?"

"I'm waiting on Pop and Jelly," she answered. "For some reason my father is the most popular guy in the church after services. He always gets bombarded with questions. I guess it must be about meals on wheels. It takes him twenty minutes to get out of the building."

Todd laughed. "Those old gals may be hungry all right, but

I don't think their interest in Walt Wolkowicz has anything to do with meals on wheels."

Andi furrowed her brow, befuddled. "What are you talking about?"

"Your pop has definitely become the senior most likely to succeed. When it comes to the over-fiftys, he's the most eligible bachelor in town. He even looks good to the forty-something divorcees."

Andi was completely taken aback. She glanced up to see Pop emerging from the church door, surrounded by chattering females.

"My pop is not a bachelor," Andi pointed out. "He's a widower. And my mom just died in October."

Todd nodded. "I know it's hard to get your mind around it," he said. "It's one of those tremendous gender inequities. My mom says everybody expects women to be in mourning for at least two years after her husband dies. But it's perfectly acceptable for men to be picking up phone numbers at the funeral."

"My father is not like that," Andi insisted. "He and my mother were very much in love."

"Of course they were," Todd agreed. "But life is for the living. And he seems very much alive."

Andi glanced up at Pop once more. He'd made it to the bottom of the steps, but a woman in a big yellow hat had her gloved hand on his arm and was staring up adoringly into his eyes. He was grinning down at her.

"Ewww," Andi muttered under her breath.

A few minutes later she caught up with her father and Jelly in the parking lot, a quartet of gone-to-seed groupies still in tow. Now that the truth had been shown to her, there was absolutely no missing it. These women all had household projects they wanted him to look at, books they wanted to share, chores they needed a man's opinion on. Mrs. Gaspar even claimed to have fifteen pounds of fresh summer sausage that needed to be cooked up on a grill.

They were fawning over her father and were condescendingly saccharin-sweet to her sister.

Andi was disgusted and decided to take the situation in hand.

"Excuse me, ladies," she announced loudly. "We really have to go. I have a rack of lamb warming in the oven and you know you mustn't wait too long to drizzle it with rosemary sauce."

Her words stunned the ladies present. Andi had never cooked a rack of lamb in her life, but she'd eaten one with rosemary sauce in a Chicago restaurant and it had been fabulous. She wanted to let these women think she was a gourmet chef. She didn't want any of them trying to load up her father with home-cooked meals.

Unfortunately, her family was as caught off guard by her remark as the widow horde.

"What's a 'wreck a lam'?" Jelly asked.

"Never mind. Get into the truck," Andi whispered.

As they pulled out of the parking lot, her father questioned her.

"What was that all about?" he asked.

"Those women," Andi complained. "Jeez, Pop, they're after you. You're still grieving and they're coming on to you, trying to take advantage."

"To take advantage?" Pop chuckled. "I doubt the ladies of the church have intentions to ravish me."

"Well, maybe not that, but they are desperate, though I wouldn't put it past Betty Broniki."

Her father laughed. "Old Bett has always been a gal who goes after what she wants."

Andi huffed. "And she wants to get her hooks into you. They all do. Making excuses to lure you to their houses and tempting you with casseroles."

He grinned at her. "Don't worry, Andi," he said. "I can't be had so cheap. At the very least I'm holding out for pierogi."

"Pop!"

"You're taking this too seriously," her father said.

"It is serious," Andi said. "Mom just died and here are these women, her friends, stumbling across her grave to get to you."

"Nobody is stumbling across anybody," Pop said. "And Ella would have thought this all a wonderful entertainment for the community."

Andi knew he was right. Mom hadn't had a jealous bone in her body. This wasn't about her mother. It was about her father.

"Pop, you're such a great catch," she said seriously. "Hard-working, honest, faithful, kind, there's not a widow at the church who wouldn't give her eyeteeth for a chance with you. I'm just worried that…that your dating skills might be a bit out of date. These women could use their…wiles in ways that you're not expecting."

"Women had their wiles back in my day as well," her father told her. "I think I can handle myself. And try not to worry. I'm not interested in a relationship with any of the women at the church."

Andi nodded, grateful.

"I like pierogi, too," Jelly announced. "But not radish."

Andi looked at her sister momentarily puzzled. "Radish? Oh, Pop said ravish, not radish," Andi said.

"What's ravish?"

Pop gave Andi a look. "It's the same as radish," he told Jelly. "Only it actually tastes worse."

"Then I sure don't want any," Jelly said.

They continued their drive home and ate their pitiful microwaved lunch around the table. Afterward Pop made an excuse to leave and took off in the truck.

It was only then, as he was driving away, that Andi realized he'd said he wasn't interested a relationship with any of the women at church. What he hadn't said was that he was not interested in having a relationship.

Chapter 5

ANDI HAD SPENT the entire weekend perfecting her business plan presentation for city council. And she hadn't skimped on the details. She put it together in a PowerPoint including current photos of the car wash building and an overlay that she drew herself of how the new business would look. She called it Corner Coffee Stop. And she was even keeping the retro lettering of the current car wash sign. It was a perfect use of the historic building, she decided. She really got into the excitement of it as she put all the figures together and speculated with growth charts and impact data. She loved doing this. She missed doing it. In the last months of job hunting she'd been so focused on her financial needs and her obligations she'd forgotten just how much personal satisfaction she got from doing something that both challenged her and allowed her to utilize her natural gifts and acquired knowledge. Just the sheer pleasure of the task had her excitement in overdrive. Presentations to the council were limited to three minutes. She came up with enough talking points to give a day-long seminar!

She boiled it all down on Monday morning, making it direct, fact-filled and to the point. From there she began practicing her delivery.

She went over it twice in the silence of the house while Pop and Jelly were out doing the rounds of meals on wheels. By the time they came home, she was ready to try her words out on living, breathing human beings.

Andi set up her laptop in the living room and had her father and sister pretend to be the city council. Jelly really got into the pretending part. She hurried upstairs to her room to retrieve a top hat that she'd worn once on a Halloween long past. Why she thought the aldermen might wear top hats, Andi didn't know, but her sister certainly looked cute in it. And maybe it helped. Andi was not one of those speakers who imagined her audience naked, but imagining the council wearing ill-fitting top hats really cut down the intimidation factor.

She went through her presentation, presented her argument. The drive-through coffee business should be exempted from the traditional regulations governing restaurants because it is not, in any sense, a restaurant. Corner Coffee Stop would not serve any person inside the building. The average length of time a customer would occupy the bay would be less than five minutes.

"This business would be an appropriate and revenue generating use of a currently vacant building. And it offers safe and convenient access to goods and services for the elderly, physically handicapped, families with small children in the vehicle or anyone on the go in downtown Plainview."

Andi ended her spiel with a "thank you" and Jelly rewarded her with cheers and applause. While she appreciated the enthusiasm, she looked for keener insight from her father.

"What do you think?" she asked her dad.

He smiled. "I think all the scholarship money for that expensive graduate school wasn't wasted."

Andi blushed. "It's not exactly what I thought I'd be doing at this stage of my life."

"You were thinking CEO of a Fortune 500?"

She chuckled and shrugged. "Closer to that than to becoming a Plainview barista."

"Well, Andi, I've always believed it's more important to like what you do than do what you like," Pop said. "You need to make enough cash to get by, but beyond that, it won't make you any more or less happy."

"When I start making enough to get by," she told him. "Then I'll try wondering about the happy part."

The council meeting was held at City Hall in an ornate and cavernous room, obviously designed a century earlier for what had been anticipated to be a much larger community. Ten rows of folding chairs sat at a distance from the curved dark wood dias. A half dozen high-back seats were arranged around the council table, each with a name plaque in front. Alderman Houseman, Alderman Gensekie, Alderman Brandt, Alderman Guthrie, Alderman Pannello. In the center was Mayor Gunderson-Smythe.

Andi, Pop and Jelly were the first people to arrive. That was Andi's fault. She'd been too concerned about being late. Now she was early which, for some reason, made her more nervous.

Pop walked around the room looking at all the old maps

and town memorabilia on the walls. Jelly pulled a big photo album out of her bookbag and flipped through it contentedly.

A staff person from the city arrived to put out copies of the agenda. Andi saw she was "Item 6." She showed it to her father.

"I'm worried that Jelly won't be able to wait this long," she told him.

He shrugged, unconcerned. "If she gets restless, then we'll leave," Pop said. "You can take the bus or call me to pick you up."

Andi nodded. "You can't let her applaud," she said. "Maybe we should tell her that."

Pop laid a hand on Andi's cheek. "Just let go of that," he said. "Jelly is not going to mess this up for you. This is not high school. The real world is much more accepting."

"You're right," she agreed, glancing across the room toward her sister. "Jelly never really messed things up for me. I always managed to mess them up for myself."

"Not tonight," Pop said. "Tonight you're going to be a smash."

Andi took heart that her father would be right.

Within a few minutes, the room filled with people, some well dressed, some barely dressed. There were senior ladies with hair that looked almost blue, and tattooed girls with hair that was definitely purple. Some men were in suits and some in shirtsleeves.

Mr. Gilbert from Code Compliance nodded to her in a businesslike manner before taking a seat among the staff.

As the council arrived, Andi silently assessed them. Mayor Gunderson-Smythe was a petite fortyish woman who reminded Andi of her kindergarten teacher. Brandt and Pannello were recognizable as older versions of men she'd seen before, but wasn't sure where. The one who really caught her attention, of course, was Hank Guthrie. Growing up she'd seen him a million times in the grocery store. She hadn't realized he was on the council.

"Why didn't you warn me that Hank Guthrie is an alderman?" she whispered to her father.

Pop seemed surprised with the question. "I didn't think it would matter. Guthrie won't put his own interests ahead of what's good for the community. The downtown needs another business. If he goes against the idea, it won't be personal."

Andi wished she had her father's confidence.

"Try not to put too much on this," Pop added. "People can always smell desperation. It's a fine idea. If it comes about, then that's great. Just remember that a lot of excellent plans never come to be. That's just how it is. The prayers un-answered are often the ones that prove to be the biggest blessings."

That was one of the things Andi most admired about her father, his absolute faith in ultimate good. But Andi preferred trusting what she could control.

The meeting was called to order with the flag pledge followed by a lengthy discussion of the minutes of the last meeting and reports from various city departments. As the talk of stop signs, potholes and sewer pipe dragged on, Andi found herself stifling a yawn. She glanced over at Jelly. Her photo book sat open on her lap, but she'd laid her head on Pop's shoulder. Andi was wishing she could take a little catnap as well.

On the other side of her, a young man in a sport coat was rapidly texting on his phone. It was then that she noticed that most everyone in the room, under the age of sixty, was focused on a phone, PDA or BlackBerry.

Why do these people come to these meetings if they're not going to pay any attention, she wondered.

But the idea that most people weren't paying attention buoyed her somehow and her anticipatory jitters just fell away. By the time the agenda reached "Item 6" she was as completely composed as she'd been in Pop's living room.

The presentation went perfectly. Andi made every point that she had in her notes.

"Exemption from these regulations can be granted by the council on grounds of reasonable hardship," she concluded. "As no expansion can be permitted on the building due to its historic designation and required setbacks to adjacent property, I believe this constitutes a reasonable hardship. And I ask the council to grant my business, Corner Coffee Stop, a variance to this city ordinance. Thank you for your consideration. I'll be happy to answer any questions that you may have."

There was a long, thoughtful moment of silence as the council members sifted through their papers.

Alderman Gensekie, a white-haired gentleman with a bow tie was frowning a little. "So, what you're saying is that people will drive up in their cars and you'll pour them a cup of coffee?" He looked at the other councilmen and then toward the chief of police at the staff table. "Is that legal, I mean to drive around with a hot cup of coffee?"

Andi tried to keep her jaw from dropping. Fortunately, everyone around him quickly assured the aged alderman that it was done all the time.

"You can get a morning coffee at all the hamburger places out on the interstate," Alderman Pannello assured him.

"Really?" Gensekie seemed genuinely surprised. "Just seems like it would be a safety hazard driving around with hot coffee."

Alderman Brandt was thumbing through her handout. "You're from Chicago, Ms. Walcowski?"

"Wolkowicz," Andi answered. "Andrea Wolkowicz and, no, I'm not from Chicago. I lived there for several years but I'm from here in Plainview. My father has owned this building since 1979."

The next question came from Mr. Houseman. It was one Andi was ready for. It pertained directly to her request for exemption on public toilet facilities and she thought she handled it well. A follow-up from the mayor was also one she'd anticipated and Andi was very pleased with the response she was getting.

Then Alderman Guthrie asked what Andi perceived as a stupid question. "These statistics about drive-through coffee, are those national statistics?"

"Yes, sir," Andi answered.

Guthrie made a dismissive sound followed by a comment that was openly skeptical. "Maybe it would have been better to somehow filter out the East Coast and the West Coast. What those people do and buy, well, that's just meaningless around here."

Both the council and the audience chuckled and began muttering in agreement to that. Guthrie was clearly enjoying his little bit of humor at Andi's expense. He was grinning broadly and looking around at his fellow council members and at the audience, but he never allowed his gaze to fall on Andi. She knew that technique from her corporate meeting days.

Marginalize the presenter by uniting the rest of the table in humor. It created an us–vs–them mentality and the person not laughing was definitely on the outside looking in.

Andi needed to counter that move as quickly as possible. If she could have come up with a snappy comeback, it would have been perfect, but she had to be careful. Any joke at the expense of the council or the community could completely backfire. So she gave up the measure-for-measure flanking with a direct assault.

"Your Honor," Andi said, addressing Mayor Gunderson-Smythe. "I'd like to request that Alderman Guthrie, as the adjacent property owner and a person who previously offered to buy this building, recuse himself from these deliberations."

The mayor nodded sympathetically and opened her mouth to speak, but before a word came out, the silence in the building was filled by Guthrie.

"Hold it right there, young woman!" he said loudly. "Are you suggesting I cannot be impartial?" His tone changed to incredulity. "I don't know what kind of people you're accustomed to encountering where you live in Chicago. But we hometown hayseeds are not so lacking in old-fashioned virtues like integrity and justice. We're not people to be swayed one way or another by a business deal gone bad ten years ago. And if you're going to disqualify your neighbors, well, in a town this size, well, we're all neighbors here."

Murmurs of agreement swept throughout the room.

"But just to reassure you on this council's sense of honesty and to counter even any perception of bias on my part, I will recuse myself," Guthrie continued. "I *will* actually step out of the building while this is decided. We are a small city, but we are a city of rules. And unlike bigger places where elected officials hold out their hands for bribes and allow businesses to operate under the assumption that the laws just don't apply to them, we here in Plainview bend over backwards to ensure fair play for everyone. And if it happens that you are to become a merchant here, I would encourage you to adopt that attitude yourself."

Guthrie then rose to his feet and made his way through the audience and out the front door, his progress slowed by shaking hands and receiving pats on the back.

Andi saw her hopes for the Corner Coffee Stop slip out the door with him.

He had successfully portrayed her as the outsider, demanding to be freed from the rules that governed everyone else. The council voted against her three to one.

Chapter 6

A GUILTY CONSCIENCE, for guilt not his own, had plagued Pete most of the weekend. He'd spent an inordinate amount of time figuring how, in these tough times, he might make it right. By Monday he almost had his ducks in a row. He didn't have the money to buy the car wash property that his father had offered on so many years ago, but he thought he might be able to manage a long-term lease on the property. That would put some money in the hands of the Wolkowicz family—maybe even more money in the long run—and he could begin working on a plan to utilize the place.

He put his ideas on hold, however, when he heard about the drive-through coffee proposal that went before the council.

"That sounds like a pretty good idea," he told Miss Kepper as he stood in her office doorway, sipping at his own cup.

"Oh no," she insisted. "It's a terrible idea. Who would buy expensive coffee on that corner? And it's like your father said, rules are rules."

Mention of his father had Pete immediately curious.

"My dad was opposed to this?"

"Mr. Guthrie recused himself," Miss Kepper answered quickly. "He didn't want to even give the appearance of bias. But he is totally correct about the rules."

Pete deliberately kept his expression blank. He didn't want to point out how Miss Kepper's own opinions always leaned heavily in his father's favor. He also chose not to remark on how little respect his father typically gave to rules. Especially if they were meant to apply to him.

He was saved from saying anything by the store intercom.

"Mr. Guthrie to Bakery, please. Mr. Guthrie to Bakery."

Pete frowned. "What could be going wrong at the bakery this early in the day?"

He hurried down the stairs and past the checkouts toward the far corner of the store. It was too early for the smell of fresh bread. The baking for that started about noon, encouraging buyers of lunch and lingering through the buyers of dinner. Mornings were sugar-filled with fluffy doughnuts and cinnamon rolls, the scent of which had Pete's stomach growling. His bowl of plain oatmeal already seemed a long time ago. He deliberately chose to ignore that.

"What's up?" he asked Beth, a plastic-capped worker arranging cakes in the display case.

She pointed toward the stainless steel doors. "They're in the back."

The prep section of the bakery was set apart from the rest of the store by a glass wall. Customers could view the clean, orderly area, but were protected from the heat and noise. Through the window, Pete could see the supervisor, Nell, standing arms crossed and tight-lipped, her expression furious. Beside her in a slouching posture that could only be described as insolent, was Cher-L, a bakery employee who was frequently in trouble.

"Oh, crap," Pete whispered under his breath. He hated negotiating between these two. He warned Nell the last time that it happened that Cher-L was her employee and he didn't want to be called in on every rule infraction. *Hey, Peterson,* he chided himself sarcastically. *This is why you get paid the big bucks.*

Forcing a optimistic smile on his face, he went through the doorway and approached the two women.

"Good morning," he greeted them both.

"Not so good for us," Nell said. "Cheryl has ruined the dough."

"My name is Cher-L!" the younger woman whose blue-striped hair was visible beneath her clear plastic cap complained. "I just made a mistake."

"Yes, well, as usual, you're better at making mistakes than making bread."

Cher-L's eyes narrowed and Pete knew she was just an instant away from name-calling, something that simply couldn't be tolerated. He quickly intervened.

"Tell me what happened," he asked.

Both women turned to him.

"You first, Cher-L," he said, hoping to counter her sense of being outnumbered by her bosses.

Cher-L turned her attention and her body to face Pete completely, as if to suggest that Nell's presence was irrelevant. The young woman's mouth was pouty and she dropped her eyes suggestively for a glance at Pete's crotch. She was accustomed to dealing with men on a very primitive level and she was undoubtedly successful with it.

"It was just a silly mistake," she explained. "I remembered to take the dough out of the freezer. But when we closed up last night I forgot to put it in the fridge."

When she said it, it did sound like a small, silly thing. But Pete knew what it meant. He glanced past her to the cart beyond. Frozen dough was floured and laid out on baking sheets to thaw. Then it had to be refrigerated to keep the dough from rising. Each morning it would be brought out and allowed to rise for fifty minutes, then it would be reshaped and allowed to rise another twenty minutes before it went into the oven.

This morning, the baking cart was laden with giant, awk-wardly shaped loaves that could never be made to look right and that would taste unpleasantly sour. Add to that the health inspection violation of leaving food sitting out and Pete was staring at a couple dozen bake sheets of money to be thrown in the garbage.

There would not be enough time to thaw, rise and bake a day's allotment. Therefore no fresh bread for sale at Guthrie's today.

"Cher-L," he said, very softly. "Why don't you change back into your street clothes and meet me in my office."

The young woman looked genuinely surprised and hurt at the suggestion. But as she turned to walk away, there was more defiance in her walk than defeat.

Pete turned to Nell and shrugged. "Throw it out," he said, sighing.

"I can put together some scratch," she offered. "Maybe twelve or fifteen loaves by lunchtime if nothing goes wrong."

Pete nodded. "Do what you can," he said.

Nell nodded.

He walked back through the store and up the stairs. He stopped at Miss Kepper's office.

"I need Cher-L's employee file."

Miss Kepper got up from her desk and walked to the vertical file cabinet against the back wall and quickly retrieved the thick pile of collected documents wrapped in a manila folder.

"Here you go," she said.

"Thanks," Pete answered. "Send her into my office as soon as she shows up."

"Okay."

Pete waited a long moment. Miss Kepper didn't say another word.

He broke the silence. "Sorry about this," he said. "You were right. I was wrong."

The older woman shrugged. "You always try to see the good in people," she said, putting the best possible spin on Pete's bad hiring decision. She didn't ask him what he intended to do. And he appreciated that. Although he was pretty sure he was out of options.

Pete walked to his office and set the file on his desk. He knew he probably should spend the time waiting for her to look through it and make sure he remembered it all correctly. Instead, he stood at the window staring out at the parking lot toward the little building on the corner. He wondered absently if Wolkowicz's daughter was there again today. Would she continue to sort the place out, or would rejection of her coffee shop have her just locking the door and walking away? Somehow she didn't seem like the walking away type.

Cher-L showed up in the doorway. The white coat and

plastic cap had disappeared. She stood there for a moment, almost posing. The blue-striped hair, heavy eye makeup and plump bloodred lips were just the beginning of her feminine allure. She was now wearing very high heels, tight slacks and a blouse that revealed more skin, both in neckline and midriff, than it covered. She deftly closed the door behind her and smiled up at him, lowering her eyes in a way that was unapologetically provocative.

She was not at all his type. But when a guy hasn't had sex in a while, he's a lot less picky. She was attractive and available.

Pete mentally reminded himself that he was nearly thirty years old. He was the head of his company. A lot of people, a lot of families, depended on him. They trusted him to make tough choices that concerned their livelihood. And he needed to make those decisions with his brain instead of his penis.

"Have a seat," he said in a tone he hoped was all business.

As Cher-L walked past him, her hips swayed seductively. His eyes were drawn to the spiderweb tattoo on her lower back and he caught sight of the top of her purple thong showing above her low-cut waistband.

Deliberately, Pete reopened the door.

She swivelled slightly in her chair, crossing her legs. "I was hoping we could have some privacy?" she whispered. "I don't want Miss Kepper to hear."

"Miss Kepper is not listening," he assured her brightly. "And she is the soul of discretion on personnel matters."

By the time he got to the other side of his desk, he could see Cher-L was frowning slightly. He hoped that was a good sign. He sat down and opened her file. He already knew what was there, but he flipped through it carefully nonetheless. There were already two serious reprimands that Cher-L has signed off on. Both in the last three months. Three strikes, you're out. It was the rule in baseball as well as the grocery business.

Pete looked the young woman directly in the eye. He kept his voice soft, but his words were firm.

"Cher-L, things don't seem to be working out very well for you in our bakery."

She bit her lip and leaned forward, offering him an excellent view down the front of her blouse. Pete kept his eyes on her face.

"I am so sorry," she said, her voice as breathy as a Marilyn Monroe impersonator. "Leaving the dough out, well, it was just awful and expensive and, oh you have every right to be so angry at me."

Her apology was spoken in such an enticingly sexy voice, Pete fully expected her next line to be a description of herself as "a very naughty girl." Forestalling that, he went straight to the point.

"I believe it is time for both of us to admit that Guthrie Foods is not a good employment fit for you."

She sat up a little straighter and recrossed her legs. Clearly, she was rethinking her assumptions about him and deciding on another tack.

"The bakery is just not quite my thing," she said. "All those old biddies, half of them crazed with menopause and the other half taking turns with PMS. It's like trying to work in the eye of an estrogen hurricane every day of the week!"

Pete understood that talking about female biology was another distraction intended to make him waver in his decision. He steeled himself for more of the same. Mention of maxi pads and monthly courses was the nuclear option for women when manipulating male bosses.

"The organization needs to work like a team, Cher-L," he said. "I believe you've tried to be a team player. I give you credit for that. But I think, by nature, you are a more…more creative sort and you'll be happier and more successful in a different type of work environment."

With a quick indrawn breath and an exaggerated jaw drop, Cher-L was smiling again. "I was thinking exactly that same thing," she told him. "The bakery just isn't the place for me. Bread is boring, boring, boring. I'm thinking that my natural gift for color and display and stuff, just makes me perfect for produce. The produce department would be great for me."

Pete wasn't about to transfer Cher-L to produce. He was not unaware of gossip that suggested she and the produce manager had engaged in trysts in the back parking lot. The produce manager was a married man with two little kids. Even if none of it was true, he had no doubt that Cher-L would use the rumors to her advantage.

"No, Cher-L," he stated firmly. "A transfer to another department is not going to be possible. We are terminating your employment with us."

She was incredulous at the idea. She needed the job. She had rent to pay and credit card bills. There were so few jobs in town. If she lost this one, where would she ever find another?

Pete kept his resolve as unmovable as stone. And continued to repeat the final verdict. She was no longer employed at Guthrie Foods.

When argument failed, she began to cry.

Pete hated tears worse than anything. There was no way

to fight back, nothing to do but live through them. In his head he knew that he was in the right, but the crying made him feel like such a heel. He sat there listening to her sobs as long as he could stand it. Finally he went for his own secret weapon. He stepped out the door and walked down the hall.

He didn't need to even speak to Miss Kepper. She obviously *had* been listening and she was waiting. Without a word, she went up the hall and into his office.

"Cher-L," he heard Miss Kepper say. "It's time to go to the bathroom, wash your face and straighten up. I'll mail your check by the end of the week."

Pete moved over to the edge of the room, not hiding, but not visible to anyone just passing in the corridor.

A few minutes later he saw the back of Cher-L as she went by. She'd stopped crying but all the confidence had gone out of her walk. She looked now to be the person he'd originally thought her to be, a lonely confused young woman in need of a job.

Andi hadn't realized how much she'd counted on the coffee stop until the possibility was gone. She wasted half of a sleepless night in denial. *They couldn't do this to her. Guthrie had been in the wrong. In the light of day, the council would see that and alter their position.* That was, of course, a complete fantasy on her part. The decision was made and, as far as the city was concerned, it was final. She could take them to court, but she couldn't afford that, and she'd probably lose anyway. There was nothing to be done. When it came to opening a small business, it was prudent to worry about striking out. But she hadn't expected to be thrown out of the game before she even made it to the batter's box.

She went directly from denial to outrage. How dare they deprive her of an opportunity to create a livelihood! How dare they deprive the community of a place to drive through and get coffee!

Andi was still furious over breakfast.

Her father was sympathetic, but not that consoling.

"It was a good idea and you presented it well," he said between bites of oatmeal. "You gave yourself a fair shot and you should be rightly proud of that. But plenty of great ideas never get implemented. I'm sure they taught you that in business school."

"Of course they did," Andi agreed, unsmiling. "But I guess they failed to mention that a venture could be rejected for no reason except a creepy old alderman takes a public affront at having his bias pointed out."

Pop shook his head and tutted. "I know you're feeling like it was all unfair," he said. "But you knew it wasn't going to be a sure thing. They call it 'granting a variance' because it's asking for an exception. You had to know from the outset that you may not get it."

She didn't answer. She had known it, of course. But she hadn't really considered it. A business, any business seemed better than a empty building. It was unreasonable that the council couldn't see that.

Andi sat, stewing, as her coffee turned tepid and her oatmeal congealed.

Jelly got up from the table, her breakfast unfinished, and raced to her room. In a minute she was back with one of her stuffed animals. She set it on the table next to Andi.

"What's this?"

"It's Happy Bear," Jelly told her. "He smiles all the time. We have to take smiles wherever we can find them." Her sister's earnestness was endearing. "Maybe you should keep him with you today," Jelly added.

Andi picked up the nearly ragged pink-and-purple bear. He had patches of missing fur, a clumsily mended right leg and one eye was completely gone, but his bright red, velour grin was completely intact.

"For a smiling guy, he looks pretty beat-up," she pointed out to Jelly.

Her sister shrugged. "Sometimes I have to hold him a lot," she admitted solemnly. "And the washing machine is hard on everybody."

Andi eyed her sister's very serious concern and forced a smile to the corners of her mouth.

"Thanks, Jelly," she said. "I'll borrow him from you. Just for today."

Jelly sighed with relief and smiled cheerily as if that settled everything.

Andi piddled away the morning, doing nothing constructive and allowing her thoughts to go over the council meeting again and again. Trying to make it all come out differently. It didn't.

As Pop and Jelly left for work, Andi aimlessly surfed the Internet. Finally she got up from the couch and went into the kitchen to fix herself something for lunch.

Happy Bear was still sitting on the table where Jelly had left him. Andi grimaced at the sight of the big, red smile on the creature's face. For an instant she envied Jelly. Her world was so much simpler than Andi's own. And she could find such happiness in small things.

That thought was immediately followed by a more truthful assessment of reality. Life was far from easy for her sister. Much of the world was shut off from her as too risky and unsafe. And there were so many things that she could never understand, but that impacted her every day of her life.

Andi straightened her spine. She was going to stop feeling sorry for herself and get busy getting on with her life. She went up to her room and dressed in jeans and a T-shirt. She pulled her hair up into a casual ponytail and put on a pair of well-aged, comfortable sneakers. After finding the keys and leaving a note on the refrigerator, she headed out the front door.

The car wash building still needed to be cleaned up and the supplies still needed to be sold. She might as well get busy at that. She had nothing better to do.

The seventeen-block trek actually lifted her mood considerably. When the sun is shining and the breeze is blowing and there is a scent of crab apple blossoms in the air, it's hard to remain pessimistic. Something would come up, Andi assured herself. Something even better than the Coffee Stop. And it would be something that Guthrie and son couldn't stop. She just needed to keep herself open to the possibilities.

Arriving at the corner of Grosvenor and Fifth Street she unlocked the door on the little building. It was better than it had been, but there was still plenty to be done.

Andi used a five-gallon jug of rust inhibitor to prop open the door, adding both light and ventilation to the inside. She began sorting and shifting. It was heavy work but, surprisingly, Andi welcomed the exertion. It made her feel like she was accomplishing something. And today, she really needed that feeling.

Andi glanced up as a shadow darkened her doorway.

"Hey, girl! I thought it might be you in here."

At first, she didn't recognize the woman. But the sound of her voice brought recognition.

"Oh, hi," Andi said. "You're the waitress from Connor's Diner."

The woman shrugged. "No, this week my sister is the waitress at Connor's Diner. I'm just unemployed Tiff McCarin out walking the streets."

With a smile Andi noted her conservative suit and sensible shoes. "That's not quite the streetwalker outfit," she said. "Even in Plainview."

Tiff laughed. "Yeah, this is my disguise. I'm like a hunter in a duckblind. Camouflaged as I look for jobs."

"I don't think you're going to find one here," Andi said.

Tiff nodded. "That's what I understand. Isn't that just my luck? I finally know somebody who's opening a business and it gets closed down before I even get a chance to beg for work."

Andi nodded sympathetically.

"Well, you look nice," she said. "Did you have interviews today?"

"Just one," Tiff answered. "And when I showed up, they told me that they'd changed their mind about filling the position. So I guess I got dressed up for nothing."

"My pop says that 'nothing is for nothing.' There's always something good that comes out of everything."

Tiff laughed. "He may be right. I passed my ex-husband on Hager Street and he was so stunned to see me looking good, he walked into a light pole. That alone was worth the extra effort with the makeup."

Andi laughed, only because Tiff was laughing.

"I guess he hasn't seen you lately."

"Only from a distance, I guess. We have a six-year-old son," Tiff said. "He goes with his dad every other weekend. But Gil, that's my ex, he just parks at the curb and Caleb meets him at the car."

"I guess that's one way to keep things civil."

Tiff agreed. "No talking means no arguing. At this point that's about all we can do for Caleb."

Andi nodded.

"What about you?" Tiff asked. "Divorced?"

"Never married," Andi answered. "Now are you going to tell me how *lucky* I am?"

"You get that a lot, I bet," Tiff said.

"I think it's supposed to make me feel better about my drastic fate."

"Does it?"

"Truth is, I'm just getting used to it. In Chicago, being twenty-eight and single makes you an up-and-comer, free and on the town. But I get the feeling that back here in Plainview it means you're an old maid."

"Yikes, I bet that does smart a bit."

Andi nodded.

"You just haven't run into the right guy," Tiff told her.

"There may not be one," Andi said. "I've got my standards set way too high. My parents had this perfect marriage, I want one just like it."

"Nobody's marriage is perfect," Tiff pointed out.

"Yeah, I keep telling myself that, but I think theirs must have been," Andi said. "They always got along, they were both very easygoing. Even with raising my sister, which had to be stressful, they never seemed to lose their balance."

"That does sound good."

"I asked Pop about it once and he told me that marriage is like any other contract—if both people aren't willing to abide by it, then it's not a deal at all."

Tiff nodded. "I sure hear that," she said. "Wish my ex had cooperated. I'm not sure which is worse, being an old maid or having a failed marriage."

"Oh, I think old maid has got to be worse," Andi assured her. "At least you caught a husband, even if he managed to wiggle off the hook."

Tiff chuckled. "You may be right about that," she said. "I guess it goes to show that a lot of the free advice you get around this town is worth exactly how much you pay for it."

Andi nodded agreement and Tiff changed the subject.

"So what's the problem with your business here?" she asked. "What's so dangerous that the city council wouldn't let you sell coffee?"

Declining to go into personalities, Andi made it simple. "We don't have the facilities to comply with the rules for a food or beverage business," she said. "So we can't open anything that serves food and drink."

Tiff nodded. "So what can you open?"

Andi shrugged. "Nothing, I guess," she replied. "We have to get approved to do anything different. And truthfully, I don't think I have any friends on the council. I think they would just as soon I stay at home and let the people in the business community come up with the new business ideas."

"I thought new blood was always supposed to be good."

Andi shrugged. "New blood maybe, but maybe not any new ideas from the Wolkowiczs. We never did fit in to the country-club set."

"So what's next?"

"I'm cleaning this place out and sorting this stuff," Andi said. "I'm hoping I can sell it all on eBay."

"You want some help?"

"You're all dressed up," Andi pointed out. "And besides, I can hardly afford bus fare, so I sure can't pay for help."

"I've got my car parked down at Conner's with all my clean laundry in the back," she said. "I'll go change into shorts and a T. I've got nothing to do until Caleb gets out of day camp. It would be nice to feel like I'm working even if I don't get paid."

A few minutes later Tiff was back, wearing Daisy Dukes and eager to help. Andi hadn't realized how much she needed an extra pair of hands until she had them. The two women managed to move everything to one side of the room so they could clean the floor. With mops from the storage closet and plenty of soapy wash water, they proceeded to do just that. The two worked well together and the accomplishment seemed to lift the mood of both of them. But they were ready for a break when someone else showed up at their door.

"What's going on?" a young woman asked as she peered in at Andi.

"Just cleaning up," Andi answered.

The young woman, whose hair was strangely blue-striped, squinted into the darkness of the building.

"Tiffany Crandall? Is that you?"

Tiff straightened, assessing the newcomer. "I used to be," she answered. "I'm Tiff McCarin now. Who are you?"

"I'm Lisa Craven's little sister, remember me?"

Tiff eyed her more closely. "Cheryl? I wouldn't have recognized you. The blue-haired stripes are really...eye-catching."

"Thanks! My name now is Cher-L. I changed it, too."

"Cher-L?" Tiff repeated it as if it were a question.

The girl nodded. "Cool, huh." She spelled it for them, including the dash. "My mom named me Cheryl which is just like an ordinary loser name. So I gave it meaning. I'm Cher-L, because that's who I am. I share L."

"You share L?"

"Yeah, L," she answered. "L is like all the good things, love and life and laughter. It's a name that really means something. It's like a stage name."

"A stage name?" Andi repeated. "Are you an actress or a singer?"

"Oh, no, nothing like that really," she answered. "I'm just getting myself prepared...you know...to be famous or something. You never know, right?"

Andi and Tiff shot glances at each other.

Tiff murmured a tepid agreement, Andi focused her attention on the mop.

Cher-L didn't seem to note the lack of enthusiasm. She walked into the middle of the floor and turned slowly in a circle as if taking the whole room in.

"I like this place," she said. "It's got good *qi,* you know, in kind of a funky way."

"Uh...it belongs to my pop," Andi said. "I'll let him know you approve."

Cher-L promptly seated herself atop a plastic barrel of wax concentrate, crossing her legs and allowing one high-heeled slide to dangle perilously from her foot.

"I've walked by this place a million times in my life," Cher-L said. "This is the first time I've seen it open."

"Andi and I are just cleaning it up," Tiff told her. "She's going to try to sell these old supplies on eBay."

Cher-L glanced around and nodded. "I guess if people will buy a piece of toast that looks like the Virgin Mary, they ought to buy boxes of old car fresheners."

Andi wasn't sure she liked equating the two.

With the shared hope that if they ignored her, she might go away, Andi and Tiff both became very focused on cleaning the floor, the mop boards, the expanse of wall beneath the windows.

Cher-L accepted the silence, but slowly she began to kick her foot. As if keeping time to music in her head, the tempo picked up until the movement was almost staccato and very annoying.

"So what are the plans here?" she asked.

"Plans? We have no plans," Andi answered.

"Come on, you're cleaning up for some reason," she said. "You must be opening up something."

Andi shook her head. "No, nothing," she replied.

"Nothing? Nothing at all?" Cher-L gave her head a small shake as if to signal she would not have her question put off so easily.

Andi didn't really want to go into it again, but she heaved a sigh and tried to get her reply short enough to tweet.

"I wanted to open up a drive-through coffee shop, but last night I was turned down for a variance, a zoning change."

The brow beneath the blue-striped bangs furrowed. "A

zoning change? I thought people were either 'in the zone' or 'zoned out'."

"This is a little different," Andi said. "It's the way cities and towns manage growth. They can limit certain kinds of businesses in some places."

"Sounds unfair to me," Cher-L said.

It *felt* unfair to Andi, but she kept that to herself.

"So they won't let you open a coffee shop."

"No."

"So what can you open?" she asked.

Andi sighed heavily and shook her head. "I haven't a clue. The only thing I can do for sure is open it up as what it's always been, a car wash."

"So," Cher-L responded. "Then open a car wash."

Andi stopped mopping long enough to look at Cher-L. Life was so easy when you didn't understand much about it. "I can't make any money with a car wash," she explained. "That's why my father had to close the place years ago."

"People still get their cars washed," Cher-L pointed out.

"They do," Andi agreed. "But the car wash business has completely changed. The way we get them washed, the technology of it, that's all different."

"As if!" Cher-L disagreed. "There's not any technology to washing cars."

"Yes, actually there is," Andi said. "And it's been pretty innovative." She leaned her mop against the wall. "In the 1960s they invented the self-service car wash, where you could get pressurized water for what people used to do with their garden hose. You put coins in, you got water out."

Cher-L nodded.

"Then for those who were a little more lazy, they came up with the in-bay automatic wash. You drive up into it and a whirl of fiberglass brushes wash and wax, and then it blows you dry and you're on your way without even getting out of your car."

"That's what I do," Tiff said. "I get a discount on it when I buy gas."

Andi nodded. "It's cheap and convenient. But it can be really hard on your clear coat finish. The people who really love their cars avoid it."

Tiff nodded. "I remember my ex saying something like that."

"So they came up with the tunnel wash," Andi said. "It's mechanized with the car moving through the different wash, rinse and wax stations. But there are no harsh brushes and all the finishing is done by hand. A perfect mix of technology and manpower."

Andi was quoting her father on that last statement. He had been very taken with tunnel wash technology. It was the reason he decided to close up and retire.

"So what's this place?" Cher-L asked.

"This is a hand wash," Andi answered. "High labor, low tech. It's very hard to compete head-to-head with a mechanized wash. Their price points can just be so much lower. And there are just way too few customers willing to pay a premium to have it done the old-fashioned way."

"You'd have to come up with some kind of gimmick to overcome the disadvantage," Tiff said. "The way Connor's Diner gives unlimited refills on drinks, so that people aren't thinking they could have eaten cheaper at a fast-food joint."

"Exactly. That's what hand washes do. They offer detailing and extra interior cleaning and buffing with pure elbow grease," Andi said. "That works for some people in some places. But in this town, with our economy, we'd have to think of something besides personal service to bring them in."

Tiff nodded glumly. "These days nobody wants to spend extra money on anything."

There was a thoughtful pause of agreement between Tiff and Andi. It was suddenly interrupted by Cher-L.

"Well, that's not true," she said. "Oh, I guess it's true about women, but it's not true about men."

"What do you mean?" Andi asked.

"Yeah, women can be pretty tight with the money, especially for something like washing a car, but men aren't."

"They aren't?"

Both Andi and Tiff were surprised.

Cher-L shook her head. "I go out to bars nearly every night and you wouldn't believe the number of guys who want to pay for my drinks. It doesn't matter if I'm alone or with girlfriends. I drink all night and it hardly ever costs me anything."

Andi sighed. "That's different," she said.

"No, it's not," Cher-L said. "It's men with money spending more than they need to for something they want."

Andi shot a glance at Tiff and saw an almost imperceptible shrug of disbelief.

"That's just guys in bars," Tiff said. "With a short skirt like that and a little bit of alcohol haze, men aren't buying beers just to be polite."

"It's not like I'm having sex with them," Cher-L said. "Trust me, I don't come so cheap. They pay for the drinks just to sit next to me and look at me and talk to me. They pay just to imagine that maybe I would do something, even when I never will."

"That's kind of a dangerous game, Cher-L," Tiff said.

The younger woman waved away her concern. "And I can spot the troublemakers ten miles off, so I steer clear," she assured them. "Most of these guys are just sweethearts."

Andi had her doubts about that. And if Tiff's raised eyebrow was evidence, she was skeptical as well.

"But what does any of this have to do with washing cars?" Andi asked.

"If you want to bring men in to get their cars washed, I think it all depends on what you're wearing when you wash them," she answered.

"What do you mean?"

Cher-L's expression was smug and worldly-wise.

"Are you going to wash a guy's car in baggy old coveralls, or are you going to be wearing just a wet T-shirt and a thong?"

Jelly sat at the dining room table. Across from her, Happy Bear hadn't even taken a sip of his tea, but then he rarely did. Jelly was looking through the photo album with Sesame Street's Big Bird on the front. It was one of her favorites. All of the snapshots featured two little girls at play.

"This is Andi and me when we were in our stroller," Jelly told her stuffed animal companion. "Mom used to take us everywhere and we would ride along, side by side together. People couldn't tell us apart."

Jelly gravely noted the Law & Order *implications. "No positive identification in a lineup. Lieutenant Van Buren would be disappointed."*

After a moment Jelly smiled broadly at the bear. "That was when me and Andi played together all the time. I like this picture book better than our school one. In school it wasn't me and Andi anymore. I had Special Olympics and Camp Courageous. Andi had…Andi had something else."

She sighed a bit sadly, but turned the page. Immediately she was smiling once more. "Look at this!" she said. "This is a fun one. See us running through the lawn sprinkler. See how we're laughing. This person is me. My swimsuit is pink. Andi's is blue." She gazed at the photo for a long moment. "I wish we could wear our swimsuits and play in the water again."

Chapter 7

BECAUSE IT WAS raining in torrents, Walt raced from the bus to the shelter of the ticket booth overhang in the parking lot at Mt. Ridley Park. He wore his cap down low to hide his face and the collar of his jacket high to disguise his profile. The secrecy and subterfuge was getting old. He understood why it had to be that way. He was sure that some men would have enjoyed it. But the rush of excitement from an illicit relationship had never held much allure for him. He'd had too much of it too soon.

The memory of those heady days of first love was clear in his mind. He recalled it all distinctly, holding hands in the bleachers of the cold empty gym. Paul had promised to stand outside as their lookout. Everybody else should have been in or around the cafeteria. But in a busy place like Plainview High School, privacy was always at a premium. Beside him wearing a pleated shirt and pristine white blouse, her dark brown hair pulled back in a ponytail, was the love of his life.

"We can't tell anyone," she'd said. Her desperate whisper somehow drew his attention to her beautiful mouth, the plump lips shimmered with the palest pink lipstick. He wanted to kiss her.

"Nobody knows," he said.

"Paul and Ella know."

"We can trust them."

She nodded. "Yes, I'm sure we can. I just get so scared." Vulnerability was unusual for her. She had such strength of purpose, such confidence in herself that it almost glowed around her like a phosphorescence. It was in many ways her most attractive feature. And to Walt's mind, her attractive features were almost too numerous to count.

"If anyone finds out, *anyone,* then the whole town will know," she said. "My family would be so angry. And so hurt. I couldn't bear to hurt them." She closed her eyes and shook her head. "Please, Walt, don't let me hurt them."

"No, no, of course we won't hurt them," he'd assured her. "But I love you. I can't bear to be apart from you."

"I know. I love you, too. But it's…it's impossible."

"Don't say that!"

"I just don't know how to make it possible," she rephrased.

"We'll find a way," he promised.

He leaned forward and kissed her then. He couldn't help himself. Their stolen moments together were too infrequent. He craved her like a drug. Her body was his nightly fantasy. But he craved her smile, her voice, her laughter, just as much.

His kiss lingered on her lips and he pulled her a bit closer, just enough to feel the graze of her nipples against his chest. He laid a hand upon her knee, inching up the hem of her pleated skirt. He wanted to grasp her tight against him, but he didn't trust himself. He was afraid that if they got started, they'd never be able to stop. There were so many people to think of, so many hopes and dreams and aspirations in their way.

As soon as their lips parted, he slid away from her, giving them each a safety zone. Walt deliberately tried to slow his breathing and shifted his legs to disguise his reaction to her nearness. He couldn't keep his eyes off her. He noticed, as she regained her self-control, the soft, loving look in her eyes melted into sadness.

How long could a couple be in love and keep it a secret? The two had kept their silence for five months. Secret steadies, pretending in public to be just friends. The days were filled with longing glances and stolen moments. Their nights went on forever, with Walt sneaking downstairs to call her on the telephone. Many nights they talked till daybreak. They didn't need sleep or food or even air to breathe, they just needed each other.

"Have you read the English assignment?" she asked.

"The English assignment?" Walt was taken aback by the abrupt change in discussion from their undying love to this week's homework. "Uh…no, I haven't yet."

"It's *Romeo and Juliet,*" she told him. "I didn't like it at all. It's…it's so sad. Both Barb and Karen are crazy for it. They say it's romantic. Star-crossed lovers with their stupid, old-fashioned parents. The girls think that it's so cool that they are our age and choose to die for love. For me it's just…it's just such…such…I don't even know a word that's bad enough. Two people who love each other ought to get to be together, to live happily-ever-after. If they can't do it in real life, at least they ought to get to do it in stories."

Walt slowly nodded in agreement. "*We* are going to live happily-ever-after," he said firmly. "You've got to trust me on that."

"I do trust you. I trust you completely about everything. But I also know that you aren't in charge of the world. And the people who are, our parents and teachers, even God doesn't really seem to be on our side."

No, God had not been on their side. Walt had to agree with that as he waited in the deserted parking lot watching the rain stream.

He caught sight of the blue Mercedes coming up the road. It pulled into a parking space under a tree far across the lot. He zipped up his windbreaker and pulled the hood over his head before stepping out into the relentless downpour.

He ran across the parking lot dodging puddles. He felt exhilarated, full of life, young. Yes, that was it, he felt young.

The passenger door was already ajar, a thin feminine hand held it open. The woman inside was bright-eyed and petite. She was wearing casual slacks, a crisp blue blouse and a summer sweater. Her hair was tidy, her makeup natural but effective. In short, she was an attractive woman. An attractive woman who looked her age.

Walt slid into the seat next to her.

"I'm getting all your fancy leather upholstery wet," Walt warned her in apology.

"I'm sure you know how much I care about that," she said. "Here, let's get this windbreaker off of you and hang it in the backseat and maybe it will dry out a little."

She tried to help him out of his jacket in the crowded small space. By the time they managed to get the dripping nylon off Walt's back and hanging on the backseat window hook, they were both laughing and they were both wet.

"So much for working well together as a team," she teased. "It's a good thing we weren't trying to get naked. Somebody could have gotten injured."

"It would be worth an injury to get naked with you, Rachel," he told her.

She grinned at him.

"You talk a good game," she pointed out. "But I don't see you hustling me off to the adult video store motel."

"No scratchy sheets on backstreets affair for me. I'm not that kind of guy," he informed her. "I mean, why buy the bull when you can get...uh...wait a minute."

She laughed. It was a sound that oozed across his skin like warm molasses.

Walt reached over and took her hand in his own and brought her fingers to his lips as he looked into her bright brown eyes. "When a man has waited as long as I have, well, he wants it in a bed of roses with all the time left in the world."

"A bed of roses is not that hard to manage," she told him. "But all the time left in the world is a bit more difficult to guarantee." She was still smiling, but her expression was more serious.

"Whatever we've got left is enough," he assured her. "As long as we can get started soon."

She nodded.

He pulled her as close to him as the steering column would allow. She rested her head on his shoulder. He breathed in the scent of her. It was fresh and lightly floral, but there was nothing cloying about it. He loved the fragrance that was, to him, so familiar and so welcome.

He felt a sudden stab of regret about Ella. Had she worn perfume or just plain soap? He was certain that his late wife had smelled lovely. In truth he couldn't remember a scent at all. Thirty-five years of marriage and he apparently hadn't noticed.

But it was unfair to compare the two women, he reminded himself. Ella never compared him. Or if she did, he never knew it. He was determined to do right by his late wife, the mother of his children. It was so easy just to get lost in the woman in his arms.

"Have I told you lately how I love you?" he asked.

He could feel her grin against his shoulder. "You could always sing it," she replied. "Though you were never that good with the Elvis imitation."

He chuckled, but kept his serious tone. "I do love you," he told her.

"I know," she answered. "And I love you. I always have. It just doesn't make things any easier."

"No," he agreed simply.

"How are your girls?" she asked.

"Fine," Walt answered. "They're doing fine. Jelly is the happiest person on earth. I know she misses her mother. And losing touch with the people at her old job, that bothers her, too. But somehow she wakes up every morning just happy and excited and that enthusiasm sticks with her all day long."

"That's wonderful," she said.

Walt nodded. "Yeah, it's one of those unexpected perks that you can't imagine springing from disability. She can be so satisfied with so little. And her sense of her own success is unflappable. I wish Andi had some of that."

Rachel made a sympathetic murmur of agreement.

"When those two were children, I thought Jelly had the hard row to hoe, but it's Andi, with all her gifts, who struggles to find her way."

"She misses her mother, too," Rachel said.

"Yes, she does. And unlike Jelly, I think she has lots of guilt. She and Ella always had their mother-daughter conflicts. Now, without the chance to make it up or say goodbye, all that remains are the 'what-ifs.'"

"That's not all," Rachel assured him. "It just takes some time to sort through that to get to the real memories."

Walt sighed. "I hope you're right."

"I heard about her drive-through coffee place," Rachel told him. "I thought that was a good idea."

"It was," Walt agreed. "I think it was. But the council just didn't go for it. I told Andi not to take it personally, but she did. She blames Hank Guthrie. She thinks he torpedoed her. I'm sure he never intended that."

Rachel raised her head off his shoulder and eyed him askance. "I wasn't there," she admitted. "But I wouldn't trust Hank Guthrie farther than I could throw him."

Walt chuckled. "If you were mad enough, you could probably throw him pretty far."

"That man is a slimy lowlife," she insisted. "He'd screw up her plans or work against them behind her back, just for his own entertainment."

Walt wasn't so certain. "You just don't like him because he cheats on his wife."

As she shook her head, a lock of dark hair, frosted with silver, escaped the confines of her neat matronly updo.

"Why Madeleine Grosvenor gave that man thirty minutes of her life, let alone thirty years, will always be a mystery to me," she said. "But I'm not talking personal, I'm talking business. There's not a soul at the Chamber of Commerce that doesn't keep a wary eye on Guthrie."

"I've never heard anybody say anything," Walt told her.

"And you won't," she answered. "He's powerful enough that nobody openly speaks against him. But he's earned his reputation as a snake in the grass."

"He's a pretty arrogant type of guy. I'll give you that," Walt said. "But he's been so blessed and he's so successful. I can't help but think that a lot of the distrust is based on jealousy."

She shook her head, but at the same time she smiled broadly.

"That's one of the things I love about you," she said. "You're always determined to see the good in people."

Walt raised an eyebrow. "You think I'm naive?"

"No, not at all," she answered. "Naive implies an ignorance of the cruelties of life and an innocence of that experience. The way you think is not based in either of those. It's more as if you choose to only see us mortals in the best possible light. And that really sort of pushes us to live up to your expectations."

"I'm no saint, Rachel," he said. "Just ask Father Blognick."

She waved away his words. "He may know your every sin. But I know *you* better than anyone else."

She placed her small hands on either side of his face. "Now kiss me you idiot," she said. "I'm not willing to wait all day."

Pete was standing at his corner office window, a cup of coffee in one hand and a Mallomar in the other, as he watched the rain come down. He tried not to let the gloom of the day weigh down on him.

The big news in the weekly *Plainview Public Observer* was about the huge expansion of Superbuy, Guthrie's competition out near the interstate. Two adjacent businesses in severe financial trouble had given up their leases to the national chain and they were inexplicably making their store bigger, just as Pete was belt-tightening his operation day by day. It was frustrating. It was disheartening. And it didn't matter how many times he told himself that it was a global economic crisis, it still felt like a personal failure.

He watched the city bus pause at the Grosvenor Street stop. Someone emerged beneath the cover of a pink flowered umbrella. There was something cheerful about bright florals on a dark gray day. He watched as its bearer moved along the sidewalk. It was only when she turned up the driveway of the former Plainview Wash & Wax that he realized it must be Wolkowicz.

He rolled his eyes and muttered under his breath, "Great, Peterson, another reason for you to feel guilty."

Why had his father pulled that reprehensible trick on the woman? First he double-crossed her dad on the sale of the property and then he deep-sixed her coffee store plan.

He took another bite of his Mallomar.

His phone rang, but he let Miss Kepper get it in the other room. He needed to get a little more psyched up before he talked to anyone. The Mallomars helped.

The intercom on his desk beeped.

"Mr. Guthrie, it's your father on line one."

Pete groaned aloud. He stuck the last of the Mallomar in

his mouth and walked across the room to sit behind his desk. He finished chewing and swallowed before forcing a smile to his face. He picked up the phone.

"Morning, Dad," he said. "I can't talk long. I'm still going over yesterday's numbers. What's up with you?"

Hank didn't bother responding to his pleasantries. "Have you seen the news about Superbuy? Damn it, boy! How could you let us get blindsided by this?"

Pete reached for the bag of Mallomars at the edge of his desk. He listened for fifteen minutes as his father criticized virtually everything that he'd ever done. Pete was not unaccustomed to this and he'd acquired the helpful ability to listen intently while removing his emotions. He'd learned the skill from watching his mother. And he'd had many years of practice on his own. Pete listened as if it were someone else's conversation and he was just an observer. As an observer, he could only marvel that the man who could never remember to show up for award ceremonies, birthday parties or parent-teacher conferences had such a steel-trap memory of his son's every misstep, slight or momentous. From his failure to make the All-Star team in Little League to the story in this morning's newspaper, it was all, to Hank Guthrie's thinking, evidence of his son's innate inferiority to his father.

"It's just like marrying that little tart of yours," his father blathered on.

Pete was immediately sucked back into the moment. There were places where his father's opinion was off-limits.

"No!" Pete stated firmly into the phone. "My divorce and my ex are not your business. Don't even go there. You've made such a mess of your marriage, you can't give anyone advice on that score. Besides, all that's history. It doesn't have anything to do with the store."

The sudden push-back shocked Hank into momentary silence. Unfortunately, it was only momentary.

"I don't give a damn about Minx or your marriage," the older man said. "But both say a lot about your character. A man who lets a woman run around on him, that's a man who's not in control. And if you're not in control, then somebody else is controlling you."

"No one is controlling me," Pete said. "And I am controlling the store. You are *not* controlling the store. So why don't you stop calling here and acting like you are."

Pete slammed down the phone. He immediately regretted it. Losing his temper was losing control.

Still angry, he got up from his desk and headed out of his office. Down the hallway, Miss Kepper's door was open and he glanced in just long enough to see her face. Her expression, one of disappointment and distress, was to be totally expected. Her loyalties were divided. She was always on Pete's side, but she loved Hank.

"I've got my phone," he said simply and moved on quickly, leaving no time for discussion.

He walked down the drab hallway to the stairs. His mood immediately lightened as he entered the light and activity of the store. He liked the store. He loved Guthrie Foods. He had since he was a kid. He enjoyed the energy and the feeling of accomplishment. He'd thought that managing the store would be like working in the store. But, of course, it wasn't always. Pete wasn't afraid of hard work, or hesitant of making big decisions. But some days the responsibility for all these employees, for his customers, for the community and to his family heritage, weighed more heavily than others. And the time spent trying to save three cents on a product or two minutes out of a workweek, turned out to be the most frustrating and the most important. It was always the one thing that only he was in a position to do.

He remembered to smile and nod at the cashiers as he passed. He stopped to help on checkout three.

"Cody, I think we should put the box in like this, upright," he said. "It gives the sack a more open form and that makes it easier to pack."

The young man nodded as he allowed Pete to help him.

The new bring-your-own-reusable-bag policy was a great money saver and good for the environment. But with carryalls of every shape and size, bagging had become more of an art than a science. In a solid-bottomed tote, the best place for the eggs was on the bottom, as long as the stuff on top was not too heavy. But if the sack had just seams or curved out, the eggs went on top, just like they do in plastic store bags. In the past, a bagger might have been free to utilize a near infinite number of store bags. Today, if the customer brought in three bags, they wanted their groceries to fit in them, and without being so heavy that they couldn't easily lift them out of their car.

Most of the baggers at Guthrie's were easily able to adapt to these changes. For Cody, a young man with Down's Syndrome, inconsistency was a challenge. But he tried hard, was quick to apologize when he messed up, and was a favorite among the cashiers.

Pete made his way into the aisles. He greeted people he knew, answered questions for shoppers and picked up trash as he went through the store. Finally, on the far end of Aisle Nineteen, he located Harvey, the stock crew supervisor. He was a weathered but wiry employee who'd been with the company all of Pete's life. He was working alongside the two guys and one woman on his team. Nearby a grocery cart was loaded almost to capacity with items being cleared off the shelf.

"How's it going?"

The older man shrugged. "This dang trail mix sure didn't sell," he answered.

Pete nodded, picking up the package.

"The price is off for the kind of demand we get," he agreed. "It may be more organic and healthy than the stuff in the bags, but it looks the same. Folks just won't pay a dollar more to try something that only *might* be better."

"They should have introduced it for the same price," Harvey said. "Then once people tried it, they could slowly move it up to cover the costs."

"Yeah," Pete agreed. "They probably did that in other markets and thought they had built enough reputation to just show up here. Our folks just don't eat as much of this grazing stuff as they do in California."

Harvey laughed. "It's 'cause we get to wear our coats all winter," he said. "We look stout anyway, we might as well eat what we want."

Pete began helping him clear the shelf. The end displays on each aisle were the most active product areas in the store. Each month merchandisers paid for the prominent placement of their products. So last month's merchandise was out and new things were brought in. It was labor-intensive for stockers, but it was very good for business.

"I'd bet you've got something better to do than follow me around today," Harvey said.

Pete shrugged. "I know you're down to a bare-bones crew," he answered. "If I don't help you, I'd need to take someone off the checkout line."

Harvey nodded.

Pete had avoided layoffs by not filling positions that came vacant, and by hiring part-timers. It helped to keep the store profitable, but it made for heavy strains on productivity.

"You know I've been thinking," Harvey said.

"That's always dangerous," Pete pointed out.

The older man grinned, adding to the joke. "I do it so rarely it doesn't pain me much."

The two men chuckled together.

"Maybe we could cross-train more of the staff," Harvey said. "If we could get most everybody competent in more jobs in the store, then we could utilize whoever is on the clock."

Pete nodded, hearing the man out. Cross-training was often fraught with push-back from employees. The extra effort required to learn a new task was frequently resented. And there often existed an entire hierarchy, in the minds of some workers, as to which jobs were acceptable and which jobs were beneath them. Pete did all he could to counter the latter mind-set, showing by example his willingness to do whatever needed doing. He was just as quick to fill in for a cashier as he was to do "cleanup on Aisle Nine."

"I haven't said anything," Harvey said. "Because I know your father was a true believer in specialization, but—"

Pete cut him off. "My father is not running Guthrie Foods."

Harvey's eyes widened and Pete realized that he'd spoken

more sharply than he should. He forced a wide grin to his face to counter his tone. "And times are a lot different now than when my dad ran the store."

The older man nodded slowly. "That's right," he said. "Times are different."

"I certainly think it's an idea worth looking at," Pete said.

"We could start small," Harvey said. "We wouldn't want to go storewide the first day. Just test the waters, see if we can get it going."

"Let me think about it for a day or two," Pete said. "And we'll talk again."

"Okay. Sure, think about it."

"And I do appreciate your input," Pete continued. "We need everybody in the store to be thinking about how to make things work better. So…so thanks."

Pete continued to help with the end displays for a few minutes before he was called to the loading dock to haggle with a driver who was a day late and half the order short.

By the time he got that sorted out, he only walked through the produce department before he was called to the checkout. He subbed for the front end manager while she took an early lunch. He cleared up over-rings and ran down uncoded prices for an hour. He didn't mind that. He wasn't so thrilled about the personal check that failed the scan-check. The scancheck was a fraud prevention system. Its compact reader could electronically verify the validity of an account and rate the risk of it at point of sale. That was good news for the retailer. Not always such good news for the customer.

Pete was called to register five. When he stepped up, the

cashier handed him what amounted to a worthless piece of paper.

"It's a code three," she told him.

Pete nodded at the cashier and then turned his attention to the customer. He didn't know her, but he figured she was about his age. She had two quiet children eyeing him and a third, a gooing cheerful infant, was strapped into the shopping cart.

"There seems to be a problem with your check," he said quietly.

Neither the mom nor the kids looked surprised.

"Maybe, you…ah…do you have a credit card?"

"It was declined," the cashier told him.

The woman looked cornered, ready to bolt. The weight of her humiliation created a heaviness in the air making it hard to breathe.

Pete glanced at the grocery bags already loaded into the cart. She was buying bread and milk, peanut butter and diapers. If she'd had a six-pack of beer or a carton of cigarettes, even a frozen pizza he might have been able to fault her. But he knew that if he had three kids and needed to feed them, he didn't know what he might have felt compelled to do.

He hesitated only a minute before scrawling his initials next to the amount on the check.

"Give me a copy of the receipt," he told the cashier. She quickly printed it out and he stapled the two pieces of paper together.

"Is this your current address and phone number?" he asked the customer.

The woman's "yes" was almost inaudible.

Pete nodded. "We're going to hold this," he told her.

"When you get some cash together, you can come pick it up. I'll give it to Miss Kepper. Her office is up the stairs over there."

"Okay," the woman said. Her voice was still tentative.

"Great," Pete said, feigning an enthusiasm he didn't feel and smiling broadly at the kids. "You have a real nice day. And thank you for shopping at Guthrie's."

As the young woman hurried out with her kids and her groceries, Pete knew he would probably never see his money. And even if he got paid, the family would most likely never shop here again. No matter how gently a situation like this was treated, it always left a bad taste in the mouth.

When the front end manager returned to her post, Pete went over to the deli section and asked them to fix him a sandwich. As he waited, he stood near the windows, watching the rain. It was no longer an angry torrent, but a steady, gentle gift to his landscaping.

When he heard his name called, he turned back toward the counter and noticed the light was on inside Wolkowicz's car wash. She was undoubtedly still there. What on earth was she doing? Suddenly, he was very curious to find out.

"Meggie, may I have two sandwiches today?" he asked the woman behind the counter.

Chapter 8

ANDI DIDN'T KNOW what she was doing. That was a very unusual experience for her. Typically, she made certain she knew exactly what she was doing. Every move she'd made in her life had involved research, list making, spreadsheets and risk analysis. Even when she might be making a mistake, like leaving the city to move back home to Plainview, she hadn't allowed herself to get by without weighing the options and the outcomes. Life was too crazy not to plan ahead.

Today, she had no plan.

She'd rejected out of hand Cher-L's suggestion of a wet T-shirt and thong car wash. That was an idiotic idea, not even worthy of consideration. She was definitely not doing anything like that. Still, she'd had the lights and water turned on in the building, and she had made no move to try to sell the stored supplies. Today she was looking at the equipment. Her father had always treated his equipment as kindly and gently as he treated his kids. But this gear had been lying around for almost a decade. The good news about not having a conveyer or an automated brush system, Andi decided, was that an old compressor that attached to hoses and wands wasn't all that complicated. The vinyl was leaky and there was a bit of rust on everything, but nothing was irreparably damaged.

She began cleaning the metal using one of Pop's old tricks. Dousing it with cola then scrubbing it down with aluminum foil. It worked pretty well.

An aging blue Taurus pulled up beneath the overhang. Andi glanced up curiously and saw Tiff emerging from the driver's seat. She was wearing cropped jeans and a scoop-necked T-shirt, her long blond hair was loose and hung down to the middle of her back. She walked around the car and opened the back door. A towheaded boy in shorts and a hoodie muscle shirt emerged. He was carrying a video game and hardly glanced up as his mother directed him toward the building.

Andi got up and opened the door to welcome them.

"Hello."

"Hi, Andi," Tiff said. "I'd like you to meet my son, Caleb."

"Hi, Caleb."

He looked up quickly with a smile and a wave before refocusing on the tiny screen in his hands.

"Whatcha playing?" she asked.

"Lego Star Wars."

"Are you good at it?"

Caleb nodded. "Too good," he answered. "I got it in *kindergarten*." He said the last word with enough emphasis to suggest the time was aeons in the past. "Nobody even plays this anymore. All the other kids have new games."

"No, they don't," Tiff corrected. "Lots of other kids have dads out of work, just like you."

Caleb shrugged and sighed.

"You've still got something to play and lot of kids don't even have that, right?"

"Yeah, right," he agreed, with only the vaguest hint of sullenness to his tone.

"So go play your game while I talk with Miss Andi."

Caleb walked across the room to an empty corner, crossed his legs and sat without once taking his thumbs off the controls.

"Don't stop what you're doing," Tiff said to Andi.

"I was just cleaning up this equipment," she replied as she seated herself on the wooden workbench. Tiff hoisted herself up beside her and inspected the pieces that she'd completed.

"Still thinking to sell this stuff?" Tiff asked.

"Yeah, yeah, I guess so."

A silence lengthened between them.

"Guess what I just saw happen in the grocery store."

"What?" Andi asked.

"I was in the checkout behind this woman with three kids," she said. "They rang her up and she handed the cashier a credit card. The card was declined. So she tried to pay with a check. But they put it in that check security gizmo and it was declined, too."

"Oh, jeez!"

"I know," Tiff said. "I knew I should just walk away, get in another line, but it was like some horrible traffic accident. I just couldn't look away."

"So, what happened?" Andi asked.

"They called Guthrie over and I thought that if it were me, I would have just died of humiliation right on the spot," Tiff said. "But he was pretty cool about it. He told her that he'd keep her check and she could come back and pick it up when she had the money. He even thanked her for shopping at Guthrie's."

"He thanked her? With a straight face?"

"Pretty much. He actually smiled at the kids. I guess it must have been about the kids. Wouldn't that be horrible?"

"Yeah, horrible."

"I felt sorry for her," Tiff said. "But at the same time I was thinking, 'I'm so glad it's her and not me!' That's exactly what I was thinking. Because I know that next week or next month, it absolutely could be me."

Andi looked at Tiff, nodding sympathetically and secretly glad that she had her father to live with and his retirement saving to live on. But she was pretty sure that Pop had never made plans for long-term support of Andi. Having one daughter that would need his help was more than enough.

"I've got to find something," Tiff said. "Even if it's not something…something that I'd normally consider doing."

Andi's brown eyes gazed assessingly into Tiff's blue ones.

"You're thinking about the car wash."

Tiff nodded. "I mean, Cher-L has a point. You don't see any of those titty-bars down on Doge Avenue going out of business. What if a guy could get a pretty good show and his car washed at the same time?"

Andi shot a quick glance toward Caleb. "Are you sure you'd want to do that?"

"No," Tiff replied. "I'm not sure at all that I want to do it.

But I *am* sure I don't want my son to see me trying to pass a hot check at the grocery store."

Andi nodded.

"And honestly, how bad can it be? I don't mean we should do the wet T-shirt or some kind of costume with pasties. But we could wear bikinis. We won't be showing off anything the whole world couldn't see at the community swimming pool."

"Yeah, I guess that's true," Andi agreed.

"I think...I think we ought to try it," Tiff said.

Andi sighed. "I've been thinking about it, too. I look at the opportunities for this building and I just don't see much. If times were better, maybe it could be some kind of office. But there's empty office space all up and down the street. We'd just be one more FOR RENT sign."

"Times are going to get better," Tiff assured her. "And when they do, well, you could come up with something entirely different. But this bikini car wash thing is something that could work now."

It could work. It was a possibility. It was an opportunity. Still, she knew there were plenty of excellent business ideas that should never see the light of day. She feared this might be one of them.

"Let's talk to Cher-L and maybe, between the three of us, we could give it a try," Andi told her.

Tiff's eyes widened.

"We're really going to do it?"

Andi glanced down at the equipment she was cleaning and then back up at Tiff.

"It's a seasonal business," she said. "I'll only be able to keep it open through the summer. And we can't know for sure that it would even make money," she said. "It's not like I could guarantee any decent wage."

"I'll work for tips," Tiff assured her. "I just need a chance."

"I'd have to ask my father," Andi said. "This is still his building and his equipment." She looked around and allowed herself a moment of remembering what the place was like when Pop had it open. "I can't imagine that he'd say 'yes' to this," she admitted, shaking her head. "He's a very straightlaced kind of guy."

Tiff shrugged. "Still, it's worth asking, I think," she said, then added apologetically. "That's why I'm here asking you. And that's why you're asking yourself."

"I'll call you after I talk to Pop," Andi told her.

As she watched Tiff and Caleb drive away, she felt a sense of deflation nearly overwhelm her. Uncharacteristically she had refused to even weigh the pros and cons. The thrill of opening her own business just couldn't permeate the disappointment of a plan based on everything that she absolutely wasn't. It was easy and pleasant to imagine herself handing out frothy lattes to friendly faces of drive-up customers. It was not so pleasurable to imagine herself in a skimpy bathing suit being viewed and judged by the same kind of creeps who had made fun of her in high school. Somehow, over the years, in all her imaginings, she'd return to Plainview in triumph having made it big in the city. Instead she was returning as a thick-thighed late bloomer, bending over car bumpers in a bikini.

Andi shuddered unpleasantly at the thought.

The equipment was looking much better and her stomach was beginning to growl. She was just thinking to brave the rain once more and head back to the house when there was an unexpected knock on the door.

Andi glanced up to see Pete Guthrie on the other side of the glass. Her brow furrowed, puzzled. He smiled at her. What on earth was that about?

"It's open!" she called out.

She watched for a moment as he fumbled with the knob. Somehow she felt no compulsion to help him. Pete Guthrie had always been the golden boy. The guy who had everything. That could have spurred envy or jealousy in anyone. But with Andi adding in her own attraction to the guy, well, resentment was just a natural outcome.

"Have you come to run me off the property again?" she asked him. She heard the anger and defiance in her voice. She wanted to sound cool and confident, but he brought out the defensive.

"Nope," he answered. "I brought lunch." He indicated the two brown paper bags he carried.

"Oh…" Andi was surprised and wary. "I…uh…I was just about to catch the bus for home."

"I…uh, I saw your light on in here and thought you might be hungry," he said.

Andi's gaze narrowed. "Is that what you do up there in the exalted corner office of Guthrie Foods? Look down on the street and think about who is hungry?"

She was baiting him.

"Hey, that might not be such a bad habit for a groceryman," he answered with an orthodontically perfect grin.

Nobody deserved to be that good-looking, she thought to herself. He looked a lot like his dad, and like his dad, time just enhanced the handsomeness.

"May I sit?" Pete asked, indicating the empty length of table beside her.

"Sure, grocery guy, I'm sure you're used to making yourself at home. I should probably charge rent."

He laughed and handed her a lunch sack. "Maybe you can put this on account."

"On account of you brought it."

"You're quick."

"I've had to be," Andi answered. "When you're a target you have to keep moving to stay out of people's way."

Pete seated himself beside her. "Were we that hard on you?" he asked. "High school is no place for fragile teenage sensibilities, but was it hideous?"

Andi wanted to answer "yes." It was very strange to have him sitting beside her as if they'd been friends. They hardly knew each other and they'd never had anything to say. It was Pete Guthrie and his pals who had made high school miserable for her. That's what she'd always thought. But looking back, they had all been more annoying than cruel. And much of her teenage unhappiness had other root causes.

"It was fine," she answered him, honestly. "I'm no delicate flower. And I wasn't back then. I had enough confidence in myself that I could take all the geek and lesbo taunts that your crew could dish out."

Pete was nodding as he unwrapped his sandwich. She felt his khaki-covered thigh against her own. He might be older, less sculpted than in his bygone days, but his legs were still muscular and masculine.

Andi crossed hers at the knee to put some distance between the two of them.

"My crew?" he asked. "Funny that you'd think of them that way. I had such a weird, diverse group of friends. Many of them had nothing in common but me. I guess I never thought of them as a crew."

He chewed on the thought a moment, but didn't dispute her.

"And I could never figure out if I was a preppy or a jock," he said. "I frequently got accused of both. Do we pick our clique? Or do other people define who they think we are? What did you think?"

"I just thought you were puffed up and lame," Andi answered.

"Oh, well, if we're being honest, then that's pretty much what I thought, too," he admitted. "But isn't that what high school is all about?"

His self-deprecation was strangely alluring. She resisted by frowning at him.

"Look," he said, turning slightly to meet her eye to eye. "If I was mean to you, I'm sorry," he said. "And for the record, I never started, repeated or passed on any comments about your sexual preference. That's really nobody's business."

"I'm not a lesbian," Andi stated flatly. "I was just a tomboy."

"Oh…well, great, fine…I mean…uh, me neither."

"You're not a lesbian?" Andi found herself enjoying his discomfiture.

"Well, no, I'm not, but that wasn't exactly what I meant. Are you going to eat your sandwich?"

Andi unwrapped it and took a bite. It tasted wonderful. "What is this?"

"It's shaved turkey with roasted peppers and goat cheese," Pete answered. "It's my favorite."

Andi wasn't sure if she was just that hungry or if it was the best sandwich she'd ever tasted, but she savored it.

"I'm completely over all that teenage angst and persecution. So don't give it a thought. I'm sure you have great high school memories," she told him. "Everybody liked you and respected you."

"Nobody even knew me," Pete said with a chuckle. "I didn't even know me. I was so busy trying to be the guy everybody expected, I didn't even figure out who I was until after college."

"Then you're ahead of me," Andi said. "I thought I had everything figured out until a few months ago. Now, day by day, I'm less and less sure."

"That's the work thing," Pete told her. "It's unsettling to lose your job, to be out of work."

"I didn't lose my job," she corrected him quickly, maybe too quickly. "I resigned and moved back home."

He nodded and chewed.

"So given your crappy high school experience," Pete said. "And with the worst economy since the Great Depression, you've decided to return to Plainview on a permanent basis."

"My mom died," she stated bluntly.

"Yes, I heard that. I'm sorry."

Andi shrugged.

"Her death made you decide to move back?"

"I knew my dad would need help with my sister," Andi said. It was the truth, but not so true that she could look him in the eye when she said it.

Pete chewed for a moment, nodding. "How is your sister?" he asked.

"Fine," Andi answered. "She's happy. Probably happier than you."

She regretted the last as being snarky, but Pete seemed to overlook it.

"She always was," he said. "In high school you two still looked a lot alike, but even from a distance I could tell the difference. She was always the one smiling and you never did."

Andi found herself surprised, and slightly pleased, that he'd been aware of her at all.

"So, besides wanting to have lunch with me and chat about old times, do you have a reason for showing up here?" she asked him.

Pete's expression sobered and he seemed to choose his words carefully.

"I just wanted to come by, as…uh…a commercial neighbor and to tell you how sorry I am that your coffee shop thing ran into trouble."

"Ran into trouble or ran into your father?" she asked.

Pete shrugged. "You aren't the first person to suggest that it might be the same thing."

Andi had obviously meant to wound, but Pete didn't show any signs of being offended. Instead he continued to chat in a manner that was as matter-of-fact as their discussion about high school.

"I want you to know that as the head of Guthrie Foods, I can assure you that Guthrie Foods has no objection to any business plan you might have for your property."

Andi's eyes narrowed and she surveyed his face with skepticism. "Is this kind of like your father recusing himself from the council vote?" she asked. "It sounds really good and makes you look really fair. The real purpose being just public relations."

"No," Pete told her firmly. "That's not what I'm after at all. What I'm telling you, with complete sincerity, is that it's me, not my father, who speaks for Guthrie Foods. And my take on it is that a rising tide lifts all boats. I want to see stores in the neighborhood succeed. If you find a way to bring customers to this corner, then I'm all for that and my company supports that."

"So you wouldn't care what kind of business I might open here?"

"If you decided to open a supermarket, I might be worried," he said, grinning at her. "Beyond that, I think whatever you decide to do here will be fine with me and I vow to say so publicly before the city council if you need me to."

The rain had stopped by the time Andi arrived back home. Pop's truck was in the driveway, but the house was empty. The thumping sound of a basketball against the driveway drew her out to the back porch.

Pop was seated on the swing. The sight of him brought a momentary rush of memory to Andi. So many times she had seen the two of them, Mom and Pop, seated on that swing. Her absence loomed large. Behind him their small backyard with its huge buckeye tree shaded everything.

"Hi Andi! Hi Andi! Hi Andi! Hi Andi!"

She turned to see a familiar face playing basketball with Jelly. "Hi, Tony," she replied.

"I made a basket!" he announced. "I made a basket! I made a basket!"

"Good for you."

"Andi's my girlfriend. Andi's my girlfriend. Andi's my girlfriend."

"Shut up and play," Jelly reprimanded him.

"Shut up and play. Shut up and play."

Andi took the seat next to her father. "What is Tony Giolecki doing here?" she asked.

"His grandma had a doctor's appointment. You know she doesn't have any help. None of her friends or neighbors are willing to take Tony on."

"But, Pop, you've got enough to manage with Jelly," Andi said. "You shouldn't have to take on another special needs kid."

Pop shrugged. "Jelly pretty much takes care of herself. Besides if we don't help, who will?"

"I made a basket!" the singsong voice announced from the driveway. "I made a basket! I made a basket!"

Tony and Jelly had been classmates since elementary school. Tony represented some of the most scary stuff about special needs kids. His diagnosis broke up his parents' marriage. They both ended up fleeing from his care and he was left with his aging grandmother who did the best she could. Tony was annoying and repetitive, prone to wandering away if he wasn't watched and he was just smart enough to get himself into a lot of trouble. His IQ was probably 20 points above Jelly's but he had none of her sweetness or biddability. He could be stubborn and belligerent. He would often take things, almost compulsively. Though he'd voluntarily handed them over at the end of a visit. And he'd had a crush on Andi that went back as far as elementary school. He told anyone and everyone that "Jelly was his best friend. But Andi was his girlfriend."

Seated beside her father, she watched the two playing basketball. Tony was more naturally athletic and several inches taller, but he couldn't stop talking. Jelly focused more clearly on the task, whether it was bouncing the ball in the driveway or throwing it up to the rim. She only needed to bide her time until Tony distracted himself to get a clear shot.

"ALL RIGHT!" Jelly hollered in celebration.

"Two points!" Tony said.

"One hundred thousand, cash or bond," Jelly corrected.

Andi rolled her eyes. "Even basketball is about *Law & Order*," she pointed out to her father. "Maybe we should try to get Jelly interested in some other show."

He shook his head. "Your mother and I tried that for years," he said. "We played a million hours of family friendly sitcoms. We got not one spark of interest from her."

"Then maybe we should talk to somebody."

"We did," he said. "We had a behaviorist assess her."

"And?"

He chuckled. "As I recall it was a very high-level technical explanation that translated into everyday English, means different strokes for different folks. Nobody's entertainment choices make sense to anybody else."

Andi raised an eyebrow at that.

"Stupid shrinks!" Andi commented with a heavy sigh.

The two of them sat there silently in the slight sway of the swing as they watched a strangely rule-free but cooperative basketball game. The rain had washed away the heat, the dust, the pollen, and the breeze that had come with it kept the afternoon from being sticky.

Pop had swapped his typical sport shirt for a faded T-shirt that advertised a long-defunct manufacturing company on the edge of town. He was still as trim and muscled as he'd been as a younger man. His secret was that he simply loved to work.

Whether it was tuning up an old car or replacing a length of pipe in the basement, he kept busy. And somehow that had always kept him healthy and strong. But he was not one of those active men who couldn't relax. Pop had spent a million hours of his life just sitting quietly reading a book or talking with his wife or Andi. He seemed to enjoy that as well as more productive pursuits.

"So, how was your day?" he asked her.

Andi shrugged. "I want to talk to you about something," she said. "And I need for you not to overreact or get too worried about me."

Pop patted her on the hand. "I always worry about you," he said. "That's my job."

Andi gave him a small half smile. "I know you do," she said. "I know you've been kind of doing double duty lately, with Mom gone and both Jelly and I to worry about."

Her father's brow furrowed with curiosity.

"I've always had two daughters," he pointed out.

"Yeah, I know," Andi said. "But Mom was pretty much the point person for Jelly. I was the only daughter that you really had to be responsible for."

Her father offered a wane smile. "I'm sure that's how it seems to you," he said.

"That's how it was," Andi said, very matter-of-fact. "Mom was in charge of raising Jelly and you were in charge of raising me. I'm not complaining or criticizing. I'm sure it was very hard to have twin girls who were so different, who had such different needs. And honestly, I think it worked perfectly for the two of you. You and Mom were always so in tune with one another. I guess that's an advantage of being…soul mates or whatever, that each of you could be both mother and father to your daughters."

Pop shook his head. "It's curious sometimes how different things look from the outside than from the inside," he said. "Your mother and I had a lot of things going for us. Not everything, but many things. If she were here, I think she'd agree that our girls have always been *our* girls."

"But she was more with Jelly and you were more with me." Andi heard herself belaboring the point, but she couldn't quite stop.

Pop didn't corroborate, instead he urged her to the point.

"I promise not to worry more than I need to," he told her. "What do you want to tell me? Are you moving back to Chicago?"

"Moving?" Andi was completely caught off guard by the suggestion. "No, of course not. I'm opening the car wash."

Once the words were out in the open, all the uncertainty and fear that she'd cloaked around them seemed released as well. It was a car wash. She knew a lot about running a car wash. And what she didn't know, Pop would tell her.

"You're opening the car wash?" The surprise was evident on his face. "I thought we went over this. The old hand wash is no longer competitive with the technology of the tunnel wash."

"I know," Andi said, nodding. "I've…we've found a way around that we think. I'm opening a…a bikini car wash."

"Bikini?"

"Yes," she told him. "It will be women only doing the hand wash and we'll all be dressed in bikinis."

For a minute he just continued to stare at her uncomprehendingly, but suddenly his face changed. And to Andi's displeasure he burst out laughing. Not a friendly, appreciative chuckle, but a deep, male belly laugh.

"I'm not kidding about this," Andi insisted.

He was nodding as he tried to regain his composure. "Oh, I'm sure you're not kidding," he said. "I can always count on you to be completely serious when it comes to business. And I know that you will always figure out a way to make something out of nothing and now you've gone and done it again."

"I'm opening as soon as possible," Andi said. "I'm determined to do this, but it is your building, your equipment, you do have a say."

He was still smiling broadly, but his eyes were more serious. "You think I would go against you?" he asked. "You're a grown woman, Andi. You don't need your pop to tell you what a hornet's nest you're going to stir up in this town."

She nodded.

"Do you think it will work?"

"I'm sure it will for a while," he said. "I'd say you're likely to get an excellent summer season out of it."

"So, are you okay with this?"

Her father wrapped his arms around her neck and pulled her close enough to kiss the top of her head. "If you told me you'd decided to take up bank robbery, I'd trust you to think it all through and know what you're getting into. Beyond that, Andi, I want you to do what you think is the right thing to do. Sometimes I may not be of the same opinion. But it's your life and your choices and that's what I want to give you. Not everyone has that."

It wasn't a rousing endorsement, but Andi was grateful that Pop wasn't going to try to talk her out of it. In fact, he seemed perfectly willing to give her as much technical advice and equipment refurbishing help as she needed.

"The ladies at the church are not going to like this," she pointed out to him, hoping that he already understood that.

He agreed. "Andi, they are just plain going to hate it," he said. "And they are going to give you grief like you've never gotten in your life. But all that's good. The madder folks are, the more attention that it gets, the better your receipts will be. That's the nature of a business like this. The push-back is worth twice as much as the push. If your customers just wanted to see some girls in bathing suits, they'd go to the swimming pool. They'll pay to see you because it's illicit and objectionable."

Andi didn't quite like the idea of being illicit and objectionable, but she knew he was probably right. They weren't going to be making the cars clean enough for surgery nor were they going to be doing lap dances for the customers. It was all about the appearance of something shady, something forbidden. That's what the customers were going to be buying.

"I made a basket! I made a basket! I made a basket! Andi, did you see me? Andi, did you see me? Andi, did you see me?"

"I saw you, Tony," she called out.

"I made a basket! I made a basket!"

The sun was getting low before Tony's grandmother showed up to get him. She seemed tired and worn-out and Tony whined to stay.

Pop invited them for dinner and the older woman accepted with gratitude. So with cooking and dinner and cleanup and goodbyes, it was nearly ten o'clock before Andi was alone in her upstairs bedroom.

From the bottom of her chest of drawers, Andi began pulling out swimsuits. She had several, and, for the most part, they were fairly modest and mostly functional. When Andi had gone to the lake or the pool, she'd been a swimmer rather than a sunbather. Skimpy bikinis weren't really for swimming. But she did find a nice-looking two-piece with a brightly colored halter-top. The swim-short bottoms were a far cry from a bikini. But she remembered the suit looking cute on her and she hastily stripped down to try it on. It felt just fine. It wasn't too tight or too loose. It seemed perfect. With that thought in mind, she stepped in front of the full-length mirror and her smile faded.

"Ouch!" she said aloud.

She turned round and looked over her shoulder to view her backside. "Double ouch!"

The equipment at the car wash wasn't the only thing that needed to be toned up.

Chapter 9

PETE'S DISTANCE FOR his morning run had increased enough that he could actually make it to the track and get around once before his progress became iffy.

Today he was trying to puff it through to the half-mile marker on the second lap. In high school, he'd discovered that creating a focal point could steady his breathing and distract him from the pain in his legs. A pace runner was ideal for this. If he could find somebody on the track who was going at the right speed, he'd just follow, focusing in on the heel of the runner's shoe or, if he was closer, the logo on the back of his shirt. This morning he was intent on a metallic silver stripe along the legs of a pair of pink shorts. As the muscles moved with each footfall, the fabric caught the light in slightly different ways altering the brightness of the color. Silver. Gray. Silver. Gray. Silver. Gray. Like a flashing beacon, it kept him moving forward.

He passed a pair of runners on the inside track. They were

moving slow and one of them was chattering. He saw them only in his peripheral vision, not allowing himself to be distracted. He could not, however, fail to hear what was said.

"Look! It's the man from the grocery store. Isn't it? Isn't it the man from the grocery store? I can make a positive ID from a lineup."

Pete ignored the weird comment. He could feel the heaviness in his legs, now. He willed away the lethargy in his limbs and urged himself into fierce concentration. Silver. Gray. Silver. Gray.

"Why is the grocery man staring at that lady's butt?"

Pete misstepped, the toe of his shoe caught on the track surface and he went sprawling across two lanes. Before he even hit the ground a body crashed into his. It was a jumble of arms and legs. Pete's hands clutched at the air, instinctively seeking something to hold on to.

The other person in the mishap was obviously doing the same thing. Unfortunately what she grabbed to break her fall was a large handful of his private parts. The cotton-Lycra liner of his running shorts was great for movement, but was never meant to hold off a frontal attack. As they slammed into the ground, he heard a sound like a squealing pig and realized it was his own voice's nonlanguage version of "letgo-a-me!"

The instant she released him, Pete scrambled to his feet.

He looked down to see that the woman he'd tripped up was none other than Andi Wolkowicz.

"Are you okay?" he managed to choke out.

"Yeah, I'm fine."

"Your leg is bleeding bad!" her companion announced.

Pete glanced up to see Andi's sister. "You should get on the horn to dispatch and tell them to send a bus."

"Huh?"

"He doesn't need an ambulance," Andi both answered and translated. "It's just a scrape. I've got a first-aid kit in the truck."

Pete looked down at his injury. Blood ran in small rivulets down his shin.

Other runners were going around them as Andi got to her feet.

"Come on, let's get that cleaned up," she said.

Pete took a couple of steps and found that he was not too steady. His knee was beginning to swell. He limped a couple of steps before Andi wrapped his arm around her shoulder.

"I'm okay," he assured her. But the shoulder was welcome and he leaned on it more than he should.

"Let me, let me help, too," the sister said, grabbing his other arm.

"It's okay, Jelly," she said. "I've got him."

"I've got him, too."

Pete was not able to lean on two shoulders, so for the width of the track, he just walked it off, with his arms around two women.

They led him to an old white truck with a sign on the door that read: St. Hyacinth Senior Service Meals on Wheels. Andi put down the tailgate and had him sit on it while she searched for the first-aid kit in the cab.

"I'm sorry it hurts, Mr. Grocery Man," the sister said.

He looked up at her and managed a small grin of reassurance. The sister looked so much like Andi and yet, not at all. It was the same face, same eyes, same complexion. The hair was different, but there was something else as well, something unique. It was that guileless smile that made her expression somehow ageless and almost otherworldly.

"Call me Pete," he told her.

"I know, Pete," she said. "I remember you from school. I'm Jelly."

"Hi, Jelly, I remember you, too."

Andi sat the red plastic box beside him and flipped it open. She pulled out a pack of alcohol pads and tore open the packing.

"I'm going to clean this up."

The damp gauze was cool against the undamaged skin and burned like fire over the scraped and bleeding places. Pete was holding his breath, trying not to wince aloud. As she leaned over him, Pete became very aware of her, the scent of her hair, the warmth emanating from her skin. With a sudden jolt of unexpected reaction, Pete realized just how long it had been since he'd felt a woman's touch. It had never been his plan to live a monkish life. But he'd also been very stern with himself, not wanting to become the kind of man his father was. Andi's nearness was like a wrecking ball, assaulting the carefully built walls he'd constructed. Deliberately, Pete focused his thoughts elsewhere. Mentally he was surveying the canned food aisle.

Green beans, string beans, lima beans, mushrooms.

His successful self-distraction came to an abrupt halt when Jelly asked, "Why were you staring at that lady's butt?"

"Jelly!" Andi scolded.

"What?" she asked, innocently.

At first Pete was so surprised, he had no idea what the young woman was talking about. Had he been staring at

Andi? No he couldn't have been, she was facing him and his eyes had been on his leg.

"I wasn't," he defended.

"Uh-huh, uh-huh," Jelly insisted nodding. "You saw him, too, Andi. When he was running on the track he was staring at that lady's butt."

Pete flushed with embarrassment. "I wasn't staring," he quickly defended. "I was…I was maintaining a focal point."

"Main taming a folkel point?" Jelly repeated.

"It helps when I run, I…" Pete struggled for an answer that the young woman might comprehend. "I look at something, I really look at it hard and it helps me do my best."

"Okay," Jelly said. She was thoughtful. "So why did you look at her butt?"

"I wasn't looking at her butt."

"Oh yeah, you were."

"No! Yes, I mean, not her butt per se."

"What's a purr say?"

"It means not exactly her butt," Andi translated.

"Right," Pete agreed. "I was not exactly looking at her butt. I was looking at the silver stripe on her running shorts."

Jelly nodded slowly. "Okay," she said. "I guess that's a good reason to wear shorts without stripes, huh. So guys won't stare at your butt."

"I…" he began.

Andi laid her hand upon his own. "Let it go," she said. "Sometimes with Jelly, you just have to let it go." She turned toward her sister. "We're not talking about this anymore."

"I'm just saying that I'm only wearing shorts that are one color."

"Enough."

"Okay."

An embarrassed silence settled around the three. Andi dabbed some antibiotic ointment on his abrasions.

"I didn't know you were a runner," Pete said, finally.

"It's my first day out," Andi answered. "When I left Chicago, I left my gym membership." As if that explained everything.

"Is that where you've been? Chicago?"

"Yes."

"And now you're back in Plainview to help your father."

"No," Jelly quickly disagreed. "Andi doesn't help Pop, I do. I help Pop deliver the meals on wheels. Andi doesn't help. Andi doesn't help at all. But she *is* going to wash our truck."

"Jelly!" Andi's tone was scolding.

"What?"

Andi glanced uneasily at Pete. He didn't understand what was going on, but figured it wasn't any of his business.

Andi retrieved a roll of emergency bandage from the first-aid kit and held it up to him in question.

Pete shook his head. "I don't think I'm going to need that," he told her as he surveyed his shin. Without the blood running down, the injury looked pretty tame.

"Still, you should probably cover these cuts with something."

"I've got some Band-Aids at home," he said. "I think I'll be able to patch myself up."

"And you're going to need some ice on that knee."

He nodded, having concluded the same thing. "I'll put it up for a half hour or so with a cold pack."

"Well, at least let us help you to your car."

"I ran over here."

"You live near here?"

"Not too far, about ten blocks, I guess."

"I'll drive you," Andi said. "You can't walk that far."

"Oh, I'm sure I'm all right," he assured her. "You need to finish your run."

"It's my first day out," she answered. "I was pretty much finished when I started. Come on, we'll take you home."

She snapped the lid back on the first-aid kit and once Pete was on his feet, she put up the tailgate on the truck.

He leaned on the truck as he made his way to the passenger door. Jelly was there first and held it open for him.

"After you," he said politely.

Jelly frowned. "I don't like to sit in the middle," she explained.

"Jelly," her sister scolded. "He's hurt and he's a guest."

"But I don't like to sit in the middle," she repeated.

"It's okay," Pete said. He hoisted himself into the truck and eased himself across the bench seat. His left knee would not bend sufficiently to accommodate the gearshift. So he tried sprawling slightly sideways, but Jelly wouldn't let him get away with that.

"Scoot over, you're hogging the whole seat!" she complained.

Pete tried to rearrange himself, but there was just no way to make himself fit easily into the small truck cab.

"My left leg is stiff," he explained to Andi. "I need to stretch it out on your side of the gearshift."

"Oh sure, of course," Andi answered.

Pete didn't look at her, but he could hear the discomfiture in her voice. He straddled the long piece of black metal, vacillating between giving Andi plenty of room near the gas pedal or plenty of room to change gears. In fact, there was not a lot of room for either.

Jelly bounced in beside him, squeezing him further in Andi's direction.

He murmured an apology.

"These trucks, they're not really all that roomy for three people," she said.

"Andi always gets to drive," Jelly said. "I don't get to drive. But I could. I know I could. But Pop says if you can't read, you can't drive. I don't know why because you shouldn't read when you're driving anyway." She hesitated. When neither Pete nor Andi responded, Jelly went for confirmation. "That's right, right? You can't read and drive. That's silly. Isn't it silly?"

"Yes, Jelly," Andi said. "It's very silly. But you can't drive because you don't have a license."

Jelly sighed heavily. "Yeah, that." Her deflation was only momentary. "I drove a go-cart once," she told Pete. "I drove really, really fast. You don't need a license to drive a go-cart."

"I guess not," he agreed.

"I wasn't speeding away from a crime scene," she clarified.

Andi turned over the ignition and the little truck sputtered to life. As she stepped on the clutch and placed her right hand on the shifting knob, she shifted into Reverse. That gear was unfortunately to the far left and all the way down. Putting her hand squarely in Pete's crotch.

He pretended that he didn't notice. So did she.

She backed out of the parking spot quickly. And once she shifted into first, Pete let out a long breath. There wouldn't be any more backing up. He'd make sure of that, even if he had to direct her around the block three times. As it turned out, he got her through the streets and to the front of his home without incident.

"This is it here," Pete pointed out. "Third house on the left."

He heard her sharp intake of breath. "What a great house!"

"Thanks."

"It must have been wonderful growing up here."

"Oh, yeah, you know it must have been."

She turned sharply to look at him. "You didn't grow up here?"

"Me? No. I bought it a few years ago."

"Oh, I thought it must be your parents' house," Andi said. "It seems like such a family place."

"Yeah, it does."

Pete didn't want to say more. He didn't want to stir it all up in his mind or be caught in some kind of long explanation. The house had said "family" to him. And he'd bought it with that idea, that ideal, as a dream on his horizon. But it had turned out to be a mirage. Now the house served him as little more than a big dorm room with high property taxes.

He glanced over at Jelly who had her earbuds in place and was quietly rocking to the music she heard playing. She showed no indication of moving.

"Maybe getting out on the driver's side would be better anyway," he said.

"Oh yeah, sure," Andi said and unhooked her seat belt as she opened the door.

Pete scooted in that direction. He heard the slam of a front door and rapid footsteps when he stepped out into the sunshine. He caught sight of Mrs. Joffee hurrying down her walkway. When she caught sight of him, she halted abruptly, then, after an instant of hesitation, she continued forward more slowly.

"What's happened, Pete? Have you been in an accident?"

"Nothing much," he assured her, surprised at her concern. "I just fell down and these ladies gave me a ride home."

She smiled at Andi. "Hello."

Andi gave her a polite nod and responded, "Hi."

"Do you need help getting up the stairs?" Andi asked him.

"No, I think I can make it."

"Let me help you that far, anyway," she said. As she offered a shoulder, she asked a question. "Who is your busybody neighbor?"

"Oh, it's Mrs. Joffee, from the department store."

"Yeah," Andi said nodding. "I thought she looked familiar, but I couldn't place her. So she's like your personal mother hen, huh."

"No, not at all," Pete said. "We get along, but typically, she doesn't pay much attention to me. I must look a lot worse than I feel."

They'd reached the bottom of the stairs. The eight steps looked very formidable, but Pete couldn't ask her to help him. If she went to the top of the steps, she might ask to see inside the house. He couldn't let that happen. She liked the house. Her first reaction to it had been the same as his own. He couldn't let her see it as it was inside. An untidy collection of still-packed boxes and dirty laundry scattered on the floor. It was a family house and somehow he couldn't bear for Andi not to see it that way.

"I can take it from here," he told her. "I'll just hang on to the railing."

She nodded. "Well, put some ice on that knee. It's already swelling."

"Yeah, I will."

"Hi, Mrs. Joffee! How is your yellow kitty cat?"

"He's fine, Jelly," the woman answered. "He's around here somewhere."

Jelly scrambled out of the truck and headed to the woman's yard as if she had done so a million times.

Andi and Pete shared a puzzled glance.

Andi didn't bother to dress up this time when she went down to City Hall. Opening a car wash where a car wash had been merely required a permit of occupancy. She paid her fee to Mr. Gilbert and made an appointment with the fire inspector to visit the property.

Mr. Gilbert seemed pleased that she'd taken the decision of the council without complaint and was now intent on opening a business that was already suited for the site.

Andi just smiled at him. Nowhere on any of the paperwork or within any of the questioning did the subject of what her employees might be wearing come up. It was merely a car wash. As such, it didn't require any special uniforms or safety gear.

She was humming to herself as she left the building. She was fully aware of what she was doing. She was not lying. Lying meant saying something that was not true. Everything she'd said about her car wash business was true. She'd just been careful not to say everything.

She called Tiff to tell her that everything was on track and to discuss the best way to make a splash opening.

"I'm thinking Saturday morning would be the best," Andi told her. "We'll have more traffic down Grosvenor Street. And more of them will be people with jobs who have to run errands on the weekend."

Tiff chuckled. "I really don't think you'll have trouble getting the word out," she said. "This news is going to be on the lips of everybody in town."

Andi laughed, too, but her heart wasn't really in it. She was determined to do this, determined to make it work, determined to snub her nose at the city fathers. But she also just wanted to make a living, she just wanted a business, her own business, without excuses or controversy.

Her father and Jelly were at the car wash when she got there. They had opened a big five-gallon bucket of white paint and Pop was rolling it on to the white brick walls.

"What are you doing?" Andi asked, astounded.

"Just thought you ladies could use a nice, clean look."

"We're tampering with evidence!" Jelly said joyously.

Andi smiled at her before standing back to assess what they'd done.

"What do you think?" Pop asked.

"I think you're a miracle worker," she said. "It's looking great."

Her father nodded. "It was amazing how easily a tired old eyesore can start looking cute and quaint."

"I bet you tell that to all the old gals at the church," Andi teased.

Pop feigned disapproval. "Polish girls are never cute, Andi," he reminded her. "They're handsome, smart and hardworking. We let the Irish girls be cute. They're better at it."

Andi laughed. It was an old joke of her mother's, as familiar to her as her own childhood and special to hear from her father's lips. It felt strangely like old times, the times when they had all been together. The times that were gone for good. She held on to the sweetness of the feeling, refusing to allow the sadness in.

"So, if you've got time to lend a hand here," Pop said. "I think we can get this done before Jelly and I have to go to St. Hyacinth's."

Andi took over his paint roller as he picked up a brush to get into the tight corners.

"So how did it go at City Hall?" Pop asked.

"Good," Andi answered. "The inspector is coming out tomorrow and with luck, we'll be ready to go by Saturday."

Her father nodded. "You might call Williard Hoskins, my old plumber. See if he can come out here this afternoon and snake these drains. Drains have always been this building's Achilles' heel. Draining is vital."

Andi nodded. "Okay, I'll give him a call."

"What are you going to do about the sign?" Pop asked.

Andi leaned her roller against the side of the building and walked out to the sidewalk where she could assess the faded red letters painted onto the brick front facing of the overhang.

"Do you think I should get it repainted?" she asked.

Her father sucked at his teeth thoughtfully. "You probably should," he said. "But with all the expense of getting opened up, maybe it could wait."

"Still," Andi said. "There's nothing like something new on the street to get people's attention."

Her father agreed. "Maybe you could hang a banner," he said. "A banner might be cheaper."

Andi was thoughtful for a moment. "You know, it would be a lot cheaper if I did it myself."

He raised an eyebrow. "Do you think you can do that?"

"Hey, Pop," she answered. "You're the guy who told me that I can do anything."

He chuckled appreciatively.

By the time her father and Jelly left for their meals on wheels deliveries, the front of the building was looking clean and bright. Before starting on the back, Andi took the ladder out to the end of the overhang and took measurements for her banner. One of the unexpected advantages of being in groups like the math club and Science Explorers was that, unlike pep club or band boosters, there was never any money for flags or decorations or signs. Andi had figured out how to do those things herself and to do them well enough that she didn't need to be ashamed of her efforts. She'd make a banner that looked good. One that was simple, readable and would catch the eye. And sometimes, she assured herself, homemade could be more appealing than anything slick, flawless and commercial.

Lunchtime came and went with her stomach growling. She remembered with sensual pleasure the sandwich that Pete had brought her. Sandwiches just like that were only a parking lot away. But she tamped down her hunger and kept working. There was nothing like imagining herself standing around here on the street in her skimpy bathing suit to encourage dieting. Just thinking about it had her stopping her work to do a dozen repetitions of lunges or wall squats. Her thighs were not going to be bikini ready by Saturday. But ready or not, Saturday was coming.

Mr. Hoskins showed up a little after one o'clock. Andi hadn't thought she knew him, but she recognized him as soon as he drove up. His aging, rusted, windowless panel van was exactly the kind of vehicle that the serial killer in the movies would always drive. Hoskins himself, however, looked more like Santa Claus than a suburban slasher. He was a short round man with a long, scruffy white beard. There were no roses in his cheeks, but his nose was about as red as Rudolph's. Andi suspected this might have been the result of forty years of Happy Hours at Glombicki's Beer Garden.

He was amiable and agreeable and seemed to know his business.

"I'll snake through this," he told her. "And then we'll send the camera down to see what we've got."

The snake he spoke of was a coil of metal wire whose movement was driven by a small motor about the size of a suitcase. The man whistled while he worked, clearly enjoying his oneness with the sewer line. His big, weathered, rather dirty hands looked incongruous with the keyboard of the laptop computer he set up on the seat of his van.

Andi found herself standing behind him as she watched with interest as the images of the inside of the underground pipe flickered on the screen.

"This is really pretty neat," she said.

Hoskins nodded. "For plumbers it's the best invention since the plunger. It can check out your pipes all the way down the lateral to the main sewer. If there's any blockage, it can show us exactly where to aug or, in the worst cases, where to dig."

"I hope I won't need any digging," Andi told him.

"Everything looks pretty good," he told her. "Good

enough for a while anyway. You see these little cracks?" He indicated an area that looked something like a roadmap etched into the side of the pipe. "Within another year or so, these will be wide enough for roots to get in. Once they do, we'll have to auger them out and sleeve this section."

Andi wasn't sure what that meant, but it sounded like it might be expensive.

"How much would that cost?"

Hoskins shrugged. "I wouldn't worry too much," he said. "Especially not yet. If your dad couldn't make a go of this business anymore, then I figure next year will probably not even be an issue for you."

Andi felt almost as if she'd been slapped. Hoskins's words were neither critical nor angry, simply matter-of-fact negativity. She was stung.

"My father is a very good businessman," she conceded. "But I have some…some new ideas for the car wash that he wouldn't have implemented."

Hoskins eyed her and nodded, but clearly he didn't believe her. If Pop hadn't been able to keep the place open, she wouldn't either.

Hoskins gave her a clean bill of health on her drains. He even managed to come up with a very official-looking piece of paper, showing that they'd been video surveyed by a certified technician licensed by the National Association of Sewer Repair Companies. He managed to hand it to her with only one grimy fingerprint.

"This seems good," Andi said.

Hoskins nodded. "I think it'll carry a bit of weight with your inspector," he told her.

He was loading up his truck when Tiff and Caleb showed up. Andi was delighted to see them.

"Have you had lunch?" Tiff asked. "I've got some cheese and crackers in the car. Or we could walk down to Connor's and get you something."

Andi shook her head. "I'm avoiding food," she said. "I tried on one of my old bathing suits last night."

Tiff laughed. "I hope it's a little string bikini."

"Well, not quite," Andi admitted.

"So, we're here to help," Tiff told her. "I figure if we're opening up on Saturday, you're going to have a million things to do. And I see that I was right."

Andi nodded. "I'll take all the blood, sweat and tears you've got to offer."

"My mom's not a big sweater," Caleb informed her.

Still, they both seemed happy to jump right in. Neither seemed lacking in work ethic or energy.

"I got a new video game," Caleb announced proudly. "My dad got it for me. It is so cool and I'm good at it. I'm already on level three and I have magic powers and I can destroy all the evil invaders and even cyborgs."

"Hey, that sounds fabulous," Andi agreed.

She put the magic cyborg killer to work on the back of the building, rolling paint. It was exactly the kind of potentially messy job that kids love to do.

"Should I help him with the high spots?" Tiff asked.

"We'll finish it off when he gets tired," Andi suggested. "I need your thoughts on something."

Tiff followed her to the building's interior.

"Last night I made up our price list," Andi told her. "We

have got to post the prices, but I don't want to come up with the cheapest sign possible. And I started thinking about these windows. We don't have any products to display, so I think they would be perfect as signboards."

Tiff nodded, but looked worried. "I hope you're not thinking that we could hand letter these. I've never been good at stuff like that."

"Me either," Andi admitted. "But I can do stenciling. So I printed out everything. It's all backward. If we cut the letters out with a hobby knife we can use the pages as a stencil for the lettering."

Tiff agreed to give it a try. It was quickly evident that she was very good with the knife. She was both quick and accurate. So Andi handed the job to her and began the measuring and marking necessary to get the lines straight and adequately spaced. But by the time they got the first line of stencils taped up, Caleb was getting bored with his painting project and making up excuses to come ask questions. Tiff finally told him it was time to take a break. The young boy gladly seated himself against one of the pillars of the overhang and focused all his attention on the tiny screen in his hands.

"So Caleb seems pretty pleased that your ex came through with the new video game," Andi said.

Tiff nodded. "He got some day labor cleaning up one of those old factory sites down under the viaduct," she said. "He showed up at our door as soon as they paid him. He hasn't quite caught up on his child support, but I couldn't fault him for spending a few bucks on Caleb."

"Of course, he could have given you the money he owes you and let you decide whether to spend it on a game for your son," Andi pointed out.

Tiff shrugged. "I don't mind Gil being the hero," she said. "Right now, I think he needs that. And Caleb needs it, too."

The tap, tap, tapping of the paintbrush against the window went on and on. It was time-consuming and exacting. Too much paint on the homemade paper stencils and they just fell apart. But when a line was done and the paper pulled away, it looked very good. And that little bit of satisfaction kept the women working for the rest of the afternoon.

Finally finished with their deliveries, Pop and Jelly arrived to help, just as Tiff and Andi were beginning to tire out.

"It looks nice," Pop told them. "You girls do real good work."

"She's not a girl, she's my mom," Caleb corrected him.

Jelly tried her hand at the task, but she couldn't seem to limit the amount of paint she got on her brush. No matter how carefully she listened, she continued to get a lot when she needed just a little. The paint would run on the paper and down the window, requiring hasty cleanup.

"This is a crime scene!" she declared after her third disaster.

"The paint roller is better for you," Andi said.

Her sister nodded in agreement. "The paint roller is better for me," she repeated.

"Why don't you help Caleb finish the back of the building?" Andi suggested.

This worked perfectly. Jelly loved to be of help. She needed to be needed. And because the boy was smaller and couldn't reach the high places, he truly needed her. Caleb wasn't as bored as when working by himself.

With Andi, Tiff and Pop tap, tap, tapping, the price list slowly but surely became a visible reality on the window. And, just as surely, the opening of the bikini car wash was headed their way.

Jelly sat on the back porch with her friend Tony. She had her photo book with the big bright purple flowers on the front. There were words on the front that Jelly could not read. Tony could and did.

"GIRLS JUST WANT TO HAVE FUN! GIRLS JUST WANT TO HAVE FUN! GIRLS JUST WANT TO HAVE FUN! GIRLS JUST WANT TO HAVE FUN!"

"Shut up and listen," Jelly demanded.

He complied, sort of. Under his breath he was still whispering and bobbing his head to the rhythm of the words.

Jelly opened the slick creaky pages of photos. Almost every one featured the two sisters.

"This is me and Andi in Easter bonnets," Jelly said.

"Andi's my girlfriend. Andi's my girlfriend."

"This one is Halloween," Jelly continued. "I'm a princess and Andi is a pirate."

"Jack Sparrow, got to find the Black Pearl."

She continued to point out the moments of the girls together. Sometimes they were dressed for Sunday school and sometimes for backyard picnics. Always two girls side by side.

Then Jelly stopped and examined a photo that showed only one of them. With glasses and braces, dressed in damp coveralls Andi stood with Pop in front of the car wash building looking up at him adoringly.

Jelly smiled. "My sister, Andi, knows a lot about washing cars."

"GIRLS JUST WANT TO HAVE FUN!" Tony blurted out again.

Chapter 10

WALT WAS AS NERVOUS as he could ever remember being. He'd hardly eaten a thing at dinner. Andi and Jelly had made pancakes; even they couldn't mess that up. And it was the best meal served in his house in a long time. After a busy and eventful day, he should have been exhausted, but he was unable to sit still.

"I'm meeting some of the guys tonight at Superior Lanes," he'd told Andi as they cleared the table. He'd tried hard to sound nonchalant.

"Oh, okay," she'd answered. "Who are you bowling with?"

He should have anticipated the question, but he was caught flat-footed. What if he named someone and Andi saw them and then mentioned it?

"Rob Sowa and Angus Bender," he told her. He was pretty sure she wouldn't see either of those fellows, unless she was wandering around the graveyard. Both had been dead for several years.

He cleaned up, slicked up and pretty much snuck out while the girls were down in the basement watching TV. He backed out into the street and then ground the gears unpleasantly as he shifted the old truck from Reverse into First.

Walt winced and gave himself a mental scolding. He needed to get a handle on himself. He was not some hormone-crazed teenager. He was a steady, serious, retired guy. With studied deliberateness, he eased up on the accelerator and gripped the steering wheel.

He resorted to an old trick he'd learned from military training: mission silence. Shutting up all the noise in his head except for what he was doing. He was driving out to the interstate. He would do that perfectly and allow no extraneous thoughts to distract him.

The army had taught him how to do that. Of all the things they'd taught him, there were very few that he ever used. If he'd known it before he joined up, maybe he wouldn't have needed to volunteer. But, back then, he'd been desperate to get away from his anger, frustration and disappointment. Military service was his ticket out of town. His best friend, Paul, had joined up with him, worried about Walt going off alone. They had planned to do their service together. But then the army discovered that Walt had grown up speaking Polish with his grandparents. And that he had a natural aptitude for Slavic languages. He'd ended up sitting in a listening post in West Germany. Paul had gone to southeast Asia.

At the bowling alley Walt parked the truck in an obvious spot beneath the light pole. He was in complete control of himself again. Still, lurking underneath that calm was an anxious excitement that he couldn't completely tamp down.

He locked up the truck and touched the key card in his front pocket before making his way to the front door of the Superior Lanes. Once inside, he glanced around to see if there was anybody he knew. The place was busy, active, loud. There might be a recession on, but you couldn't tell it by this place. Spotting no one familiar, Walt headed toward the far end of the building. He came to a deserted hallway beneath a neon sign with an arrow. RESTROOMS. He strode purposefully in that direction, but when he got to the door marked MEN, he didn't even hesitate. He continued on to the end of the hallway and out the back exit.

A hundred yards away, across a mostly deserted parking lot, was the side door to a Vacation Inn Express, a low-cost, national chain motel, newly built to cater to business travelers and people driving along the nearby interstate.

Walt touched the key card in his pocket for perhaps the thousandth time. And with a careful eye out for anyone who might observe him, he hurried across the distance.

He slid the card down the reader and heard the click of the lock releasing. He pulled open the door and went inside. His footfalls were silent on the carpeting as he walked to the elevator.

His nervousness, held at bay for the drive, now returned with full force, along with an anxiety that was wholly new.

Now, he thought, *now, after all these years, all these dreams, what if it's a disappointment? What if I am a disappointment?*

On the third floor he got off and followed the directional signs to the number she'd given him. When he reached the appropriate door, he hesitated only an instant as he took a deep breath and then with fumbling hands he used the key card again.

Inside the narrow room with its nondescript furniture and window view of the bowling alley, she sat on the edge of the bed. Her brown eyes were huge with the same kind of uncertainly that he felt himself. But it was her elegant, beaded after-five attire that caught him off guard. Inexplicably a smile spread across his face.

"Hey, Rache," he said. "Don't look so scared. It's only me."

Dressed in beige silk and pearls, she was seated, back straight and legs crossed elegantly at the ankle, her matching handbag clutched in her lap.

He held out his arms to afford her a better view of his own wardrobe choice, jeans and a polo shirt bearing the name of a local sports team.

"Obviously I'm underdressed for this occasion," he said.

She smiled up at him.

"I'm pretending to be on my way to the Juvenile Diabetes Gala," she said. "And you?"

He shrugged. "I'm out for a night of bowling."

"Whoever imagined that we would turn out to be such liars," she said.

Walt shrugged as he took a seat beside her. "We've had a lot of years of practice," he admitted.

She nodded and sighed. "We sure have," she said. "I'm tired of it," she said.

"Me, too."

He wrapped his arm around her waist. "Have I told you, 'I love you' yet today?"

She feigned serious concentration. "No, I don't believe you've actually mentioned it."

"I need to get that on my calendar, so that I don't forget," he teased.

"Perhaps I could buy you one of those handheld phone-things my boys have," she said. "They go off with little buzzing noises right and left to remind them of some important something."

"Really?"

"Yes, you just program in what you want and it buzzes to remind you."

He nodded solemnly. "So I could get a 'tell Rachel you love her' reminder every day?"

"Absolutely," she said.

"You should get a marketing campaign together," he told her. "If you could get the word out on this before Father's Day, I think you'd get rich."

She grinned broadly at him. It was a smile unchanged for forty years. "I'm already rich," she told him in a manner both teasing and matter-of-fact. "Rich enough to attract a much younger man. One who wouldn't show up in his bowling shoes."

"These aren't bowling shoes," he said, looking down at his two-toned suede ankle boots.

"Well, you certainly could have fooled me."

"Take that back, woman," he said. "I don't let gals speak badly of my comfortable footwear." He grabbed her foot and held it up to near eye level. "Especially when they are wearing something like this? Two thin leather straps attached to a ladder. How much did these set you back?"

"Those are designers," she answered. "I don't remember how much they cost, but I do think they could probably be exchanged for a mountain of bowling shoes."

He pulled the strappy sandal off of her foot which he set on his knees and began massaging its aching muscles. "Now, doesn't that feel better?"

She didn't answer, but made almost a purring sound.

Walt planted a kiss on her instep.

"That's a good start," he said.

"A good start for what?"

"I want to kiss every inch of you," he told her. "And I was always the kind of guy who started out at the bottom."

He placed his second kiss on her ankle and she laughed. "I think kissing every inch of someone is something that you do to a twenty-year-old. Most of my inches are now covered with wrinkles."

"You know," he said. "I should have done it when we were twenty. But I didn't. *We* didn't. That was then and this is now. And now…well, kissing is about the only service I'm absolutely sure I can perform."

"Oh, Walt, don't worry about that."

"I do worry," he said. "I went to see my doctor this week and asked him to give me some of those little blue pills."

"You didn't?"

"I did," Walt said. "Of course I did. When you've wanted a woman for forty years and she finally agrees to meet you at a motel, of course you'd want to be prepared. I wasn't a Boy Scout for nothing."

"What did he say?"

"He said no," Walt told her. "He said I've got to under-perform before I qualify for help. Sounds like a lot of Main Street business ventures these days."

"Well, let's just hope you're one of those firms who's too big to fail," she said.

"Rachel!"

They both giggled like kids.

"Shame on you!" he teased.

"Darling, when you've waited for this as long as I have, a woman has got no shame," she answered.

"I'll do the best I can," he promised.

Rachel moved over to sit on his lap. "We love each other," she told him. "That's enough to satisfy me."

She brought her lips down on his. She tasted warm and sweet and familiar. He pulled down the zipper on the back of her dress and drew the fabric slowly down to her waist, revealing a beige lace bra that confined two small, but still lovely breasts. He pressed his lips against one before laying her back against the bed and discarding her dress completely.

"You are so beautiful, Rachel," he said. "Inside and out. And I have been in love with you all my life. I just hope I can do justice to the way I feel."

She ran her manicured nails along the front of his shirt before tugging it over his head.

"I'm happy just to hold you in my arms," she told him. "If we can't make the earth move, well so be it. I always thought sex was a bit overrated."

"Oh, really?" Walt commented, smiling. "With a little luck, perhaps I can change your mind on that."

The Friday night before her big Saturday opening, Andi stayed up late perfecting her banner. It was a six-foot piece of canvas that she'd cut from an old camping tent she'd found in the garage. With the help of stencils, she'd put on one word in bright red letters. BIKINI. She was going to hang it at the top of the existing sign painted on the front of the building overhang. It would cover up the word Plainview, making the sign read: BIKINI WASH & WAX. Once the paint dried, Andi used the steam iron on the back side of the fabric to make the lettering further adhere to the canvas. She didn't expect it to last forever, but she did need it to survive a rainstorm or two.

The most problematic part of the whole banner plan was how to hang it. She couldn't really figure out any way to attach it to the bricks, so she put a grommet in the top two corners and decided to tie it with ropes to the rafter tails of the roof. She wasn't totally sure that would work, but it seemed like the most reasonable solution.

Andi draped her finished product across the dining room table and admired her handiwork. It looked good. It was eye-catching. And catching eyes appeared to be the major objective of her business plan.

She let out a little puff of disgust.

"Mom would be so proud!" she commented facetiously.

She would have undoubtedly been shocked, Andi thought. Then again, maybe she wouldn't have. Maybe she would have said, "hey, go for it."

The truth was, Andi admitted to herself in the silence of her parents' home, she didn't have a clue about what her mother had thought about much of anything.

Bitterly she recalled her last conversation with her mother. Or, at least, she recalled being on the phone. She remembered her mother's voice, husky with exaggerated breathing.

"You need to come home," Pop told her, when he got on the line.

"I can't get away right now," she'd explained. "It's all crazy here at work. Nobody goes out for lunch, 'cause they think they might not have a job when they come back."

"She's very sick."

"She can't be that sick," Andi had insisted. "It's like two days ago she had a really bad cold."

"And now she has pneumonia," Pop answered. "I'm looking at her, Andi. I think you'd better come home."

"Sure, Pop," she'd said. "I'll come home."

Andi could remember how annoyed she felt. The stress she'd been under had been tremendous. She'd been putting in long hours every day and more on the weekend. And now she'd agreed to spend four hours on the interstate. She worked the rest of the day. Went home, showered, packed and grabbed some dinner to eat on the road. It was a little after eight when her cell phone went off. She saw that it was Pop and heaved a big sigh before putting a smile on her face to answer.

"Hi, Pop. I'm sorry I'm running late. I should be driving up to the door by, maybe, 11:30."

There was a long pause. "Okay. Okay." His words were very quiet, almost stilted.

"Pop?"

"Andrea…sweetie, your mother passed away about…about fifteen minutes ago."

Standing in the dining room, more than six months later, the memory of those words still had the power to make Andi feel sick to her stomach.

She took a couple of deep breaths and then pulled out one

of the dining chairs and sat down, wearily holding her head in her hands.

Why were you so wrapped up in yourself? Why wasn't there more time? Why didn't you leave that day as soon as you hung up the phone? And the ultimate of guilt-inducing questions. *When exactly did you plan to get to know your mother?*

Andi heard the key turn in the front door lock. She heard her father tiptoeing through the living room.

"Hi, Pop," she said.

He startled at the sight of her. His brow immediately furrowed with annoyance. "Are you waiting up for me?"

"Waiting up? No." The suggestion was ludicrous. "No, I'm working on my banner for the shop. And I'm sure I couldn't sleep anyway. My stomach is full of butterflies and my brain is racing in overdrive."

His face relaxed and he nodded. He stood beside her chair, assessing her handiwork. "It looks pretty good," he said. "It's definitely not professional work, but I think it will do very nicely, at least until you scrape together some cash for a real sign."

"Thanks," Andi said. She was grateful for his praise and for the vote of confidence. He'd not suggested that she *might* eventually have to pay for a real sign, he spoke as if she would. Pop was always on her side and she needed him there.

She glanced up to tell him just that. To thank him for being in her corner every step of the way. Then she noticed something that distracted her from the words in her head.

"Pop? You hair is wet."

He stepped back slightly. There was a wariness in his expression. "I…uh…I had a shower at the gym."

"The gym? I thought you were at bingo tonight?"

"I was, but…uh, some of the guys got bored and decided to go shoot some hoops. So, I went with them."

Andi nodded and offered a knowing glance. "I've never known you to be much of a sports player, bowling one night, gym the next. I suspect something entirely different."

When he didn't respond she continued, her voice teasing.

"I think you're still trying to get away from that trail of lonely church ladies who follow you around like puppy dogs," she said. "I can only imagine that the rare time you show up for bingo just sends all hearts aflutter."

Her father sort of chuckled, but it sounded almost humorless. "I'm going to get some sleep," he told her. "I think you'd be smart to do the same."

Andi knew he was right. And she tried. She marched upstairs, got ready for bed, climbed in, turned out the light and lay there. Her mind couldn't let go of everything. The larger issues, her family, her finances, her future loomed before her, intermittently crowded out by thoughts of 1099 tax forms, water use fees and schedule coverage. There were so many things that she needed to remember and she was afraid she might forget, that she finally got up, found a paper and pen and made a list to carry in her purse. Then just as she settled back into the covers, she was assailed once more. So she got up, found a sticky note and stuck it on the bedroom door. It read: *Don't forget your purse.*

She eventually slept, if fitfully. At 4:30 a.m. she decided it was practically morning, so she just got up and got started. She was surprised at how much energy she had. She quickly showered and dressed. She put on her modest two-piece. In lieu of a swimsuit cover, she put on the old coveralls. Certainly modesty was not going to be the company policy, but at least she was going to be decently covered when she started her day. She spent an inordinate amount of time in front of her mirror carefully applying waterproof makeup. She put on a bit more than was appropriate for daytime wear, but she assured herself the situation called for it.

"Besides," she told herself in the mirror. "You'll be lucky to get anyone to look at your face."

Downstairs she ate a pear and a piece of dry toast. She had never been a fan of dieting, but the anticipation of being half-dressed on the busiest corner of downtown gave her extraordinary incentive. At the kitchen table she drank an extra cup of coffee, went over her list, made sure she had everything she needed to take with her. At last she was sure she was ready. Completely and perfectly ready.

At that moment, she nearly lost her nerve. *What was she thinking? A bikini car wash? That was a crazy idea? It was low class. It was misogynistic. It was beneath her dignity!*

She deliberately held back the negativism running through her head. And mentally perused a better list of criteria. *Was it in her skill set? Yes, it was.* She'd been washing cars since she was eleven years old. *Was it a reasonable business plan? Yes, it was seasonal and relied heavily on a gimmick, but it had a likely chance to make a profit.* And finally she asked herself, *Do you have any other choice?*

She didn't even bother to answer that one. She got to her feet, gathered up her things and headed to the front door. The buses wouldn't be running this early on a Saturday. She thought about taking Pop's truck. She could call him later to come pick it up. But in the end, she loaded everything in tote bags and set off on foot through the early morning streets of her neighborhood.

With everything that was on her mind and all the anxiety that she was feeling inside, it came as a complete surprise to catch herself humming. And the song, rather than one from her teenage music years, was one that Pop used to sing at his shop. The tune came to her effortlessly, but she couldn't quite remember all the words. It was something about the sun is always shining somewhere. And that the smart thing to do would be to make it shine for you.

That's what she intended to do today. To get some personal sunshine in her direction.

It was full dawn when she arrived at the shop. She unloaded everything she'd brought. And began getting ready for the day.

The most important and critical thing she needed to do was hang the banner along the top of the sign on the overhang. She decided that it was best to get that done early. It was her first source of advertising.

She carried the extension ladder outside. It was heavy and a bit clumsy, but in the last few days, she'd been doing a lot more lifting, both through work and with her attempts to tone up. So she was able to maneuver the big bulky apparatus out to where she needed it. She made certain it was anchored properly and as level as possible. She judged the height she needed at about ten feet. So she was careful to lean it at a safe one to four angle. The last thing she needed on her first day of business was an accident.

She climbed the ladder and screwed a hook into the base of the rafter tail. Then she tied the cord she'd attached to the banner to the hook. She had to get down and move the ladder to the other side of the overhang to screw in the second hook and tie up that side of it as well.

Once down from the ladder, Andi observed her handiwork with some satisfaction. It was bright, it was readable and it clearly announced:

BIKINI WASH & WAX

She hardly had a moment to worry if it was eye-catching, before she heard the screech of brakes. She turned to see two guys in a truck, stopped in the street, openmouthed and staring at the sign.

"We open at nine," she called out to them.

The two responded with whoops and cheering.

Okay, she thought to herself. Two potential customers. At least the community was capable of giving a warm welcome.

Welcome wasn't even the half of it. By eight-thirty, a full half hour before they were scheduled to open, there were already two cars waiting.

Tiff arrived a few minutes later wearing an ankle-length sundress. She was jittery and in a rush.

"Am I late? I had to wait for Gil to pick up Caleb. I got here as early as I could."

"You're right on time," Andi said.

"Oh, good. Are you as excited as I am?" Tiff asked.

"Yeah, yes, I think what I'm feeling is excited," she answered. "Though it might be the kind of excitement you get when your car breaks down on a railroad track."

Tiff laughed and shook her head. "Yeah, I admit to that railroad track feeling, too. Well, should we start washing cars or wait until the time we're scheduled to open?"

Andi shrugged. "I can't decide," she said. "In Pop's day, if someone showed up early, he'd go ahead and get started. But somehow I'm thinking that having a line of customers waiting can only hype the business, get more attention and translate into more customers."

At that moment a burst of car horns and whoops and hollers caught their attention. They turned immediately to look out the front windows. Cher-L was walking up the driveway. Her blue-striped hair was braided into an elaborate updo. Above the waist she wore only two tiny triangles of faux black leather held in place by lengths of shiny silver chain. The skirt wrap that was her coverup, was a thin, gauzy black material that was mostly see-through, except for the darker, spider web pattern woven into it. The look was completed with lace-up, high-heel vixen boots.

"Oh my God," Andi said.

"How's she going to work in that?" Tiff asked. "I hope she's not thinking she's going to stand around while you and I do the car washing."

"It doesn't matter what she's thinking," Andi said. "That's not what's happening."

Cher-L walked breezily into the building, beaming. Her typically bored, worldly-wise and jaded expression was gone. She looked surprisingly young and inexplicably happy.

"This is going to be so great!" she said. Then spinning around like a little girl with a new dress she asked. "Don't I look fabulous? Oh, and you haven't even seen it all." She whisked off her skirt to reveal the small piece of black leather-look material that made up the rest of the swimsuit. Less than a half inch of fabric spanned the sides beneath the pelvic bone. The front trailed down in a U shape, dangerously low. The back was only a few inches wide covering about half of her buttocks.

"It's called a Brazilian bottom," she told them. "At first glance it seems a lot more modest than a thong, but it's nicely revealing as well."

"I hope you're not planning to wear those boots," Andi said.

"No, of course not," Cher-L said, eyeing her as if she'd lost her mind. "I would never risk getting these wet. But they sure weren't wasted walking across the parking lot."

Cher-L set down her big black tote bag and pulled out a pair of black flip-flops. "Look, I painted the little silver chains on the top myself." She showed off her artwork proudly. "I used metallic gray fabric paint with a rigger brush. I think they turned out extremely excellent and completely unique. Just perfect, huh?"

"They're great," Andi admitted. For herself, she'd thrown in a pair of ratty sneakers. Why did the idea of ensemble matching flip-flops suddenly seem more professional?

At exactly nine o'clock, Andi peeled off her coveralls.

"Good grief! What are you wearing?" Cher-L asked.

"It's a swimsuit, a two-piece," she answered defensively.

"Uh, yeah, like the kind of two piece you wear to Girl Scout camp," Cher-L pointed out.

"She's right," Tiff agreed. "The guys who show up here with their cars are going to expect to see…well, a lot less suit, a lot more girl."

Andi shook her head. "I'm not exactly a beauty queen. I think I might be better off in something not quite so revealing."

"No way," Tiff said, firmly. "You can't weasel out on me. I'm the first grader's mom who still hasn't lost all the pregnancy weight."

"You look great," Andi declared.

In fact, Tiff's blue-striped string bikini did reveal a bit more hips and thighs than was strictly fashionable, but her curves were far more voluptuous than chubby.

"If I'm showing up here skimpy," Tiff told her. "You have to, too."

"No need to argue," Cher-L said. "I've got the solution right here." She pulled a small plastic shopper's bag out of her tote and handed it to Andi. The name on the outside was Joffee's Manhattan Store.

"What's this?"

"A bikini," Cher-L said. "I bought two. I was going to take it back, because I like this black one better. It will be perfect for you."

"I don't know," Andi said. When she pulled it out of the bag, she recognized it as the super-sexy red thong suit she'd seen in the window. "Oh no, I *really* couldn't wear this."

"Wow!" Tiff said.

"This will make you look like an extreme hottie," Cher-L coaxed. "I'm going to be jealous."

"I'm not wearing this," Andi said.

"Yes, you are," Tiff said. "This is a bikini car wash and that is a real bikini."

"It's more revealing that either one of yours."

Tiff nodded. "That's only fair," she said. "You're the boss. The boss always sets the highest standard."

"Or in this case the lowest."

"Try it on, at least," Cher-L said. "If you're not woman enough for it, well, we'll let you know."

"Go!" Tiff told her, in a tone that her son, Caleb, was undoubtedly familiar with.

Andi went into the bathroom and tried on the suit. It seemed impossible, but wearing it made her feel more exposed than if she was naked.

"I can't do this," she told herself aloud as she perused her bare flesh. "I can't go out there like this." Then she straightened her back and looked herself in the eye. "If you can't wear it, then you can't have this business. This is the kind of business it is. So either wear the suit or close down. Your choice. Nobody is making you do anything."

She gave herself one long last look and then stepped out of the restroom.

"Okay, let's go," she said. "We've got cars to wash."

Cher-L applauded.

Tiff was nodding. "Good for you," she said.

When the three stepped outside the confines of the little building, the crowd of men waiting together in a little huddle sent up a cheer, immediately followed by hoots and whistles. Then everyone laughed. It didn't seem dirty or dangerous. It was fun and friendly. Andi refused to allow herself the weakness of being self-conscious. She was going to let these men ogle her in a swimsuit, but she was not going to get caught up in that. She was going to focus on business.

"Men, let's get this started," she called out. "Who's the driver of this red Pontiac?"

"That's me!" A balding guy in his midlife crisis announced.

"Drive it in under the overhang," she told him.

The man gave a kind of victory shout and pumped the air with his fist. The other guys were cheering him, as if he'd just led the team to victory.

She turned to Tiff and Cher-L. "Remember," she said. "Women care about the inside of a car. Men care about the outside. So, it looks like we'll be focusing on the exterior. It's got to be perfect. The bikinis may get them in here, but a quality service is the only thing that will get them back."

Tiff nodded. Cher-L just shrugged.

There was no more time for training. The driver of the vehicle got out of his car and Andi went to talk to him. From a distance he'd been a cocky loudmouth. But standing face-to-face with Andi he was soft-spoken, polite even deferential. Not at all the smart-aleck chauvinist she was expecting.

Maybe it's one of those chicken or egg questions, she thought to herself. *Is he talking to me like I'm not dressed in a bikini, which makes me feel more confident. Or do I seem so confident that it doesn't occur to him to talk to me like I'm wearing nothing but a thong bikini.*

Whichever it was, within moments of opening her business, Andi was feeling pretty comfortable in the uniform. Even the jokes and the whistles didn't bother her. She was working hard, but it all seemed like fun. Cher-L did a bit of posing, especially when one of the guys brought out a video camera. She tried to make the water run down her body suggestively, but that was very hard to do with a power hose. So she contented herself with just splashing against the fenders.

And the cars! They were working as fast as they could, but the line didn't get shorter, it got longer. Long enough that they were double-parked down Grosvenor. And shiny, perfectly cleaned vehicles were rolling off the lot. Cash was filling up the register. It was everything Andi could have hoped for. Until the police showed up.

Chapter 11

PETE WAS RUNNING LATE. It was after ten o'clock when he pulled his car out of the driveway. He'd not been sleeping well. He was staying up late watching bad late-night comedy that never made him laugh. Then once he finally forced himself to go to bed, he would toss and turn all night. He was worried. And it was the kind of worried that was hard to get a handle on. The kind where a dozen different problems vied for attention, none of which, by themselves could really throw you off. Together, however, they created a seemingly insurmountable hurdle.

The economy was bad. The cost of his employee benefits was through the roof. He was being underbid by the big-box chain stores. He was being undercut by his father.

Most of that was unfixable, but he continued to lie awake and ruminate on it as if a solution could be found. Always, adding to that, was pent-up sexual frustration.

He really should take the time to go out and find himself a girlfriend.

Pete was never going to be a player kind of guy. He was just not going to be able to go out and score a new girl night after night. Even if he wanted to, *who has that kind of time?* he asked himself.

That was why marriage to Minx had been so perfect for him. She was so beautiful, impeccably charming, the ultimate arm candy. She was only so-so in the sack, but quantity had been more important to him than quality. And she was totally involved with her own life, her friends, her shopping, that she was able to give him limitless hours to concentrate on his job.

He was yawning as he drove down Grosvenor Avenue. Perhaps he should get Miss Kepper to put an ad in the paper for him.

WANTED: Attractive woman to share house. Some cooking, light housekeeping, occasional sex. Fringe benefits and long-term commitment possible.

Pete chuckled. *Yeah, Peterson,* he thought to himself. *Imagine the line of job seekers Miss Kepper would come up with for you. The only attractive women she ever recommends are over forty and with big angry husbands.*

He thought about the two candidates she'd come up with for the advertising job. One was a retired second-grade teacher. The other, claiming newspaper experience, had delivered the *Plainview Public Observer* door-to-door for fifteen years. He didn't think either of them would know a concept-driven advertising campaign if they saw one. How on earth could he expect them to plan one?

As he neared the store the traffic slowed to a crawl. This was extremely unusual. In fact, traffic was pretty unusual just on its own. He assumed that it must be a fender-bender up ahead. He hoped it didn't involve any of his employees or any company vehicles. He finally realized that the cars in the right lane were all lined up for something. It wasn't until he got to the entrance to the parking lot that he realized that they were lined up for the car wash.

Well, that's good, he thought to himself. After the way his dad messed up Wolkowicz's last business proposal, he really hoped she'd be able to make a go of washing cars on that corner again. And if the line and the crowd of people standing around was any indication, she must be having an excellent opening day.

He was whistling by the time he parked his car. He made his way into the front door of Guthrie Foods. The minute he stepped inside he felt something different. It was nothing negative. Just a strange titter of excitement that would have been imperceptible to those who didn't work in that building day after day. It was noticeable enough to cause Pete to pause.

He saw Neal, the produce manager, struggling with an unruly mound of cantaloupes. No one else in the department was in sight. Pete rushed over to help. Together they quickly got the stack stable and in no danger of falling to the floor.

"So, what's up this morning?" Pete asked him.

"Did you see the car wash as you came in?"

"Oh, yeah, I did," Pete told him. "I think it's great."

"You do?"

The man's response wasn't so much surprised as skeptical. Pete didn't like that so much. He was sure that it was because his father had been unwelcoming to Andi's prospective coffee business on the street. He didn't want anybody to think that he agreed with that, that it would continue to be the policy of Guthrie Foods to kneecap anyone who had the audacity to try to open up nearby.

"Business is good for the neighborhood," he told the produce manager. "Any business is good."

Neal's eyebrows went up. "Well, it certainly does bring people into the area," he agreed. "But not everybody is happy about it."

"They're not?"

The produce man wiped his hands on his apron. "I'd say the employees here are split about 50/50 on it," he said. "And it's not just women vs men. Some folks just think, 'well good luck and good for her' and others are shocked or think it's bad for the neighborhood."

"Well, I think it's great," Pete said. "I want to do everything I can to support the place. So just tell anyone who asks that they can expect to see me driving a much cleaner car in the future."

Neal gave a strange little chuckle.

"You should do the same," Pete told him. "I'm sure you've got plenty of weekend chores without having to wash the car. When you take your break, wander over there and see what they can do for you."

The produce manager shook his head. "I don't think my wife would be too crazy about that," he said. "It's all right for a single guy like you, but I sure don't want to get myself into hot water."

Pete couldn't imagine what he was talking about.

"Why should your wife even care who washes your car?" he asked.

Neal rubbed his bald spot in lieu of scratching his head and gave Pete an incredulous grin. "Well, she does," he answered. "And even if she didn't, Cher-L is working over there. Even a stupid man would know to keep his distance."

Pete was surprised to hear that his former employee was working there. It seemed like a much more laborious job than Cher-L was really cut out for. But then, jobs were hard to find.

"Good for Cher-L," he said. Pete was pretty sure that everybody in the store knew she'd been fired, but it was important to keep a positive attitude about anyone who'd once been in his employ. "I hope she does well. And I honestly look forward to seeing her."

Neal made a strange choking sound.

"You're not the only one who feels that way," the man said, laughing. "Several of the fellows are already talking about getting a close-up view without the white coat and plastic cap."

Pete didn't quite know what he meant by that. He went on about his business, doing a complete walk-through of the aisles, greeting his employees with a "good morning" before heading up to his office. He glanced in on Miss Kepper as he passed. Her chair was empty as was the room. Although her schedule was officially weekdays, more often than not she put in a few hours on Saturday morning as well. A second later he heard voices down the hallway. She must be in his office, he thought. He continued down to his door and stepped inside.

A trio of young guys guiltily jumped back from the window. He recognized them as a bag boy and two members of the stock crew. Pete couldn't imagine any reason why these guys would be in his office. And one of them was trying to hide something palm-size and yellow behind his back.

"What's going on?" he asked.

Darnell, the bag boy, quickly answered, "Nothing!" His voice was at least a half octave higher than usual.

All three looked embarrassed. The two older guys mumbled unintelligibily.

It was then that Pete noticed the opened packaging lying on the floor. He bent over and picked it up as they eyed him warily.

The paperboard and plastic had come from the store's toy aisle.

"Jungle Jeff Safari," he read aloud. And then the words underneath. "Real Binoculars."

"I was going to put those back," Brian, the eldest of the three told him. Then quickly he restated. "Actually, I was going to buy them."

Pete held out his hand and Derek, who'd been trying to hide the pilfered product behind his back, placed it in Pete's hand.

He held the yellow plastic and continued to eye the three questioningly. There was nothing to see out his window but the parking lot and the car wash. Looking at the parking lot would not require binoculars.

"What? Are you spying on Cher-L?"

They all blushed very guiltily. Pete knew the young woman was not particularly well-liked at the store. She'd been lazy and a bit of a troublemaker. But why would anyone want to spy on her at her new job?

"We were just looking," Brain admitted defensively. "There's no law against looking."

"No," Pete agreed. "There is no law against looking. But you don't have to do it from my office or with company merchandise. Maybe you should just get back to work."

"Yes, sir," all three agreed. They made a hasty exit.

Pete was left holding the binoculars. They definitely couldn't go back into their packaging. He held them up to his eyes. He saw nothing but brown. When he glanced to see what he was aiming at, he realized that the brown was his desk. He walked over to the window. There was still a crowd over at the car wash. Through the binoculars he saw several guys standing around. As he panned across the line of cars he suddenly saw a naked woman's backside bent over a bumper. He was so startled that he nearly dropped the binoculars. He quickly put them back in place, not sure that he could believe his eyes.

Yes, it was a nice-size, generously rounded female backside that was virtually naked but for a tiny triangle of red material that disappeared between the cheeks of her bottom.

It was not until she stood up and turned around that he recognized her.

"Wolkowicz?" he whispered aloud.

He wouldn't have known her, but then he'd never seen her like this. Everything that had happened that morning, everything that had been said suddenly made sense. It was so obvious. As obvious as the excellent curves of Andi Wolkowicz. Who knew that such a woman lurked beneath those baggy coveralls? Pete was stunned, amazed, virtually dumbstruck and he couldn't stop looking.

"What on earth are you doing?"

Pete startled as Miss Kepper stood in the doorway. He resisted the impulse to hide the binoculars behind his back.

Thankfully, the phone rang, saving him from having to answer.

The policeman, Officer Mayfield, was all business. Andi could appreciate that.

"We've had complaints," he said. "Several calls came into dispatch."

"There is nothing illegal about washing cars," Andi said, defensively.

"No, ma'am, there's not," he agreed. "However this line of cars double-parked, that's illegal. And all the gawkers driving by at ten miles an hour, that's snarling traffic.

"Perhaps if you gir—uh—women put on some cover-ups that might be helpful."

There was a whine of complaint from those patrons standing about. Someone in the crowd yelled something like "Why don't you go after some real criminals!"

Andi didn't want to stir up any trouble. She glared in the direction of the offending comment.

"The policeman is just doing his job," she said, to anyone listening, but mostly to Officer Mayfield.

"I don't know what we can do about the fellows driving by," she said.

"Well, you can tell these guys who are loitering here and those double-parked to come back when there is not a line," he said.

Andi hoped that time would never come.

"I'll give them all appointments," she said. "That way everybody who's not on the lot can *loiter* elsewhere."

Officer Mayfield wasn't so sure that would work, but Andi was convinced, or at least she accepted it as a viable option. It would be better to have the crowd standing around waiting. It hyped up the place, making it a desirable location, but rationing services could also build business. And although there was some concern that, once they left, they might not come back. Andi had faith in her smart-aleck, big-talking, testosterone driven customers. If a woman in a skimpy bikini asked them to meet her at a certain time, only a serious setback could keep them away.

Andi left the car washing to Tiff and Cher-L for several minutes as she walked down the line of waiting cars, explained the situation and gave out return times with no waiting. She quickly discovered that the street was not a good place. Face-to-face, the guys might be leering but they were nice. Just driving in the anonymity of their cars and with buddies to egg them on, they hollered out things to her that weren't just suggestive, they were suggestions.

Andi feigned total deafness. If they wanted to get a reaction from her, they needed to step up and get their cars washed. Her customers, however, had perfect hearing and to her surprise, they didn't appreciate hearing her insulted. The verbal altercations were rapid-fire and intense. It was a strange world when a near-naked woman on the street can evoke reactions that probably should have been reserved for mom or sis.

Officer Mayfield was still standing around and watching the proceedings when she got back. He was mostly watching Cher-L who was posing provocatively for him, as she had done for one fellow or another through most of the morning. Andi couldn't tell if the policeman liked what he saw or was merely watching for something he could arrest her for. His young, square-jawed face didn't show so much as a hint of expression. And regulation sunglasses hid whatever secrets might be in his eyes.

"They're all leaving," Andi told him with forced cheerfulness. "Sorry about getting things so backed up. It's…it's our opening day and it's all new and lots of people are showing up. By next week we'll be old news and the crowds will dwindle down."

"Are you still going to be wearing what you're wearing?" the policeman asked.

"Uh…yes," Andi answered.

"Then I expect you'll draw more than your fair share of attention all summer."

Andi couldn't tell if that was a criticism or an encouragement.

The young policeman turned his back on Cher-L. He stood facing the street observing the traffic.

"Just to let you know," he said to Andi quietly. "There are a lot of people who are calling in wanting to know what's going on in this place. Wanting to know who let you open this business right in the middle of downtown."

"It's a car wash," Andi replied simply.

Officer Mayfield turned to eye her soberly. "So I see," he said. "Just make sure that's the only business you're trying to run down here. If you, or any of your girls start trying to make a little cash on the side, you can be sure I'll be back here to shut you down."

He walked back to his cruiser, and Andi hurried to help with the interior vacuuming of a ten-year-old Corolla.

"So what did he say?" Tiff asked.

"Basically, beware of prostitution," Andi answered.

"As if!" Cher-L exclaimed, laughing as if it were some great joke.

Pop and Jelly arrived about one o'clock. They had brilliantly brought takeout for Andi as well as her employees. Everyone was hungry.

They took turns eating inside the little building. It had gotten pretty hot in the afternoon sun, but Pop turned on the big noisy fan making it bearable.

Jelly was bright-eyed and animated. She loved all the noise and activity. She thought every horn that honked was somebody saying "hi" to her.

"I want to come to work here," Jelly told her sister. "I can wash cars. I want to work here."

"No, you can't," Andi told her.

"Why not? I can wash cars. I can wash cars good. Why not? I want to work here."

"No, you can't," Andi said. "That's it, no discussion. The answer is no."

"Objection overruled!" she declared.

Andi shook her head. "I said, 'no.' And no is no."

"That's…that's…that's testimony not in evidence."

"It's enough in evidence to keep you from working here," Andi said. "You already have a job. How could Pop deliver the meals on wheels without you?"

That mollified her sister somewhat, but she continued to mutter under her breath.

"I can wash cars. I can wash cars in my swimming suit. And

I have a better swimming suit than you. Mine fits me. It doesn't have my bottom all hanging out of the back."

Andi sighed and hid a smile. She could always count on Jelly to tell it like it is.

When she finished eating, Andi hurried back outside. She found Pop quickly and efficiently applying wax to a newly cleaned vehicle.

"You don't have to do that, Pop," Andi said.

He grinned, without bothering to look up from his task. "That girl with the blue hair thing," he said. "She's not much of a worker. If you mess up a waxing job, well, the owner will see the evidence of it every time he looks at the car."

"I'll try to do some more training with her," Andi said.

Pop shook his head. "She doesn't take to training much. I tried to show her but she didn't pay any attention. I finally gave up. It's easier just to do it myself."

Andi hoped that he was wrong about Cher-L. Andi hoped she could learn to do the job.

"I don't mind," he said. "I always enjoyed making a beautiful machine look its best." He raised his head and grinned at Andi. "But I'm not wearing one of those little bathing suits."

Andi laughed. "I do need your help, Pop," she admitted. "But I don't want you to do any more than you want to do. And I'll have a talk with Cher-L. I'll get her over here to help you whether she likes it or not."

Pop's brow furrowed. "Well, Andi," he said. "It's your business and you need to run it your way. But if it was me…"

He hesitated, obviously giving her time to voice her lack of interest in his opinion.

"Tell me," she said. "If it was you?"

"I'd put Cher-L to work as the greeter, taking orders," he said. "That way she gets to talk to all the customers, which I think would suit her just fine. And her standing around trying to look sexy for the customers wouldn't get in the way of getting the job done."

Andi nodded as she considered her father's idea. She'd been trying to deal with both the sales and the cash and help with the labor. Dividing that up and giving it all to Cher-L would be placing a little more trust in the woman than she was truly comfortable with. But it might make the work go faster.

"Thanks, Pop," Andi said. "It's a good idea, I think we'll give it a try."

Immediately she went over to the young woman, who was doing some kind of little dance as she toweled off a big Chevy SUV.

"Cher-L, I need to speak to you for a minute."

Her doelike brown eyes were wide with fear, guilt. Apparently most of her past interactions with bosses had not been good. Andi decided this one was going to be different.

"I'm really pleased with the work you're doing," Andi told her, deliberately leaving out any of the problems with car waxing. "You're a natural with the customers. And customer service is really what a business like this is all about."

Andi watched as her expression changed from wary and defensive to incredulous.

"Uh…thanks," she said.

"I'm giving you a bit of a promotion," Andi said. "I mean we're all equals here on the job, but I want to use your natural abilities in a more specialized way."

"Well, sure."

"I want you to greet the customers, find out what service they want, write out the tickets and take their money. Do you think you can do that?"

"Uh…yeah," she said, obviously excited. "You mean I won't have to actually wash the cars anymore?"

"You have to help out, a little here, a little there, but yes, basically you're not actually washing the cars."

Her face was all smiles. Smiles and near disbelief. "I'm like…oh wow, thanks, really thanks."

"I'll help you through the first few," Andi said. "But I'm counting on you to take it over."

To Andi's surprise, Cher-L took her new position very seriously. She was still flirty with the customers, but she was very careful in handling the money. Andi was quickly able to turn that job over to her and help Tiff do the labor.

And despite Andi's dictate to the contrary, Pop enlisted her sister, Jelly, to do vacuuming of the car interiors. Since he was supervising and Jelly was fully clothed, Andi couldn't come up with a decent excuse to oppose the suggestion. And they did need the help.

Cars continued coming, even as the ones sent away earlier showed up for their appointments. It was great, if exhausting.

A number of guys just hung out around the place, watching. Some were waiting for cars to be washed. Others had already had theirs done. They now took up a significant space in the Guthrie's parking lot behind the building. Andi decided it was better to get Guthrie mad at her, than to have the police show up again.

The afternoon grew hotter and her arms grew tired. The sexy bikinis were merely attractive decoration on what was very physical work. Andi consoled herself with the fact that she could give up trying to run off her chunky thighs. A couple of weeks of this and she was going to be brown and buff.

A beat-up Taurus with a gray primer bumper pulled into the driveway around the other cars and screeched to an abrupt halt. A man jumped out of the driver's side and after grabbing something in the backseat, hurried around the vehicle.

It all happened so fast, Andi didn't even have time to move. His face was a mask of fury and he was headed straight for Tiff. For an instant of horrified terror, Andi thought Tiff was being attacked. But as the man ran toward her, her coworker appeared more angry than frightened.

"Gil! What are you doing here?" Tiff asked angrily.

The man swathed her in a blanket, holding it closed in front.

She jerked away from him, but kept the cover wrapped around her, tucking it efficiently under one arm.

"What am I doing here?" he said. "What are *you* doing here, nearly naked in public?"

"Hey, buddy!" one of the men in the crowd called out. "Leave the lady alone." As he stepped forward, another man caught his arm.

"Domestic dispute," the second man said quietly.

His words stayed the intervention, but every eye was on the couple, seemingly ready to step in if things got out of hand.

If the man was even aware of the attention of the crowd, he gave no indication.

"How could you do this?" he asked her. "How could you

parade yourself like this? Have you got no pride at all? No sense of what people think of you?"

"What people think of me?" Tiff repeated his question angrily. "I'll tell you what they ought to be thinking. That I'm a single mom. A single mom with an ex who has trouble paying regular child support. So I'm working, making a living, earning money to take care of my child."

"Doing this, being out here prancing around wearing next to nothing for all these creeps to slobber over and fantasize about," the man said.

He nodded toward the crowd and the creeps in question did not appear to appreciate the description. They were restless now and murmuring.

Tiff was silently defiant.

"What can I expect to see next?" Gil asked. "Will you be giving lap dances down at The Horny Toad?"

"This is honest labor," Tiff declared. "And unlike some people I don't shy away from that. I'm not like *some* people who think that some jobs are beneath them. I don't have lists of things that I won't do. I don't let my son do without because I can't take jobs that I'm too smart or experienced or skilled to do. I take the jobs that are there. And if you've got a problem with that, well, hey, it's just more fodder for the evil ex-wife complaints that you make to the boys in the bar."

"I'd never say a word against you!" Gil snapped back. "Not because I owe it to you or because you don't deserve it. I don't do it because I care about our boy. I can't even imagine what he thinks seeing you like this."

Tiff's gaze shot to the car with the gray primer bumper. Andi's did, too. There in the backseat, peeking out the window was a very confused and unhappy-looking Caleb. Andi was fairly certain that it wasn't the sight of his mother in a swimsuit, nor the implications of ogling that his father found so offensive, that were responsible for the expression on the little boy's face. It was the spectacle of his parents arguing loudly and in public.

Tiff took a startled breath. She hadn't realized that he was in the car.

"Why did you bring him here?" she whispered to her ex-husband through clenched teeth.

"I didn't bring him here," Gil answered. "I was taking him out for ice cream. I was driving down a public street. He looked over here and saw you…he saw you like this."

Tiff peeled the blanket from her shoulders and threw it at Gil. Then she walked over to the car to squat down next to the back passenger door. The little boy rolled down the window.

"Hey, Caleb," she said. "What's up?"

Andi couldn't hear the little boy's reply, but she turned back to the front fender she was working on. She felt guilty, personally guilty. There was no logic to it. She'd given Tiff a job, that was a good thing. She just wished it was one she didn't have to be embarrassed about in front of her son.

Jelly was seated in the rumpus room. Upstairs, Pop was cooking dinner. Jelly was hungry. It had been a long day and a lot of hard work, but it had been fun, too. It was so good being with Andi, being a helper to Andi. A Law & Order rerun was playing on the TV, but Jelly wasn't paying close attention. The Assistant D.A. was Serena Southerlyn, not one of her favorites. Instead of really watching, she was leafing through the shiny silver-and-black photo book that bore a growling black panther, the high school mascot, on the front.

Inside were photos mostly of her sister. Andi looked young and happy, if a bit dorky with her big, messy-looking hair and oversize eyeglasses. Andi with the math team. Andi with the National Honor Society. In Jelly's favorite, her sister's grin was wide as she held high over her head, as if she'd just won a sports championship, the modest plaque for Outstanding Enterprise in Junior Achievement.

"Andi can do anything," Jelly stated with absolute conviction.

Chapter 12

THE PHONE CALL was from Pete's father. As usual, he waived any friendly greeting and went straight to complaint.

"Why didn't you call me about that sex business opening on our corner?"

"Uh…well, Dad, I don't think there is a sex business on my corner," he said, with a lot of emphasis on the word *my*. "I think it's a car wash."

"It's a car wash featuring sluts in skimpy clothes," Hank said.

"Sluts? One of those women worked for us up until a week ago," Pete pointed out. "And Andi Wolkowicz? She can't be a slut, I don't think most people even knew she was a girl."

"The sneaky little bitch is doing this just to get back at me!"

"Earth to Dad!" Pete told him sarcastically. "When you screw people over, sometimes they'll retaliate. But this doesn't even seem like a payback thing. She's just trying to make a living. What does it matter to you? I'd think you'd more likely be a frequent customer than a shocked citizen."

"My constituents are in an uproar," Hank said. "If she's going to do this kind of thing, she needs to take it down on Doge Street. I've called the police. I'm going to get that place shut down."

"Shut down for what?"

"Good God, Pete! Are you still that naive? You don't need a reason for things if you know the right people."

Through the next hours, through the day, Pete tried, unsuccessfully, to concentrate on his work, his business. Instead his mind was constantly drawn to the activity across the parking lot. And a dozen times, he found himself standing at the window with the toy binoculars trying to see what he could see.

Finally he locked them in his bottom desk drawer, so that he wouldn't be so tempted. Then he immediately took a package of Mallomars out of his small office refrigerator and ate every last one.

If a man doesn't get to have sex, he told himself, *then at least he should be able to eat whatever he wants.*

The atmosphere at the store continued to be heightened with tension. The employees were doing their jobs, the customers were buying their groceries but underneath the noises of creaking shopping carts, chirping bar-code scanners and piped-in music there was a hum of whispered chatter that was nearly as tangible as a crackle of electricity.

"Guthrie! Guthrie!"

Mrs. Meyer waved him over as she stood in the checkout line. He forced a good groceryman smile on his face and hurried to her side. She was buying one tomato and a small box of teabags.

"Have you seen what's going on right outside your door?" she asked him.

He nodded. "Yes, ma'am," he said, brightly. "Isn't it nice to have one of our empty downtown buildings open up with a new business."

After his discussion with his father, Pete was absolutely committed to taking the opposite view from the one Hank was so convinced about.

"Surely you're joking!" Mrs. Meyer replied. "This is no joking matter, young man. This is a scandal and an outrage."

"With all due respect, ma'am," Pete said quietly. "I'm not joking and it's not a scandal. It's just a car wash."

"Have you not seen what they're wearing?" Mrs. Meyer asked. "Or should I say, what they are *not* wearing?"

Immediately the very pleasurable image of Andi Wolkowicz bent over a car bumper flashed in his mind. He could feel the blush rising in his neck. He knew his ears must be vividly red and silently cursed his own pale skin.

"Washing cars means getting wet," he told the older woman. "Appropriate clothing for workers getting wet might be a rain slicker. But it's so hot in the summertime, I think an ordinary swimsuit is a fine idea."

"An ordinary swimsuit!" The woman huffed self-righteously. "In my day a young woman would be arrested for showing up at a beach wearing something like that."

"Uh…I guess…what's that slogan? 'You've come a long way, baby.'"

Mrs. Meyer was not amused.

"We may be downtown, Mr. Guthrie, but this is still a family area," she said, adamantly. "There are three churches within five blocks of that place. And Curtis Elementary School is not far away."

Pete nodded slowly. "I believe the elementary school is closed for summer recess. And the churches, well, I doubt the car wash will be open on Sunday mornings."

Her brow came down angrily and her mouth thinned to one straight line.

"If that's going to be your attitude, Guthrie," she declared. "Then I…I am taking my business elsewhere."

She handed him her tomato and tea bags, haughtily raised her nose in the air, marched past those ahead of her in the checkout line and sailed out the front door.

Pete glanced around to see that every eye in the store was focused upon him.

Smart move, Peterson! he said to himself, sarcastically. *Get right into the middle of a controversy. Great show of business acumen.*

Outwardly he gave everyone a nice smile and went around asking the supermarket version of *what up, dude,* "Are you finding everything you need?"

Saturdays were notoriously busy and this one seemed especially so. He wondered absently if the increased volume of shoppers was actually caused by the bikini car wash. There were certainly more people on the streets than he'd seen on any Saturday in recent memory.

More people in the store, of course, meant more sales, but it also meant more questions, more complaints, more spills, more over-rings and more shoplifters.

He caught a couple of the latter in the act. He turned onto the beverage aisle and there were two young teenage boys trying to stuff a six-pack of beer inside their pants. The problem of typical summer clothes having not apparently occurred to them. It was possible to hide merchandise under a coat or jacket. But when all you're wearing is a T-shirt and some low-rise shorts, there weren't many places to stash stuff. The two had broken up the beer box and had stuck individual cans in their pants pockets and in their underwear. They would never have been able to walk out the front door like that.

At the sight of him, one of the guys froze in place. The other took off running. Pete made no attempt to chase. Instead he picked up his phone and with one button he had Neal, the produce manager, on the line instructing him to apprehend the boy at the door.

"Do you have a gun or a knife?" Pete asked as he approached the boy still standing in the aisle.

"Uh-uh," the boy answered, shaking his head.

"Okay, let's go."

The boy, who was only about fourteen, Pete guessed, did as he was ordered. The metal cans on his person clunked into each other noisily as he walked. These boys were either idiots or they were very new at this. Pete hoped it was the latter. He had a no tolerance policy for shoplifting.

He got a beep on his phone. It was Harvey, the stock crew supervisor.

"Guthrie," Pete answered.

"Neal and I have got the kid," he said. "We're on our way to Neal's office."

"I'll meet you there," he answered and then hung up. The young guy beside him was still clanking and hanging his head down low, his chin almost lay against his chest.

The produce manager's office was in the back of the store. An empty, windowless room, it was designed so that nobody would want to spend any time there, including the produce manager. Pete clicked a switch that turned on the ceiling fan, but that also activated the video camera. Holding someone against their will in a secluded area of the store could be a litigation nightmare. They needed their own record until the police arrived.

Pete indicated that the boy should sit on one of the mostly dirty, uncomfortable-looking plastic chairs. He did so, bending in half to lay his cheek on his knees. He wrapped his arms around his head creating a kind of figurative hiding place.

Lingering in the doorway, Pete gave the kid a little space. Almost immediately he could hear small shaky sobs sneaking out from the boy's throat.

When Neal and Harvey arrived with the fleet-footed accomplice, the young guy straightened up and pretended that he was being tough. Neither fellow looked the other in the eye.

Pete continued to hang around as Harvey made the boys put their haul on the desk. Between them they had five beers. And the kid who ran had two candy bars that he'd tucked into the access pocket of his tidy whiteys. Pete cringed. *Who would want to eat that chocolate?*

Pete began filling out a company report form. He asked the boys their names. The tearful one was Devon Pardue. Pete was pretty sure he'd heard the name before. The boy's parents probably shopped in the store. The runner identified himself as Bradley Terrington, Jr. Pete almost groaned aloud. Brad Terrington, Sr. was a prominent man at the country club. He was perhaps a decade older than Pete and played golf with Pete's dad. He was also argumentative, a bit of a hothead and well-known for always needing to be right.

Peterson, he thought to himself, *it might have been smarter just to let that kid get away!*

That hadn't happened and now, he would have to throw the book at the kid, no matter how hard his father retaliated.

Officer Mayfield arrived before Pete had even finished his stern lecture about the dangerous road of a life of crime.

Mayfield was twentysomething, blond with very short cropped hair and a permanent pale mask around his eyes from countless hours wearing sunglasses. He allowed Pete to finish his admonishments, but didn't bother with any of his own. He ushered the two young guys out the rear entrance of the building and into the police cruiser. Once both the boys were in the backseat, he accepted the yellow copy of the form Pete had written up. They all knew the drill. Someone on the staff caught a shoplifter nearly every week. In the summer months it was more often.

"Thanks for coming," Pete told the policeman.

Mayfield shrugged. "It's my job," he stated factually.

"I appreciate it nonetheless. Holding somebody in the produce office for any length of time is tough on us. It makes the store shorthanded and it's just very unpleasant for everyone. So thanks for showing up so quickly."

"I've been stuck on this corner on and off all morning," Mayfield told him. "With all the traffic snarled up and the cascade of citizen complaints coming into dispatch, this is the busiest place in town today."

Pete nodded slowly. "You're talking about the car wash?"

The guy nodded.

"I think my father was one of the complainers," he said.

"Your father, the alderman?"

"Yeah."

"I talked to him personally," Mayfield said. "I'll tell you like I told him. I can't shut down a business just because the surrounding businesses don't like it. We've got to have some evidence that they are in violation of a state law or at least a city code. He's going to talk with the Joffee brothers and other merchants on the block. He's hoping they'll join him in a zoning complaint. They're calling it an S.O.B."

"An S.O.B.? Andi Wolkowicz is a woman. And the downtown merchants shouldn't be banding together to call anybody that."

The officer eyed him curiously for moment and then explained the acronym.

"S.O.B. means 'sexually oriented business,'" he told Pete. "And city code precludes the downtown from the establishment of any sexually oriented businesses."

"Oh." Pete was relieved that it wasn't getting quite as mean as it sounded. "Well, just to get my opinion on the record, the place is fine with me. I don't think it's a sexually oriented business, and I don't think it will hurt the downtown merchants. Truth is, I think it's generated more shoppers in my store today. As far as I'm concerned any reason to make people come downtown is a good reason."

Officer Mayfield nodded. "It's good to know that everybody is not lined up against her," he said.

Pete shrugged.

"I've been keeping my eye on things over there," the policeman said.

Pete looked at him closely to see if he was making some little joke. The man appeared completely serious.

"I came here from Cincinnati P.D.," he continued. "Down there I learned a bit about the gals that work in S.O.B.s. These women at this car wash, they're just washing cars. But not everybody is going to make that distinction. Their critics won't. And many of their customers won't either."

"Thanks for not allowing the screeching of angry voices to get the best of you," Pete said. "And thanks for taking these kids off my hands."

Mayfield gave him the very slightest of nods. "I'll get them down to the station, put them in the box until Mommy and Daddy get there," he said, glancing back at two occupants visible through the police car's passenger window. "The young one, I've never seen him before. The Terrington kid, I've picked up a couple of times. Nothing major, just nuisance problems. I just hope his parents take petty theft a bit more seriously than they have truancy and vandalism."

"Whatever you need me to do, just let me know," Pete said.

As the police cruiser drove off, Pete headed back inside the store. He needed to get word to Andi about what Mayfield had told him. If the downtown merchants were out to get her, and he was sure his father was, then she needed to be warned.

When he opened the back door a blast of welcoming cool hit him in the face. It was getting very hot and he was grateful for the air-conditioning. He thought for a moment about Andi Wolkowicz working out in the sunshine all day. The bare backside image flashed through his mind again. By now, however, he was getting accustomed to it, beginning to enjoy having it in his thoughts to drift in and liven up a tough workday. He sure hoped she remembered to put some sunscreen on those gorgeous round butt cheeks.

After the unexpected visit of Tiff's ex-husband, the buoyant mood of the afternoon had been spoiled. They continued to work and talk and smile at the customers, but the atmosphere was chilly, even in the hottest of the afternoon sun.

Jelly had gotten so fixated on what had happened that Pop finally had to take her home. She kept repeating over and over that "it's time to get that perp off the street." And she needed to "call the D.A. for a warrant."

The constant repetition of this negative litany was making things worse. She could see it on Tiff's face. And there was just no explaining to Jelly.

So Andi was glad to see them go, though the help she'd gotten from her family had been critical to the work they'd managed to get done.

Andi couldn't recall having ever been so tired. Her arms ached so much it was hard to drag a towel across a car hood. Her back screamed in protest every time she bent over. And her legs were so exhausted, she was unsteady on her feet.

When she began turning cars away at 5:30, she did it without the slightest sense of regret. She'd lost sight of her business model and her need to make money. All she cared about was closing down on time and going home.

Tiff and Cher-L obviously felt the same. As soon as the last car rolled off the lot, both of them were putting on their coverups eager to head for home.

Andi was hot and sweaty and couldn't bear to drag on her coveralls. She found one of her dad's old workshirts hanging on a nail outside the bathroom. She slipped it on over her swimsuit. It didn't come down much further than her thighs, but she did feel covered. Buttoning it up, she ran her hand across the name embroidered above the pocket. Wolkowicz. She wondered if her father had been proud of her today or if he'd been embarrassed. Her mother would have been embarrassed, she thought. Then, immediately she shook her head. She didn't have a clue what her mother was like, what she wanted or believed in, she didn't know a thing about her mother and now she never would.

That rumination caused Andi to tear up. More evidence of how tired she was. She blinked away the emotions that had drifted to the surface and tried to get on with her business.

She didn't think her brain was sharp enough to even count the receipts taken in, let alone compare it with the tickets. She just stuffed everything in a bag and stowed it in the safe. Tomorrow was soon enough to celebrate their success.

The tip jar was another matter. The three women counted it together. Their plan that morning was equal thirds, but acknowledging the help they'd gotten from Pop and Jelly, they split it 4 ways, allowing those two to split their quarter. That seemed equitable to Andi, especially since Pop and Jelly weren't drawing any wages.

Everybody was happy to have some actual cash in their pocket.

"I'm just so glad we're not doing this again tomorrow," Cher-L said. "I'd planned to go out tonight and now I can even afford it, but I'm just beat. I'm going home and going to bed."

As Cher-L left, Tiff was gathering up her things. Andi walked over and gave her a hug.

"Thanks for working so hard today," she said. "I just want

to tell you that I think you're a good person and a great mother. Caleb is lucky to have you."

Tiff nodded, apparently not trusting herself to speak.

"See you Monday," Andi said.

As Tiff went out the door, Andi eased her aching body down on the bench at the back wall. She needed to change from wet sneakers to dry ones for what felt like the longest walk home ever.

She put her head against the wall and closed her eyes.

Or maybe, she thought, she would just sleep right here, sitting up.

She heard the door open again and assumed it was Tiff.

"Did you forget something?"

"You're actually a difficult woman to forget," a male voice answered.

A startled surge of adrenalin shot through Andi as her eyelids snapped open and she sat up straight. Pete Guthrie stood in front of her.

"Don't sneak up on me like that!" she said angrily. Her heart was pounding.

"Sorry," he said. "The door was open."

Inexplicably and embarrassingly, Andi felt tears gathering in her eyes. Exhaustion, unexpectedly jolted by fear, had pushed her emotions, already close to the surface, over the top.

She couldn't cry. Women in business don't cry. Or if they do, they don't stay in business very long. She steeled herself against it.

"Oh gosh, I'm sorry. I'm sorry," Pete repeated.

He sat down beside her and put a comforting arm around her shoulder. That just made it worse.

She would not cry! She would not cry! She insisted to herself as she squeezed her eyelids tightly closed. A lone tear escaped and trailed down her cheek.

Stupid, stupid, girly-girl reaction, she reviled herself.

Then she realized that high school hottie, Pete Guthrie was right next to her. He was warm and smelled good and had a muscled arm around her. Andi knew exactly how to send her emotions in an entirely different direction.

She pulled away slightly and looked up at him. His expression was one of friendly, gentlemanly concern. Andi decided to wipe that look right off his face. She snaked her arms around his neck, and planted her mouth right on his.

The chemistry of kissing was something Andi had learned in college, both through practical experience and textbook research. It was a human conditional response that produced a surge of hormones and an exchange of pheromones.

Andi's intent was to send Pete some of hers. She was caught off guard with the quality and quantity she got in return. Perhaps it was the exhaustion or maybe the emotion, but kissing Pete Guthrie felt strangely like an overdue homecoming, all new, different, yet completely familiar and welcoming. More than just welcoming, it was stimulating. A tiny spark within her developed into a cloud of sexual combustion that flamed up with an almost audible whoosh of intensity.

Suddenly neither of them could quite get enough. Andi moaned deep in her throat. He sucked in breath through his nostrils and pulled her more tightly against him.

"Wow," she said, when they separated.

"Wow yourself," he answered.

She pulled away and moved down the bench, putting a little bit of safe distance between them. She leaned back once more against the wall and he did, too. Andi was very surprised at her reaction. Where was that exhaustion she had felt? The sadness that had made her cry? Her whole body was now wide-awake, the blood humming through her veins like a taut violin. The heaviness that had weighed on her all afternoon had vanished.

"I don't know what that was all about," she said finally.

"Me neither," Pete answered. "I guess I should apologize, but I warn you, it's going to be really tough for me to drum up any pretense of regret."

His honesty was so close to her own reaction that she laughed.

"I've had a really tough day and I'm so tired, I don't know what I'm doing," Andi said, adding, "That's my explanation. What can you come up with?"

"Well," he said, thoughtfully. "I haven't had sex in like a year. That's a pretty good excuse, I think."

"Sex? I'd forgotten about sex," Andi answered. "But I'm beginning to remember."

Their laughter slowly tapered off into silence. They continued to sit there, quietly, companionably. It was nice.

Pete finally spoke. "You said it was a tough day, but with all the traffic over here," he said, "I'm guessing you had a good number of sales."

"Yes, we did," Andi told him. "That was what was so tough about it. A few more days like this and I'm done for. I worked my butt off."

He nodded. "I saw your butt earlier today," he said. "Very nice."

She grinned at him, amused. "I didn't know that you were funny."

"I didn't know that you were a girl," he replied. "I guess that makes us even."

"I was never much of a girl," she said. "All the girls were somewhere fixing their hair and doing their nails. While I was hanging out down here drinking soda pop and listening to guys complain about their drive trains and transmissions."

"It probably saved you a lot of grief," Pete said. "I understand that hair and nails stuff gets pretty tedious day after day."

"I guess we shouldn't knock it if we haven't tried it," Andi said.

"I was married to it…for a while," he answered.

"How'd that work out?"

He gave an oversize shrug. It was a gesture both comedic and self-deprecating. "Apparently I'm a better supermarket manager than I am a husband," he said. "Or at least I think that I am. My father might disagree."

"Ah…your father," she said. "How is the great public servant?"

"Not too happy," Pete answered. "That's actually why I came down here. Not that I wouldn't have come just to share that great kiss, but I did have other motives."

"Hmm, well, I don't know if I'm disappointed or relieved," she teased. "What's up with Alderman Guthrie?"

"He's out to get you," Pete said. "Some of his constituents have been giving him grief over this place, so he's maneuvering for a way to shut you down."

"Why am I not surprised at this?" Andi asked rhetorically.

"He didn't give me any of the details," Pete said. "But I talked to Officer Mayfield. Apparently my dad is attempting both to band the downtown merchants together against you and to have your business deemed ineligible for this zoning code."

"Ineligible how?"

"He's trying to say that you're a sexually oriented business," Pete told her. "Like a strip club or an adult video store, the city can zone you away from churches and schools and residential neighborhoods."

"I'll fight him," Andi declared. "I won't just give in. He'll never win that in court." But even as she said it, she could hear the defeat in her own voice. He wouldn't have to win in court. He could just hire a handful of lawyers, get a couple of legal actions filed and delay her until she ran out of money. She couldn't afford to go to court. She didn't say any of this to Pete. Maybe Mr. Wow-he-sure-knows-how-to-kiss was on her side, but blood is thicker than kissing partners.

"I need to go home," she told him instead.

He nodded, though she sensed it was a little reluctantly. "Go ahead and lock up and I'll walk you to your car."

"I'm sort of car-free," she joked. "I couldn't keep up the payments, so now I'm on foot."

"Then I'll drive you home," he said.

"You don't have to do that."

"Just doing my civic duty, ma'am," he said. "I can see that you're nearly dead on your feet. I wouldn't want you to collapse on the street wearing just a shirt over that skimpy red bikini. For the sake of public decency I'd better drive you home."

She made sure the building was secure while he walked over to the Guthrie Foods parking lot to get his car. Her muscles still ached and she could hardly stoop or bend, but she felt surprisingly alert and alive and optimistic. Intellectually, she knew that was wrong-headed. If Hank Guthrie and the other downtown business owners were allied against her, they'd find a way to hurt the business, to shut it down, to shut her out of her opportunity. But somehow Pete's support loomed large. If Pete was on her side things couldn't be so bad.

Had he said he was on her side?

No, she didn't remember him saying anything. But she did remember the feel of his lips. Andi couldn't stop herself from smiling.

His car pulled under the overhang. She was surprised at his car choice. He drove a sensible, nondescript sedan. Somehow that just didn't mesh with the flashy, high school dreamsicle that she still remembered him to be.

She headed to the passenger door. He raced around the car and grabbed for the handle just as she did, actually covering her hand with his own.

"I think I can open my own car door," she told him.

"I think my mother wouldn't want you to," he answered.

Andi shrugged and gave him a facetious sigh of resignation. "Well, okay, we wouldn't want to upset your mother."

He handed her into the car. She couldn't help but feel uncustomarily elegant, even in a man's shirt and a skimpy swimsuit.

"Where am I headed?" he asked as he took his seat behind the wheel.

"Jubal Street, between 11th and 12th," she answered.

He pulled out onto Fifth and headed in that direction. He glanced over at her.

"What?" he asked.

"Huh?"

"You have a kind of faraway look," he clarified. "What are you thinking about?"

She was thinking about him, the nearness of him, the scent of him. That was not exactly how she chose to answer.

"I was just imagining myself as one of the popular girls that were always in your car in high school."

Pete sighed. "Are we back to talking about high school again?" he asked. "High school memories are the bane of small-town existence."

His words were spoken with such drama, she chuckled. "What do you mean?"

"Everybody else in the world gets to move on with their lives, to grow and change," he said. "But not here where people still remember you from high school."

"We're all shaped to some extent by things that happened in our teens," she said. "That's not unique to small towns."

Pete shook his head. "Maybe not completely," he said. "But in big cities, you almost never work with the same people who knew you in high school. You don't have to do business with them or have your children grow up with their children. In cities, who you are is just whoever you grew up to be. But in small towns, you can never run away from your adolescence. If you were Pizza Face at fifteen, you're still called Pizza Face when you move into the assisted living center."

"Well, that's a depressing thought," Andi said.

He nodded. "Yes, it is. I think if all those city dwellers who fantasize about moving back to the simpler life in small towns had any idea how long memories are here…well, they'd start holding on to those crowded subway lines for dear life."

Andi laughed lightly.

"And it's not just our generation," Pete continued. "All the bad blood between my father and yours dates back to some teenage jealousy that my dad hasn't been able to get beyond."

"Really? Pop never talks about high school," she said. "Or really anything about the past. He never even talks about my mom. And I know he's got to miss her so much."

In the dim light of the dashboard she could see Pete nodding.

"This is it up on the left," she said. "The place with the truck in the driveway."

He pulled to a stop on the street in front of her house.

Andi reached for the door handle, but Pete got out and rushed around the car to open the door for her once more.

"I'll walk you to the door," he said.

"Why? It's twenty feet. I think I can make it on my own."

"I…uh…I thought I might kiss you again."

"That's probably a really bad idea," Andi said.

"Yeah, I'm sure it is," he agreed. "But I'd still like to."

He was beside her as Andi made her way up the front walk. He didn't take her hand or touch her in any way, but she was completely aware of his nearness. She shouldn't kiss him again. It was way too dangerous to kiss him. She quickly discounted that thought. The kiss they shared had to have been a fluke. Kissing wasn't *that* good. It was just kissing and it was probably better for her to kiss him again and realize it was ordinary than to carry that memory around to taunt her every time they ran into each other.

At the bottom of the porch steps, she stopped and turned to face him. She slid her arms up around his neck and he bent down to encircle her waist with his hands. There was no fumbling, no bumped noses, their lips found each other perfectly in the darkness as if they'd been doing this for a lifetime. It was hot and sweet and amazingly passionate. Andi didn't want it to end. She ached to be closer to him, pressing herself full-length against his body. His arms held her tightly, stroking her. Andi's knees were turning to jelly and she leaned heavily against him.

Their mouths separated as they each gasped for breath. He should go. Andi knew that. She needed to unclench the grasp she had on his shirt and send him away. That's exactly what she needed to do.

"Let's sit down," he said.

"Yeah," she agreed.

Pete seated himself on the top step. Andi seated herself in his lap.

Suddenly he grasped her hips. "Don't wiggle!"

"Sorry," she answered, recognizing that was exactly what she'd done.

She heard him whispering under his breath.

"What did you say?" she asked,

"Nothing."

"It sounded like Q-tips, cotton balls, cuticle remover."

"Aisle Twelve," he explained. "I'm getting a grip on myself by forcing myself to visualize Aisle Twelve."

That really made her laugh. They started kissing. Once they started, it just seemed crazy to stop.

"I should go," he said against her throat.

"Uh-huh," she agreed.

"We're not thinking straight."

"No, we're not."

"I'm going to leave now."

She nodded. "In a minute, just a minute." Andi wasn't quite ready to give up this moment, this feeling.

He ran one long finger down the buttons on her shirt. "I want to look at you," he said. "May I look at you."

They both fumbled to get the buttons undone. He reached for the string at her back as she untied the one on her neck. Carelessly she tossed away the expensive triangles of red material. In the darkness she looked at him looking at her.

He kind of whistled under his breath and then added, "You're beautiful."

"Thanks," she answered. It was a stupid thing to say, but her brain wasn't functioning well.

"I said I was just going to look but…"

She raked her fingers into his hair and pulled him toward her. It was the only encouragement he needed. His mouth was on her breasts and shards of sexual arousal splintered through her body. She forgot his admonition not to wiggle and she moved atop him in an instinctual rhythm.

Andi couldn't tell where his moaning stopped and hers began.

A minute later he grasped her around the waist and laid her back on the porch.

"If we don't stop, we're going to do this right here on this porch," he told her, stating the obvious.

"Yes, we've got to stop," she agreed, but then added a trailing off, "I guess."

"Let's go to my house," Pete said. "I've got a nice, comfortable bed at my house. Maybe we'll come to our senses before we get there."

Andi nodded eagerly. "Let's go to your house."

Chapter 13

SUNDAY MORNING WALT sat in his regular church pew, with Jelly beside him. Andi had been so sound asleep that he hadn't had the heart to wake her. Now he was very glad he hadn't.

"It is your responsibility as head of your family to control your daughter," Emmet Kurkamer told him emphatically. "This is a shame and an embarrassment for the whole community."

"No one needs to be ashamed or embarrassed," Walt answered him. "My daughter is running a car wash, nothing more."

"It seems to me that it is a great deal more," Emmet insisted. "Have you seen it?"

"No, I haven't and I won't," Emmet told him. "My wife passed by coming from the grocery store and she is beside herself with shock that you've allowed this. She's phoned every woman in the parish and she's talked incessantly of nothing else since yesterday afternoon."

"Well," Walt said to him. "I'd say that as head of your

family it's your responsibility to tell your wife to shut the hell up."

The man's jaw dropped in shock before he stormed away.

"Pop, I don't think you're supposed to say 'hell' in church," Jelly whispered to him.

"It's okay, sweetie," he told her. "Church is the one place where mentioning hell is almost a requirement."

He shouldn't have lost his temper with Emmet. Walt knew that. But he was not the first person who'd spoken about the car wash, he was about the tenth. From the moment he and Jelly had parked the truck, he'd been besieged with complaints. He'd tried to answer the first few seriously, but he'd figured out quickly that no one seemed to want answers, they wanted to state their opinion.

And added to that, an altar boy had handed him a note from the priest, requesting Walt make an appointment to speak with him on a matter of urgency. Walt had no question about the topic to be discussed.

He sat through the service, trying to force his attention on the liturgy and the sermon. That was why he'd come. To worship God as he always had in the same church where his parents had, the building erected when the town was new by immigrant grandparents like his own. It was a solemn, sacred thing to do. But today, he couldn't seem to do it. The current brouhaha brought forth unhappy memories from the past, memories steeped in anger and disappointment. As he sat there he recalled it all. Everything that had been said. Everything that had been done. His parts of it and those that had been out of his control. Walt sat as the music played, as the choir sang. Walt sat and he just got mad.

When the final benediction was said and the procession filed out, Walt stood, ready to do battle. His face must have revealed some of what he felt as several people approached him, but as they neared, they'd turn away, not willing to speak.

He walked Jelly outside to a bench beneath the shade of the large sycamore in the churchyard.

"I need you to wait here for me for a few minutes," he told his daughter. "I'll try not to be long, but even if I am, you have to wait."

"Okay, Pop," Jelly answered.

"What are the rules?" he asked her.

"I don't talk to strangers and I don't leave with anybody, not even people that are friends, not anybody. You are coming back for me, so I got to stay put."

"Perfect," he told her, giving her a thumbs-up.

Walt went back into the church, making his way to the door of the vestry just as the priest, dressed in street clothes, was coming out.

Father Henryk Blognick was a man of significant age. He had grown up at St. Hyacinth's and returned as a priest over forty years earlier. With his rotund body and just a fringe of hair along the edges of his bald head he appeared like a fat and jolly Friar Tuck, until looking into his eyes. His sense of moral rightness and his own confidence in his ability to discern that, made him less empathetic and more judgmental. And since the parishioners of St. Hyacinth's were, by and large, trying mightily to stay on the straight and narrow, the priest's personal prejudices were rarely brought to light.

He seemed surprised to see Walt, surprised and annoyed.

"Wolkowicz," he said. "I meant for you to call for an appointment. I am due in the rectory almost immediately."

Walt was sure he was due there, due to eat lunch.

"I'm a busy man, Father," Walt said. "With all the work I do here in the parish, you should know that. Whatever you have to say to me, I'd suggest that you say it now and say it quick."

Someone passed unobtrusively through the corridor behind them. The priest lowered his chin and spoke in more whispered tones. "I had hoped to speak to you in a more private setting."

"Why?" Walt asked. "Do you think that everybody in this church doesn't already know my business? Aren't they the very ones who've asked you to stick your nose in it?"

"I wanted to speak to you about your daughter," Father Blognick said.

"My daughter? Which one, Andrea or Angela?"

"It's Andrea, of course, who has prompted my concern," he said.

"Funny, you've never expressed a great deal of concern about my girls before," Walt said.

"All the young women of the parish remain in my prayers," he assured Walt. "And if I see any one of them making a misstep, it is my duty to say so."

"And you believe my Andrea is making a misstep."

Blognick nodded gravely. "I have reports about this business that she's opened. It's very unseemly."

Walt widened his stance and folded his arms across his chest. "It's a car wash," he stated without equivocation.

Father Henryk shook his head and made a tutting sound. "Perhaps that's what she told you," he suggested.

"Are you saying my daughter is lying to me?"

"I don't think Andi is truly a bad girl," Father Blognick assured him. "But these young women learn bad ways when they go off to the city."

"Oh, I see," Walt said. "I guess what you're saying is that I should have kept her home like her sister. Forget how smart and talented and ambitious she is and keep her here in Plainview under my thumb."

"Under your thumb is a bit harsh," the priest said. "I'm aware that she is a grown woman with a mind of her own. But as long as she's living under your roof..."

"As long as she's living under my roof, she's my business and not anybody else's, including yours, Father."

"I'm your priest. I would be remiss if I didn't speak up about this...this..."

"Car wash," Walt filled in the blank. "It's a car wash."

"Walter, I don't believe the men of this community are lining up on the street in the simple hope of getting their cars washed."

"You think they have other reasons?" Walt asked.

"I am certain of it."

"Well, whatever reason the men might have for lining up," Walt said. "My daughter's reason for opening the business was to make a living washing cars."

Blognick's brow furrowed. "You can't have seen what is going on down there."

"Have you seen it?" Walt asked.

"No, no, of course not," the priest answered. "But I have heard. My phone was ringing and ringing yesterday. The community is shocked, truly shocked."

"I bet they are," Walt said. "All those school-yard tattle-tales are now grown into busybody gossips. And you do nothing but encourage them."

"Surely if you saw what they saw…"

"I was there myself," Walt said. "Jelly and I were both helping out. And I'll tell you what I saw. I saw a nice long string of clean cars pulling out of that lot."

"But washing cars in such an immodest fashion," Father Blognick said. "It's titillating. It appeals to man's basest nature."

"Man's basest nature doesn't need much to titillate it. If I'm any judge, the fellows around here stay titillated pretty much all the time."

"That may be true," Father Blognick admitted. "But it's no excuse for your daughter's behavior."

"I don't believe a word has been said about my daughter's *behavior* at all. It doesn't seem like it's her *behavior* that anyone finds objectionable. It's how good she looks in a swimsuit."

"I wouldn't dream of suggesting that Andrea is doing…anything unmentionable," Blognick said. "But this is a conservative congregation in a conservative town. So I must caution you to keep an eye on her."

"That seems to be the problem," Walt said. "The whole town can't seem to take their eyes off of her."

"You are taking this far too lightly, Walter," the priest said. "Your daughter is exposing her body in public for money. She is provoking lust and that is one of the deadly sins."

"So is gluttony," Walt pointed out. "But that hasn't seemed to keep you from the table."

That shot clearly landed. The old priest's eyes widened in shock.

"Walter, is there some problem, some issue here, that I don't know about?"

"No. Absolutely not," he answered. "You know every issue in my life and have had more than a bit part in most of my problems."

"Whatever are you talking about?"

"I'm talking about Rachel."

"Rachel?" The priest first appeared puzzled and then incredulous. "Gracious heavens! That was nearly forty years ago. Surely you're not still harboring a grudge over being denied a youthful fancy?"

Walt's jaw tightened, his words were sharp. "She was not a 'youthful fancy'. She is the love of my life. I have missed her beside me for forty years."

Father Blognick gave a dismissive huff. "You were much better off with Ella," he said. "You two had an exceptional life together."

"Ella and I made the best of what we had," he answered. "A friendship and a mutual respect. That's not the same as a real marriage, but we took out of it what we could, some comfort and companionship and a couple of kids."

"Shame on you for even saying such a thing," the priest said. "And your wife barely cold in the grave. You should be on your knees every day giving thanks for the wonderful partner you were given, instead of pining over that spark of teenage rebellion that could only have distanced you from God and your church."

"I clearly see now that what I would have lost would only have been your narrow-minded opinion and the silence of a few wagging tongues. I'm sure I could have learned to live happily-ever-after without either."

Walt turned and strode out of the doorway and down the hall to the vestibule and out the front door. He was still angry, but he also felt amazingly free. He'd broken the bonds that had held him captive too long and he felt suddenly as if the weight of the world had lightened considerably.

Jelly was still seated under the tree looking at her picture books. He waved her over and she rushed to his side, gushing about a police car that had passed by on the street and speculating, in *Law & Order* lingo, about the nature of their Sunday morning patrol. Walt was hardly listening.

As soon as Jelly got into the truck he dragged his cell phone out of his pocket and made a call.

"Rachel," he said, as soon as she picked up. "I think it's time."

Pete Guthrie awakened on Sunday morning with a smile on his face. His whole body was relaxed, refreshed and languorously limp. Well, not completely limp. Some of him was not limp at all and he rolled over to point that out to the woman beside him.

The other half of the bed was merely a tangle of bedsheets. He felt a strange clutch of disappointment in his gut.

She was gone.

A flash of something red caught his eye and he got out of bed to retrieve the tiny piece of thong bikini bottom that had somehow made it to the ledge of the windowsill. He picked it up with one finger and eyed it for a long, pleasurable moment as that not so limp area tightened in anticipation.

She's got to be in the house, Peterson, he assured himself. *Not even Wolkowicz would walk across town wearing nothing but a shirt.*

"Andi!" he called out.

He walked to the bathroom and tapped on the door. "Andi, are you in there?"

She wasn't. And she wasn't in the hallway or downstairs in the kitchen or even on the patio or the front porch. She was completely gone. He felt a tremendous sense of disappointment. It was strange. The house seemed empty without her. And yet, the house was always empty and she'd only been with him a few hours.

He began to rationalize her absence. She still lived at home. If her father woke up and she'd never made it home from the job, he'd for sure be worried. And the way gossip flew through this town, she probably couldn't dare be spotted leaving his house. Still, he wished she'd awakened him. He would have been happy to drive her home. Of course, maybe she knew that if she woke him up they would have just done it again.

Pete smiled at that thought. *Wow* was the only descriptive word he could think of.

Then another word came to mind: *hungry*. Pete headed into the kitchen, eschewing his usual milk and Mallomars breakfast he decided to make pancakes. He found an aging packet of mix in the cabinet and had almost enough milk, stretching it with a little water. He stirred it all together.

On the best mornings of his childhood, his mother had always made pancakes. Saturdays or Sundays, just the two of them laughing and joking in the kitchen, was a special time. It was only as a teenager that he realized what these unexplained absences of his father meant. His mother had kept her smile firmly in place and her focus totally on her son. Willing away the question of "why didn't Daddy come home last night?"

He poured round circles of batter on the hot griddle and watched the bubbles slowly appear on the top of each pancake.

He was humming to himself as he thought about Andi. She was smart and funny and beautiful. Uninhibited and enthusiastic in the sack. They fit together so well. How come he hadn't noticed that in high school?

"If you had, Peterson, you would have saved yourself a world of grief."

Minx had been so…it was not fair to compare, Pete knew that. Everybody had their strengths and weaknesses. Minx had certainly dressed for success, she'd always looked good on his arm. She was sophisticated and witty and charmed everyone she met. But she'd been no great shakes in the sex department. It had all been a negotiation for Minx. Whether it was a smile or a blow job, everything in their relationship had some kind of price.

He flipped the pancakes.

There was no sense with Andi that she had been granting him favors. She'd been intent on her own satisfaction. And achieving that involved mutual pleasure. That was what he'd thought that sex was supposed to be. Pete was very glad that he hadn't been wrong about that.

Once the pancakes were on a plate and swimming in maple syrup, he carried his breakfast outside on the patio. The sun was already high enough in the sky to wipe out most of the shady spots, but he sat near the edge of the house, where a nice breeze made for a very pleasant morning.

Pete had only had two, very good-tasting bites, when he heard his cell phone. He was up like a shot and racing into the house. His expectation was high. It had to be Andi.

When he grabbed the device off the counter his smile faded. The caller ID indicated Phoebe Johannson, one of his cashier supervisors.

He snapped it open and held it up to his ear. "Guthrie," he said.

The crisis was mild. Phoebe had car trouble, her husband was already on the way to pick her up, but Pete needed to cover for her until she could get to the store.

Assuring her that it wouldn't be a problem, Pete knew he needed to get there as quickly as possible. He grabbed his plate of uneaten pancakes from the patio and put it in the sink. He raced upstairs for a quick shower and got dressed.

At the last minute, just as he was retrieving his keys and his wallet, he spotted the red swimsuit bottom.

Hey, Peterson, when you find something that somebody lost, it's a priority to return it to the owner.

With that thought in mind, he stuffed the small red thong in his pocket. The prospect of returning it to Andi had him whistling as he headed down the front porch steps.

"Morning, Mrs. Joffee," he called out to his neighbor.

The woman was using a garden hose to water her flowers, her face completely obscured by an oversize floppy hat.

As he drove to the store, his brain kept concocting reasons to detour down Jubal Street. He imagined catching sight of her getting her morning exercise, sweaty from exertion, her running shorts damply clinging to the generous curve of her backside. Or maybe she was just waking. Yesterday had been physically demanding. Maybe she was just getting up, drinking a cup of coffee. He imagined her standing barefoot on her front porch, wearing one of those flimsy, girly nightgowns with that well-satisfied look glowing from her complexion.

A car horn interrupted his reverie and he realized he was driving too fast. He braked just as he passed St. Hyacinth's. Perhaps that was where she was, spending the morning at church. Pleading forgiveness for everything wonderful that happened last night.

By the time he reached the store, minus the detour to drive by her house, he was convinced that nothing whatsoever could darken his mood.

The Sunday Morning Slugs, a designation this shift of workers had more or less proudly named themselves, were accustomed to a more languid pace. Traffic in the store was always light until after eleven and shopper and staff alike were always a little bit sleepy, a little bit quiet.

That was not at all how Pete felt. He was in a great mood, full of energy, full of enthusiasm. He was joking, laughing, truly enjoying himself at a job he loved. And if the thong bikini bottom tucked way down in his right pants pocket was a part of that, then so be it.

The whole mood of the store lifted. All the smiles were genuine and all the offers of assistance were sincere. It was exactly what he wanted for Guthrie Foods every day of the year. It was the high concept that he'd been searching for and he was surprised and amazed to find it existed inside him.

By the time Phoebe arrived, he was eager to go up to his office and get his ideas down on paper.

The entire upstairs was dark and empty. The blinds were drawn in his office. He opened them and immediately spotted the Jungle Jeff Safari binoculars on the windowsill.

If you couldn't keep resist looking before, how will you ever keep your eyes off her now? he asked himself.

He opened a package of Mallomars and sat down at his desk to concentrate. On a notepad bearing the logo of a prominent food conglomerate, Pete wrote down his thoughts about his own responsibility for calibrating the atmosphere at Guthrie Foods. Somehow there had to be a way to make friendliness and familiarity as much of a product in their store as coffee or bread. And to use image and advertising to sell that product.

He noted every idea that came through his head, the brilliant, the so-so and the completely idiotic. It was the only way he knew to push his mind from the mundane into the creative.

He tapped his pen thoughtfully upon the desk. This was a start, but he really needed to brainstorm it with someone. What a luxury that would be! Bouncing ideas off with a co-worker that he trusted would be such a help. Just seeing a reaction to the things he said would be beneficial.

His father came to mind, but he quickly discarded that idea. Nothing he could ever come up with would appeal to his father. Hank was way too competitive to engage in collaboration. He would dismiss everything out of hand just because it came from Pete.

Maybe he could talk with Miss Kepper. But he wouldn't be unguarded enough. He couldn't imagine himself voicing his less brilliant thoughts in front of her. It would be like discussing boogers with your teacher. Just not done.

Perhaps he should try a discussion with one of the assistant managers. Neal? Harvey? He'd have to think about that.

Pete worked on his notes for a few minutes more, until he

was down to just doodling in the margins. It was time to put it away and move on to more pleasant tasks. He felt for the swimsuit in his pocket and smiled. Returning the woman's property was a top priority.

Whistling, he went to the bathroom and combed his hair. He eyed himself critically in the mirror. He was no longer the high school hunk. Now he was just a goofy groceryman. But he felt more comfortable as the latter.

A goofy groceryman with an important errand, he thought to himself. Within minutes he left the store and made his way down to Jubal Street between 11th and 12th. Finding the house was not as easy as he thought. In the darkness he hadn't noticed a color and the structures on this block, though all distinctive, were all two-story row houses with front porches and narrow driveways. Wolkowicz's truck was nowhere in sight. He was about ready to start knocking on doors, when a flash of something red caught his eye. A small bit of material seemed to be caught in the bushes near one set of porch steps.

It's a good thing your throwing arm is still accurate.

He parked his car in front of the house and walked to the front door. On the way, he rescued the other piece of the thong bikini and stuck it in his other pocket. Now he had a double reason for showing up.

He rang the doorbell.

He waited. And waiting made him nervous.

Maybe you should have brought flowers? he thought. Then quickly discarded the notion. *That would be totally lame, Peterson. Get a grip!*

After several minutes he realized that nobody was going to answer. He felt disappointed and then concerned. She'd walked all the way across town in the middle of the night. Something might have happened. It wasn't as if Plainview was crime-free. He was walking down the steps when he heard the distinct sound of a basketball bouncing against a sidewalk. He recognized it because plenty of his teenage afternoons had been spent on the same activity. He walked around to the side of the porch and peered down the empty driveway toward the garage in the back.

Dribbling inexpertly was the person who looked like Andi, but not quite.

Pete walked toward her along the side of the house. The old brick foursquare was well shaded and looked lived in. The trim sported a new coat of paint and the tawny red brick seemed solid. The shrubs had been well tended and the little pots of flowers were indicative of a real apprecia-tion of the place. The basketball hoop was attached to the garage. It looked, Pete thought, about regulation height. A deck on the back of the house overlooked the makeshift court area. A well-worn porch swing served as prime seating for any game.

"Hi, Jelly," he said. "Is…is Andi home?"

She stopped dribbling and looked over at Pete curiously.

"Andi's a slug-a-bed," she announced. "I know you. That's why I can tell you that. I don't talk to strangers when my family is not around. But I know you."

"Okay."

"You went to my school and now you work at the grocery store," she continued. "And you watch women's butts when you run."

"Uh…well, not exactly."

"Are you here on a material witness warrant?"

"I beg your pardon?"

"No use trying to skate on this one. You're going down. And you haven't done hard time until you've done it in Dannemora."

Pete was practically speechless on that. "Uh…well, I guess I'd better go."

"Do you want to play basketball with me?"

"Basketball?"

"I remember you played in school and I play, too. I'm really good at it."

"If your sister's asleep, I should really go," he said.

"Please. Please, please, please, please, please, please." She clasped her hands together in supplication. "Pop says I'm not to wake up Andi. But he went out and the TV is full of baseball. And I've been looking at my picture books for hours. Please, please, please play basketball with me."

Pete was a little uncomfortable. He didn't recall her ever crying or screaming or really causing trouble in school. But he didn't really know her and he'd spent almost none of his life around handicapped people. He had no idea how a person was to interact on a one-to-one basis.

Hey, Peterson, what could a couple of basketball games hurt? he asked himself. He had nothing better to do.

"Sure," he said.

Jelly immediately passed the ball to Pete. He had to leap sideways in order to catch it. But he did catch it which prompted Jelly to inform him of her skill.

"I'm a really good passer," she said. "And I make a lot of baskets. Do you make passes?"

"Sure I do," Pete said.

"Okay, pass it to me and I'll shoot."

He sent the ball her way. She dribbled in for a layup. Or perhaps what she thought was a layup. It was mostly just making her way directly under the basket, pausing and shooting straight up. That she missed it didn't seem to bother her at all. Pete rebounded and gave her another crack at it.

"I'm waiting on the forensics," she told him.

He had no idea what she meant by that. "Well, take a shot while you're waiting," he suggested.

Jelly giggled as if he'd said something very funny. Maybe he had.

Chapter 14

THUMP. THUMP. THUMP. The distinctive sound of a basketball bouncing against the driveway awakened Andi. She rolled over and a moan escaped her lips. She hurt everywhere. Her arms and legs ached. Her back was sore. Her hips, her stomach, her chest, places she didn't even know she had muscles had muscle aches. Even inside her, delicate female parts were complaining of overwork. Not a good idea, she decided, to wash cars all day and spend half the night playing sexual acrobat.

That memory popped her eyes wide open.

"I had sex with Pete Guthrie," she said aloud.

Bad idea. A very bad idea. She'd been exhausted into idiocy. Not him. Not now. In her right mind she would never have done something like that. She had never done something like that. She'd never slept with a guy on a first date.

"Wait, there was no date," she reminded herself. He had just walked into her business and she'd fallen into bed with him.

She threw an arm over her eyes and groaned again, this time more in humiliation than pain.

He was handsome and sexy and such a good kisser. And she'd been feeling pretty sexy herself. After spending a day half-dressed and attracting a lot of male attention, all those whistles and catcalls must have gone to her head. She didn't even have the excuse of alcohol. She'd been cold sober and totally drunk on her own sexuality. What a mess!

Andi pushed off the tangle of sheets that covered her and rolled into a sitting position.

The thump, thump, thump outside her window continued. She could hear voices, but not what was being said. Occasionally, Jelly's high-pitched giggle was discernable. Maybe she was playing with Pop. Or perhaps Tony Giolecki was spending the day again.

Andi got to her feet with the minimum of moans and groans and shuffled to the bathroom in the hallway. She turned on the water in the tub and then sat down on the toilet, holding her face in her hands.

"What were you thinking?" she asked herself. The very last thing she needed was to get involved with somebody in Plainview. And thank God she was still on the pill. She liked how it kept her regular and kept the blues at bay. Now she was grateful she wouldn't spend the next few weeks worrying that a careless night would result in lifelong responsibilities. "You are such an idiot!"

She grabbed a clip from the top of the vanity and wadded her hair together on the top of her head. Discarding her modest cotton nightgown, she stepped into the tub and eased her weary body into the hot water.

She'd always found something magical, comforting, in the sound of running bath water. It made just enough noise to drown out every other sound in the house, limiting a scary, dangerous world to one warm, safe place that was clean and cozy.

In her rough, tomboy childhood, it was only here, in the privacy of her bath, that she'd allowed herself to think girly thoughts. To imagine herself as a pretty princess hidden amidst the bath bubbles. There was something wonderful about that. Maybe how hard-won it had been made it more precious to her.

For most girls, getting privacy in the bath was de rigueur. For Andi it had not been so easy. She was probably ten or eleven when her mom was still insisting that she and Jelly wash up together. Bathtime was as much a learning experience as the rest of her sister's day. Mom insisted that Andi's life should model appropriate behavior for Jelly. And it didn't matter if it was in church in school or in the bathroom.

Andi understood it now, of course. They were a family and Jelly's disability required the help of the whole family. She'd even understood it then. She loved Jelly and her sister needed her. If Andi didn't watch her, teach her, show her, then Jelly would make a bad mistake, maybe even a dangerous one.

Still, she used to fantasize about being an only child.

When it came to her home and her mom, Andi's only identity seemed to be as Jelly's sister.

It was different at the car wash with Pop. There she knew she was special. And even at school where she excelled academically and kept a low profile socially. All her teachers had adored her. The other students had mostly ignored her.

What had Pete said last night? In small towns, who you were in high school is who you are forever.

She wasn't sure she agreed with that. She was pretty sure that nobody would suspect that the math geek tomboy of her teenage years would have rolled out of a lust-filled bed to walk across town at three o'clock in the morning wearing stolen clothes.

Andi laughed for the first time that morning.

In the darkness of Pete's bedroom, she hadn't been able to locate her swimsuit. She found her shirt on the floor of the hallway. As she was getting up her courage to walk home bottomless, she'd spotted his running clothes hanging out of the laundry chute. She slipped on his dirty, sweaty oversize clothes and walked out the door.

She still couldn't believe she'd had sex with him. And it was difficult to regret it. She'd forgotten how good sex could be. Or maybe it had never been so good. Certainly her college boyfriend, Brent, had never been so thorough. And the affairs she'd had since had been less than spectacular, even in the beginning.

Pete Guthrie knew how to light up places in her that had been in darkness forever. She sighed and allowed herself a satisfied smile. And then abruptly sat up in the tub, splashing water over the side.

"Of course he's good in bed," she told herself. "He probably did every cheerleader and majorette in high school. And now that he's Plainview's most eligible bachelor again, he's probably got them lining up at his door!"

She turned off the tap. The basketball thumping outside could be heard once more.

Pete was undoubtedly like his father, Andi decided. Wasn't that what people always said. A man grows up to be like his father. And Pete's father was an infamous philanderer. Pete was probably the same way.

She crawled out of the tub and began to dry off.

Last night had probably been just an ordinary Saturday night for him. Pick up a woman and take her home. No big deal.

He'd said he hadn't had sex in a year.

Andi thought about that for a moment and then shook her head. He was just talking, just being charming.

The sinking sense of disappointment hung with her. But she tried to spin it. It was better if it meant nothing to him, she assured herself. It was a crazy mistake on her part and she was not about to allow it to happen again. He undoubtedly knew that this morning as well. If she just kept her distance, he would, too.

The worst thing about that, Andi realized, was that she liked talking to him. He was smart and funny and on her side. She thought they probably could have been friends.

Nothing kills friendship quicker than sex.

"I might as well stick a fork in it," she told herself in the mirror. "This relationship is done."

Back in her bedroom, feeling better physically and mentally, Andi donned a pair of shorts and a T-shirt. She made her way downstairs to the kitchen. Breakfast was over hours ago. The coffeepot was clean and empty. On the counter there was evidence of sandwiches made for lunch. Andi quickly put one together for herself.

The thump, thump, thumping was even louder downstairs and individual voices could be heard. She paused to listen. The other voice in the driveway wasn't Pop. And it wasn't Tony.

She cut her sandwich in half and headed toward the back deck. She took one big, hungry bite just before opening the back door.

The swing was empty, but the driveway was not. The man she was avoiding was not avoiding her.

"Hi!" he called out and waved.

"Wah da woo ooing weer?" Andi asked with her mouth full. "Huh?"

She swallowed. "What are you doing here?" she repeated.

"I…I guess I'm shooting hoops with your sister," he answered.

"I like Pete," Jelly declared.

"Thanks," he said to her.

"Pete is really good at passes," Jelly continued. "He can throw a pass better than anyone. You should get him to throw a pass at you, Andi."

He laughed. "I think I already did," he said, giving Andi a conspiratory wink.

She was in no mood for conspiracies or innuendo or seeing him while wearing an old T-shirt and her hair in a wad.

"I'm going to eat my sandwich," she said.

She walked across the deck and took a seat. To her dismay, he urged Jelly to practice her free throws and he came up the stairs. And seated himself on the swing beside her.

He smiled at her. It was that wholesome, handsome smile. The one that melted girls' hearts. Andi wasn't falling for it.

"I guess I look funny with no makeup," she said.

"You look beautiful," he told her. "It's like you're all lit up from within."

"Oh, yeah, right," she said. "Does that line usually work for you?"

His smile faded. "I don't think I've ever used it," he said.

Andi turned her gaze to her sister's basketball practice. Pete watched, too. They sat next to each other in silence for several minutes. She hoped he would just excuse himself and go home, but he didn't.

"So what are you doing here?" she asked again.

"I...I woke up and you weren't there," he said. "I wanted to make sure you got home all right."

"I made it home fine," she told him.

"I would have driven you," he said. "Next time, wake me up."

"Next time?" Andi turned to glare at him. "You're assuming a lot, aren't you?"

He hesitated before answering. "Maybe more than I should," he said. "It was...it was so good for me and I thought...I mean, that it sure seemed like it was good for you."

Andi could recall perfectly how loudly and persistently she'd expressed her approval. She couldn't get away with a lie, even in the clear light of day.

"It was great," she said. "It was great. So, thank you very much."

"Uh...I don't think 'thanks' are really called for," he said. "It was mutual. Fantastically mutual. You and I are just good together."

She nodded. "So, I guess we should just keep doing this because it feels really good, huh? Is that what you're thinking? I don't know how they are up at United Methodist, but at St. Hyacinth's they really frown upon that."

"Hmm. They're not all that big on it at United Methodist either, but I wasn't going to call the deacons to get their opinion."

"Whatever," she said. "It happened. We can't change that, but it doesn't mean we ever repeat it."

Pete nodded thoughtfully. "So you're thinking that last night was just a one-night stand kind of thing," he said.

"Right," she said. "It's the only reasonable way to look at it. Sort of a summer vacation hookup, without all the expense of a vacation."

"I get it," he said. "What happens at Pete's house stays at Pete's house?"

"Exactly," she told him. "We were just two people who got drunk and crazy and ended up sharing a bed."

"Except we weren't drunk," Pete pointed out. "We were both completely sober and in our right minds."

"We must have been crazy," Andi said. "It couldn't have happened any other way."

"But it did."

"Yes," she agreed. "We did it. It was great. Now we get back to our lives."

He didn't immediately respond and the silence between them lengthened.

Jelly called out for them to watch her. They both dutifully did.

"I'm disappointed," Pete said finally.

"Did you think that we were going to have some tacky affair or something?"

"I don't know about 'tacky affair,'" he said. "But I thought we made a connection. I thought we had something to share."

"Not me, not now," Andi told him. "The timing's all wrong. I'm home to help with my sister. I'm trying to start a business. It's not the time for me to try to share anything with anybody."

He nodded and gave her a tight smile. But after only a moment it broadened.

"I guess this means you aren't willing to split your sandwich with me. I left my breakfast in the kitchen and only had Mallomars for lunch."

His obvious attempt to lighten the mood deserved a reward. She handed him a half of sandwich. He took a bite.

"Mmm, very good," he said. "That's what I always heard about the girls at St. Hyacinth's. Excellent cooks."

"I don't cook," she said.

"Me neither," he answered. "We have that in common."

"That's about all," she said.

He nodded. "Except for dads who watch over us and a lifetime in Plainview."

"Watch this!" Jelly called out. "Approach the bench!" Immediately she dribbled in for a layup. "Two points."

Pete and Andi applauded.

"It's not a bench," Pete told her. "It's called a goal."

The young woman gave him a long-suffering glance. "I know that," Jelly said.

"It's *Law & Order* lingo," Andi explained to him. "It's her favorite TV show. She talks *Law & Order* all the time."

He considered that thoughtfully. "I guess it's better than getting your language from *South Park* or MTV videos."

"Yeah, I think so," Andi said. "Though I know it looks weird from the outside, when you're inside it all makes sense."

Pete nodded. "That's true about a lot of things."

Andi didn't ask him to expound on that. She needed to keep it light, to keep it shallow. He'd come over to…to be her boyfriend. She was glad that he was taking the refusal so well. And she was glad that he was a nice guy. At least she didn't have her lapse with some terrible man that she'd spend the rest of her life trying to forget.

"I guess I'd better get going," he said.

"Let me get your clothes," she said.

"My clothes?"

"I borrowed your running clothes to walk home in," she said.

"Well, that relieves my mind," he said. "'Cause I've got your bikini in my pocket and the idea of a shapely young woman walking through the city of Plainview virtually unclothed might completely unhinge the more conservative of the population."

She laughed. She couldn't help herself. Then she hurried upstairs and located his sweaty clothes where she'd left them in her laundry basket. She took them out to the deck and handed them over.

He pulled the two small pieces of red material out of his front pocket and gave them to her.

"Thanks for bringing this back," she said. "This is my work uniform. I'm sure I'd get my pay docked if I showed up without it."

He chuckled.

"Well, I guess I'll see you around then, Wolkowicz," he said.

"Yeah, sure."

They stood facing each other uncertainly for a moment. Finally Andi offered a handshake. Pete took it, but then he leaned forward and planted a kiss on her cheek.

"Bye."

He headed down the stairs. "Thanks for the game, Jelly," he said.

Andi's sister offered a "you're welcome."

At the bottom of the steps he turned. "I really will see you around," he said. "I have binoculars in my office."

★ ★ ★

The fireworks of Saturday night and the respite of Sunday in no way prepared Pete for all hell breaking loose on Monday morning. He arrived at his office to find the hallway crowded and a meeting going on in the conference room.

He greeted people he saw as cordially as his befuddlement would allow. He spotted Seth Joffee who returned his nod of greeting.

"Could you step into my office a minute," Pete said.

His neighbor's son, comanager of the nearby Joffee's Manhattan Store quickly complied. Seth, the younger brother, was just a couple of years older than Pete himself. The two had never been friends, but always friendly. They'd known each other since Little League.

Pete shut the door behind him.

"What's going on?" he asked.

"You don't know?"

Pete shook his head.

"Then you must be the only one," Seth told him, handing over a bright yellow flyer.

Pete read the document aloud. "Merchants and Citizens Alliance for Morality."

He glanced up at Seth, surprised. Then he read the rest of the announcement inviting everyone to the organizational meeting at Guthrie Foods.

"This is about the Bikini Car Wash?" Pete asked.

Seth nodded. "Yeah, there are some people really stirred up about it," he said.

"All these people?"

Seth shrugged. "It's hard to tell who's angry and who is just being careful. For us, foot traffic in our store was better on Saturday than we've seen in months. Dave and I were practically doing the happy dance. But if it starts to sour, well, we just don't want to be on the wrong side of this issue."

Pete nodded slowly.

"Guthrie Foods is the anchor of this whole downtown neighborhood," Seth continued. "If you're going to be opposed to this then we are, too."

"Guthrie Foods is not opposed to the car wash," Pete said.

Seth raised an eyebrow and chuckled lightly. "I guess your dad didn't get the memo. He's the point man for the organization."

Pete's brow furrowed and he shook his head. "He might have volunteered our meeting room. But my father's on city council. He can't take the lead in an advocacy group."

"He's not the actual chair of the group," Seth said. "The chair is Doris Kepper. You're father is just the guy doing all the talking."

"Oh crap!"

Seth nodded agreement.

The two went back into the hallway and Pete stayed on the edge of the crowd. He didn't need to see his father. Utilizing a microphone, his voice could be heard even by those who couldn't even get close to the conference room door.

"This is a community of families, decent families," Hank was saying. "We can't allow women tainted by big-city immodesty to come in here and undermine the moral fiber of our young men and boys."

Pete raised an eyebrow. It was the same kind of "she's not one of us" argument he utilized against Andi's coffee shop idea.

"We all know what this kind of business means," Hank continued. "They say they only wash cars, but the truth is they are washing young minds. Washing minds free of all the values that our families and schools and churches have tried to teach them."

There were mumbles of agreement. Pete could see several people in the hallway nodding.

"I don't want to say these women are bad. Maybe they are just rudderless and naive. Perhaps they don't fully understand that the men they attract to this…this business, if you can call it that. These men become hangers-on, vagrants. They're susceptible to alcohol abuse and drugs."

There were hisses of fear and disgust.

"And it's not only the boys in our community that are irreparably injured by this," Hank went on. "Think of the young girls, riding by on the city bus. They're headed to vacation Bible school or piano lessons and they are confronted, on our public streets, with this insidious evil. This subjugation of women. Is this the self-image we want for our daughters?"

"No," someone shouted.

"Hell no!" someone else agreed.

"As merchants and neighbors, parents and grandparents, we must take a stand against this lewd public display. I ask you, fellow citizens, what next? Will we see peep shows and prostitutes on our sidewalks. The road to obscenity and debauchery is a slippery slope, and you and I can both see the city of Plainview beginning to slide."

Pete walked back into his office and once more he closed the door. He walked over to the phone. Took one deep breath before picking it up. He dialed 911.

The dispatcher answered almost instantly.

"I need the fire marshal," Pete told her. "I've got an over-occupancy of the second-floor conference room area at Guthrie Foods. It's a dangerous safety hazard and I need the crowd dispersed."

As soon as he'd finished his call, Pete walked over to his window and picked up the Jungle Jeff Safari binoculars. He spotted Andi almost immediately. She was wearing a sundress swimsuit cover and was busily engaged in sweeping the lot clean. Just keeping the place up was a big improvement for the corner.

He watched her, trying not to get distracted by his memories of Saturday night. She'd been very certain about their timing being wrong. He couldn't argue with that. But he wasn't willing to just move on. There had been something special between them and he wasn't about to write it off without finding out what it was.

He still had his eyes on her when she straightened and focused her attention on something in the street. Pete scanned over to see what she was looking at and saw Plainview's hundred-foot ladder truck was turning into the Guthrie Foods parking lot.

Well Peterson, that's not going to be all that helpful with this morning's customer count.

The long firetruck pulled up directly in front of the store main door. A half dozen guys got out and walked inside. At least they were wearing T-shirts instead of helmets and protective clothing.

It was only a couple of minutes before they reached the hallway.

The fire marshal, a grizzled old veteran of a very dangerous profession, didn't waste any time. As soon as he came upon the crowd in the hallway, he started moving people out of there.

"Clear this hallway!" he called out. "You'll need to move downstairs. We've got to clear this hallway."

As he worked his way toward the conference room, people generally recognized the voice of authority. They began leaving.

"What's going on?" he heard his father ask. "What's going on?"

When the fire marshal made it to the doorway of the conference, Hank voiced the same question directly to him.

"We need to move people out of this room," he announced.

"We're conducting a meeting," Hank answered.

"Yes, sir, but the placard here on the door clearly states this room's maximum capacity at thirty," the man answered him. "There's more than twice that number in here. That's an unsafe situation. We need to remedy it immediately. Let's clear the room now, people. Make an orderly departure if you will."

As men and women began filing out of the conference room, Pete headed in that direction. He could hear his father furiously berating the aging, white-haired fire marshal as if he were some snot-nosed kid.

"I'm sorry," the man told him evenly. "Safety concerns are not negotiable. Once we became aware of the problem, we had no choice but to clear the area."

"Who notified you?"

The fire marshal shook his head. "I don't know who called it in, but once we're notified of a situation, we have to check it out. You were clearly in violation. I have no choice. I have to follow the law."

"The law!" Hank said the word as if it were a curse. "I *make* the law, do you understand that?"

"Yes, sir, I do," the fire marshal answered. "That's your job and mine is to carry it out."

His father's jaw was tightly set, his eyes glaring. Pete knew from experience how angry his father could get. Hank was enraged.

"I'm going to have to write a citation," the fire marshal said firmly.

"Give it to me," Pete told him. "It's my building, my store, my responsibility."

The old fire marshal nodded and stepped closer to the doorway where Pete stood. He pulled out a pad and began writing on it.

His father had begun pacing. His complexion was dark as a beet and his expression furious. Nostrils flaring, he kept slapping his fist into his palm.

He stopped directly in front of Miss Kepper and addressed her angrily.

"Doris, we must have a traitor on the store staff," he said. "You have to find out who it is and give him his walking papers. And I mean today! I will not tolerate disloyalty."

"I don't think we can ever know for sure who did it," Miss Kepper told him. "It's not the kind of thing that anyone would admit."

"I admit it," Pete spoke up immediately. "I called it in."

All three faces in the room stared at him incredulously.

"What?"

"You?"

"Yes," he answered. "There were too many people here. They weren't authorized to be here. I'm responsible for the people in this building. I knew it was a safety hazard. I had no choice but to call the fire marshal."

"Damn it! You disrupted our meeting," his father complained.

"No meeting was ever cleared with me," Pete said. He glanced over at Miss Kepper. "Was there some reason that I was not informed?"

The woman's expression was concerned. "Mr. Guthrie called the meeting," she said. "I just...I just assumed that he could do that."

"Understandable error," Pete said. "But in the future the answer is 'no.' My father cannot call a meeting without my approval. He can't, my mother can't, my Aunt Sylvie out in Idaho can't. And you, Miss Kepper, or should I say Madam Chair of the...what is it? the Merchants and Citizens Alliance for Morality. You cannot either. We're running a grocery store here, not a lobbying firm."

"Why you worthless girly pissant! You don't tell me what to do!" his father hollered.

"I can as long as I'm CEO."

"Don't push me, boy. I put you in that job and I can take you out of it!"

"Can you?" Pete asked, his tone deliberately conversational. "Replacing me takes a majority vote of the board of directors. There are only three of us on it. You vote me out. I vote me in. Shall we have Miss Kepper get my mother on the phone in China? I'm sure she'll be interested to know that you're now putting our family business squarely in the middle of a controversy. And that you, after sixty years of being a self-serving philanderer, have inexplicably become the spokesman for decency and morality."

Hank's face was so red it looked like he might explode.

"Do you want Miss Kepper to call her," Pete prodded. "I'm willing to take my chances with her vote if you are."

"You are just like her," Hank screamed at him through clenched teeth.

"Thank you, as always."

Powerlessness was not a feeling to which Hank Guthrie was accustomed. He did not allow people to dispute him. He certainly never allowed that from his son. Being shown up in the presence of Miss Kepper and the fire marshal was more than he could take. In furious frustration he grabbed a pitcher of water from beside the lectern. He hurled it in Pete's direction. Pete dodged unnecessarily, his father missed by a mile. But the pitcher shattered against the wall in a hail of broken glass and splattered water.

Hank cursed vividly and stormed out of the room.

Pete turned to the old fireman beside him and offered him a tight smile. "My father is having a bad day," he said. "I'm sure that I can trust your professionalism in what is repeated about this incident."

The fire marshal tore off the piece of paper from the top of his pad and handed it to Pete.

"The fine is $250," he said. "I came here, I cleared a room and I wrote you a ticket. There's nothing else to say."

"Thank you," Pete said.

The fire marshal half turned and tipped his hat. "Ma'am," he said. "Mr. Guthrie."

As soon as he was gone, Pete crossed the room and set the ticket on the table in front of Miss Kepper.

"Pay this out of Miscellaneous Expenses, please. And could you ask Meggie to put together our best goodie basket and have it sent down to the station house."

"Yes, Mr. Guthrie," she answered.

There was something in her tone that was new. Pete noticed it immediately. She had never been even remotely disrespect-ful. But this was, he realized, the first time he'd ever heard respect. He almost felt badly. As if he should reassure her that he understood why she'd done what she had done. But he knew better than that. She wasn't a member of the family. She was an employee. And she had messed up. She had assumed. She had forgotten who was her boss. And Pete knew the woman was smart enough never to let it happen again.

"Do you still want me to try to locate your mother?" she asked.

Pete shook his head. "I don't believe that will be necessary," he said. "Why ruin her vacation."

Jelly sat in the rumpus room looking again at the big brown photo book that smelled like the attic. On the TV in front of her, Detective Rey Curtis was having trouble with his wife. Jelly understood that. Sometimes even people who love each other have trouble.

She showed him the old black-and-white photos of the long-ago prom with fake palm trees and streamers hanging from the ceiling.

"This is my mom," she said, holding up the picture of two couples dressed in elegant formal wear from another era. She moved her finger to the other side of the photo. "This is Pop."

There was another picture of the four of them sitting together at a table. Pop had his arm around another woman, a dark-haired woman who looked familiar, but Jelly didn't recognize her.

Another photo showed Mom dancing with a very tall man with a square jaw and a big grin. Her mom was smiling, too. Smiling in a strange, dreamy way that was not so much like her.

"Mom was so happy," Jelly told Rey. "I don't know why. But when she's looking at this guy, she looks so happy."

"That's the way the groceryman looks at Andi," Jelly revealed, lowering her voice to just above a whisper. "But Andi doesn't look happy about it at all."

Jelly turned the page and there, posed within the center of a big heart strewn in crepe paper flowers was the strange man and Mom. They were kissing.

She studied the photo for a long moment. "I wonder if he's got her swimming suit in his pocket?" she asked.

Chapter 15

THE FIRST FULL workweek of Andi's new car wash business was both profitable and problematic. Although nothing could compare with opening day, she was continually surprised by the steady stream of customers who pulled in and paid cash.

They were able to reduce the schedule so that all three of them weren't needed all the time. Tiff came in as soon as they opened. Cher-L showed up in early afternoon. During that period of time when both were there, Andi could run errands and do paperwork. The latter was rapidly becoming a burden.

The new anti-bikini group, Merchants and Citizens Alliance for Morality, or M-CAM, the acronym they now called themselves, was very busy on numerous fronts trying to shut her down.

Every day they filed some sort of complaint. Mr. Gilbert from the city administrator's office or occasionally Officer Mayfield, would show up to deliver their latest salvo. Sewer and water use were being scrutinized. M-CAM tried to suggest that her permit of occupancy should never have been issued without an environmental impact study. The car wash shouldn't have received uncontested approval of a "grandfathered" business since it had been closed for so many years.

The status of Andi, Tiff and Cher-L was being carefully looked into. The quick, one-page agreements that clarified their employment as part-time, contract workers, had been written up by Andi. She had never imagined that a succession of Hank Guthrie's golf buddies, all high-priced lawyers, would be second-guessing every word. And she'd received a warning about allowing Pop and Jelly to help. If they had no contracts and weren't being paid, they were not allowed to volunteer.

The insurance company that had formerly been most concerned about fire hazards and vandalism, now contacted her father about the necessity of upgrading the liability. The insurance guy, another golf buddy, insisted that with the building as a target of community organizations, the current coverage put his company at greater risk. What he wanted for that risk was almost doubling the premiums.

Andi had her father respond by filing a grievance and requesting a hearing. That would at least stall any changes for a month or two.

And then there were the protestors.

A gaggle of middle-aged, middle-class women stood on the sidewalk most hours of the day carrying signs and harassing customers. Their placards were an unlikely mixture of feminist agenda and Midwest puritanism. BIKINI CAR

WASH DEMEANS WOMEN or I WAS NAKED AND YE CLOTHED ME! Andi's favorite was DOES YOUR MOTHER KNOW WHERE YOU WASH HER CAR?

For the most part, Andi wasn't bothered by their presence. It was like free advertising right on the street. And if some customers shied away because of them, others were emboldened.

Most of the women allied against Andi were strangers. But several times she spotted former friends of her mother's, or matrons at St. Hyacinth's.

One morning a woman cackled angrily at Tiff. The woman had come boldly up under the bay with her sign that read SIN! SHAME! NOT IN OUR CITY. She was calling out names like *hussy* and *harlot*. Tiff was cool and calm in ignoring her, but Andi decided to step in.

"Officer Mayfield has made it quite clear that the protestors must stay on the public sidewalk," she told the woman. "Are you going to get off this private property or am I going to call the police?"

"You'd better be calling a moving van," the woman answered. "We're going to run you out of this town, back to that sinful place you came from." Then she looked over at Tiff. "And you'd better be calling your attorney. We'll see that your son is taken out of this filthy life for good."

Once the woman made her threats, she did retreat to the sidewalk.

"I was born in Plainview," Andi screamed at the woman's retreating back.

She began vigorously polishing the fender of the car Tiff was working on.

"What a nasty old biddy!"

Tiff nodded. "She's Gil's aunt."

"Oh gawd!" Andi said.

"I just want to be totally straight with you," Tiff said. "I am determined to keep this job and make as much money as I can here. But if it comes to a custody battle, I…I'll have to quit."

Andi nodded. "I understand. I hope it doesn't come to that."

"I don't know what's going on," Tiff said. "Gil's not a perfect guy, but he's always tried to be a good dad and never threatened Caleb's happiness, no matter how bad things got between the two of us."

"But you do think he might do something now?"

Tiff shrugged. "I don't know. He won't talk to me. All I know about him is what Caleb tells me. And, of course, he wouldn't discuss this stuff with our son."

"Well, at least there's that," Andi said. "There are guys out there who wouldn't hesitate to try to turn his child against his mother."

"Gil's not like that. He's a family guy. A loving guy," she insisted. "I've never thought…I've never thought that he actually quit loving me. Our troubles have all been about money. It kills him not to be able to support his family. And I think this, me working at a job like this, I think it embarrasses him on a lot of levels. It's not just guys are looking at his wife. It's also that he couldn't make a decent living, so now his wife has to do this kind of work."

"I'm sorry, Tiff."

The woman straightened and pulled down the back of her blue-striped bikini that had the tendency to ride up.

"Don't you be sorry," she said to Andi. "I'm glad to have this job. I'm making enough, just in tips, to put groceries on the table. I'm going to be able to pay my rent next month and the car insurance. I'm not lying awake at night worrying about how I'll keep a roof over our head. You're a lifesaver for me and Caleb. And if that offends the sensibilities of Aunt Carrie, well, the old bag can go fart herself!"

Andi laughed. "I wouldn't mind seeing that."

"But we wouldn't want to smell it," Tiff piped in.

Unlike Tiff, Cher-L was having a great time. Andi worried, however, that everything she was earning was being spent on new swimwear. She showed up in a new bikini nearly every day. Some days she was lacy, girly. And others, she was a vamp. But all of the suits were small and the customers seemed to be appreciative. Cher-L laughed and giggled and flirted with the customers, but she was also perfect on the money and great at selling a little more service to every guy asking for a basic wash.

One customer spent an inordinate amount of time talking to her. She was sweet and smiling, but she seemed serious as well. When he finally got in his huge midnight-blue SUV and left, she was practically jumping up and down with enthusiasm.

"Do you know who that was?" she asked Andi.

"Who?"

"Micky Sveck!"

"Who?" Andi repeated.

"He's the owner of The Horny Toad," Cher-L said incredulously. "He hires all the talent for the shows. He thinks I have exactly what it takes to be an exotic dancer. Is that totally cool or what?"

"You want to be an exotic dancer?"

"Maybe," she answered. "I mean you've got to be really sexy and know how to move and stuff and wouldn't that be great?"

"Uh…maybe, I guess," Andi answered lamely.

Cher-L was too thrilled to even notice. But the man's visit had been a boost to her confidence. That afternoon she was even more fun and flirty with the customers.

As the week went on, not all of those who patronized the business were men. Several older women showed up.

The well-heeled, well-coifed, Mrs. Olivia Meyer was one of the first. Andi personally shined up her aging Lincoln until it looked nearly new.

The woman inspected it with her nose in the air and then huffed a reluctant approval.

"I was against you when I first heard about this," she told Andi. "But I simply hate having to fight all that traffic out to the interstate. It's nice to have my car cleaned up here, close to home."

"Well, we appreciate your business," Andi said.

"And as for these skimpy swimsuits," Mrs. Meyer said. "I was young once, too."

Andi smiled appreciatively before the woman added, "Of course, I was never as hippy as you are, dear. You can't put on so much as an ounce of fat or you'll be positively pear-shaped."

"Uh, thanks for the warning," Andi replied.

She decided later that she could put up with all the digs that Mrs. Meyer could dish out. The lady told all her friends about the place and very shortly a number of aging widows were getting their cars cleaned at Bikini Car Wash.

Bekka Kozlowski dropped by as well with the family minivan.

"I think you're very brave to get out here and try to make a living," she told Andi. "I'm so glad I have Todd. I don't know what I'd do if I was a single woman on my own in this economy."

Andi detected a bit of *schadenfreude,* delight in the bad luck of others, but not so much. And Andi was willing to take encouragement anywhere she could get it.

Where it came from most was Pete Guthrie. He showed up in the mornings with bagels and muffins. On days when they were particularly busy, one of his employees, most usually one of the guys, would show up with a sack of sandwiches at lunchtime. And he'd taken it on as a regular thing at closing to drive Andi home.

"You don't have to do this," she told him.

"Yeah, I think I do," he answered. "You've made it clear that you don't want to date me. So it looks like being your chauffeur is about my only chance to get you alone."

It was notable however that on none of these chances to be alone, did he attempt to renew the passion in their relationship. He never tried to touch her, kiss her. He never even took her hand. He drove her to her house. She said goodnight and got out.

At least that was mostly what happened. He would usually ask her about the day and she took the opportunity to unload most of the troubles swirling around in her head. Pete was a good listener. She trusted him. And he didn't jump in with a fix for every problem. Most of them were not easily fixable and he seemed to understand that a lot of working them out was just stating them aloud.

"Your father is bringing an agenda item up at the next city council meeting to change the definition of sexually oriented businesses," she told him.

"I heard a bit about that, but I don't have the details," Pete said.

"Well, I guess now the city's current definition is based on the amount of clothes you wear. Nudity and seminudity fall into the sexually based business determination."

"Okay."

"M–CAM was thinking that *we* are a seminude business," she said. "But the city attorney says no. The term came into use in lieu of 'topless' which was too crude and descriptive to be used in legal documents. Expanding seminudity to include bikinis is just not possible, because they are permitted at public parks and pools. They are, legally, clothes, so wearing them, in the way they were meant to be worn, cannot be considered seminudity."

"So that's good."

"It's completely good," Andi told him. "It makes us a completely legal downtown business."

"So what's my dad's next move?"

"He wants to change the definition from what we have on to what our motivation might be," she said. "He wants to have the definition of sexually oriented businesses to be based on whether or not they appeal to 'prurient interest.'"

"How does that work?" Pete asked.

"I don't think it will," Andi said. "One man's 'prurient interest' is another man's ordinary enthusiasm. Can you close down a movie theater for showing R–rated films? Or shut down a restaurant because one of the waitresses has big boobs?"

"I think there are some people in this town who would be all for that," Pete said.

Andi nodded. "And the crazy thing about this for me," she said, "is that if this were happening to somebody else, I don't know which side I'd be on. I've never been the 'hot mama' type. I've always thought that women who came to business meetings in short skirts were undermining the workplace for all of us."

"Different kinds of jobs have different dress requirements," Pete said. "The cashiers at Guthrie's wear slacks and polo shirts. The women in the bakery have on white coats and plastic hairnets. And Miss Kepper shows up in a business suit when it's a hundred degrees outside."

"Ah…Miss Kepper," Andi said. "That woman is a thorn in my side. The brains behind your father without a doubt."

Pete nodded agreement. "She is really a nice person," he assured her. "She wouldn't be involved in this except for him."

"I don't know," Andi said. "She didn't like me on sight. And I wore my very best dress to my job interview."

Pete leaned forward slightly and turned to stare at her. Even in the dim light of the dashboard she could see the surprise in his face.

"Job interview? You had a job interview? With Guthrie Foods?"

"Yeah, about a month and a half ago," she said.

"I never saw your application."

Andi shrugged. "Figures," she said. "It was a part-time position, mostly setting up ads for the paper. I was way over qualified, but she was definitely not impressed."

"You've got experience in advertising? I thought you were like a math teacher or something?"

"A math teacher?" Andi was surprised. "No, no. I still like math, but in college I guess I got bitten by the business bug. I got a summer job as a runner at the Chicago Board of Trade. I just found it incredibly fascinating, so I changed my major."

"You went into advertising?"

"I dabbled in it," she said. "I took an internship on the Miracle Mile, but ultimately I decided that I wanted to run businesses, not just hawk them. So I took a job at Milo Corp and worked myself up to a really nice position as a corporate contributions professional."

"That's a terrific breadth of experience," Pete said.

Andi chuckled humorlessly. "Yes and all that fabulous education and experience has brought me here, to arguing that a piece of red string in my butt crack qualifies as clothing."

He reached over and took her hand. "Don't get discouraged," he said. "Lots of people are on your side, lots of people you don't hear a word from. It's only those who are offended who are making noise. Wait, let me qualify that statement. Those who are offended, plus my dad and Miss Kepper."

Andi laughed.

Walt pulled the truck to a stop at the curb in front of faded, crumbling row houses.

"Mrs. McKenna," Jelly announced.

For a person who could not read or write, she had a fantastic memory. She knew every house on every street they visited and all the clients who lived there.

The two got out and walked to the back of the truck. Walt let down the tailgate and opened the hot food compartment of the delivery cabinet and began retrieving the container with the day's entree and vegetables. He set them on a tray.

Jelly opened a white paper bag which he filled from the adjacent cold food compartment—a half pint of milk, a container of sliced fruit, a couple of pats of butter. From a giant plastic bag a dinner roll was added on top.

"Okay, that will do it for Mrs. McKenna," he said.

"Pop!" Jelly complained. "She is going to want her dessert."

"You could tell her we were robbed and then we could eat it," he teased.

"We don't joke about our job," his daughter said firmly.

"No, we don't," Walt agreed. "We've got a little bit of pudding here to give her."

"That's good," Jelly said. "'Cause I think she eats that first."

Pop made sure both compartment doors were fully closed. Maintaining quality temperature during the food transport was one of the most important aspects of his job. Afterward, he just leaned against the truck and watched his daughter work.

Jelly walked slowly and carefully to Mrs. McKenna's front door. She rang the doorbell and waited patiently for the older lady, getting around on a walker, to answer.

Because the older woman had trouble navigating, she allowed Jelly to walk into her house. His daughter would put the hot food on the table and the cold food in the refrigerator.

A minute later, Jelly, laughing and waving, was on her way back to the truck.

"Mrs. McKenna is silly," she told him enthusiastically. "She's going to hook up reins to her Chihuahua and make her walker into a dogsled. That's very silly."

"Yes it is," Walt agreed, as he headed the truck down the street for their next delivery. He was pretty sure Mrs. McKenna had thought up that story and saved it all morning to tell Jelly.

That had been one of the surprises of bringing his daughter along with him. When the sheltered workshop that she'd attended since high school closed down in the bad economy, Walt had been very concerned. With ordinary people out of work all over town, what would happen to the sudden influx of handicapped people who were hard to place even in boom times? These special people accustomed to daily interaction, useful occupation and paychecks that they'd earned on their own, suddenly found themselves alone at home with nothing to do.

Walt had looked into other workshop situations, but it would have meant moving Jelly out of town and into a group home in a nearby city. The two had talked about it. But he and Ella just couldn't send Jelly away. Then Ella died and Andi came home. After that, Jelly had no interest in going away.

So, he'd decided to take her on deliveries with him. Initially he'd had her stay in the truck. Then he got her to help him get the right meals on the tray. Finally he'd allowed her to go to the doors. He wasn't at all sure how his frequently crabby, occasionally disoriented clients would take to having Jelly as their delivery girl.

They loved her. From the very first day, everyone just treated her wonderfully and seemed delighted to see her.

Of course, Walt loved Jelly and he knew her to be lovable. But the world wasn't usually like that. As an amateur student of human nature, he watched and waited and tried to understand the meaning of the day-to-day reaction.

It took him several weeks, but he finally hit on what he believed to be going on. These people, these older, vulnerable people who were much in need of care from their community and reminded daily of the abilities and faculties slipping away were being given an opportunity to give back. A person who was, in her own way, more vulnerable than they, showed up at their door. By being nice to Jelly, it was as if they could say, "yes, I still have value to this community."

"Mr. Lassiter," Jelly said a few blocks later as they pulled to a stop in front of a modest duplex.

They got out, did their job. They put together the components of the meal. Once more he deliberately forgot the dessert. It was important for Jelly to keep focused on the details. If he didn't make mistakes, she might not watch so carefully.

Mr. Lassiter met her at the door. He was a very tall, very thin man in his mid-eighties. He took his meal from Jelly and gave her some wild animal stickers that had arrived in his junk mail. Jelly was as delighted with his gift as if it had come from a fancy store and cost a fortune.

"I can use these to decorate my picture books," she told the old man. "I love my picture books and I love these pretty animals."

In a few moments they were on their way again.

Down one street, up another, they made their way through Plainview's older neighborhoods, where most of the senior citizens tended to reside.

Jelly was mostly content to watch the houses go by, but sometimes she could be chatty and silly. Walt had grown accustomed to listening to her. And to her repetitive jargon. Walt actually enjoyed it, although he'd been counseled to discourage it.

"It's not good to let her rely on this TV dialogue," the doctor had told him. "She should be forced to communicate in a more conventional manner."

Walt nearly rolled his eyes as he remembered. Conventional communication! This from the medical establishment locked into code words no one else could understand.

Multiple developmental delay.

Atypical skills progress.

Impeded cognitive function.

"My daughter is retarded," he'd stated flatly one day.

"We don't use that word, Mr. Wolkowicz," he was told.

"Why not? It's a good English word that everybody on the street understands."

"It's a pejorative word. Young people use it as a slur."

"Then I want my daughter to get used to hearing it on a kinder level," he said. "We can't stop the world from making noise, but we can all choose to filter it through our best experience."

As he drove through the streets with his daughter, Walt was certain that he and Ella had done the right thing. They had kept her close, protected her from the worst of the world and given her as much freedom and independence as she could manage.

Jelly was their shining accomplishment. Walt was pretty sure that no one from the outside would see it that way. Andi was so smart, so focused, so hardworking. They were both extremely proud of her. But Walt was pretty sure that given any environment, Andi would have thrived. She just had it in her to be an achiever. He was equally certain that if they had allowed Jelly to be hauled off to an institution, she would not have prospered into the young woman at his side.

When they didn't turn on Weymouth Avenue, Jelly voiced a protest.

"Pop! Mrs. Feldheim!"

"Remember," he said. "Mrs. Feldheim isn't there anymore."

"Oh yeah," Jelly said, nodding slowly. "Did she take a

powder?" the young girl asked in a deep voice reminiscent of a tough New York City detective.

Walt masked his chuckle by clearing his throat. "No, she's not dead," he reminded her. "She's gone to live in a nursing home, closer to her children."

"Is that bad or good?" Jelly asked him.

"It's neither, sweetheart, it's just different."

Jelly thought about that for a moment.

"I don't like different," she said.

"I know."

"I wish nothing is ever different."

"Changes can be good," he told her.

She looked at him uncertainly.

"Mom died," Jelly said. "That wasn't good."

"No, it wasn't," he agreed. "But then Andi came home."

Jelly's face immediately brightened into a big smile. "I like Andi," she said.

"Me, too."

"New things are always going to happen, Jelly," he told her. "Some of them will be good, but some of them will be bad. But what we need to try to do is accept the bad and try to find the better parts of it."

Jelly squinted at him, her brow furrowed. "Bad is just bad."

Walt nodded. The gray areas of life were hard enough for typical people to cope with. He wasn't sure he really could make Jelly understand.

"It was very sad and bad for your mom to die," he said. "But we don't cry about it all the time, do we?"

"Mom would want us to live happy," Jelly parroted what she'd been told.

"And how do we do that?" he asked.

"We remember the happy times," Jelly answered. "That's why I have my picture books. So I can remember."

"That's right," Walt said. "We remember the happy times and it helps us live happy. And then new things happen that are happy, like Andi coming home."

Jelly nodded.

Walt knew that if he was ever going to try to speak to her, now would be a very good time.

"I'm thinking of some other new things that will make us happy," he said.

"Okay," Jelly said.

"I know you like my friend, Rachel," he said.

"She's nice."

"Yes, she is," Walt said. "And I want her to spend more time with us."

"Okay."

"I want her to live with us," Walt said. "So we could see her day and night."

Jelly's face clouded over immediately. "She can't have my room."

"No, I wouldn't give her your room," he reassured her.

"If you give her Andi's room, Andi will crowd me."

"I wouldn't give her Andi's room either," Walt said. "She would share my room with me."

Jelly thought about that for a long moment.

"Is she your girlfriend, Pop?"

"Yes, she is."

"Then you need to marry her," Jelly said.

Chapter 16

A COOL FRONT blew into Plainview and with it a drenching rain. That shut down the car wash in a way that the Merchants and Citizens Alliance for Morality never could. Pete's Jungle Jeff Safari binoculars just sat on the windowsill gathering dust as he attempted to concentrate on the ad sheets for next week's paper. It was ridiculous that, in a job market as bad as this one, that he hadn't been able to find some competent person to do this job. Though, since finding out that Andi had been turned away, Pete was fairly sure that others might have been as well. It was in Miss Kepper's authority to do that, but Pete really wished that she hadn't. And he wasn't sure how to change the status quo. If he just walked in and took away some of her responsibilities, it might look like retaliation for her leadership of M-CAM. And when you were the boss, how things looked really made a difference.

He glanced down at his work and sighed. It was fine. It highlighted a few selected items and offered some coupons to those who had an appreciation for them. But it was boring, ordinary, lacking anything that would compel the reader to say, "This is my store. This is where I shop."

The big-box chains had national ad campaigns with catchy jingles or rock era anthems to get stuck in a customer's head. Guthrie Foods couldn't afford more than a Web page and a weekly insert in the local paper. And he felt as if he wasn't even making the best of that.

He stopped what he was doing and pulled the notes he'd made out of his desk.

Make friendliness and familiarity as much of a product in their store as coffee or bread.

How did he do that? How did he convey that?

He'd tried to talk to Harvey about it one morning. Harvey said it was a fine idea. Pete hadn't needed approval, he needed feedback and some ideas about how to implement it. None of that had been forthcoming.

He headed for his little refrigerator to get another bag of Mallomars, but resisted at the last minute. He was trying to cut back.

Out of habit he walked over to the window. The rain was still coming down with intensity. Watering all the summer lawns and garden flowers, but trapping everyone inside houses and buildings full of gray gloom.

Then he noticed a light on in the car wash. Andi was there. She must be doing paperwork or sorting supplies or something. Pete immediately walked across the room. Grabbing an umbrella from the stand he headed out. In the hallway just outside the door, he stopped abruptly, turned around and went back to his desk. He gathered up his ad sheets and his notes about his new store advertising concept, wrapped them in a couple of large plastic bags and went looking for just the help he needed.

As he traversed the puddles in the parking lot, Pete didn't second-guess himself too much. Yes, she'd made it clear that she didn't want to get involved any further with him. People who didn't want to get involved really ought to stay out of close proximity. He had not done that. But then, he was not at all opposed to the idea of being further involved with her. He had made a point of showing his material support for her business and her employees with coffee or sandwiches. And he'd tried to show his personal interest by giving her a ride home. He was hoping to wear down her objections. Maybe their timing wasn't perfect, but time changes. And when Andi felt settled enough, secure enough, through her grief enough to start looking around for a boyfriend, Pete wanted to be standing right in front of her.

But today, this was not about her. This was about him.

He lowered his umbrella as soon as he stepped beneath the overhang. Through the glass he could see Andi inside. She was seated in front of a makeshift table with papers spread across it. A small lamp provided a working light casting a welcoming glow that was like a halo around her.

He tapped on the door glass. She glanced up and smiled. She had such a gorgeous, feminine smile. Pete couldn't imagine how he once thought her to be kind of butch. She waved him in.

"I hope you haven't brought me something to eat," she said. "You are feeding us so well I'm beginning to think that's your method of closing us down. Get us all so fat our customers are repulsed."

Pete laughed. "Guys are almost never repulsed by near-naked women, no matter what their body shape might be."

"You may be right," she said. "But my theory is that I can show a lot less skin when I have less skin to show."

"Actually you can't eat this," he said. "But I was hoping you'd take a look at it."

"Sure." She began stacking her papers, each pile perpendicular to the one beneath it.

"What are you working on?" he asked.

"Ordinances for defining sexually oriented businesses," she said. "Your father is going to come at me with both barrels. I've got to be ready."

Pete nodded sympathetically. "I shouldn't interrupt."

"No, please," she told him. "I'm getting cross-eyed reading all this legalese."

Pete stripped the plastic bags from his rolled-up papers and laid them out on the top of her table.

He didn't say anything. He just let her look at what he'd done. He dragged up a chair and seated himself beside her.

She pointed out a typo which was quickly corrected.

"What do you think?" he asked.

Andi glanced over at him and back at the ad mock-up. "It looks fine, Pete," she told him.

"Exactly," he said. "It looks fine. Boring, unspectacularly fine."

She grinned at him. "Were you hoping for a grocery ad masterpiece?"

He shrugged, his words self-deprecating. "I've been wracking my brain trying to transcend the ordinary. My brain is now completely wracked, so I'm hoping your head has some wrack space."

"Hey, what kind of advice can I offer?" she asked him.

"Add some photos of women in swimsuits and you'll triple your readership."

"Well, there is that, but it's not quite what I was looking for."

He watched her surveying the mock-up. Giving it her complete attention.

"Tell me what you are looking for."

Pete tried. "I've…I've been looking for some kind of new advertising concept," he said. "I know I need to give customers a reason to come to my store, a reason beyond the weekly coupons. My big-box competitors have coupons that are just as good as mine. They can undercut prices. They have national ad campaigns. I'm not sure if *I* were just a guy out there looking for a place to buy bologna and cheese, if *I* would have any good reason to come to Guthrie's."

"That doesn't sound hopeful," Andi said.

"Then just like ten days ago, I stumbled on it," he said. "I just realized what it is that I need to sell, but I don't know how to sell it. I don't know how to express my feelings into some kind of marketable slogan."

"Okay," she said. "Try to explain it to me."

She had turned her attention to him. She was eyeing Pete with the same degree of concentration that she'd used to survey the mock-up. It was intense and dispassionate. Pete felt almost intimidated by the naked vulnerability of exposing his thoughts and feelings to her. He reminded himself that *he* had come to *her.*

"Sunday mornings are, like, the worst," he told her. "Everybody is tired and it feels like we're the only people who have to work and it's just not the best day."

She nodded.

"But this particular Sunday...well, this was *our* Sunday," he said. "It was the Sunday after our Saturday night together."

He could see Andi's guard go up immediately. There was wariness in her eyes. She adjusted her stance, folding her arms across her chest.

"I was just so...I was so happy," he said. "I was happy and relaxed and feeling great. And my employees picked up on that. They were happy and relaxed and feeling great, too. It was contagious. None of them had spent the previous night wearing out the bedsheets with sexy you. But they all began to smile and laugh and be as optimistic and in tune with the world as I was."

Andi said nothing.

"I realized that I could reset the tone of the business," he told her. "I think that I can make Guthrie Foods a sunnier, happier place to work. We're implementing a new cross-training program and I think we can use that to add a sense of camaraderie that maybe we've been missing."

She nodded.

"At Guthrie's we're a family," he said. "We've been a family for eighty years or more. We always talk about that in staff meetings, and it's become nearly a cliché. But what I think we've got is one of those families that doesn't know or like each other that much. Maybe it's time that we become friends."

He allowed Andi to think about that for a moment.

"Making the workplace more fun, creating a sense of closeness, that's very good for employee retention," Andi said. "Although in this economy, I can't imagine you'd have a lot of trouble with turnover."

"We don't," Pete said. "Our resignation rate is the lowest it's been in a decade. But this isn't about keeping our employees. It's about keeping our employees happy. That Sunday, the staff caught the smiling, optimistic bug from me. And I immediately saw them transmitting it to the customers. We had the most consistent customer service we've had in a long time. Far fewer patron problems or complaints. Everybody was glad to be in that building. They were enjoying buying their groceries there."

Andi leaned back in her chair, eyeing him thoughtfully.

"That's what I want to sell," he said. "I want to sell, 'hey, you want to come to Guthrie's because it's not a miserable, boring experience to buy groceries.'"

Andi chuckled. Pete heaved a sigh of relief when he heard it. He was worried that having mentioned the effects of their fabulous hookup, she might just turn off from listening to the rest.

"I don't think 'miserable' and 'boring' are words typically suggested for any advertising slogan," she said.

"Right," he agreed. "And this is where I get stuck. How do I say the positive things that I need to say, without pointing out the negatives of the status quo?"

She took out a pad of paper, tore off a few pieces for him. Pete dug his pen out of his pocket.

"Let's take, like, a minute and write down positive words," she suggested.

They did that. Then they looked at their lists, marked the synonyms, and came up with two that shared large places on each list.

"Friend and home," she said.

Pete chuckled. "That sounds more like your dad's job with the meals on wheels."

Andi laughed, too. "I think we can work with this," she said. "I think we can come up with a slogan that says these two things to people."

Pete liked how she used the word *we. You should have put that one on your positive list, Peterson,* he thought.

"But now we're back to the mock-up," he said. "Even if we have a great slogan, just printing it in big letters on our grocery ad doesn't change a thing."

Andi agreed.

The two sat together silently staring at the mock-up.

"How big do these coupons have to be?" she asked suddenly.

"Huh? How big? I don't think size matters."

"At least in coupons," she said, grinning.

"What!" He laughed, feigning insult. He was sure that her sudden influx of humor meant she had a great idea.

"Why don't we change the ad to be less about groceries and more about people."

"Oooookay," he said, slowly thoughtfully.

"What if part of the ad was a lighthearted look at some of your employees. 'Joe Smith, butcher, wins local bowling tournament.' Or 'Jane Jones, cashier sees youngest of four sons sworn in as Eagle Scout.'"

"Now that's an interesting idea," he said.

"It forces everybody on the staff to pay more attention to each other and it draws the customers into that familiarity. 'Yeah, I know Joe, he's the guy who butterflies those pork chops for me.'"

"Oh, wow. That could be great," Pete agreed.

"You wouldn't have to use your whole page. Just a little portion of news up here, maybe a photo."

Pete was nodding, the synapses in his brain now firing at warp speed. "It would draw people to the ad. Even those who don't clip coupons or look for bargains would stop on this page."

"And it's easily transferable to your Web site," she said. "Those people who get their news from the Web instead of the local paper would have a reason to stop by your site. And if you're going to go to the trouble to put up weekly news, of course you can put up your specials and your printable coupons."

"That's a great idea," he said. "It's an absolutely great idea."

"It makes Guthrie's itself a source of hometown news," Andi said. "None of those national retailers are going to be able to do that."

"Hometown news," Pete repeated, just above a whisper. "Guthrie Foods Hometown Friends."

She nodded. "How about...maybe... Shop at Guthrie's: Wholesome Foods from Hometown Friends."

"That's great!" he said. "That's just exactly what I want to say." He repeated the words aloud.

Andi nodded and laughed. "It is great."

"It's exactly it."

"Exactly."

"Once you hear it, it's so obvious."

They were both laughing, celebrating the success of their collaboration and repeating the words and marveling at how perfect they were in conveying the feeling they wanted. In a rush of certifiable silliness they even tried them in different voices. First a high halting soprano, then low and languid as Barry White, with a thick Polish accent like immigrant grandparents and even as quacky as Donald Duck, the words were good.

In the midst of those buoyant moments, without forethought or agenda, Pete leaned forward and kissed her. It seemed totally reasonable and natural. Yet as soon as their lips touched, it was something more.

A friendly peck instantly turned into total recall of the well-matched passion they'd shared.

"Bad idea," she told him as she wrapped her arms around his neck.

"Sorry, so sorry," he whispered against her throat.

The rain against the windows provided the barest minimum of isolation, but it was enough to make both of them incautious. Pete's brain was fuzzy with testosterone, but still he marveled at how good she was at this. How naturally she seemed to know just how to move her lips against his own.

Within minutes she'd moved from the nearby chair to his lap. He was crazy for her, but not just nuts in general.

"Let's go to my house," he said. "Let me go get the car and we'll go to my house."

"It's the middle of the morning," she pointed out.

"We're making out in front of windows on the busiest corner in Plainview," he countered.

"We shouldn't."

"Maybe not, but let's do it anyhow."

They second-guessed each other through the entire trip. So much so that by they time they made it to the door of his bedroom, neither one could get away with suggestions that they were swept up in the moment or that they didn't know what they were doing. No more excuses of being intoxicated with passion.

He wanted it.

She wanted it.

They did it. And did it. And did it.

Pete's cell phone beeped at him a number of times which he ignored. Finally as they lay exhausted, naked and drenched in sweat, it rang again, He picked it up, glancing at the caller ID. He cleared his throat and then hit the talk button.

"Miss Kepper, is there a problem?"

The problem was that he'd disappeared and hadn't answered his phone for three hours.

"I went out to SuperMart to check out that new display promotion we heard about," he told her. "I locked my keys and my phone in the car. I've been waiting in the rain for a locksmith. I've got to go by the house and get showered and changed. I'll be in the office later."

When he clicked the end button, he tossed the phone back on the floor and rolled over to face the naked woman on the other side of the bed.

"That was a pretty good lie on such short notice."

Pete leaned up on one elbow. "It must be genetic," he said. "I always wondered how my dad could always come up with the most outrageous stories just out of nowhere. I'm now convinced that sexual motivation must be a tremendous spark to creative lying."

She smiled at him. She was gorgeous. Her eyes were heavy-lidded and dreamy. Her pale skin, framed by tan lines, was still flushed with evidence of her last orgasm.

"I could get used to this," she told him.

"I sure hope that you do," he agreed. "Repeat business, that's what I'm all about."

She laughed.

"You know, I never imagined that being in bed with a woman who was laughing was anything but humiliating."

"You're not humiliated?" she said. "What about if I ask for another go, just a quickie. Are you up for that?"

"A shower is about the only thing I'm still up for," he admitted.

But she joined him in the hot water and proved to him that he wasn't completely played out. It was nearly another hour before the two were dressed and headed out to his car.

They were both still laughing and teasing as they left the front porch. They ran arm in arm like silly teenagers. Then, as he held open the passenger door for her, he couldn't resist stealing a kiss.

As he straightened he came eye to eye across a distance of barely twenty yards with his neighbor.

Her expression was so shocked and incredulous, Pete thought to himself, *Jeez lady, have you never seen me bring a woman home?*

Then he realized that she hadn't. In all the years he'd lived there, Andi was the only one.

And with the two of them all kissy and fresh from the shower, it was undoubtedly obvious that it had been a little afternoon delight. Just the kind of thing that set tongues to wag in small towns.

"Afternoon, Mrs. Joffee," he called out. Thankful that the woman could be trusted not to further damage Andi's growing reputation.

It was standing room only in the city council chambers. Walt was glad he'd decided to leave Jelly at home. She did not do well in noisy crowds of people, and if the crowd began verbally attacking Andi, as Walt suspected they would, he was certain his daughter would jump to her twin's defense. Social conflict was difficult to sort out, but for those with intellectual impairments it could sometimes be impossible.

The Merchants and Citizens Alliance for Morality were in attendance, carrying signs and wearing matching T-shirts that declared No Near Nudity In Our Neighborhood! Plenty of others had also squeezed in. Whether they had picked a side or just wanted to see the show was not immediately evident. But the air-conditioning of the old building was not sufficient to cool the tempers of the more strident in the crowd.

Beside him, his smart, clever, beautiful Andi was calm. So deliberately calm, it felt unnatural. He wanted to grab her and hug her. He wanted to protect her. He wanted to lash out at those who were being unfair to her. The padded bumpers inside her crib had once softened any hard knocks from an unwise move. But she was not his little baby anymore. She was a grown-up woman who had to face the consequences of the decisions that she made. She had to stand up for herself. And because he loved her, he would stand beside her.

Walt glanced at the crowd behind him once more and spotted Rachel at the back near the door. Their eyes met and he allowed himself the tiniest of smiles just for the sight of her. She was here for Andi, too. Though his daughter didn't know it.

With the hammer of the gavel and an official notation of the time, Gunderson-Smythe called the meeting to order. Walt was old enough to remember her when the mayor was a gangly teenager with acne and braces. She seemed very self-possessed now and not in the least intimidated by the size of the gathering.

They all stood for the pledge of allegiance. Then the minutes of the last meeting were approved. Before they could move to the first item, Alderman Gensekie requested a change in the agenda.

"It just seems to me, Penny," he said, addressing the mayor by her given name, which sounded to Walt's ears to be slightly misogynist and generally disrespectful. "That most of these good people have come here to be heard on item number four. It behooves us, as public servants, not to waste their time and move that discussion to the beginning of the meeting."

There was a smattering of applause. To which the mayor quickly responded with her gavel.

"There will be no outbursts of any kind in this meeting," she warned. "No clapping. No speaking out. No demonstrations. Any violators will be immediately removed from the room."

Her sternness may have been as much to counter Gensekie's informality as to acquaint those new to the council chambers with the standard rules. The mayor turned to the man at the end of the table with a look that would have withered most in the room.

"Is that a motion, Alderman Gensekie?"

The white-haired man in thick glasses and a seersucker suit, chuckled in a strange, almost sneering, way.

"Sure, if that's the way you want it, Penny," he said. "I so move."

"Second," Hank Guthrie piped in quickly.

The mayor's sigh was almost undetectable. "It has been

moved and seconded that item four on the agenda be moved up for immediate consideration. Do we have discussion?"

The council was silent.

"All in favor?"

"Aye," was the unanimous response.

The mayor snapped down her gavel. "If the clerk will read item four, please."

A short, round woman wearing a snug-fitting business suit and teetering on high heels made her way to the microphone.

"Proposed," she read. "An amendment to City Zoning Code Section 21-4.1. DEFINITIONS. To add 'or any business relying upon prurient interest or directly appealing to prurient interest. Any business whose public presence is salacious or encourages salaciousness.' And to add Section 21-4.8 OTHER. 'Any other shop or business of any kind that council shall deem to be inappropriate in the zone in which it is proposed to open. Said shop or business will be restricted to Zone D2 only and will not be permitted within one thousand feet of any school, church, child-care facility, public building, historic landmark or city park.' Amendment submitted by Alderman Henry Peterson Guthrie, III."

With that the clerk left the podium.

The mayor thanked her. "Do we have a list of citizens to be heard on this issue?"

As the mayor perused the list, there was a bit of a tussle in the crowd and a couple of polite *excuse me's* before young Guthrie appeared at the end of row next to Andi. Her briefcase had been occupying that chair and she'd politely refused it to several people. She immediately put it on the floor, as if she'd been holding the place for him. He smiled at her as he seated himself removing any doubt that the seat was saved for him.

That exchange piqued Walt's interest. Of course, the fellow would be interested in Andi. She was, in Walt's perhaps slightly prejudiced opinion, the brightest, best-looking single girl in town. But the idea that Andi might be interested in him. That was new. Neither of his daughters had had a date in high school. He'd never got to play the protective papa frowning over his newspaper at a pimply swain waiting nervously in his living room. Jelly's only boyfriend was Tony and she testified early on that kissing him was stupid. Andi had never talked of kissing at all. She'd spent all her teenage years in blue jeans or coveralls. And he wasn't deaf to the gossip that she was gay. Despite lack of evidence to the contrary, he'd never quite believed it. He really didn't care. If there was anything a man could learn from having a disabled daughter, it was how to have perspective. Andi had always been a wonderful daughter. Throughout her childhood their family lives had completely revolved around Jelly. If Andi resented the lack of attention, the constant requirement to accede to the needs of others, she never voiced it. But he and Ella had both understood when she took the first chance to get away, and why she chose a college some distance from Plainview and a life's work that would always keep her far away from her hometown.

But she was home now. And she was the first person the mayor called upon to speak. Walt watched her as she made her way to the podium, notes in hand and head held high. She was wearing her sleek, tailored blue dress that she saved for occasions that called for self-confidence. Andi had that tonight in spades. She gave no indication of stress or concern.

There was not one hurried move or clumsy gesture to indicate the height of the stakes. Win or lose, Walt couldn't imagine a prouder moment.

"Mayor Gunderson-Smythe, Aldermen of the Council," she addressed with due deference. "I thank you very much for the opportunity to speak in opposition to Alderman Guthrie's prurient interest amendment."

Walt hid a smile. First one to speak always got to name the discussion. Walt was pretty sure that Hank Guthrie would be more interested in calling this amendment something like "public decency" or a more neutral "restrictive zoning."

He glanced over at Greta Steiner, reporter for the *Plainview Public Observer* who was writing that down. "Prurient interest amendment."

Score one for Andi's side.

Walt listened as Andi made her points. The current zoning ordinance on sexually oriented businesses had served the community admirably well for over forty years. The definition utilized during that time was specific to certain types of businesses that were actively involved in the sale of sexually oriented materials or nude entertainment. Her business was washing cars.

Gensekie began the questioning with a snort that could only be interpreted as skeptical.

"So, young lady, you're trying to convince this council that all you're doing out there on the public street, mostly naked, is washing cars?"

"I'm not 'trying to convince' you," Andi said evenly. "I'm stating as a fact on the record that is exactly what we are doing."

"Most people who wash cars don't choose to do so wearing a skimpy bathing suit," the alderman pointed out.

Andi nodded. "And most gentlemen sitting on this council don't choose to wear a bow tie, sir. But I doubt you would want to infer that alters the type of job you do."

Gensekie's hand immediately went to his throat and he glanced quickly down the table as if noticing for the first time that he was the only man sporting the atypical neckwear.

The man's brow furrowed and his superior grin flattened in anger.

"A bow tie is not a bikini!"

"No sir, it is not," Andi agreed. "So I can assure you that I will not wear one to wash cars."

A ripple of laughter swept through the crowd. The mayor tapped her gavel threateningly. Gensekie's face was beet-red. She had gotten the better of him and he didn't like it.

"Have you no shame, young woman?" he asked, pointing his finger at her accusingly. "You are not fooling anyone. You're little better than a stripper or a prostitute luring young boys into sin!"

"If I am luring anyone into anything," Andi replied evenly, "I'm luring them into driving through our streets in cleaner cars. That could be considered community beautification."

"Miss Wolkowicz," the mayor growled sternly. "You have already made your statement, please limit your response to questions specifically asked."

"Yes, ma'am." Andi nodded politely.

"Alderman Pannello," the mayor said. "I believe you have a few questions."

"Yes, thank you, Your Honor," he replied before turning his attention to Andi.

"The current definition of sexually oriented business

includes various levels of nudity or seminudity," he said. "Are you certain that your mode of dress at this car wash does not constitute seminudity?"

"I am certain it does not," Andi answered. "We are wearing swimsuits. The same swimsuits that can be seen at any public swimming pool in town, at our local lake. The same swimsuits that are worn by teenage girls tanning in their own backyards."

"These suits are commercially produced?"

"Yes, sir," Andi answered. "I have mine here." From within her briefcase she produced the little red thong that she wore. "This is by far the skimpiest of the swimsuits that my employees wear. As you can see, it has sufficient material to cover both the nipples and the genital area."

She carried it up to the council table and set it down in front of Alderman Pannello. He did not look at it at all, but scooted it toward Alderman Brandt.

Brandt picked up the thong bottom and held it up in the air for the audience to view. A rustle of angry disapproval was evident among the M-CAM members.

"Girls may dress like this is California. But they don't go around like this in Plainview!"

"Alderman Brandt!" the mayor chided. "You are out of order. Alderman Pannello, do you have another question?"

"Yes, Your Honor."

"Ms. Wolkowicz, you have not altered this suit in any way?" Pannello asked. "And you purchased it in a traditional retail establishment here in this state?"

Andi nodded. "It was purchased at Joffee's Manhattan Store," she answered. "Located less than a hundred feet from my car wash." Andi glanced back behind her. "I saw Mrs.

Joffee here in the crowd. I'm sure that if the council were interested she might be able to provide numbers on how many of this swimsuit and similiar suits have been purchased here in town. Joffee's has been a successful business in this community because they carry those items that people in Plainview want to buy."

It was a good point and Walt was glad that Andi had gotten the opportunity to make it.

Alderman Houseman brought up the suggestion of screening the area. "It seems that most of the complaints come from the passersby on a public street," he said. "Perhaps a privacy fence around the property."

Andi was deliberately open to the subject.

"If screening us off from the street would be agreeable to the council," she said. "Then I would be willing to do it. However, I do need to point out that the building has been designated for historic preservation. So any architectural additions will require some special exemptions."

The council murmured thoughtfully. Alderman Pannello and Mayor Gunderson-Symthe were nodding.

"Maybe a tall hedge," Houseman suggested.

Hank Guthrie was the last to question her. Though *questioning* wasn't exactly what he did. It might have been better described as inferring. Walt had known Hank virtually all his life. And although the two had never been friends, Walt had never really had a quarrel with the guy. Lately, however, he wasn't too happy with him. Hank had, for some reason, taken a deliberate dislike of Andi. Walt feared it was some kind of payback for something, but he honestly didn't know what. But maybe it wasn't about him, Walt thought as he cast a quick glance toward the younger Guthrie, seated just on the other side of Andi's empty seat. Maybe Hank thought Andi was after his son and didn't like it.

Whatever the reason, Hank Guthrie was sure laying the sarcasm on a little thick for a fellow who could not, in anyone's estimation, cast the first stone.

"Do you allow minors to patronize your business, Ms. Wolkowicz?"

"Our patrons are drivers, Mr. Guthrie," she answered. "People with dirty cars."

"But many of these 'drivers' are young boys of sixteen or seventeen," he said.

"Some may be," she admitted. "Though that age group traditionally doesn't have the pocket money to afford having someone else wash the car."

"Exactly!" he said as if she had just proved his point. "Those young men would not be lined up, spending their school lunch money to have their car washed. They are obviously there for some other reason."

Andi shrugged. "The reasoning of teenage boys has long been a mystery to me," she said. "Why *do* they wear their pants like that?"

There were a couple of titters in the audience but Guthrie ignored them.

"I know exactly why they are there," he stated adamantly.

Andi smiled. "Yes, I have heard that about you, Alderman."

The room exploded. There was laughter, but also anger. He'd goaded Andi into a cheap shot. Yes, Walt thought, the old lecher probably deserved it, but it didn't do anything to make Andi's businesslike, reasonable case.

The mayor pounded the gavel for order. "I will clear the room!" she threatened.

Andi was asked to take a seat, with the stipulation that she might be recalled for further questions. Then followed a long line of citizens wishing to be heard on the subject. Most of them were from the newly formed protest group, expressing fears that ranged from distracted drivers on Grosvenor Avenue causing fender benders to the imminent demise of civilization as we know it.

Many of the speakers, Walt knew personally. Even if he didn't, when they stated their name and address, as required, he felt a sense of community kinship. He suspected it was the same for everyone else as the crowd listened politely, even though some of the finger pointing in Andi's direction was accusatory.

"How can our young girls grow up with self-respect when they see these women debasing themselves for money?"

"Why should our community cater to the lowest common denominator of moral behavior?"

"What do our children learn when they see their mothers, their sisters, prancing around nearly naked?"

Walt spotted Gil, Tiff's ex-husband, in the crowd. He thought that was probably the same question he wanted to ask. But surprisingly, the man kept his seat and kept his thoughts to himself. Walt gave him credit for that. He may disapprove of his wife's work, but he wasn't going to say so in public.

Not all the speakers were negative. There were a couple of old ladies who, surprisingly, declared Andi a godsend.

"I am Olivia Meyer and I live at 411 Whitherbone," an older woman announced, identifying herself. "In my day if a woman showed her knees it was a scandal. Well, it seems to me that the complainers of today must be the children of the fuddy-duddies from back then. If you can't stand the sight of a pretty girl in a bathing suit, then I'd encourage you to avert your eyes while the rest of us get our cars washed without driving all the way out to the interstate, and support a local business in our downtown core."

The final speaker was the last arrival, Pete Guthrie.

He stood and walked to the microphone without a glance toward Andi. He pulled out a small slip of paper, presumably notes and spread it out on the podium.

"I'm Pete Guthrie and I live at 1927 Hartley Row. I am Chief Executive Officer for Guthrie Foods, Inc. and store manager for the site at Grosvenor Avenue at Fifth Street."

Pete was looking at the mayor. Every other person in the building was looking at Hank Guthrie. The man sat stiff and silent. His mouth had thinned into one straight line and his eyes narrowed angrily.

"I want to officially go on record as saying that Guthrie Foods has no objection to the business currently being operated at the corner of Grosvenor and Fifth by Ms. Andrea Wolkowicz," he stated. "For some time now, those of us with downtown retail businesses have been dismayed by the number of empty buildings on the street. The concern is that without more shopping variety along that corridor, we could ultimately become an abandoned downtown area, like many we know in surrounding towns and cities. Since the opening of the Bikini Car Wash, we have seen increased foot traffic and higher sales in our store. Other retailers in the area have also expressed to me anecdotal evidence of the same in their stores.

This is a good thing and I believe it is something that should be encouraged."

He glanced up for a moment, observing the council before returning to his notes once more.

"But despite much of what has been discussed here tonight, the purpose of the amendment being offered is not to judge the value of Ms. Wolkowicz's business. It is to change the definition of the term 'sexually oriented business' from one with very specific parameters, to one so flexible it might best be described as 'I know it when I see it.' The changing of city code is rightly the job of the council and, as I would not want you telling me how to run my grocery, I would not presume to tell you how to run the city."

Again he glanced up and smiled at the seated officials.

"What I do wish to point out," Pete continued. "Is that typically when new statutes are added to city code or existing ones are altered, the businesses currently in operation are not affected. Grandfathering of existing commercial ventures that were permitted prior to the adoption of changes has been the consistent and virtually unanimous policy since the inception of this council in 1834. So I would respectfully wish to point out to you and to the good people of Plainview, that adopting this amendment will not and should not affect continuing operation of the Bikini Car Wash."

Hank Guthrie slammed his fist on the table so hard that everyone in the building, including Mayor Gunderson-Smythe, jumped. Pete did not jump. He didn't even flinch. He gave his father a cool, even look that was not triumphant, but it was fearless.

Chapter 17

WHEN THE CITY COUNCIL voted down Hank Guthrie's amendment, it offered Andi a reprieve. However, even before she'd left the building, the guy told her through clenched teeth that it wasn't over. The next day the protestors were back on the sidewalk as if their lost gambit had never even occurred.

Andi didn't mind. They seemed to attract more customers than they drove away. The insults had grown more infrequent, and as the days lengthened into the longest and hottest of summer, their number dwindled and their fervor lagged. It was hard to be indignant when the sweat ran down your back like a river and your industrial strength antiperspirant was failing.

It was hot for Andi and Tiff and Cher-L, too. But they had the shade of the overhang and the cooling spray of water. The three were getting better and more efficient at the job as days went by. They no longer had lines of customers waiting. But they had steady business and repeat customers. That was the measure of success for Andi. Sure, a lot of folks would pay to ogle the girls and see what all the fuss was about. But if they would come back to get their car washed a second time, then she knew she was well on her way to being not just an oddity, but a service.

About a week and a half after the council meeting, a big windstorm blew in overnight. There were a few tree limbs down in the neighborhood and reports of power outages in the areas along the interstate. When Andi arrived at the car wash, she initially thought everything was fine. But after several strange jokes from her first customers of the day, Tiff showed up with a revelation.

"Have you seen your sign?" she asked with a chuckle of her own.

"My sign?"

"Your banner on the front of the overhang," Tiff answered. "I guess it must have gotten a lot of buffeting last night. Or in-the-buff-ing or something."

Andi walked out to the corner to see what she was talking about. Her sweet little banner, so like ones she'd made for high school math club, had slipped down during the night, revealing a hidden word and hiding ones that were important. The sign that had read:

BIKINI
WASH &
WAX

Now said:

PLAINVIEW
BIKINI
WAX

"I guess we're expanding service in a whole new way," Tiff joked. "Perhaps I can sign up volunteers for in-service training."

Andi laughed and rolled her eyes.

"Now that might put some life back into the Merchants and Citizens Alliance for Morality," she said.

"I'll call Pop and have him bring the ladder down here," she said.

She walked across the hot pavement and inside the building to do just that. While she was on the phone, she heard a car pull up. She assumed it was just another customer and that Tiff would handle it. It was only after she hung up that she turned her attention outside to see Gil McCarin, his car parked on the far side of the overhang, talking to Tiff.

Andi immediately went to her purse and dug her cell phone out of the bottom of it. She flipped it open and hurried outside.

They weren't yelling and Gil had not thrown a blanket around her, but Andi wasn't any less wary.

"I have Officer Mayfield on speed dial," she announced in a tone that she hoped conveyed a real threat. "Tiff, do I need to call him?"

Gil frowned at her, but then turned his attention back to Tiff. "Do you really think I would hurt you?" he asked his ex-wife.

"You *have* hurt me," Tiff answered. "When you gave up on yourself, you gave up on us. I guess that's about the biggest hurt a husband can inflict on a wife."

Andi felt like she was eavesdropping and quickly retreated to the inside of the building. She didn't know that much about the problems between Tiff and Gil, but she knew how much Tiff loved Caleb. And she knew that if Tiff decided that Gil could make custody trouble, she'd be gone in a skinny minute. Andi understood that, of course. The way Andi felt about it was strange. The righteous indignation of the M-CAM members only encouraged her. It made her want to be outrageous. But the reality that her brazen business venture might mean trouble for Tiff and Caleb, really gave her pause.

A gray minivan pulled up under the overhang. Andi hurried out to meet the pudgy guy in plaid Bermuda shorts and offer him an excellent deal on a complete detail.

The guy was only willing to go for a basic wash and wax. Andi took his money and he took a seat on a shady bench, more interested in his book than the women around him in bikinis.

Tiff quickly hurried over to help as Gil drove away.

"Is everything all right?" Andi asked.

She shrugged. "Who knows?" Tiff replied. "He's not yelling, so I guess that's an improvement."

Andi agreed.

Pop showed up a few minutes later. He and Jelly needed to be at the church for meal on wheels by 10:30 a.m., but he brought the ladder and took the time to rehang the banner. It took him only a few minutes, but he was not optimistic about its future prospects.

"Temporary signs are meant to be temporary," he pointed out to Andi. "That one is getting faded and ragged. Don't you think it's about time to invest in a sign painter?"

Andi nodded reluctantly. "I don't know, Pop," she said. "It seems so permanent."

He eyed her skeptically. "Isn't this a permanent business?" he asked.

"Yes…yes, of course it is," she said. "But it's a summer business and…"

"And you're looking toward next summer?"

She nodded. "Who knows what the next summer will bring."

Her father chuckled. "Truth is, Andi," he said. "I think these men would pay to let you girls wash their cars in snow-suits and mukluks."

Andi grinned at her father. "I don't know if you're right about that, Pop."

She was about to get on about her business, when he fore-stalled her.

"Do you think you could take off a little early this evening?" he asked. Andi was surprised at the request. "Sure, probably," she answered.

"I'll have to work it out with Tiff and Cher-L. What's up?"

"I want to take you out to dinner," he said. "Kind of a little family meeting. I want to talk about something."

"O…kay," she said, dragging the word out slowly. "It's not something that you can just tell me?"

"Let me buy you dinner," he said. "I don't remember the last time I took my girls out to a restaurant."

Andi nodded. "Great," she said with feigned enthusiasm. "What time?"

They agreed on eight o'clock. Andi cleared it with Cher-L who agreed to close up for her. Through the rest of the day, Andi was busy. But the surprise invitation had made her curious and concerned. She knew it had to be associated with bad news. Good news just bubbled out of people. It was only the unpalatable that required food and drink. Her speculation ranged from some horrible health issue that Pop had been keeping secret to his being forced to give up volunteering for meals of wheels because of her notoriety. The latter was infuriating. But the former was terrifying. Her mother's rapid, unstoppable decline and death still loomed large in both grief and guilt. If something were to happen to Pop… Andi couldn't even complete the thought. She fearfully recalled all those mysterious appointments he had in the last several months. Nothing…please God!…nothing could happen to Pop.

By the time she got home from work, a little after seven, she wasn't in the best of moods. And the first thing she saw, when she went upstairs to shower, was Jelly in the dress she'd worn for their mother's funeral.

"Take that off right now!" Andi snapped at her sister.

Jelly, who'd been smiling at her own image in the mirror, was caught off guard by the sudden, unexpected vehemence directed at her. Her face clouded over. It looked at first like she might cry, but instead she set her jaw obstinately.

"You are not the boss of me!" Jelly insisted. "Pop said to dress nice and this is my nicest dress. I never get to wear it."

Andi deliberately modulated her tone. "It's just not the right dress to wear to a restaurant," she said.

Jelly didn't believe her. "Grown-up women wear black dresses to dinner," she said. "I am a grown-up woman."

"Yes, you are," Andi agreed. "But I don't think…" She trailed off, but then focused on a new direction. "Would you like to wear my designer dress?"

Jelly's eyes narrowed and she looked at her skeptically. "Why would I wear a diner dress to a restaurant?"

"Not diner, designer," Andi corrected. "My blue dress, you know, the one that I wear for special occasions."

Jelly's eyes opened wide and her jaw dropped. "You would let me wear your blue dress?" she whispered.

"Yes I would," Andi answered.

Jelly's anger was completely forgotten as she followed Andi into her room. She was giggling and excited as Andi pulled the Escada out of her closet and removed its protective plastic cover. Andi gave it only the most casual of glances before handing it over to Jelly. It was a symbol, she thought, of how far she'd come. The dress was everything grand and hopeful and ambitious that she'd planned for herself. And now it was a hand-me-down for her sister.

Andi rushed through her shower and makeup. Deciding after a couple of attempts with the curling iron just to pile her hair on top of her head and call it a style. Thanks to the car wash her skin was now attractively tan and her arms amazingly buff. So the simple, cool sundress she chose looked fabulous and with a pair of perilously high strappy slides, it was dressy enough for any place in Plainview.

When she went downstairs, Jelly was giggly and excited and ready to go. Pop, on the other hand, seemed nervous. He was dressed in his very familiar, utilized-once-weekly suit, but his crisp white shirt was brand-new, as was his tie. The tie, with blue variegated lines atop a pewter-colored background really freshened up his traditional Sunday gray. Andi was surprised to see her father looking so sharp, almost fashionable.

"You look great, Pop," she told him. "So where are we headed?"

"Delmonico's."

Delmonico Prima Vera, known by locals as simply Delmonico's, was located on the side of a hill near Mt. Ridley Park. The only place more fancy or expensive was the country club and anyone who'd ever eaten there concluded that Delmonico's served better food.

Pop ignored the optional valet parking and found a space for his old white truck near the far edge of the lot. They walked the distance with Jelly managing to hold up all ends of the conversation on her own.

"I look really nice in Andi's blue dress and I get to go to a fancy restaurant because I have good manners 'cause I never eat with my fingers or blow bubbles in my drink like Tony Giolecki does. I don't wear high heels because I could fall over and break my leg. Andi doesn't mind if she breaks her leg 'cause she doesn't have to carry meals to people's houses, but I do and I couldn't if I had to be on crutches the way Mrs. Pietras was after she had the operation on her foot."

Andi listened absently and glanced over at her father occasionally. His thoughts appeared a million miles away.

When they stepped up to the desk of the hostess she asked if they had reservations.

"Yes," Pop answered. "Wolkowicz. I'm supposed to have the small private deck at eight o'clock."

"Yes, sir," the young woman said, smiling at him very broadly. "If you'll follow me."

Andi had only been in the restaurant a couple of times and she'd always eaten in the main dining area. They were led upstairs and down a hallway into a corner room that had floor-to-ceiling windows on two sides. The view of Mt. Ridley, and their pleasant little small town, was magnificent. In the center of the room was a table for six with snowy white linens and an abundance of very breakable-looking stemware.

"Jelly, you're going to need to be very careful," Andi warned.

Her sister nodded, eyeing the elegant table decor with great trepidation as if it were set with explosives able go off with one false move.

"So, what's the deal, Pop?" Andi asked. "Did you win the lottery?"

"No, but I do hope it will be…well, a bit of a celebration."

Celebration, Andi thought. Nobody, not even Pop, would announce some dreaded disease like a celebration.

"The chef helped me to select the wine when I came in on Monday," Pop told the waiter.

"Yes, sir," he answered. "Would you like me to serve it now or wait for the rest of your party?"

"The rest of our party?" Andi asked.

Before the question could be answered, the hallway door swung open once more and three well-dressed strangers were ushered in.

No, Andi thought. They weren't strangers, she recognized all three. And Jelly did, too.

"Mrs. Joffee!" she said, excitedly. "Andi let me wear her blue dress, don't I look really nice?"

"Yes, you look very nice," Mrs. Joffee answered.

"Rachel," Pop interjected. "This is my other daughter, Andrea."

"Yes, of course."

The dainty little woman took Andi's hand and smiled up at her.

"And you probably know my boys, as well," she said. "Andrea, Angela. This is Dave and Seth."

She politely shook hands with the Joffee brothers.

"You can call me Jelly," her sister told them. "That's what everybody calls me, so you can call me that, too."

"I remember you from school," Seth said.

Jelly nodded. "So are you the fall guy?" she asked him. "Your brother will be out on parole in three to five, but you'll be making license plates until your reservations in hell."

"I beg your pardon."

"Oh, Jelly is just playing around," Pop interjected quickly. "I'm Walter Wolkowicz," he told the guys as they shook hands.

"Mr. Wolkowicz," Dave acknowledged.

"Please, call me Walt," he said.

All six of them stood together for a long moment, everyone smiling falsely bright. Andrea had a pretty good idea what this must be about and she wished her father hadn't sprung it on her as a surprise.

"Why don't we all sit down," Pop suggested. "I'll get the waiter to bring us a cool glass of white wine. Does that sound good, Rachel?"

"Yes, lovely," she said.

As Pop stepped out of the room, Mrs. Joffee glanced around at them all again.

"Come, let's sit," she said, taking Jelly's hand before Andi even thought to reach for it.

She took a seat at the end of the table, with Jelly across the corner from her. As Jelly frequently required a little help at restaurants and this one was unfamiliar, Andi knew she needed to be close. She sat down beside her sister. The Joffee brothers sat opposite them.

Pop returned with two waiters and a couple of bottles of wine.

"I didn't ask you boys if you want a cocktail," Pop said. "I'm sure they can make anything here at the bar."

"A glass of wine is fine," Dave said. Seth nodded agreement.

"What about you, Andi? Is wine okay?"

"Fine," she answered, reminding herself that she needed to keep her wits about her.

"I don't drink wine," Jelly said. "It stinks funny and it's really gross if you think like Father Blognick that it is blood. I'll have a Scotch, neat, the way Jack McCoy drinks it."

"I don't think so, Jelly," Pop said quietly. "Would you fill her wine glass with water, please. So she can toast with us."

The waiter quickly did as he was bid.

"We're going to have toast," Jelly said, sounding disappointed. "I thought we might at least get a hamburger or something."

"It's not toast like a breakfast," Andi assured her, sotto voce. "It's a toast like...well...like a pep rally or something."

"A pep rally?" Jelly looked incredulous.

Andi felt exactly that way.

Her father stood. "Rachel and I weren't exactly sure how to bring this up," he began.

"Then maybe you shouldn't," Andi interrupted. She glanced around quickly, embarrassed for her father and for herself. He was such a nice guy and he always tried to do the right thing, but recruiting the Joffees into her camp was just unnecessary. "This was very nice, Pop, to try to line up support for me from one of the most influential downtown businesses, but really, it's not that big a deal. Any support is always appreciated, but I don't think we to need to…to twist any arms over this. I have a legal right to run my business. I'm going to fight for that right and I believe that's the end of it."

"We're okay with you running the car wash," Seth told her. "We don't see any downside with it. And our foot traffic has improved."

His brother, Dave, agreed. "I think this meeting must be about the property itself." He turned to Pop. "I heard recently how Hank Guthrie welched on the sale." Dave then glanced toward his mother at the other end of the table. "Are you now thinking to buy that corner, Mama?"

Mrs. Joffee didn't immediately answer, but looked over at Walt for a moment. He shrugged and sighed heavily. She stood and walked around the table to stand beside him.

"This is not about you, Andi," Pop said. He looked over at the young men on the other side of the table. "And it's not about you, either, or about property."

"Is it about me?" Jelly asked.

"No," Pop answered. "Though you are going to be one of the people most affected."

He glanced down at Mrs. Joffee again and then smiled at her before he cleared his throat.

"Rachel has done me the honor of agreeing to be my wife," he said. "We're going to be married."

There was a moment of completely stunned silence around the table.

"For real?" Jelly asked, loudly and enthusiastically.

Andi was thinking the same thing, but without her sister's joyous optimism.

"Yes," Pop answered. "It's for real."

"And you'll be my new mom?" she asked Mrs. Joffee.

"I'll be your stepmom," Rachel answered. "Your mother will always be your mother, but I want to love you and be a part of your life."

"Cool," Jelly said.

"Hold on, hold on," Dave said. "This is…this is surprising and…unexpected. We haven't talked about this at all. Are you two sure you've thought this through?"

"Oh, yes," Pop said. "We've thought it through."

"We've thought it through and thought it through and talked it to death," Rachel added with a light laugh that had Pop joining in.

"How could you have thought it through that much?" Andi asked. "Mom has only been dead for six months."

"It's almost ten months," Pop corrected her. "And we're going to wait a full year out of respect before we make it official."

"Oh, well then, if you're waiting a full year that's fine," Andi said, her tone heavily laced with sarcasm. "Grass isn't even growing atop her grave yet, but you certainly can't let any grow under your feet."

She wasn't the only one who had a problem with their engagement. Seth Joffee's tone was heavily laden with sarcasm. "Uh, Mama, in case you haven't noticed, this guy is not Jewish."

"Yeah," his brother agreed. "Don't tell me you're planning to become a Catholic?"

"We're each keeping our own religion," Rachel said. "We

respect each other's beliefs. And since our children are already grown, there won't be any sticky decisions about how to raise the kids."

"This is just too fast," Andi said. "You hardly even know each other. How long can you two have been seeing each other? A few weeks, a month?"

"And let's be clear about this for sure, Mr. Wolkowicz," Dave said. "If you're thinking that you've hit the jackpot with a rich widow, let me assure you that we will insist on a very strict prenup. You won't take anything from this marriage beyond what you bring into it."

"Pop's not like that," Andi defended. "He doesn't care about money. He's just lonely." She turned her attention back to her father. "Pop, I know you miss Mom. But you can't just jump right back into marriage with the first woman who makes eyes at you."

"My mother doesn't 'make eyes' at anyone."

"Well, I doubt they met over bingo in the recreation hall at St. Hyacinth's."

They were all talking at once and the level of discourse got louder and louder.

Suddenly Jelly covered her ears and cut through the noise.

"HAVE YOU PEOPLE GOT A PROBLEM OR SOME-THING?"

There was a moment of stunned silence before Jelly added, "Let Pop and Mrs. Joffee talk. They are the ones who are getting married."

The obvious logic of her mentally handicapped sister's words caught them all up short.

"Thank you, Jelly," Pop said. "Rachel and I will answer all

of your questions, or at least all of them that we think you have any right to know."

Rachel smiled, appreciating his humor.

"This isn't some whirlwind courtship," she said. "We've known each other almost our whole lives."

"And," Pop added. "We've been in love with each other for over forty years."

"What?" a chorus of three potential stepsiblings asked in horrified unison.

"Rachel and I fell in love in high school," he said, with a confirming glance toward her. "Our families, our religious communities were completely opposed. We wanted nothing more from life than to just be together. But we allowed our parents to talk us out of it. Believe me when I tell you that we have no intention of allowing our children to do the same."

Rachel nodded. "When we told our parents, we did it separately. I told mine, Walt told his. They would never even agree to meet each other. So we decided that we'd make our families sit down together before we even spoke a word."

"It's important to us that our children approve," Pop said. "But we want to make it clear, this is our decision and we've already made it."

A stark finality of silence settled around the table. Andi glanced at the two thirtysomething guys across the table from her. Their expressions reflected much of what she was feeling.

"So you two have...have..." Seth was loath to say it, but managed to get it out. "You two have been...uh...*close* all this time?"

"No we have not," Rachel answered her son, sternly. "We

made our commitments and we honored them. We never tried to see each other, we never even spoke until we were both free."

"And so you flew from Mom's funeral straight into her arms," Andi accused.

"Andrea, there is no need for that tone," Pop said. "Ella knew all about us. She was there. We were a foursome. Rachel and I and Ella and Paul."

"Paul?"

"Paul Gillette," Pop answered. "My best friend and the love of your mother's life. He was killed in Vietnam in 1969."

Andi felt as if the bottom had just dropped out of her world and she was suspended in dangerously frightening midair.

"Ella and I were both suffering broken hearts," Pop said. "It's what brought us together and we made the best of it."

"You made the best of it?"

He nodded. "We had a full life with a happy marriage with wonderful children. Neither of us wasted a lot of time wishing it were different."

"You children can never understand what it was like for us," Rachel said. Addressing her sons she added, "Your grandparents lost family and friends in the concentration camps in Poland. That I would give up our heritage and marry a Pole was more than they could bear. And I couldn't bear to hurt them. I grew to love your father, just like my parents said I would. I regret nothing in the past. But I would regret not taking hold of our future."

"Irv was an honest, decent man," Pop said. "I don't need to tell you boys that. Because I loved Rachel, I wanted her to be happy. And I am grateful that she was." The two shared a smile. "And as for my Ella," he continued looking at Andi. "I have no doubt she would be happy to see us together at last."

Andi couldn't argue. She didn't know what to argue. She couldn't claim to know her mother better than Pop did. It had become completely clear to her that she did not know either of her parents at all.

"So, if there are not any more immediate questions…" He let the words hang out there in the silence for a moment. "Pass your mother's glass down this way, David, I'd like to propose a toast."

The piece of crystal was handed down the table and she held it daintily by the stem.

Pop raised his toward her. "To my beautiful Rachel, whom I have loved so long. I wish to spend every day of the rest of my life with you."

She smiled at him, her eyes glowing with admiration. "And to our two families," she added. "Very soon to be one."

Jelly cheered and gulped down her water. Pop and Rachel eagerly brought the wine to their lips. The two Joffee brothers drank as well, though a bit reluctantly.

Andi gazed at her glass as if it contained poison, but she did manage to choke down a sip.

Jelly decided it was necessary to convene a grand jury. Since Jack McCoy was not available, she took on the role of prosecutor herself. She lined up all her dolls and stuffed animals in rows, poised for attention. Then she carefully explained the gravity of the situation to Happy Bear, Quaky Duck, Baby Dimples and the rest assembled.

"Andi was mad and Mrs. Joffee's sons were mad and it was like nobody was happy for them but me," she explained.

Her words were acknowledged with complete silence in the Jury Room, located on the floor space between her bed and the closet.

"I think it will be great to have Mrs. Joffee as my new mom. My stepmom she calls it. I will never step on her, of course. But that's something Andi might do."

Still the jurors were uncommitted.

"I have a picture book I'd like to put into evidence," Jelly announced.

She opened the creaky, old photo album that had so many photos of her mother in high school. Jelly flipped through until she came to the ones with the prom. She held the book up and pointed out to the assembly one particular photo.

"See this one," she said. "I thought this girl looked familiar. It's because she is Mrs. Joffee. And Pop is kissing her. So he must love her. I rest my case."

Chapter 18

THE FIRST STOREWIDE cross-training at Guthrie Foods went pretty well, Pete thought. There had been only minimal bellyaching as they started out. There were cashiers who didn't want to stock. And there were ham-handed meat clerks who just couldn't get the right buttons on the registers. But Pete presented the exercise as a great adventure for the employees and a way to learn how to appreciate each other. His upbeat attitude continued to be contagious and he thought it had gone very well.

As he neared nine o'clock, he was eager to pick up Andi and tell her everything that had happened. That had become the best part of his day. He stored up incidents he wanted to share with her. And he listened eagerly to what she had to tell him.

"I've never talked so much in my life," he'd told her one night as they lay in his bed together in the aftermath of intimacy. "It's crazy. Minx and I needed to deliberately try to have conversations. The only spontaneous ones we ever had were arguments. But with you, I just never seem to run out of things to say."

"Yeah, most of my exes weren't big on talking either," she admitted. "But you, heck I practically have to stick a boob in your mouth to shut you up."

"Well, okay, I'll go for that!"

They laughed and joked and made love and Pete was convinced that he had never had it so good.

So he was humming happily to himself as he left Guthrie's and walked out to his car. He loved his job. He loved his life. He loved Andi. He hadn't told her yet, but he didn't think it was going to be a big surprise. Maybe it was too soon to say so. If he rushed it, he might scare her off or she might doubt his sincerity. Timing was important. Just like in business or baseball, if your timing was off, well, it might not be fatal, but it could be a lot harder.

With that on his mind, something seemed strange when he pulled into the car wash. He saw a figure retreating hurriedly into the building. The vehicle under the overhang, an oversize Cadillac SUV, peeled out noisily and barreled down the street. Pete pulled his sedan into the spot just emptied. There was no light on in the building, but he saw shadows of the person who'd just gone inside. Something was wrong.

He put his car in Park and stepped outside. He knocked on the glass door.

"Andi?" he called out.

There was no answer. He grasped the doorknob and it turned. He took one step inside.

"Andi?" he called out again.

"She's not here," came the answer. The voice was gruff and choked, but still familiar.

"Cher-L?"

"Uh-huh."

"It's Pete Guthrie," he said. "What are you doing in here with the light off."

He immediately reached for the switch.

As soon as the light came on, she slid down on the floor behind the desk.

"No please, I don't want anyone to see me."

Pete ignored that. He walked around the desk to where she was crouched down, hiding her face in her hands.

He squatted down in front of her. "Cher-L," he asked quietly. "Are you all right?"

"I'm fine. I'm fine," she said as she dropped her hands to her lap. But she didn't look fine. She looked terrible. Her lipstick was smeared along her jaw. And the remains of brilliant black eye makeup had coursed down her cheeks in long black streaks.

"What happened?"

"Nothing."

"Then why have you been crying?"

She didn't deny it. "I just...I just..." The answer trailed off unspoken.

"Did somebody hurt you? Did one of the customers hurt you?"

"No! No!" she answered quickly, but then dissolved into tears once more.

She'd covered herself with some kind of black fringe shawl and she tried rather unsuccessfully to wipe her eyes on it.

Failing that, she used her forearm, as her right hand continued to be clutched into a tight fist.

Pete glanced around and spied a box of tissue on the desk
and handed it to her.

She offered a tearful thank-you just above a whisper.

He remembered her in his office, crying. Then he'd been
able to just walk away and let Miss Kepper handle it. He sure
wished the old lady was here right now.

"Do you want me to call Andi?" he asked.

Cher-L's eyes went wide with fear. "Oh no, please don't
call her. Please don't. She'll fire me for sure. Please, I just can't
get fired today. Please."

Tears were coursing down her cheeks again, but she
denied them.

"I'm fine, really I'm fine. Just go. I'm fine."

Leaving was exactly what Pete wanted to do. "Well, if
you're sure you're all right," he said.

She nodded rapidly. "I'm okay," she assured him. "I'll get
myself together and I'll go home. I'm okay."

"Do you want me to give you a ride?"

"Oh no, absolutely not. You go on. I'll be fine."

"Are you sure?"

She waved him away. "Go. Just go."

That was exactly what he wanted to do. He walked out the
front door and around his car. Maybe he'd stop by Andi's
house. He really wanted to see Andi. And maybe they'd both
come back and make sure Cher-L was okay. But no, Cher-L
didn't want Andi to know anything about this…whatever it
was. She said it would get her fired. What could have
happened to make her cry and also get her fired?

He sat down in his car. He had one hand on the steering wheel and the other on the ignition. But he never turned it over. He couldn't.

Pete got out of the car and went back into the building. When he opened the door, he could hear her sobbing harder than when he'd left.

He'd never had a sister and he'd hardly known his ex-wife. But he was sure that if Andi were crying, she'd want a friend to sit beside her.

So that's what he did. He slid his back down the wall and sat next to her on the floor. He just sat there. He didn't try to put an arm around her or pat her hand or touch her in any way. He was pretty sure that Cher-L would be quick to misinterpret such a gesture. Pete just sat there, listening to her. Not asking questions. Not offering comfort. Just making sure she wasn't alone.

She quit trying to hold back. She poured out all the wordless sadness and misery and shame that had dogged her since adolescence. And Pete sat silently as she let it go.

When she was down to sniffs and hiccups, Pete finally spoke. "What happened?"

"Nothing," she answered.

"Something," he disagreed.

Her whole body trembled with the effort to release the truth she wanted to hold back.

"The worst thing that has ever happened," she said. Then after a moment she disputed herself. "The same thing that always happens."

Pete took that in with as open a mind as he could manage.

"Tell me," he said.

"It was Micky Sveck," she said.

"Who?"

"Micky Sveck. The guy who owns The Horny Toad."

"Oh, that guy," Pete said, recalling a short, beefy guy always seen with an expensive suit and a cheap girl.

"He…he came by here several times and he talked to me about dancing at his club," Cher-L said. "I was, like, really flattered, because that must have meant that he thought I was really gorgeous and sexy and all that."

Pete mentally raised an eyebrow. He'd been to The Horny Toad a few times in his life and it was his considered opinion that gorgeous, sexy, even attractive women were in very short supply. He didn't say that to Cher-L. He just listened as she continued.

"So he came by again this afternoon and told me that he wanted to hire me, but I needed to audition. I told him I was closing up at nine and he said he'd come by to pick me up."

Cher-L shot a glance at him and then shook her head, as if disgusted with her own naivete. "I thought we'd go to the club and maybe it was like amateur night. I've been working up a routine to do on stage. Then he shows up and says I need to prove I can do a lap dance cause that's where the money is made. I was just trying to show him that I could be sexy. Then it went too far and I couldn't seem to figure out how to stop." She closed her eyes and then as if the memory was too vivid that way, she opened them quickly. She looked over at Pete, pleading for understanding. "I don't know why I did it. It's not like I wanted to. I don't even like him. And he's ugly and sweaty."

She began crying again. This time much more quietly which somehow made the pain deeper.

"Cher-L, we all make mistakes," Pete said. "If you asked for a show of hands in this town of who's slept with somebody they shouldn't have, maybe the only person without a hand up would be Father Blognick, and I'm not even that sure of him."

"You're exaggerating."

"Maybe a little," he admitted. "But lots of us have messed up more than once. I guess that makes up for those folks who never do at all."

Cher-L shook her head. "Tommy Gilhoolly was a mistake. DeRoy Crandall was a mistake. Micky Sveck, was a lot more." She held out her hand and opened the fist that she'd held so tightly closed. Inside was a crumpled wad of green paper bearing the image of Andrew Jackson. "He paid me twenty dollars." Her words were quiet. "That's what he saw me as, a twenty-dollar whore."

She let the bill slip out of her hand and then covered her face as if she couldn't bear for Pete to look at her.

How did this happen? he wondered. How could someone so young get so completely off on the wrong foot in the world? Maybe he should never have fired her? he thought.

Peterson, don't go there, he warned himself. *You didn't cause this. But maybe you can figure out a way to help her out.*

He gave himself a couple of minutes to work it out in his head. He checked his wallet and retrieved all four twenties that he found there.

"Cher-L, listen to me," he said, decisively. "I need you to be proactive about this."

"Proactive?"

"You need to take control," he clarified. "Tonight Micky

had all the control, but you've got to change that. And you are the only one who can."

He held the four twenties up so she could see them. They varied in age and wrinkles. He threw them on the floor with the one she'd got from Micky and quickly swished them all around so neither of them could tell one from the other. He picked up the stack of bills and handed them to her.

"Tomorrow morning, I want you to go into the doctor and get yourself checked out," he said. "This guy could have some disease and if he gave it to you, you need to catch it right away. This money should pay for your doctor's visit."

"You shouldn't have to give me money," Cher-L said.

"I'm not giving you money," Pete answered. "That's what Micky did. I'm making an investment in a person, a friend, who I believe in. A friend I have respect for. But, Cher-L, you're going to have to start having some respect for yourself. Promise me that you'll take this money and go to the doctor."

"I will," she said.

"And I promise you that no one will ever hear a word about this from me," he said. "What I know about you is that you are pretty and funny and flirty. You have a wonderful laugh. And Andi tells me that you're very competent with the money and the paperwork. And that you're just as friendly to the old geezers who show up here as the young bucks. Those are good things about you, Cher-L. It's time to start putting the bad things behind you and start building on what is good."

She swallowed hard. "It's easy for you to say. People like you and Andi just never screw up like I do."

He raised a skeptical eyebrow. "You don't count a failed marriage? Mine was a pretty big screwup."

She shrugged. "Okay, maybe that," she admitted. "But Andi is practically perfect. And she's just *so* lucky."

The younger woman's tone was surprisingly rife with envy and more than a little resentment.

"Lucky?" Pete asked rhetorically and then shook his head. "Not so much," he answered. "She has a father who barely managed to scrape together a living, a sister who is mentally handicapped and needed all the attention in the family, a mom who died too young and now a business that half the community is opposed to. If Andi is 'practically perfect', she's made herself that way by sheer willpower alone."

"You like her, don't you?"

He nodded. "I do like her," he said. "And I admire her. She's smart and creative and not afraid of what other people think of her. I see those same qualities in you, Cher-L. Why do you think I hired you to work for me? It wasn't because there was no one else. And it certainly wasn't because you gave the appearance of being just a cookie-cutter employee."

Cher-L choked out a laugh. It was the first real evidence of her dark clouds lifting.

"That was your mistake," she said. "Cookie cutter is part of the bakery's job description."

A spattering of gravel hit the glass of Andi's bedroom window. It didn't wake her. She wasn't asleep. After the surprise engagement dinner, her mind was racing.

She'd managed to get through the meal without screaming, throwing anything or stomping out in a huff. All three actions had been distinct possibilities.

One action that had not been possible was eating dinner. Sitting in the best restaurant in town and she couldn't even choke down the walnut-and-endive salad she ordered. It looked beautiful and smelled even better, but her stomach was tied up in knots.

Jelly had no such problem. She cheerfully ate and chatted and celebrated.

"I've never had a brother before and now I have two!"

Mrs. Joffee's sons looked as unhappy about that as Andi felt. It was crazy and no amount of wine, prime rib and crème brûlée would make it less so.

After what seemed like hours of conversational torture, they finally made it back home. Andi held her questions until Jelly headed up to bed, but she could remain silent no longer.

"I don't understand this, Pop," she said. "I don't understand this at all."

She followed her father into the kitchen. He got himself a glass of water from the tap.

"It's not really all that complicated," he told her. "We love each other and we want to get married. Oh, I'm not imagining that everybody in town is going to think it's the best idea since sliced bread. Father Blognick is sure to give me a few choice words. I don't know if they're as gossipy at the synagogue as they are at St. Hyacinth's, but I suspect Rachel's rabbi and his congregation may not take it any better. But she and I are clear. It's not about them. It's about us."

"Am I included in that 'us' equation or are the children of your 'marriage of convenience' not that important anymore?"

Pop's brow furrowed and gave her a look very familiar to her childhood memories of disobedience.

"Andrea Katrine!" he scolded. "I expect better than that from you."

Andi was duly chagrined.

"Sorry, Pop," she said. "But I…I feel like my whole life has been turned upside down. I always thought you and Mom had a perfect marriage and now I find out you never loved each other. You were both in love with other people."

"I did love your mother and she did love me," he insisted. "There are different kinds of love. For us it was just different."

Andi nodded unconvinced. "The kicker to that, Pop, is that different means inferior."

"No, it does not," he said. "Different is just that, different. Think of you and Jelly."

"What about us?"

"Which one of my daughters do you think I love?" Pop asked. "You, Andi, I've urged to flight. Go out, discover the world, find yourself. I've cheered on as you left home. I let you build a life in Chicago that had nothing to do with me. And when you threw it away to come home, I gladly welcomed you in. I've stood beside you as you've made choices and I've let you make them, even when I didn't agree. That's all proof that I love you."

"I never doubted that you love me, Pop," Andi said.

"So what about Jelly?" he asked. "I have kept her at home with me from the very first. There were people who thought she should go away to an institution when she was just a toddler. I wouldn't let her go. She's never been out on her own. Never given a chance to make a life away from me. I never let her drive. Never encouraged her to date. When her sheltered workshop closed, I could have allowed her to move into a group home in another city far away, but instead I took her to work with me, made her my assistant on a volunteer job. And that's proof that I love her."

He put both hands on the kitchen table and leaned forward.

"So let me repeat the question," he said. "Which of my daughters do I love?"

Andi just looked at him. There was no need to answer. Of course he loved them both.

"I loved Rachel, so I had to let her go," he said.

He pulled out a kitchen chair and seated himself. Andi followed his lead.

"I don't know if you've ever had your heart broken," he said. "As your pop, I really hope not. Because it is awful. The pain was so fresh at first that I couldn't bear to be in the same town with her. I couldn't stand by and watch her marry another man. I joined the army as an escape." He closed his eyes and swallowed hard. "Paul and Ella, all they wanted was to get married and live happily ever after. But they loved me. So Ella waited and Paul followed me into the service to keep an eye on me." He shook his head. "That didn't work, of course. I got sent to Germany and he went to Vietnam. I can't tell you the guilt I felt when he was killed. It was partly penance that brought me home to face your mother. I wanted her to revile me, hit me, to tell me how much she hated me for tearing her apart from the man she loved. But that's not what happened. We shared our grief and we opened our hearts."

"You said you married to make the best of it," Andi pointed out.

Pop nodded. "We did. Maybe we could have just stayed friends. Maybe our hearts would have healed and we would have both found other people. But I don't think either of us were ever much into maybes. We enjoyed our life together. We were blessed by you two wonderful girls. I have no regrets. And Ella certainly never expressed any."

A long silence ensued at the kitchen table. Andi still felt sick and scared and somehow guilty. Should she let Pop enjoy the happiness he'd found? Did she owe it to her mother's memory to make things as tough on him as she knew how?

"I just wish you would take this slow, Pop," she said. "You and Mrs. Joffee, you've both changed. You're different people than you were in high school. How can you be sure that it will work out for you two?"

Pop chuckled lightly. "Andi, there are no guarantees. Surely you've learned that already," he said. "Love does sometimes fade. Marriages do go bad. But life is short. It's also dangerous and complicated. None of us can risk letting something go that might be so very good."

Andi thought about Pop's words again as another smattering of gravel hit her bedroom window. She got up and walked over to peer outside.

Pete was standing in the driveway. He waved to her and then called out in a loud whisper. "May Andi come out and play?"

She quickly put on some shorts and a T-shirt. She carried her sneakers down the stairs. He met her at the front door with a kiss.

"Sorry about waking you up," Pete said. "But I missed you."

"You've got it bad, Grocery-boy," she said.

"I do," he admitted. "Truly, I do."

Andi sat down on the steps and pulled on her shoes. Pete took the opportunity to slide his hands along her body.

"Let's run," she said.

"Run? That was not exactly the exercise I was thinking about," he admitted.

She playfully slapped away his hands. "Run first, sex later."

They headed down Jubal Street toward's 12th. The heat of the day had been whisked away by a soft steady breeze. Except for crossing Grosvenor, the streets were mostly empty. She followed her usual path through the neighborhood and toward the track. The movement. The rhythm. The breathing. She needed it. She needed it to help her let the rest of things go. To let it all go. All the worries over the business. All her concerns about Tiff and Cher-L. All the unsettling information about her parents. Just her feet hitting the pavement one step after another, somehow that made it all better. And to have Pete beside her, that was best of all.

She noticed however, after only a few moments, that Pete was no longer beside her. He fell behind and she realized that he was farther and farther back. Finally when she reached the sidewalk at City Park, she pulled to a stop allowing him to catch up.

"What's the deal? You usually set the pace. Have you got a cramp?"

He shrugged. "I just don't run that well in my loafers."

"Oh gosh!" Andi said, looking down at his feet. "I guess I didn't notice you are still in your store clothes."

He laughed. "Yeah, the tassels on these loafers were never meant to fly."

Andi was shaking her head in disbelief. "I'm so sorry," she said. "I just wasn't thinking of anything but me."

"Hey, it happens," he agreed.

He reached out a hand and she took it. They continued around the perimeter of the park at a much more sedate stroll.

"So, surely you didn't just come from work," she said. "It's got to be later than that."

He glanced at his watch, but then had to stop and press on the LED to read it. "Twelve-seventeen," he said. "I got off at nine and went by to pick you up."

Andi slapped herself in the head. "I should have called."

"It's okay. Cher-L told me that you were having dinner with your dad. Did you have a good time?"

"I wouldn't describe it quite that way."

"Okay…what's up?"

"Pop announced that he's getting married."

"You're kidding?"

"Nope."

"Well that's great! I mean. Is it great or not?"

Andi shook her head. "I have no idea," she said. "You'll never guess who's the lucky bride."

"Don't tell me it's Mrs. Meyer, I don't think I could bear it."

"It might be better if it was," Andi said. "It's your neighbor."

"My neighbor?" he repeated.

"Rachel Joffee."

"Oh wow! That's wild. Do Dave and Seth know?"

Andi nodded. "They were at dinner," she said. "Jelly's already calling them her brothers."

"Jeez, I bet that was a kicker."

"I'm still reeling."

"She's a nice person," Pete said. "And you have to admit that, for a senior cit, she's pretty hot."

Andi covered her ears. "I'm not listening," she said.

Pete laughed. "Is that something your sister does?"

"It must be genetic."

He wrapped an arm around her waist.

"I'm being an idiot, aren't I?"

"You'll never hear that from me," he said.

"I guess I hear it from myself."

"Is it Mrs. Joffee specifically that you don't like?"

"I don't really like thinking of Pop with any other woman but my mom. I thought they were perfect together. But I guess I got that wrong."

She quickly explained her father's revelations about both his lifelong attachment to Rachel and Andi's mother's lost love.

Pete whistled appreciatively.

"That is a lot to take in," he said.

"I just feel like everything I ever thought I knew about my family was wrong," she said.

"I…think maybe I understand," Pete said.

She glanced over at him, surprised.

"Not like it's the same thing at all," he said. "It's totally different and I don't want you to think I'm equating it at all."

"But?"

"I was in Junior High when I found out that my dad was unfaithful to my mother," he said. "Now, unlike you, I always knew there was something not quite right about our family. But I always assumed it was some sort of failure in me. My father was never happy with me. No matter what I tried to do, somehow he never completely approved."

Pete chuckled humorlessly. "He still doesn't. Anyway, when I found out that he played around and that he had women all over town and even Miss Kepper at the office. I was just stunned. I was angry, too. But mostly I was just stunned. It seemed like every family photo was a lie printed on a page."

Andi nodded.

"Now, I didn't know your parents, except in passing," Pete continued. "But everything I know about them seemed true and genuine. And I feel very certain they could never have raised such cool daughters if their relationship had been totally flawed."

"Pop says he loved my mom," Andi told him. "That he just loved her differently."

"Do you have trouble believing that?"

"No, not really," she admitted. "It's just that every relationship I've had in my life, I've held it up to the mirror of my parents' marriage and found it lacking."

"So now you've discovered that the bar you set was perhaps unrealistically high," Pete said.

Andi sighed and nodded thoughtfully.

"That's lucky for me, I think," he added grinning.

Andi put an elbow in his ribs in retaliation. "Hey, you're making jokes and I'm having a crisis here," she said, though her tone was just as irreverent as his.

He wrapped his arms around her, as if defending himself from further digs, but in fact he pulled her into an embrace. "I love you, Andi," he said. "And if your standards ever get low enough to love me back, well that would be pretty amazing, wouldn't it?"

"My standards are outrageously high," she assured him. "And I've become *so* picky. No man will do for me who hasn't had at least one dry run on this marriage thing. He needs to be a recovered high school hottie who now owns his own business. He's got to stand up to his holier-than-thou neighbors, put up with his holier-than-nobody father and be able to play basketball with my sister. And I think I need to add the ability to run for several blocks wearing loafers with tassels."

"Good grief," Pete said. "With those requirements you sound very much like a woman destined to be alone...almost."

He kissed her then. It was a sweet, tender kiss, completely chaste and totally intimate.

"Let's walk over to my house," he suggested. "And I'll hold you all night long."

"What about your car? It's parked in front of my house."

"That will sure fake out the gossips, won't it."

They laughed together and began walking faster.

"It's going to be all right, Andi," he told her. "This thing with your dad, give yourself some time. Grief is different for everybody. Your father may be ready to move on. And you can be okay with that. But you don't need to let it rush you. Give yourself the time you need to be okay with the loss of your mom."

Chapter 19

PETE WAS HAVING a particularly good day. That was to be expected, he thought. *Peterson, you're a lucky guy.* After a gloriously sleepless night, he'd eaten breakfast at dawn with the woman he loved and then walked her home. From there he'd come on into work very early and in the quiet solitude before the store opened, he'd managed to put together the very first of his new "Hometown Friends" ads. He'd set it up as a sidebar accompanying the typical coupons for crackers and bath tissue and skirt steak. Their first "featured friend" was Nell Zawadzki from the bakery.

Pete looked at the little bio piece and smiled. Who knew that Nell, in her white coat and plastic hairnet, had managed to send four children to college. Three to state university and one to M.I.T. She'd grown up in Plainview, married a high school sweetheart who bagged groceries at Guthrie's. He got her a job when he left to be an electrician's apprentice. She was still in the bakery after forty-five years and had no plans to retire.

"I love my job," she was quoted in the article. "The wonderful people I meet every day coming into Guthrie Foods make my work such a pleasure."

Pete smiled. That was exactly what he wanted. That was exactly what Guthrie Foods needed. And although he recognized his own contribution to this very welcome development, he knew that Andi had played the most important role.

He opened the store, which surprised his cashier supervisor, Phoebe Johannson.

"Am I not on first shift this morning?" she asked, concerned.

"You are absolutely on first shift," he confirmed. "I'm in my office early this morning and I thought I might as well open up. I was coming downstairs anyway for a cup of coffee."

He was in a great mood and once more he saw how easy it was to set the tone in the whole store.

Back in his office, he did the final proofreading on the layout. The last thing he wanted was having his ad show up on the late-night shows as some blooper that read, "maxipads, assorted flavors."

A few minutes before nine Miss Kepper arrived, greeting him with the perfect mixture of supervisor respect and longtime acquaintance familiarity.

"Would you like me to run that over to the newspaper?" she asked.

"No, but thanks. I want to do it myself this first time, so I'm sure they understand exactly what I'm wanting from this and don't second-guess me and screw it up."

She nodded and politely retreated to her own office.

At exactly nine o'clock, Pete went over to his window and utilizing the Jungle Jeff Safari binoculars he took a gander over at the car wash. At first the place looked deserted. Then he spied Andi crossing the street. Dressed in a bright pink sundress and wearing a big hat and flip-flops, she was ready for her workday.

"Amen to American entrepreneurship," he whispered aloud.

On his way to the offices of the *Plainview Public Observer*, he stopped at the car wash to drop off a bag of Guthrie Foods' own handmade paczki, a kind of Polish jelly doughnut, from Nell's grandmother's recipe. Just showing up with food was enough to get him a smile and a kiss.

"Totally worth it," he told Andi.

The meeting with the ad supervisor at the paper went well. He was a little hesitant at first. It wasn't what they'd always done and he was not completely amenable to change. But Pete was flawlessly patient and polite. Within an hour, the guy was on board with doing exactly what Pete was paying him to do.

It was closing in on eleven o'clock before he got back to the office. He heard his father's voice before he saw him. Hank was seated on the edge of Miss Kepper's desk. He was flirting with the old gal. It was all Pete could do not to roll his eyes.

He gave his father a quick nod and "hello," hoping against hope that he was there only to see Miss Kepper.

"Pete, I need a word with you," he father said, loudly.

"I'm in my office," he answered without hesitating or turning back. Hank would find him without any help or invitation and he'd tell him exactly what he thought. Pete had no doubt about that.

He retrieved a bag of Mallomars out of his fridge. But he only ate one. They still tasted really good, but the truth was, they no longer seemed to comfort him as they once had. Maybe he didn't need that kind of comfort anymore.

Pete was perusing the distribution center plan-o-gram when his father walked in. Hank groaned as he took a seat.

"What's wrong?" Pete asked. "Are you getting too old for my stairs?"

Hank shook his head. "I think I overdid it at the golf course yesterday," he answered. "I only played eighteen holes, no more than usual, but it was hot and maybe I didn't drink enough water. Whatever, I woke up this morning feeling pretty achy and sore."

"Sorry about that," Pete said.

"When's your mother coming home?" Hank asked. "She's been gone all summer."

"I got an e-mail from her a couple of days ago," he answered. "She was headed out on a Li River cruise to see Karst topography."

"What the devil is that?" Hank asked, grumpily.

"I don't have any idea," Pete admitted. "But she sounded very enthusiastic about it."

Hank shook his head. "Don't marry a woman who isn't interested in the store," he warned.

"I won't."

Hank snorted. "The way you're headed, you'll never find any woman at all."

Pete didn't rise to the bait, he only smiled and cast a surreptitious glance out the window.

"Men who don't get enough sex go crazy, you know that," Hank warned.

"I'll try to keep that in mind," Pete said.

"But I didn't come here to talk to you about sex," Hank said. "Not even about you going behind my back to support that Bikini Car Wash."

"I didn't go behind your back," Pete said. "I did it right in front of your face."

"Humph," Hank snorted, as he ran his hand thoughtfully along his aching arm.

"I came here to ask you to give up on this dadgummed cross-training," Hank said.

"Oh, you heard about that."

"Doris tells me everything, you know that," he answered.

"Our first cross-training day went very well," Pete told him. "I'm going to keep it up. Once a week for a while and then maybe add some more. I don't actually want people doing each other's jobs, but I do want them competent enough to do them. And knowledgeable enough to appreciate what their coworkers are doing."

"That's just business school crap," Hank said. "We don't do that here at Guthrie's. We want people to gain competence in their own job, not get confused about who does what."

"We didn't do that at Guthrie's," Pete said, surprised at his own lack of anger at the interference. "Times have changed, Dad. We're working with a really short staff. If someone is sick or late or quits, we don't have all those part-timers you used to have to fill in. Now we've only got us. And each one of us has got to be able to fill in where we can."

"In my day…"

"In your day it was different," Pete said. "You ran a great store, you made a lot of money for the company, you were a big success. You made the decisions that worked for you, that worked for then. I've got to make the decisions that work for me and work for now."

"You don't just throw away the past like it's washed up."

"I would never do that," Pete said. "Guthrie Foods is a tradition in this town. Tradition is important. But if we can't compete then tradition won't save us."

His father sat there staring at him silently for a long moment.

"I guess you're right," he said, finally.

Pete tried to keep his jaw from dropping. "You know, I didn't want to retire," he told Pete. "I wasn't ready to quit. But your mother said she'd divorce me if I didn't hand the business to you. Maybe I should have let her. I never see her anymore anyway."

For a moment Pete didn't know what to say to that. Finally he asked the only question he could. "Do you want your old job back?"

"Would you give it to me?" Hank asked.

Pete sighed heavily. "Not happily," he answered. "But yes, I would."

Hank's whole face changed. He didn't look as pleased as he looked flabbergasted.

"Why would you do that?" he asked. "That's crazy to give this up."

Pete shrugged. "I can build something else if I need to," he assured his father. "I love this job. But you're my father. And if you want to sit in this chair, I think you've probably earned the right to do so."

Hank just looked at him and finally chuckled. "Well, I didn't expect you to give in," he admitted. "You are so much like your mother. If you didn't look like me and play sports, I'd have a hard time believing you're my son."

"But I am," Pete told him.

"Yes, you are," Hank answered. "And I like having you as the head of Guthrie Foods. I just wish…I just wish things were a lot more like they used to be."

Pete nodded. "They're just not. And there's nothing I can do to change that."

Hank nodded. "I guess I'd better get going," he said, rising to his feet. "I'm having an early lunch with a young lady. I met her in Merchants and Citizens Alliance for Morality. Kind of a stubby little brunette, but nice curves. She's thirty-seven and only been divorced about eight weeks."

Pete raised an eyebrow. "Have a nice lunch, Dad."

As his father walked out of the office, Pete picked up the plan-o-gram once more. He'd just glanced down at it when an unexpected noise brought his attention back to his father. In the hallway, Hank stumbled. Pete's first reaction was surprise. His dad was a natural athlete, strong and sure-footed. It was on his lips to tease Hank, make a joke about his misstep, when he realized his father was clutching his heart and falling.

Pete was out of his chair and across the room in a flash and managed, somehow to catch his father before he hit the floor. His eyes were wide, his face ashen.

"Miss Kepper!" Pete called out. "Call 911!"

The woman stepped out of her office for one instant. Just long enough to give a startled scream and then she was on the phone.

"Where am I? I need to get to the store," Hank said.

"You're at the store, Dad. We're going to get you an ambulance."

"Maddie? Maddie, is that you?" he asked.

"No, Dad, it's Pete. Mom's in China, remember."

"I need Maddie," he said. "I need to tell her something."

"You can tell her when she gets home," Pete assured him. His father moaned.

Miss Kepper came running out of her office. "The ambulance is on the way," she said. "I alerted Phoebe to wait at the front door and direct them up here."

"Good," Pete said.

She knelt down on the other side of him with the ease of a girl. But the concern in her expression accentuated the lines of age on her face.

"What happened?" she asked Pete.

"I don't know," he answered. "Maybe it's a heart attack."

"I have an aspirin in my purse, aren't you supposed to take an aspirin?"

Miss Kepper didn't wait for an answer but rushed to her office, returning momentarily with a glass of water and a small white pill.

Pete raised his father into more of a sitting position to make it easier for him to swallow the aspirin, but it quickly became clear that he was not going to be able to do it. He choked and gasped and water ran out the side of his mouth.

Miss Kepper crushed the pill with her thumbnail and spread the dust on his tongue.

He seemed to appreciate that and opened his eyes.

"Is that you?" Hank's voice was strangely weak as he reached out a shaky hand.

"Yes, it's me," Miss Kepper answered, clasping his fingers in her own. "I'm here, Hank. I'm right here."

"I have to tell you," he groaned out.

"Don't try to talk, save your strength," Miss Kepper said to him.

"I have to tell you. I'm sorry. I'm sorry things didn't work out so well for you. You know that I always loved you."

"Yes, I know. I've always known," Miss Kepper told him.

His father made a strange sound, part choking, part moan. Pete tried to raise his head a bit so he could catch his breath. He was looking straight into his father's eyes when the light went out of them. The dark widened pupils that had viewed the world for sixty-six years narrowed to tiny pinpoints and saw nothing at all.

"No! No!" Miss Kepper screamed. "Don't leave me!"

Pete said nothing as he held his father in his arms.

The funeral of Henry P. "Hank" Guthrie, III was held at Plainview United Methodist. It had to be delayed for several days as Pete's mother made her way from the wilds of southern China to the Midwestern landscape of Plainview.

But she did arrive, arrangements were made and the service was held in a reverent and tasteful manner.

Andi attended with Pop by her side. The church was filled to capacity and they were lucky to slip into a seat near the back. She glanced around and spotted the Joffees near the front. Rachel smiled and waved. From the corner of her eye, Andi thought she saw her father wink at the woman. She hoped she'd just imagined that.

In attendance were people from virtually every civic organization in town. His buddies from the golf course were there. As were several members of his college football squad, Cornbelt Conference Champions of 1965. And four rows of

Guthrie Foods employees were seated directly behind the family pew.

The eulogies went on forever. There were stories about his childhood and growing up in a busy grocery store. Remembrances of parties at the country club and Rotary projects. Mayor Penny Gunderson-Smythe gave such a glowing review of Hank's accomplishments as alderman that it almost sounded like a campaign speech.

Through it all Andi watched Pete, or what she could see of him, seated at the front with his mother.

Madeleine Grosvenor Guthrie was a chic and attractive widow in a suit of plum-colored tweed. Pete was beside her, looking unaccustomedly formal in a dark suit. Sitting with them, instead of among the employees, Miss Doris Kepper was adorned in unrelieved black.

There were songs and Bible readings, candles and prayers and afterward they all filed out to reassemble at the burial.

Andi and Pop decided not to go to the cemetery. Pop needed to pick up Jelly and get to St. Hyacinth's for the lunch delivery. Andi asked him to drop her off at the car wash. Tiff was covering it. And having worked the place alone herself, Andi knew it was tough.

When she arrived, to her surprise, Tiff had recruited her own help. Gil McCarin, dressed in a pair of lime-green swim trunks, was soaping up the rims of a big, mud-encrusted pickup.

Tiff was hosing down the truck bed.

"How was it?" she asked.

Andi shrugged. "Good. Sad, but a lot more talk about his life than his death."

"You look great," Tiff pointed out. "I love that dress on you."

Andi glanced down. "I bought this for my mother's funeral. I could never wear it, but I guess for another funeral it's perfect."

Tiff nodded.

Andi gave a small head nod toward Gil and then asked, feigning innocuousness, "What's up?"

Tiff blushed. She offered a shrug. "I think Gil decided that if he couldn't beat us, he'd join us."

"I never wanted to 'beat' you," Gil said, rising from his squatting position to face Andi. "It just took me a while to come around." He turned to Tiff. "Are you finished with that wand?"

She nodded and handed him the water hose.

Tiff stepped down from the truck's open tailgate. She stood, first on one foot and then the other, not seeming to know what to do with her hands, as no bikini ever had pockets.

"Spill it," Andi said. "You obviously have something to say."

"Gil and I are…we're working on getting back together," she said sheepishly.

"Wow," Andi responded.

"I…I told him that he'd have to prove that he was willing to work at anything to support his family," she said. "So he's here, helping out just for tips."

"That's great," Andi said. "I mean, it's great if you're sure."

Tiff shook her head and gave Andi a self-deprecating grin. "I'm not sure about anything," she admitted. "But I do still love him and we both love Caleb. It's seems like in hard times like these maybe if we pull together things will be easier than trying to make it alone."

Andi hugged her friend, wishing, hoping for the very best for them.

"Well, if you two have got this under control," Andi said.

"I think I'll go over to the Guthries' house. Pete asked me to come by, but I didn't want to leave you in the lurch."

"Go," Tiff said. "Me and my assistant here, we've got it covered."

Andi laughed.

She dug her phone out of her small clutch bag, intending to call Pop. But when she saw the time, she knew he and Jelly were already deep into their delivery route.

Maybe she should just walk, she thought. Then she glanced down at her shoes. Four-inch high-heel pumps were not exactly crosstown hike compatible. She could put on her sneakers, carry her pumps and then change when she got there. But would she carry the old sneakers around? Hide them in the bushes? And how hot and sweaty would she get in the interim.

She needed a ride.

Andi was thinking to wait until Tiff and Gil were finished with the pickup and ask if one of them could give her a lift. But just then, she noticed a shiny blue Mercedes pulling up to the curb across Fifth Street at the side entrance to Joffee's Manhattan Store. The two Joffee brothers exited the vehicle.

Without thinking twice, Andi began walking in that direction. As soon as Rachel caught sight of her, she rolled down the window, but her expression was wary.

She was an attractive woman, Andi couldn't deny that. Her hair was as much silver now as brunette, she was trim and petite with a lovely smile. Momentarily Andi compared her with her own mother. Ella Wolkowicz had been a big-boned blonde with sad eyes and a gentle smile. Had these two women actually been high school friends? It was off balance to think that Rachel Joffee had known her mother in a way that was so different in the way that Andi knew her. And it was just plain crazy-making to think that Pop had loved this woman, this stranger, so long ago and now, too.

"Hi, Andi," she said.

"Hi, listen, are you going over to the Guthries' house?" she asked.

"Well, yes, I was just on my way there," she answered. "I dropped the boys off to get their cars. They hate to be 'trapped' somewhere with me. They want to be able to leave when they want to leave."

Andi nodded. She could appreciate the feeling.

"Pop and Jelly are already out doing meals on wheels," she said. "Could you give me a lift over there?"

"Absolutely," Rachel said. "Get in."

Andi walked around the car, opened the door and slid into the passenger's seat. The two women smiled at each other, but with a certain amount of trepidation on both sides.

Rachel put the car into gear and pulled away from the curb. At the stoplight, she turned left onto Grosvenor Avenue.

"It was a lovely service today for Mr. Guthrie," Andi said, sort of practicing her small talk for the after-funeral gathering.

"Yes, it was very positive, very uplifting," Rachel agreed. "That was Maddie's influence, I'm sure."

"I don't know her," Andi admitted. "But she's a very attractive woman."

"She looked great today," Rachel agreed. "She was all rested and tanned. Still, what a terrible thing to come home to."

"Yes," Andi agreed politely, thinking that the conversation was going very well. It would not be a good idea for Andi to go prying into this woman's relationship with Pop or accusing her of moving too fast. "It was so nice for so many of the Guthrie Foods employees to show up. The store was closed for the day, but nobody twisted any arms to make anyone show up."

"They're a good company to work for," Rachel said. "They always have been."

Andi nodded vaguely.

"How long have you and Pete been dating," Rachel asked.

"Oh, we haven't," Andi answered quickly. Then realized she'd been caught in a lie. Or maybe an inconvenient truth. Rachel had obviously seen them together. "We've been sort of seeing each other for about a month," she admitted. "But we're not officially dating. I haven't said anything to Pop about him."

Rachel nodded as if she understood. But, of course, she couldn't. Andi wasn't sure she understood it herself.

"There is so much going on right now," Andi felt obligated to explain. "My business is all up in the air and my mom's death and now…now you and Pop getting married. With all that, I don't know how straight I'm really thinking. And I don't want to blindly jump into anything. I mean, just because he's the most eligible guy in town, doesn't mean that I should get involved with him."

"Wait a minute," Rachel said with a teasing smile. "I believe that my sons are actually the most eligible guys in town. Though I hope they are both looking for a nice Jewish girl."

That statement gave Andi momentary pause.

"So, it's okay for you to marry a Catholic, but you wouldn't want your sons to do it."

"I'd hope," she answered thoughtfully, "that if they decided to do that, I would be able to be happy for them. You know what they say, 'the heart wants what it wants.' And that's as true for the mother thinking about daughter-in-laws as it is for young people looking for brides or grooms."

Andi regretted her question. She was sure that Pop would not appreciate having her ask it. She had undoubtedly said something she shouldn't have. As the silence between them lengthened she humbly tried to backtrack.

"I hope that didn't sound like a criticism of you," Andi said.

"No, it's okay," Rachel assured her quickly. "I understand just how little sense it all seems to make. We start out in life thinking things are supposed to sort out easily and that everything ties up neatly. Then we find out that almost every question has at least two good answers that may be completely opposite of each other. We just have to feel our way through it, making the best decisions we can. Sometimes we make the wrong choices. But I'm not sure we ever even know that for certain."

"What do you mean?"

"Well, like Walt and I," she said. "If we'd gone against our parents and married, we'd have had forty years of wedded bliss by now. Paul would probably not have gone to the army and he and your mom would have had a lot of good years. So that seems like a good choice. But if we'd made it, it would most likely have cut us off from our families just when they needed us. And you children, you and your sister are the light of Walt's life. And my boys, for all that they drive me crazy sometimes, are the best sons in the world. I'm not sure I'd be willing to give them up."

"But you and Pop would have had kids," Andi pointed out.

"Yes, that's possible. But they wouldn't be the ones we have," she said. "I guess, the upside is that it really cuts down on the regrets. Personally, I don't waste a minute on regrets, they're useless."

Andi heaved a sigh and shook her head. "I have enough for both of us," she said. "Big things, little things, I've messed up a lot. And some of them I can never make right."

"I'll bet some of them have to do with your mother."

Andi felt her face flush with embarrassment. "How could you know that? Has Pop said something?"

"No, of course not," Rachel told her. "It's just that when people die, especially people we love, there are always things we did or didn't do that haunt us. It's part of the grieving process."

Andi nodded. She was glad that Pop hadn't talked to Rachel about her. Andi should never have left town. Or she should have come home sooner. She should have tried to know her mother better. She should have... So many "she should haves."

"You are very much like her, you know," Rachel said.

The words startled Andi out of her thoughts, but surprised her, too.

"I'm more like Pop," she said.

Rachel nodded. "You are like him. But I see Ella in you as well. We were not close in the last thirty-five years, but we were good friends in high school. You are, in many ways, how I remember her. She was so smart and she was fearless."

Andi glanced at the woman skeptically. "Fearless?" she repeated.

"Absolutely. You didn't see that in her?"

"No, not really." Andi thought of her mother. Sewing matching dresses. Baking cookies on rainy days. Making a papier-mâché menagerie with Jelly. None of those things really called for courage. "My mom was more the happy homemaker type."

Rachel agreed. "Yes, I suppose she was that, too. But I saw her willing herself to go on living after Paul died. Determined to have a happy marriage with Walt and defending her girls relentlessly against the status quo in this town."

"She had to defend Jelly," Andi said. "People can be so backward and suspicious of anyone who is different, no matter what the reason."

"Yes," Rachel agreed. "She defended your sister. But she defended you, too. I suspect that the same ladies that find your current business venture so abhorrent, were also quick to suggest that going off to Chicago to have a career did not compare favorably with staying home in Plainview and getting respectably married."

Andi recognized a vague memory of that very thing being said a number of times in her own hearing. Her mother had only laughed lightly and waved away the advice with unconcern.

"I have Jelly to stay home with me," her mother had said, time and time again. "I want Andi to go out and see the world."

At the time, she'd not thought that much about it. There were a lot of silly women in church with outdated ideas. And Father Blognick was not much better. But she'd interpreted her mother's response as typical of the structure of her family. Mom and Jelly were a team. Andi was not on their team. Andi was with Pop and therefore where Andi went, what Andi did was not so critical, not so much concern to Mom.

"Pop and I spent a lot more time together," Andi explained. "We like the same things. We understand each other."

Rachel nodded. "You are a terrific father-daughter pair," she agreed. "But, think about it. Walt would never have defied Hank Guthrie. If Hank put Walt out of business, he would have just shrugged and walked away. He would never have dignified such pettiness as worth the fight."

That was true, Andi realized. Hank reneged on buying the car wash. Pop hadn't gotten angry or threatened a lawsuit, he'd just ignored it and went on about his life.

"And you can be sure," Rachel continued, "that Walt would never have done something like opening a bikini car wash, wagging his finger in Hank's face and daring him to do something about it."

"No, he wouldn't," Andi agreed.

"But I'm thinking that's exactly what your mother might have done," Rachel said.

Andi let those words sink in as Rachel drove down the wide, pristine boulevards of Plainview's wealthier section of town. Since the bombshell at Delmonico's, Andi had been emotionally flailing with the unwelcome idea that her family had not been quite what she'd thought them to be. Now, for the very first time, she considered that perhaps the reality of who and what her family actually turned out to be was something more complex, more well-rounded, simply better than her stilted, adolescent understanding had allowed for.

Chapter 20

HIS PARENTS' HOME, the house where he'd grown up, was bursting at the seams with the friends, acquaintances, officials and alumni who had come to comfort the family. Pete was very tired of smiling and of saying, "thank you." Big parties, crowds of people, were very draining, especially so when you were still reeling from loss. He had to force himself to come up with things to say. And he was not all that good at it. All he wanted to do was hide out someplace until all these people went home. But he didn't do that. He stood in the archway between the front hall and the formal living room, conversing with all comers. His father, ever gregarious, would have loved the idea of all these people in his house talking so nicely about him. Pete decided that it was the last thing he could do for his father, make his final gathering friendly and memorable. So he smiled and nodded and listened to the people who talked to him. And explained over and over exactly what had happened.

"It was apparently massive and irreversible," he said to Dr.

Schott, the retired pharmacist. "The EMS was there within minutes, but the doctor said they couldn't have saved him even if he'd been in the hospital when it happened."

The old man who'd known Hank all of his life nodded sadly.

Pete accepted the words of sympathy that were offered. He imagined that humans had come up with this way of honoring the dead to make it easier on the family. After you'd said the words aloud a hundred times to a hundred different people and accepted their expressions of grief, there was no way that you could continue to deny your own. It was there, you had to face it.

Fortunately most people were eager to get the mournfulness behind them. They easily bridged to happier times, recalling memories that provoked smiles, even laughter.

"We were on the sixth hole," Claymore Reddy, a heavily tanned golfing buddy with snow-white hair, said to him. "I'd bogeyed on five but your father was still two strokes back. He went with a wedge and I thought, 'good God, Hank, that's the worst choice you could make' but you never could tell him anything so I didn't try. And when he swung…"

Pete didn't hear the rest of the story. The front door opened and he saw Andi. He wanted to rush over and hug her to him. He'd missed her so much. It had been nearly a week since he'd seen her. Even longer since he'd touched her. He called her on the phone every night and they lay in their separate beds in separate houses sharing the day's happenings and sound of each other's voice. Phone sex was not nearly as good as the real thing. And staring into her eyes, instead of into the darkness of his bedroom, would be such a gift.

"Excuse me," he said, as soon as Mr. Reddy got the remembered golf ball onto the long-ago green. "I need to greet these ladies."

Pete waylaid Andi before she was three steps inside the door. She looked so different in her stiffly tailored black dress. But her smile was still the one he remembered, her lips were the ones he wanted to kiss.

"You came!" he said, just a little above a whisper. It was only when he took her hand in both of his own that he realized who was with her.

"Mrs. Joffee," he said, greeting his neighbor more formally. "Thank you for coming."

She gave him a motherly hug. "I'm so sorry for your loss, Pete," she said. "How is your mother doing? Maybe I can help her?"

"I think she's on the patio," Pete said. The older woman hurried off.

"I've never been so glad to see anyone in my life," Pete whispered to Andi. "I thought you were going to have to work."

"Tiff's husband is filling in for me," she said. "It was a beautiful funeral, Pete. How's it going here?"

"You know I'm not so good at this sort of thing," he said.

"I think people are very forgiving at times like this," Andi assured him. "We almost expect things to go badly. At my mom's wake, Jelly got into her *Law & Order* lingo and demanded that Father Blognick 'exhume the body.'"

Pete groaned and chuckled. "Gosh, I can just hear her saying that."

"Trust me, no one felt much like laughing at the time."

"That's the first time I've laughed all day," he said. "You're good for me, Andi Wolkowicz."

"All the guys in town feel that way," she said. "And today I'm not even wearing my red thong."

He loved her naughty grin. "I just want to hide out somewhere and talk to you," he confessed. "But I've got to hang with all these people."

"Absolutely," she agreed. "Go, mingle, be consoled. I can manage my way through the room. And I promise I'll be the last to leave."

She drifted off and Pete continued moving through the house listening to the stories of these old friends of his father's. Still knowing that she was here, knowing that she would be here for him when all these people were gone, gave him a second wind. He could run as many miles as he had to, as long as she was at the finish line.

And it got easier. As time went on more of his buddies congregated together for whatever talk they shared in common. And the friends of his mother seemed content with a quick word. So Pete was mostly talking with people from the store or other business people in the community. That was more shop talk and he was better at that. It came much more easily to him.

The crowd had dwindled down to perhaps a dozen people. The caterer was restacking the food on fewer trays, rather than bringing out more. Pete caught sight of his mother, patiently listening on the edge of an impromptu group discussion with the mayor about potholes. Pete walked over and took her by the arm.

"There's someone I want you to meet," he said.

They found Andi in the living room. She was seated on the chintz couch next to Miss Kepper. She stood up quickly as they approached.

"Hello, ladies," he said, including Miss Kepper in the greeting. "Mom, I want you to meet Andi Wolkowicz."

His mother smiled. "Oh, of course, you're one of Wolkowicz's twins," his mother said offering her hand. "You're all grown up now. And I wasn't back in town ten minutes before hearing all about your unusual car wash venture."

"Uh…yeah," Andi answered.

Pete could hear the nervousness in her voice.

"Andi's my…my…" The hesitation was a genuine dilemma. They were sleeping together, but they'd never had a date. He was in love with her, but he'd never once called her his girlfriend. The word *girlfriend* just sounded stupid next to what he felt for her. "Andi's mine," he finished finally.

His mother's jaw dropped open. He heard a startled little puff of disbelief from Miss Kepper. Andi's cheeks blushed bright red. It was within that little bubble of stunned silence that he noticed that Andi held an empty glass.

"Let me get you some more wine," he said, taking it from her. "Miss Kepper?"

She handed over her glass as well.

"Bring me one, too," his mother said.

As soon as Pete moved away, he regretted it. *Peterson, what kind of idiot drops a bombshell and then leaves his woman to pick up the pieces?*

He filled the glasses as rapidly as possible and kept his head down so that no one would approach him for even a fast word of conversation. He was back in the living room in less than two minutes. All three women were now seated. His mom and Miss Kepper on the couch, Andi in the chair angled beside it. Pete passed out the drinks and then, rather than standing or dragging up more furniture, he sat on the arm of Andi's chair.

"So Andi has been telling us about your new high-concept promotion for the store," Pete's mom said.

"I wondered where you came up with such a brilliant idea," Miss Kepper said. "I had no idea it came from Andi."

"Oh, it didn't," Andi piped in quickly. "It was Pete's idea entirely. He just let me work on it with him."

"Andi certainly inspired it, even if she didn't come up with it," Pete said. "I think it was mostly a collaboration. We work very well together."

As he spoke, Pete looked both of the older women directly in the eye. He wanted it clear that he was putting up with no interference in his relationship with Andi. Not at home. Not at work.

"Well, it sounds like a great new direction for Guthrie Foods," his mother said.

"The initial response has been very positive," Miss Kepper said. "Our store sales are up and it's been like a vitamin shot for employee morale. Everyone is happier, working harder. Some of that is probably the cross-training, but a lot of it is the Wholesome Foods, Hometown Friends concept."

"You've been doing cross-training?" Mom asked incredulously. "Hank always spoke very derisively of cross-training."

"In the end, I think, I won him over," Pete said.

"He was always very proud of the way you ran the store," Miss Kepper said.

Pete wasn't sure if she really spoke for his father or for herself, but either way, he was willing to take the compliment.

They talked for a while longer, several people left, including Mrs. Joffee. They all rose to their feet to say goodbye. Rachel and his mother embraced.

"Are you going to need a ride home?" she asked Andi.

"I'll be fine," she answered.

"Thanks for bringing her," Pete said. "I'll see that she gets home safe."

"I'm sure her father might ask 'safe from whom?'" Rachel teased. Then she gave Pete a hug as well. "I have been telling her what a good guy I think you are. The neighbors always know the truth."

"Uh, thanks, I think," Pete answered, teasing a bit himself.

After Mrs. Joffee left, his mother made a great suggestion.

"Why don't you kids sneak off somewhere for some time alone," she said. "I'm sure Pete could really use a break."

Pete studied her face for lines of weariness or stress. "Are you sure you can handle the rest of the guests by yourself?"

"I'll be fine," his mom insisted. She reached over and grasped Miss Kepper's hand. "Doris will help me. We're old, dear friends. We'll do this together."

Pete looked at Miss Kepper. She was smiling at him. She looked more vibrant, healthy, younger, than he ever remembered seeing her. "Go on," she said. "Helping out the Guthries is my life's work."

"Thank you," he told her.

He clasped Andi's hand and they made their escape.

"Do you want another glass of wine?" he asked her.

"I only want to be with you."

"Come on."

He led her upstairs and down a long hallway. The last door was the guest suite. He stepped inside. The rarely used area had the look of a perfect designer room, the kind seen in magazines, with no personal mementos or family heirlooms. As perfect, beautiful and lifeless as a statue.

On one side of the room, French doors led out to a lush second floor balcony, verdant with climbing vines and pots of blooming flowers. They passed through the doors and found a small bench with a view of the backyard foliage and the dark gray swimming pool.

Pete sat down and pulled Andi into his lap. He kissed her and held her tight against him, thinking he never wanted to let her go. But, of course, he did. He wasn't so blinded by desire that he could forget that they were in his mother's house and she had guests downstairs.

"It feels so good just to hold you," he said. "I don't like being away from you for days at a time. I like having you in my arms."

"I like it, too," Andi said.

He smiled, pleased. "I was worried about you when I left you alone with Mom and Miss Kepper. I hope they were nice to you."

"Oh yeah, they were great and I know they were shocked. Your mom was very sweet and said nice things about my parents," she told him. "And Miss Kepper…" Andi rolled her eyes. "Miss Kepper talked about how impressive I was when I came into interview for the job at Guthrie Foods."

"Impressive?"

"That's what she said, 'impressive,'" Andi quoted. "And then she told your mom and I that the only reason she didn't hire me on the spot was because she thought I was so much 'your type,' and she worried that we might get involved."

"Oh, wow."

"Do you believe that?"

"I don't have any idea what to believe about anything," Pete said. He hugged Andi close and then added, "But if she did think that, then she was exactly right. You are my type and I am *so* involved."

Andi rewarded him with a peck on the lips.

They sat together silently for long moments, lost in thought.

"Miss Kepper," he said with a heavy sigh.

"What about her?"

"This really weird thing happened when my father died," Pete said. "I haven't talked about it because I was kind of trying to sort it all out in my own head. I don't know if I can. I may need your head, too."

"What happened?"

"I saw my father as he collapsed and I ran into the hall and really caught him before he hit the floor. Miss Kepper came out of her office and I sent her back in to call an ambulance."

"Right."

"My dad was kind of confused. He didn't know where he was. He thought I was Mom, then he said he needed to talk to Mom, that he needed to tell her something."

Andi nodded.

"Then Miss Kepper was there and she was holding his hand and he seemed so glad to see her," Pete said. "He told her that he loved her. That he had always loved her."

"Oh my God."

"Miss Kepper didn't hear him asking for my mother. But I did. And it wasn't clear to me whether the words he said were meant for Miss Kepper or if he thought Miss Kepper was my mother."

"Did you say anything to Miss Kepper?" Andi asked.

"No," Pete answered shaking his head. "And I didn't tell Mom about it, except to say that he asked for her in the end."

They sat silently for a few moments. Pete was reliving it all in memory. Andi sat beside him, rubbing his shoulder comfortingly.

"I'm pretty sure that my father didn't love Miss Kepper," Pete said. "But I'm not so sure he really loved my mother either. What do you think?"

Andi gave it a moment or two more of thoughtful pondering. "You know, Pete, I don't think it matters what is really true," she said finally.

"Huh?"

"Miss Kepper waited all her life to hear those words from your dad," she said. "If it was a lie, then it was a good one. She certainly earned it. It was a monumental private moment. I doubt very seriously that she would ever tell your mother about it."

Pete nodded. "And even if she did, Mom has been so disappointed by my father so many times over the years, I honestly think that she's become nearly immune to it. And if it was meant for Mom, if she could have heard it firsthand, I don't think it could have made even a dent in the problems those two have had over the years. He told her he loved her all the time, but it never changed the way he treated her. This wouldn't have changed anything either."

"But it sure changed things for Miss Kepper," Andi said.

Pete agreed.

"It's so hard to know what is true and what's not true. Even the people who are relating the facts can't be sure."

"So what do we do?" Pete asked.

"I think we try to live our lives and be happy," Andi said.

Pete leaned forward and planted a little peck on her lips. "I think I can live my life happy if I get to live it with you."

"You know, I think with the right kind of contractual agreement, we could probably make that happen, Mr. Guthrie."

He kissed her again.

"What they say about you in town is that you're the kind of businesswoman who gets her way in every deal."

"This kind of deal allows no cheating," she said. "We need to try to be as honest with each other as we can. And we won't waste too much time trying to make sense of things we can never really be sure about."

"Do you want to shake on it?"

"I'd rather try to find out if any of those bedrooms have locks on the door."

"You are scaring me, woman," Pete said. "This kind of risky behavior is not what we're accustomed to in Plainview."

"I'm fearless," Andi said. "I think I get that from my mother."

Lovers Leap Overlook at Mt. Ridley had to be the most beautiful site in town for an outdoor wedding. The first autumn cold snap had signaled the trees to turn their leaves to red and orange, yellow and gold. But today, barely a year after her mother's death, the sky was blue, the sun was warm and it was a perfect day for a wedding.

The bride wore a ruthlessly unadorned ankle-length gown of metallic champagne satin. The three-quarter-length sleeves and the multiple strands of sparkly jewels around her throat were the only concessions to a woman of a certain age.

The groom, in a new gray suit with a pink rosebud in his

lapel, was grinning like a fool. Or perhaps grinning like a man who'd waited a lifetime for this day to come. And most of that life he never believed that it would ever happen.

Beneath the gauzy canopy, Father Blognick seemed distinctly uncomfortable. Rabbi Goldman wasn't any happier.

At the four corners of the structure stood their four children. Andi and Jelly were in matching dresses of deep fuschia. The first time they'd had matching clothes since grade school, Jelly had enthusiastically pointed out.

On the opposite side, the Joffee brothers looked positively dashing. Also slightly dangerous, their matching expressions daring anyone to say anything unfavorable about the unexpected choices of the happy couple.

Andi watched the ceremony with a surprising sense of peace. Pop and Rachel loved each other. Anyone who doubted that only had to look into their faces.

Pop thought that Andi's mother would be happy for them. That she would wish them well and be glad they were finally together. Andi didn't know about that. She didn't know her mother well enough to speculate. And even if she did, it would be just that, speculation. Her mom had gone on to heaven and Pop was still here. The vow, "'til death do us part," meant just that. No holding on to the past allowed. Besides, the future was worth embracing.

Andi had reluctantly put the CLOSED FOR THE SEASON sign in the car wash window. It had been a strangely sad, but also celebratory moment. She'd stayed open all summer. She'd paid two employees who might have spent the summer out of work. After paying her utilities, she'd still managed to make a profit. She called that success.

Initially she'd set the town on edge, but in the end there were no protestors, no legal maneuvers, no problems really to speak of. People got accustomed to seeing the staff in their swimsuits and it got to be no big deal.

Unfortunately, that was true for the customers as well. After the initial burst of waiting lines, it became a car wash, not an event. Toward the end, it was as much Mrs. Meyer's group, the senior citizens who didn't want to drive to the interstate, as the ogling men who kept them in business.

She gave a casual glance across the crowd. There were people here who'd openly reviled her as a modern-day harlot. And there were also some who'd championed her as a heroine. But mostly, they were just people from her hometown. People who had regular hopes and dreams, some of which had been busted to bits in the last few years. But they were trying to put them back together, piece by piece.

As the mixed message marriage ceremony concluded, Father Blognick blessed them. And Pop stomped a piece of crystal with his foot. They were pronounced man and wife. They kissed each other, waved to the crowd and then walked arm-in-arm through the pathway between the chairs.

Andi watched a bit nervously as Jelly and Seth paired up to walk behind them. Her sister's chin was high and proud. She didn't miss a step. Andi and Dave walked behind them.

"So my official stepsister, what's next?" he asked.

"We drink, we dance, we eat cake?"

"What about the hora?" Dave said. "Don't we need to get those two dancing up in the air in chairs?"

"Just don't drop them," Andi said. "At their age somebody is bound to break a hip."

But the reception proceeded without incident. Everybody was on their very best behavior. There seemed to be almost a competition going on between the ladies of St. Hyacinth's and those from the synagogue. Sort of like, "we'll show them that we can be more open and welcoming than they ever could!" Whatever, it was working. And Andi was grateful.

The party pretty much started without the principals as the family posed near the scenic ledge for photo after photo after photo.

"Do I get these in a picture book?" Jelly asked a half-dozen times. "Do I get these in a picture book?"

The photographer assured her she would, but Jelly had her doubts.

"Perjury will get you time upstate," she warned the poor man. "Remember you're under oath!"

Andi hardly got a moment to hug the happy couple and wish them well. The caterer, looking desperate, called her away. The cranberry-mango chutney was missing and she couldn't serve the turkey breast without it.

Andi spent at least the next hour being the point person for every possible emergency. Including more guests than flatware and an inexperienced server pouring the toasting champagne into the dinner glasses.

"Hi Andi! Hi Andi! Hi Andi! Hi Andi!"

Tony Giolecki and his grandmother were among the guests. Tony wasn't used to such a big, fancy party. But he looked good in his Sunday suit and was obviously having a nice time.

"Andi's my girlfriend," he told the caterer and the waiter and guest after guest after guest. "Andi's my girlfriend. Andi's my girlfriend."

"Tony," she said. "You'd better go find your grandma and eat your dinner, because when the dancing starts they'll take the food up."

"I gotta eat," Tony agreed. "I gotta eat. I gotta eat. I gotta eat."

Andi didn't get to eat. By the time everything was running smoothly, she hardly had time to slip into her seat at the head table for the toasts.

Dave's was clever and entertaining, he had the crowd laughing.

Andi's was more heartfelt.

"I've always known how lucky I am to have my pop," she began. "He is just the kind of guy you can always depend on. He's the guy who, when you need help, will always be there with a wrench or a hammer or a shoulder to lean on. Today, he's getting a helpmate of his own. Rachel, I hope that you and Pop have a hundred years of life together and are as blissfully happy as you deserve to be."

Andi raised her glass sincerely and the applause was spirited.

When the dancing started, people finally got up and started moving around again. Andi shook a hundred hands and smiled until she thought her face might break.

She spotted a small familiar young fellow in the crowd. He hurried toward her, followed by his parents.

"Caleb," Andi said. "Don't you look all grown up."

"This is my first time to be at a wedding, that I remember," he said. "And it's pretty cool."

"I'm glad you like it."

Just as Tiff and Gil stepped up to join them, Caleb added, "We're going to have our own wedding. And I get to be in it this time."

"What's this?" Andi asked, looking hopefully at Tiff.

"We told Caleb to keep it a secret," she said.

"Sorry, Mom."

"Well, this kind of secret is sure to get out," Andi said. She smiled at them both. "Well, best wishes, congratulations, whatever. I'm happy for you."

Tiff shrugged, a little embarrassed. "We're back together and it's working. So…so we decided to make it official."

"That's great. That's so great." She hugged Tiff and shook hands with Gil.

"We're going to wait a couple of months on the wedding," he said. "I've just been accepted into an eight-week course at the hospital. If I pass the test, I should get steady employment. So we'll have double reasons to celebrate."

"Congratulations!" Andi said. "What are you going to be doing?"

"I'm going to be a nurse's aide," he answered. "There's a lot of opportunity in that, both at the hospital and in home health care. I've got a lot to learn, but at least I already know how to carry a bedpan."

They both laughed as if they were delighted by the prospect.

"I'm really happy for all of you," Andi told them.

They were obviously happy for each other, too. Andi later saw Tiff and Gil on the dance floor together and thought they looked exactly like what they were, a young couple in love.

But they weren't the only young couple in attendance. Andi caught sight of Cher-L in the crowd. It was a wonder that she recognized her. Since the closing of the car wash, she'd lightened her black-and-blue goth hair to a light ash-brown. And she was accompanied by a very handsome, buff-looking guy who was somehow familiar. Andi figured he must have been one of the customers at the car wash.

When they finally ran into each other, Cher-L hugged her excitedly.

"It's so good to see you," she said. "I've missed you."

"I've missed you, too," Andi said, only realizing it was true when she said it. "I love your new hair."

"Oh, thanks," Cher-L said. "I did it for my new job. It doesn't really scare people off the way the old hair sometimes did."

"You have a new job?"

"Oh, I haven't told you?" Cher-L shook her head. "It is so totally cool. Of course, it's not a real *real* job. I don't get wages, just commission, but I'm doing good. I'm working at Spangler's Used Cars out by the interstate. I thought, you know, I know cars and I know how to sell people stuff. So I just went out there and proposed myself. So far, it's working great."

"Oh, Cher-L, that is fabulous. I'm so proud of you."

"Oh, that's another thing," she said, sheepishly. "I'm just plain Cheryl again. That really works better and I don't have to spell it or explain it all the time."

"Well, okay, Cheryl. If it's what you want, then I'm very glad about that."

"Thanks. Me, too."

"And who is this handsome guy you're not introducing me to," Andi said. "I promise I won't try to cut in." She addressed the familiar young man directly. "Hi, I'm Andi Wolkowicz."

"Doug Mayfield," he said, taking her hand. "I guess you don't recognize me out of uniform."

"Oh…oh, of course, Officer Mayfield. It's good to see you again. So glad you could come and that you could bring our Cheryl."

He winked. "I try to see she doesn't go anywhere without me."

They all laughed.

Jelly came by and dragged the two back out on the dance floor. She motioned for Andi to come as well, but she declined.

Andi had spotted Pete several times in the crowd, but somehow, every time she headed in his direction, she got called away. She spoke for a few moments to his mother. Madeleine looked great. She was doing a big remodel of her home.

"I'm really just getting it into some sort of condition for sale," she told Andi. "I want to move into something smaller. So I'm trying to get all the work done this fall and winter, so I can put it on the market in the spring."

Andi nodded. "Pete told me that you were going to Chile and Argentina this winter."

"No, I've decided against it. I haven't spent enough time in town the last few years and I just want to stay home, I think."

There was something slightly insincere about her answer, but Andi had decided that she no longer cared that much about what people thought was true.

"I actually gave my reservations and my travel plans to Doris," Madeleine said.

"Doris Kepper?"

"Turns out that she always dreamed of retiring and doing some travel. Now she can."

That bombshell sort of rested at the back of Andi's mind. Pop came and got her to take a turn about the floor.

During an awkward fox-trot to "They Can't Take That Away From Me," she asked him about it.

"Miss Kepper is going to retire from Guthrie Foods," she told him.

"Really?"

"Yes, and Pete hasn't mentioned it at all. I mean I know I've been busy with your wedding, but I'd think he would have mentioned it."

"I guess it just didn't come up," Pop said.

"Do you think it just didn't come up?" she asked. "Or do you think it didn't come up on purpose?"

"I don't get what you mean."

"Pete knows how desperately I'm looking for a new job. And he knows how more than qualified I am to do that one," she said. "Do you think that he doesn't want me to know about it so that I won't apply? It's a family business, but I'm sure they still have rules about hiring people you're dating. And giving a plum job to your girlfriend, even if she's qualified. I guess that would look really bad. Is that what he's thinking?"

"I don't know, Andi. I think you'll have to ask him."

Andi thought about that for a moment. "Are you sure I shouldn't just wait for him to tell me? Or should I ask him?"

"I think you should ask him," Pop answered. "And it looks like your chance is walking right up."

A second later, Pete was there, cutting in. He looked so good. What had made her think that he was not still the high school hottie? The guy was gorgeous.

"You're a difficult woman to get my hands on," he told her.

"Oh, I don't know, you manage it fairly regularly," she answered.

They danced together, smiling at each other for a couple of minutes.

"Did I mention you look beautiful today," he said.

"No," she replied. "And you didn't tell me Miss Kepper was leaving either."

"Ahh," he said. "The Plainview gossip machine still hard at work. News really spreads fast in this town."

She nodded. "Was there a reason you didn't tell me?"

"Yeah," he answered. "There's always a reason of some kind."

"You didn't want me to apply for her job."

Andi stated it as a fact and then swallowed hard. She was determined to be okay with this. There were good reasons not to hire her and she was not going to allow her longing for the job to override her sense of doing the right thing.

"I'm doing away with that position," Pete said. "Executive secretary is kind of an antiquated job. We're such a small company, even the executive does most of his own paperwork. So why have a whole position tied up in something like that."

"Oh."

"I've been talking about it a great deal with the management board," he said.

"The management board? That's just you and your mother."

He nodded very soberly. "And that's one of the problems," he said. "Two people are not a board, they're just partners. What if we disagree on something. Then it's just her against me. We need a tiebreaker. We need to add another person to the management board. Someone who'd be willing to put some hands-on time with the company."

Andi nodded.

"And since we're a family-owned company, it really should

be a family member," he said. "Guthrie Foods in all its history has never had outsiders on the management board."

"Well, who do you have in your family?" she asked.

"There's Aunt Sylvie out in Idaho," he said. "But she's almost eighty and I doubt she'd want to relocate. We have some Grosvenor cousins in town, I think. But they've never been involved in the business."

"I guess people can learn," she said.

"Yeah, sure, whoever takes the seat will have to put in a lot of time learning the business," Pete agreed. "But those guys are not the ones I have in mind."

"Who then?"

"I have an outrageous plan," he said. "I mean it's something so crazy that you might even have thought it up."

"Hey," she complained.

"You *are* the Bikini Car Wash entrepreneur after all," he pointed out.

"Anyway, this idea is really out there and it's totally fearless."

"Tell me."

"I'm going to get married and put my wife on the board."

"Huh?"

"It's a proposal, Wolkowicz, please don't make me get down on one knee. I can do it, but it would really be embarrassing."

Andi stopped in mid-quickstep and nearly fell over his feet. He had to wrap his arms around her waist to keep her upright.

"So what do you think, Andi," he said. "Great benefits, you get a job, a house and a man who loves you. It seems like a good deal if you want it."

"I do!"

Jelly lovingly clutched her brand-new photo book. It was pale green with little white ribbons on it. She ran up to her new room at the back of the big house. That's what she called the place she lived now, the big house. It was a big room and Andi had helped her fix it up so that it was a young lady's room and not with a bunch of stuffed bears and bright colors. Jelly still had the stuffed bears. She kept them on shelves in the closet. And when she wanted them, she'd bring them out to sit on the bed or the chairs or wherever they wanted to sit.

She snuggled up in her window seat that overlooked Pete's house. No one was at home, of course. They were in Italy, but only for a week more, Pop promised.

Jelly opened the book and there she was on the first page. She was wearing the beautiful green dress that was in her own closet this very minute. And her hair was very cute and she was holding a bunch of flowers. Beside her, Andi looked good, too. They didn't have matching dresses. Andi's was white and gigantically poofy. They were standing by the big tree in front of St. Hyacinth's. They were both smiling.

Jelly let out a heavy sigh. This was why she loved the photo books. It was as if she could live the good moments again and again and again.

* * * * *

QUESTIONS FOR DISCUSSION

We hope the following book club questions will enhance your enjoyment of this book.

1. Why is wearing a bikini at the pool different than wearing one on Main Street?

2. Pop wanted Andi to have choices, even when he didn't agree with them. When must you allow your own children to risk a bad choice?

3. Successful fathers and their sons often have difficult relationships. Are the seeds of this implicit in a competitive personality?

4. Guilt played a big factor in Andie's relationships with both her mother and sister. Why wasn't guilt an issue for her with her father?

5. Do we ever outlive high school if we don't move away?

6. Tony's grandmother had no one to help her care for her grandson. Special needs families sometimes require special help. What services are you aware of in your community?

7. Religious differences kept Walt and Rachel apart for decades, yet Rachel didn't want her sons to marry outside the faith. Is her position hypocritical or just practical?

8. Grassroots protest groups can be necessary and effective for drawing attention to problems in the community. What did you think of M-CAM? What mistakes did they make? What would you have done differently?

USA TODAY BESTSELLING AUTHOR

PAMELA MORSI

Jane Lofton has everything she ever dreamed of: a high-powered career, a fabulous home, a wealthy husband and a beautiful daughter. Of course, David *also* has a new girlfriend spending his old money. Brynn *also* has a therapist helping her articulate her contempt for her mother. And Jane *also* has...

...an obligation to the Man Upstairs. A chance meeting between her BMW and an eighteen-wheeler prompts Jane to make a deal: let her live and she'll dedicate herself to Doing Good. Whatever that means. But when her country-club life crumbles, Jane is faced with an even bigger challenge—salvaging her soul.

The

Social Climber

of

DAVENPORT
HEIGHTS

Available wherever books are sold.

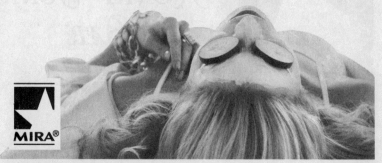

MIRA®

www.MIRABooks.com

MPM2842TR

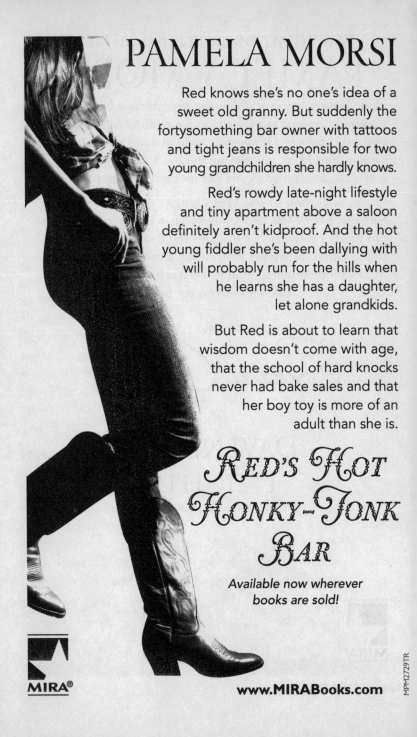

PAMELA MORSI

Red knows she's no one's idea of a sweet old granny. But suddenly the fortysomething bar owner with tattoos and tight jeans is responsible for two young grandchildren she hardly knows.

Red's rowdy late-night lifestyle and tiny apartment above a saloon definitely aren't kidproof. And the hot young fiddler she's been dallying with will probably run for the hills when he learns she has a daughter, let alone grandkids.

But Red is about to learn that wisdom doesn't come with age, that the school of hard knocks never had bake sales and that her boy toy is more of an adult than she is.

Red's Hot Honky-Tonk Bar

Available now wherever books are sold!

MIRA®

www.MIRABooks.com

MPM2729TR

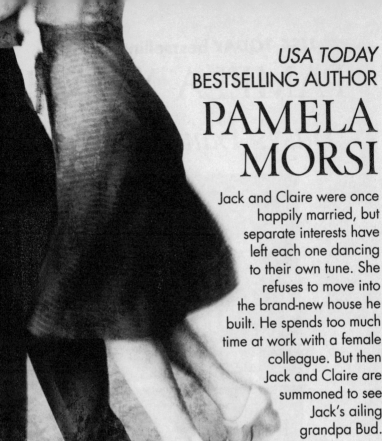

USA TODAY
BESTSELLING AUTHOR

PAMELA MORSI

Jack and Claire were once
happily married, but
separate interests have
left each one dancing
to their own tune. She
refuses to move into
the brand-new house he
built. He spends too much
time at work with a female
colleague. But then
Jack and Claire are
summoned to see
Jack's ailing
grandpa Bud.

Bud and Geri danced
through life together
as friends and devoted
spouses. They always knew
what mattered most in life.
And if Jack and Claire can remember the
bond they once shared, they might be able
to rediscover what's wonderful about love....

Last Dance at Jitterbug Lounge

Available wherever trade
paperback books are sold!

MIRA®

www.MIRABooks.com

MPM2519TR

USA TODAY bestselling author

PAMELA MORSI

Bitsy's Bait & BBQ

Fishing, food and life lessons!

Available wherever trade paperbacks are sold.

www.MIRABooks.com

MPM2423TRR